A Desperate Plot

She shook her head again. "Alain, you haven't been in prison like I have. Everyone talks about rescue and escape. That plan has been tried many times, in many prisons."

"Did it work?"

"Sometimes it did, sometimes it didn't. Your trick of having Jimmy stay inside is a good twist. But it doesn't matter, now. We can't disregard Duval's warning. Just be thankful he was here to tell you."

Alain shook his head. "I don't think you understand, dear. If it was only a mixup and they came for you by mistake, that sort of thing can be straightened out. But this is Reynaud de Gonillons we're dealing with. Who says he was even taking you to the Tribunal? You wouldn't be the first person to disappear into nowhere at a time of upheaval."

Her face blanched, and she grasped the bars as if she were going to fall. Her voice came in a husky whisper. "I never thought of that."

Savournon Today

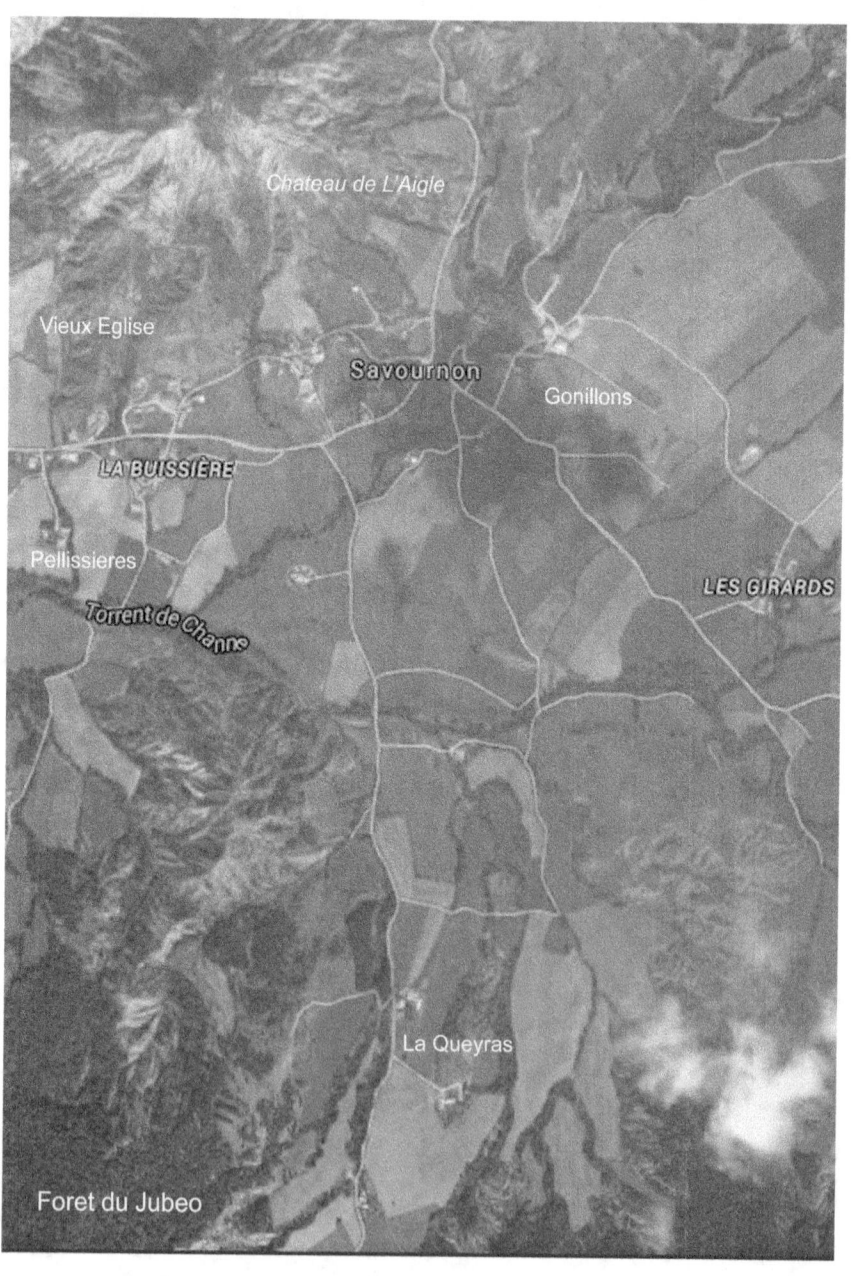

STORM OVER SAVOURNON

Gordon A. Long

AIRBORN PRESS

Delta, 2015

STORM OVER SAVOURNON

Published by
AIRBORN PRESS
4958 10A Ave, Delta, B. C.
V4M 1X8
Canada

ISBN - 978-0-9921243-9-7

Printed by Createspace

Cover Design and Photography by Gordon A. Long

Angélique's portrait is from "The Letter" by Vladislav Chahursky (1850 - 1911)
Alain's picture is John George "Radical Jack" Lambton, (1792-1840) 1st Earl of Durham (a figure from early Canadian history), painted by Thomas Phillips (1770 - 1845)

Fell Type Fonts are digitally reproduced by Igino Marini. www.iginomarini.com

Other Books by Gordon A. Long

"World of Change" Series:

Book 1: Out of Mischief
Book 2: Into Trouble
Book 3: Mountains of Mischief

Sword Called Kitten Series:

Book 1: A Sword Called...Kitten?
Book 2: The Cat with Many Claws

Non-Fiction

Why Are People So Stupid?
Expressive Poetry Performance

Thanks

To all my beta readers for their kind words
To Dusty Hagerud for his design assistance

Contents

Introduction

In 1993 my wife and I withdrew our children from school, took leave from our teaching jobs and left the country to travel around the world for a year. We couldn't afford to be on the road for all that time, so we found Savournon, a small village in the *Departement des Hautes-Alpes* of France. There were 198 people in the village, and the mayor (who was our landlord) was quite happy because our little family put the population over 200. I don't know if that was only symbolic or if it meant he got more grant money, but in any case, we were content to help out. We put our sons, then 11 and 13 years old, into the local school and lived in that beautiful valley for 6 months, walking the local paths and getting to know the area, its history and its people.

During that time, I got the idea for this book. I went to the *Prefecture* in Gap and researched what happened in the valley of Savournon during the Revolution. This material, along with the wonderful scenery of the area, was a great inspiration and source of ideas for me. The French bureaucracy may be onerous, but it has its advantages. The government archives maintain an amazing number of original historical documents, all available to the general public. I have actually held in my hands the lists – on odd-sized bits of light blue paper, written in an ornate hand, the ink faded to sepia colour – detailing the relief supplies that were handed out in that area during the famine of 1788. Thinking of the man who wrote those lists sparked my imagination. What was his background and education, with such beautiful handwriting? Why were the papers all different sizes? How did he feel when the relief supplies were insufficient, and he had to divide them up among starving people? I just had to put that person in my novel.

Likewise, the scenery around Savournon was a great impetus to my creativity. At first it was a pleasure to just get out and enjoy the area. Later, I hiked the valley and the

ix

mountains with my sons, discussing the scenes from the story, deciding where people would walk, what they would see, how long it took to go from one point to the other. While I had to jazz up some of the architecture – in a past era residents were taxed on how many floors their house had, so the owners of Chateau Savournon lowered the roof one story – all of the landscape is still pretty much as described in the book. Take away the electrical lines and the pavement and I don't think the town would be much different from how it looked 200 years ago. Much smaller now, of course. In the 1800s there were 1500 people in the valley, mostly subsistence farmers.

A note: while most mountains of the world are called mountains – "Mont Blanc" or "Table Mountain," or even "The Eiger" – the peak that dominates the south wall of the valley at Savournon is simply named "Revuaire," as if it were an individual, not a landmark. At least, that's how it sounds to me. You see how a person can get caught up in a landscape.

1. Reunion

May 29, 1788

"Hitch up the horse, will you, Alain, and then get on your good waistcoat. We have an appointment at Chateau Savournon."

"The carriage? The *chateau* is only the other side of the village. Why don't we walk?"

His father grinned. "This is a formal call. If you are going to be an eminent lawyer, you must learn the importance of appearances. When we go to the *chateau* on business, we go in the carriage."

As the horse trotted along the cobbled street between low, sandy-stuccoed buildings, M. Jouvent gazed around. "Don't you love this place?"

Alain glanced at the nearby house of Andre Lazare, one of the poorer farmers in the valley. The roofline sagged and the tattered thatch was so old it was almost black. "Not all of it."

François Jouvent shook his head. "There are poor folk in every town, son. Look up. Look at the fields, the mountains."

Alain gazed back over his shoulder at Mount Aujour, head and shoulders above all the lesser ridges that hemmed the valley in. "Some of it is pretty spectacular, I must admit." He regarded his father. "But not very big. Hardly room for two lawyers, and no space to expand."

Jouvent put an arm around his son's shoulders. "And when you become a lawyer, you can go wherever your business takes you. But for now, why not enjoy the beauty of where you are?"

"You just want me to be happy, because a happy clerk does better work."

"*Ah, bien*, you see through me in a moment." He glanced over at his son. "Speaking of beauty, I hear *sieur* de Bardel's family came back from Grenoble with him."

"And this is why we're putting on airs?"

The older man smiled. "I must admit that I usually walk when I'm visiting Charles. When Madame Marie-Françoise de Charrette is in residence, it doesn't hurt to be more formal."

"Mme. De Charrette." Alain's mind dredged up a vague image of a tall, haughty lady in an elegant plum-coloured gown. He recalled her poise, like a fantastic purple bird, strutting elegantly among lesser creatures. He turned to his father. "I don't understand, *Papa*. Look at this place." His hand-sweep took in the rustic valley, hemmed in by rugged cliffs, the sharp tor of the Chateau de l'Aigle hanging over the village, Revuaire's dark wedge shading the farms along the southern rim. "How does an elegant lady end up married to a down-to-earth farmer like *sieur* de Bardel in the back-of-beyond like this? They just don't...match, you know?"

Jouvent sighed. "I don't pretend to understand the whys and wherefores of the Second Estate. Arranged marriages, for one thing."

"I never thought of that. But it explains why she spends all her time in Grenoble. I wonder what brings her here now?"

His father grinned. "Same answer, son."

"I suppose if it's for business reasons, we'll soon find out."

"And if it isn't, we won't ask." His father gave him a quick glance. "And I gather Angélique is here too. You remember her, *n'est-ce pas*?"

"How could I forget? It's been several years, but I did visit the *chateau* with you the last time she was at home. I was expected to 'run along and play' with this little pea-chick, all got up in curls and ribbons. And you reminding me to be a gentleman. Did you really think a boy of ten was going play with an eight-year-old girl and be a gentleman at the same time?"

2

His father looked mildly concerned. "I don't remember there being any problem."

He grinned. "There wasn't. As it turned out, she was more interested in showing me her collection of lizards."

"Lizards?"

"Lizards. Oh, each had his own little house, and they had names and she made up stories about their adventures. But they were most definitely lizards. She was driving the stableboys mad, badgering them to catch flies for her pets. I was quite relieved, as I recall. She wasn't difficult to entertain. More like the other way around."

They turned off the main road onto the drive that ran along the ridge in front of the *chateau*. "Well, I don't expect she'll be showing you lizards today."

"I suppose not." Alain grimaced. "But I doubt that the plumage has changed."

As they pulled up, a groom stepped to the head of their horse. The two got out of the carriage, mounting the wide, steep steps to the front door. Jouvent glanced up at the stone-trimmed façade towering four stories above them. "I'll leave it up to you. If you're having a terribly boring time you can always say I need you to take notes. It wouldn't be a lie. You have done it before."

Alain reached over and rapped the heavy brass knocker, cast in the shape of a hawk's head. "Thank you, father. I appreciate the thought." He turned an earnest look at the older man. "You know, if I can manage it without offence I should stay at the meeting. *sieur* de Bardel is an important man. If I'm going to get ahead in my vocation, I need as much contact as I can with people like him."

"That's a good attitude, son. He is our most important client. Let's see how it goes."

The door swung open at a dignified speed, and a footman in livery bowed them in. Alain glanced at his father, raising his eyebrows. This wasn't the usual treatment at Chateau Savournon.

By way of answer, Jouvent gave his name to the new footman and stated his business, adding, "I gather Madame de Charrette is down from Grenoble."

The servant, a young man of great self-importance, nodded gravely. "Yes, *monsieur*. We arrived just last night, so she is not receiving at this time. Perhaps another day."

"Since this is a business call, I had not expected the pleasure in any case. Please convey my respects to Madame."

The footman condescended to bow and led the way to the double doors on the right side of the entrance hallway. He flung them open with a flourish, announced "Mon*sieur* Jouvent" in a loud voice, ushered them in and stepped out, closing the doors with a show of efficient silence.

Charles de Bardel, dressed in his usual workaday waistcoat and *cullotes*, was sitting at a writing desk in one corner of the big reception room. His business papers, books, files and other paraphernalia took up a much smaller part of the room than usual. Alain kept his grin to himself. *The lady of the manor makes her presence felt.*

The *seigneur* got up and came over to greet them, offering chairs and genially playing the host. Alain looked around the elegant room, wondering again at the behaviour of the Second Estate. Charles de Bardel, arguably the most important man in the district, was more affable and informal than most of the other landowners with whom Alain and his father came into regular contact.

He wondered where the famous daughter was. *I hope she's as easy to entertain as before. Maybe some of her father's charm has rubbed off. What does a kid that age talk about?* Most fourteen-year-old girls in the district spent their time giggling and making elaborate fluttering with their fans. A smaller number were comfortable with subjects such as riding, hunting and who could throw a dagger the most accurately. He feared that Mademoiselle Bardel would not be

4

of the dagger type and hoped fervently that she would not be a flutterer.

His thoughts were broken by the guilty realization that the pleasantries were over, the business had begun and he should be listening. His father had come to discuss the details involved in selling a piece of property. This was not a simple matter. *But Papa can handle it. We know what we're doing.*

De Bardel was worried about the transfer of the peasant's feudal dues to the next owner. "How do you place a value on them, in this day and age when much of the work is now done for wages?"

Jouvent laughed. "Much easier than before. If the peasant owes you so many days work per annum, you can calculate the monetary value based on an average daily wage." He leaned forward. "That is, you do if you are selling the property."

"And if I am buying?" The *seigneur* looked puzzled.

"Then you ignore the value, as you will receive little of it."

De Bardel looked more bewildered than ever. "I don't understand. My peasant tenants discharge their duties for the most part, and I perform mine in return. Where is the problem?"

Jouvent leaned in and spoke lower. "Charles, I have been your lawyer for a good many years, now, have I not?"

"Yes, but..."

"So I can tell you something which may be of use to you, and you won't take it amiss or be insulted?"

"Considering what I have trusted you with in the past, I suppose I can rely on your motives, even if I feel the urge to take offence." The *seigneur* frowned in concern. "Come, now, François. What is this all about?"

"Charles, I know you consider it a virtue, but you spend too much time here on your land."

"This argument is nothing new. A man cannot run a property he does not know. Many do, I am well aware, but they are at the mercy of their managers. How better could I spend my time?"

"I applaud your reasoning, but it puts you out of touch with the political winds blowing through our realm. Unless the present state of affairs improves, serious change is inevitable. And the first thing to be thrown aside will be the feudal dues and obligations."

The lord frowned. "Where do you get this strange idea?"

"I was in Grenoble last month on a case, and members of all the Estates there are discussing it. If a storm is blowing up, one can never be too well prepared."

Alain's chest warmed with pride. *My father is intelligent and aware. Some day, important men will listen to me like that.*

This important man was frowning. "I suppose. But on what facts are these fears based?"

"The government is in serious financial trouble."

"I have been saying it for years. Where does that lead us?"

"The aristocracy are too often away from their land, spend too much money on vapid entertainment, and do not pay their taxes. One more poor harvest, one more rise in the price of bread, and we will have a nasty revolt."

Alain had heard all this many times before, but the fact that Seigneur de Bardel was interested caused him to pay closer attention.

As he listened, he became aware of a pleasant odour, like lilacs, which were not in bloom at the moment. Out of the corner of his eye he caught a glimpse of lace, just off to his left. He sprang to his feet. His father broke off, looked around and then rose, as did de Bardel.

"My dear Angélique. How long have you been standing there? I'm sorry if we bored you with all this political talk. Of

6

course you remember M. François Jouvent, and his son, Alain?"

Alain tried to collect his scattered thoughts. This was the girl who had showed him the lizards? He had expected, at least...*what did I expect?* This was no child. *Quelle stupidité.* She lived in Grenoble, moving in social circles far above those of Savournon. Why should she not dress and act like a young lady? Why should she not wear a delicate perfume and arrange her hair up in such a way? *But why do I have to feel like checking to see whether my shoes are shined and worry about those hairs that always stick out around my left ear?* He clasped his hands behind his back to keep from picking lint off his jacket.

The cause of this small fuss preened for a moment, but then adopted a serious mien.

"Of course I remember these two gentlemen. How do you do, *messieurs*? And please, do not stop your conversation because of me. I was fascinated. Are you saying that there will be a revolution? Like in the British Colonies in America?" Her eyes brightened and her colour rose. "What part of the country will break away?"

"Not that kind of revolution, Mademoiselle. An uprising of the poor people of the whole country, demanding more rights, more freedom, and the means to put food in the mouths of their families."

Alain shot another glance at her. The girl he remembered had been stocky. Not any more. Why did her neck have to be so slim and her dress reveal so much of her...he forced his eyes back to his father, who was just finishing his usual lecture on the state of the economy. *Why does she find it so interesting? I've heard it a hundred times. Well, maybe she doesn't know everything.* His spirits rose. Or came back towards earth, he didn't know which. *Well, maybe she's stupid.*

"But M. Jouvent, my tutor told me that overseas trade has increased by a factor of five in the last twenty years. Surely that will help?"

She wasn't stupid. *A tutor, not a governess. That sounds like a serious education.* He didn't want her to be boring. *What do I want?*

"My dear, I can't allow you to quiz M. Jouvent like that. I'm sure he has better things to do than teach basic economics to a youngster. Why don't you and Alain run along, now, and leave us to our business."

Angélique was leaning forward, and her look of rapt attention fascinated Alain. Now her brow clouded. "Father! I was just learning some new ideas. Ideas you should listen to! And don't tell Alain and me to 'run along,' like you did six years ago. If you do not find our topic of conversation to your liking, I am sure we can find more suitable company."

Her nose (*long, perhaps, but delicate and straight*) rose and she swirled, ending up right beside him, her hand held out. *Merde! I'm supposed to offer my arm. I hope she didn't notice...* He thought a brief thanks to his mother for all those hours of practice in "proper manners," and allowed his training to take over.

As they reached the end of the room the big double doors swung open as if by magic, and the two of them, side by side, swept through. Angélique held her poise long enough to thank the footman, whose name seemed to be Albert. Then, swinging around, she looked up at Alain and laughed. He felt the warm pressure of her hand, still resting on his arm.

"We sure told them, didn't we?"

"Well, Mlle. de Bardel, you certainly did. I was happy to provide whatever moral support I could."

"Please don't 'mademoiselle' me! I'm the one who showed you my lizards, remember?" She pulled his arm, leading him into a small sitting room and settling him on a delicate chair. "I recall you were very patient about the whole thing."

"I don't mind lizards." He sat gingerly. "I appreciate them. They catch flies."

He had always wondered what people meant by a musical laugh.

"But not a lizard named 'Fripouille' who has a big house in Lyon and a box at the Paris Opera?"

He found himself in the strange position of defending her to herself. "I thought it was quite...inventive. In fact, I chuckled to myself about it for weeks."

He was pleased to see a faint blush rise in her cheeks.

"I was quite young then."

Inspiration struck. "You seem to have changed since. I can see why the village children said your father had brought a pretty lady with him from Grenoble." To his ears the phrase sounded stilted, but he was gratified to see her cheek darken further. *I'm beginning to catch on.* Then she glanced up at him sideways to see if he was joking, and something about the look sent him back to stuttering youth again.

There was an embarrassed pause, at least for Alain. Angélique wasn't the type to be held up for long. "I'm getting a new pet."

His grin grew with his relief that the awkward moment had passed. "May I assume it's larger than a lizard?"

"Quite a bit larger. It's a horse! A full sized hunter. They're sending her up from Marseille this week. Will you come riding with me when she gets here?"

He agreed with glee. That she would be one of the riding sort was too good to believe. *Well, maybe not...* "I...uh, I probably don't ride the same as you do. I...don't wear a fancy costume, and all that. Around here, we mostly go hacking through the bush. We don't do more than three or four formal hunts a year." *Or one or two, if at all.*

"Marvellous! You know, when we decided on this horse, Mother bought me a gorgeous riding skirt, all frills and lace. I tried to make her understand what it would look like after

I'd fallen off a few times, but she just sniffed and said, 'Ladies do not fall off their horses,' so I gave up. I'll ride in a regular old riding skirt, all right?"

"That would probably be best. Do you remember the area around Savournon at all?"

They fell to discussing the various rides around the valley. He told her about some of his adventures in the rough areas of the foothills, and she responded with a few hilarious tales of the formal hunting expeditions she had taken part in. Alain was disappointed when Albert appeared, standing very still and obvious until they could ignore him no longer.

"Mademoiselle, if you please, M. Jouvent has sent me to tell M. Jouvent that the business is finished."

Alain cast a rueful glance at his companion. "Duty calls, I'm afraid."

She smiled back, and he felt a distinct pang somewhere in his chest. "I'll send you a message when my mare arrives, and we can go riding, all right?"

"That would be wonderful." He bowed more formally than necessary and turned to the footman. "You may show me out, now, Albert." Out of the corner of his eye he caught Angélique turning aside to hide her smile. Then he was away, following the uniformed back of the servant through the hallway to where his father was waiting.

Alain was silent for most of the short trip home. The elder Jouvent noticed. "She's grown into quite a young woman, *n'est-ce pas?*"

Alain stumbled back to reality. "Huh...? I mean, yes, I suppose so."

His father laughed. "She didn't have any lizards this time, I would guess. Did you see how she had all of us under her finger because we didn't notice her? She's a smart one, the young *mademoiselle*."

"*D'accord.*"

M. Jouvent reined the horse into their stable yard and stopped. He turned in the seat and looked at Alain. "She's also beautiful, stylish, personable and rich. Everything an ambitious young man might want in a girl."

Alain stared at his father. "What do you mean?"

Jouvent shook his head. "You know what I mean. She's a desirable young lady, and I imagine you two got along very well. Much as I dislike to, I must remind you of two things. First, she spends most of her time in the society of Grenoble. With a large selection of rich, handsome, suave and probably older men. Second, even if she was interested in you, she is nobility. She can't marry a commoner without scandal, and even if she wants to, her father will have a match organized to cement a business or political alliance."

Alain felt the blood rush to his cheeks. "He wouldn't! Anyone can see how he dotes on her! If her happiness were at stake, he wouldn't force her into anything like that."

His father gathered his satchel and stepped out of the carriage. "I don't want to disillusion you, son, but when it comes to marriage contracts, the Second Estate sees things differently from you or me. Besides, she may have her father wrapped around her finger, but what about her mother?"

"Oh."

"I see you remember the mother well enough. Perhaps Mme. de Charrette would consider her daughter's overall happiness to be furthered much better by an alliance to one of the great houses, as opposed to someone she might, in her youth, find briefly appealing."

"It isn't fair!"

"Oh, you're right there. But it's true. So I suggest you temper your dreams, or at least recognize them for what they are. Dreams." Jouvent turned and walked into the house, leaving Alain to take care of the horse, his mind twisting and worrying, torn between daydreams and bitter reality.

2.   To Trap a Rat

June 6, 1788

Alain was in the grip of conflicting emotions all the following week, but he had no occasion to visit the *chateau* and heard no word from Angélique. He moved at more of a wander than his usual brisk pace as he carried out his errands around town. At noon one day he headed out for a walk to think. *And perhaps, if I stroll near the chateau...*

"Hey, Alain!"

He turned. Two figures pelted up the street towards him, one short and slight, the other almost as tall as Alain himself, but heavier. He grinned. Few of the village children, even those his own age, would treat him with such familiarity.

But the baker's children, Edmond and Aimée, went their own cheerful way, treating the world as their equal. He had always rather envied them their self-sufficiency. It must come from being twins and the fact that their mother had died years ago; M. Sarrobert, busy making a living, had to leave his children to their own devices. In any case, Alain found their attitude refreshing. *They're always polite to me, anyway. In fact, I quite like them.* He waited while Edmond dashed up then turned to gesture to his sister, who moved at her own speed.

If Le Bon Dieu was making twins, you'd think He'd have made them more alike. To be fair, I was pretty small at thirteen. He'll catch up to his sister later. "So what's got you two in such a lather? The bakery on fire?"

The boy's wooden clogs clattered impatiently on the cobblestones. "Don't be silly. If the bakery was on fire we wouldn't be calling you."

He looked to Aimée for support. As she arrived in her more dignified manner she smoothed her bright-striped apron self-consciously, but gave her brother an understanding smile. "It isn't that serious, Alain, but we

12

thought you might know something, your father being the lawyer and all. Is anything being done about the thefts?"

"So that's what it's all about. The rats got into your *boulangerie* too, didn't they? Nibbled a loaf of bread?"

Edmond had regained his breath. "Two times, now. And each time nothing broken and only one loaf taken. What do you think of that?"

"I think maybe someone isn't counting very well." He pinched the boy's skinny arm. "Or maybe someone has been nibbling a bit extra to build up his strength. Don't you agree, Aimée? He could use some more weight."

Aimée smiled, but Edmond ignored the jest. "You know better, Alain. I keep perfect record of every loaf. The burnt ones, the broken ones – every one. If I say there's a loaf missing, then it's missing. And I've kept extra careful count since the first theft, so last night I was doubly sure."

Alain gave up trying to get a rise out of the younger boy. "I suppose so. In fact, your father and some of the other shopkeepers were in our office today, asking for advice on how to demand help from the *seigneur*."

"What did he say? Can they?"

Alain led the way to a low stone wall in the shade of a thatched cottage nearby. "He thinks they can. If the guilty party is one of our people, we are expected to deal with it ourselves. Especially for such small thefts."

He raised his hand to forestall the outcry. "*Mais oui*, they build up after a while, but the bailiffs have more to do than chase after some local ne'er-do-well who slips a loaf of bread and a trinket now and then."

Edmond was following closely, his eager face turned upward. "But in this case...?"

"We've decided that it looks like someone from outside the village, and as such it's the *seigneur*'s problem as well."

"So what are they going to do?"

Alain leaned back and grinned. "Guess."

Aimée ticked off the points on her fingers. "Exactly what *Papa* always complains about. They will make a committee and discuss the problem forever. Then they will get your father to look at it. He will give them his ideas and then they will discuss it again. When they are all happy, they will take it to *sieur* de Bardel. He will take it to his lawyer…"

"Who also happens to be my father…"

"…so they won't take long to agree on what should be done. Then the *seigneur* will send his bailiff to find out all the stuff everyone already knows…"

By this time, Edmond was almost hopping off the wall. "But that could take weeks! In the meantime, the thief will have robbed us some more and left town, snickering at us. That's terrible!"

Aimée leaned back and laughed at him. "That's how it works. Could you do any better?"

He was on his feet in a flash. "Why not? I'm here, ready to start right now. I know the town. If only I knew what had been stolen, and from where, I bet…"

Alain couldn't help being impressed by the small boy's enthusiasm. *For a thirteen-year-old, he's very confident. Maybe…* "As it happens, I know what was stolen and where. I took down the details for my father this morning."

"Will you help us?"

Alain had much more on his mind than such children's games. *But…if we were successful, it wouldn't hurt to look good in the eyes of a certain well-bred young lady.*

He looked at the two youngsters. They were children, really, although Aimée had the size and the maturity of a much older person. *But I can practise being a leader. That will be good training.*

"Why not? It would be a laugh to put one over on the village council."

Edmond was already two steps down the road.

"Where are you going?"

"To your office. We need that list."

"That's not a good idea. Do we want everyone to guess what we're doing? Besides, we don't need it. The list isn't that long. I can remember it."

"Great. Where should we work? We can't sit around on the street and plan this. Let's go to our house!"

"Not now, Edmond..."

"Come on, Aimée. Don't be such a worrywart. *Papa* is sleeping, and we can sit in the shop. No one will bother us until opening time this afternoon."

"I suppose so." The girl shot a shy glance at Alain. "If that's all right with you?"

"If you're sure your father won't mind."

"Oh, no. As long as we're quiet. He starts work before sunup. He has to sleep after lunch."

"Since your brother is already half-way home, I guess we might as well follow him."

She laughed again with a tolerance that should come from a much older sister. "Oh, he tends to rush off sometimes."

They followed, their own paces lengthening in anticipation.

* * *

Alain leaned over the big work table in the kitchen of the *boulangerie*. The room was dim and warm and aromatic with yeast and baking bread. The mixing bowls and spoons all shone, everything hung in its proper place. He finished the list and turned it towards his two confederates.

"That's it?" Edmond looked at the scrap of paper "No wonder they're not in a hurry to act."

I have to cut off any negative line of talk. "Let's go through the list again. You can tell a lot about a thief by what he chooses to steal."

Aimée nibbled a fingernail. "An old wool cloak, a tin pot, a fork, a cup. Household things, or what you would take on a journey. But the fancy scarf and the lady's gloves?"

"Frippery. Things that appeal to gypsies." Alain thought some more. "Or things he could sell for money."

"The rest was food. And not too much of it, unless there are other thefts that no one has noticed. Maybe he's not very big."

"Maybe he's living off the land, like the foresters do sometimes."

Aimée frowned. "Maybe he's a big, nasty outlaw, and he's just picking up snacks in the town."

Must keep morale up. "Maybe he's a little guy who doesn't know a thing about living off the land, and that's all he's eating. If so, he'll be out looking tonight. Nothing was reported stolen yesterday, perhaps because of the storm, and he'll be hungry."

She looked more cheerful at this. "So what should we do?"

"We think. Maybe we can tell where he lives by where he does his thievery."

"There is another *boulangerie*; why ours twice?"

"He took the cloak from the bush behind Pierre's house, where his wife had left it to dry."

"And the cup was on the wall of Hughe's upper field."

"Up at the foot of the *serre*." One shoulder of the Eagle's Nest stretched down towards the town, and the fields fell away on either side of it.

Edmond snapped his fingers and jumped to his feet. "There was smoke up at the *vieux eglise* yesterday."

"Edmond! Quiet! You'll wake *Papa*. What do you mean, smoke?"

16

The boy sat down and talked in a rushed whisper, as if afraid that if he didn't say it now it would never come out. "I saw smoke coming up out of the ruins up on the *serre*, but I didn't think anything of it. Could have been a shepherd cooking his lunch. But what if it wasn't!"

Aimée frowned. "It would be silly for someone who was hiding to show where he is. He should have used dry wood and put his fire under a tree so the branches would spread the smoke."

Alain looked at her with more respect. *Where did a girl learn poacher's tricks?* Still, he didn't want Edmond to be wrong. "All the other facts fit. Maybe this fellow doesn't know much about living in the open. Maybe he's sick or weak from lack of food, and can't get a proper fire. He must have needed one yesterday, after that rain we had in the morning. Maybe he couldn't find any dry wood."

Edmond jumped up again. "Let's go and check."

"I don't think we should." Aimée shook her head. "If there is someone there we'll scare him off. We should set a trap for him."

The "we" was not lost on Alain. He listened as they rattled on at each other, their voices blending, incomplete sentences dropping as communication flashed between them. He began to feel left out. *If I'm going to be the leader, I'd better get in on the planning.* He followed the conversation more closely.

"What if we're wrong and he's dangerous? What if he's an escaped convict? He could hurt someone."

Alain nodded. "We must proceed very carefully, reconnoitre fully before we show ourselves."

Aimée looked at him. "I don't know what reconnoitre means, but if we are going to be careful, that's fine with me."

Alain felt a brief warmth in his cheeks. She had pricked the balloon of his self-importance neatly, but there was nothing with which to take offence. In a small town, one couldn't help but hear rumours. Edmond had done very well in the parish school as far as it went, and Aimée had been running her father's shop for years. They were poorly educated, perhaps, but not dull.

Edmond broke in, unaware of the awkwardness of the moment. "Bird calls would do." He looked up to see the others watching him, questions on both faces.

"Bird calls. Signals. We'll have to wait spread out on the hillside to be sure of finding him. Whoever sees him can signal the others. Maybe an owl hoot. Then, we should have a signal for moving in…"

"…and one for pulling back." His sister finished.

"The pull back signal needs to be stronger in case of an emergency. Perhaps a nighthawk?" Alain pursed his lips and called.

"We can learn that."

Alain nodded. "It's not hard. And we'll also need a… somewhere to meet if we pull back."

Aimée nodded in her turn. "A rendezvous point."

He glanced at her, but she was all innocence. Had she noticed his change to a simpler term? *If she's willing to let it go, so am I.*

Edmond was pacing again. "There are more problems to solve. We assume that someone is hiding in the old church up on the shoulder of the Chateau de l'Aigle. He is coming out at dusk to steal things, then going back when it gets full dark, to eat whatever he stole and sleep. Right?"

Alain and the girl nodded.

"So we have to figure that he is awake in the late afternoon. If he follows the routine of the predatory animals, he's asleep now and he'll wake up when the evening starts to cool."

Aimée worried the fingernail again. "If we wait for him to return, how will we know where to wait, and how will we get into position without being seen? When should we go?"

"We have to wait until almost dark." Alain shrugged. "If that doesn't fit the schedule of our burglar, then I guess we'll leave our card and come back another day."

He was rewarded by smiles on the other two faces. "So we meet somewhere at dusk?"

"We should come from the west. He won't climb up along the ridge, because he'd have to come past the *chateau*, where there are people about all the time."

Alain looked again at the smaller boy with respect. There was a sharp mind inside that small head with the big ears and the pointed chin. "Good idea. How about the little ridge that juts out to the west?

"It overlooks the *eglise*."

A glance at Aimée confirmed her opinion. "We agree. So we can meet at the top of the ridge at dusk, coming up the west side. Be very quiet." He grinned. "I guess I don't need to tell you."

He had another thought. "Is there any chance there are more than one?"

Aimée looked grave. "I have been wondering about that, too. We do have our danger signal."

"There wasn't enough bread taken for two. Almost as if he expected to be back for a fresh loaf in a day or so. If there's a problem, we split up and run for help. We should be able to get away from any stranger in the dark." Edmond slanted his head towards the hill. "Aimée and I played in those gullies all the time when we were small."

Alain smiled. "I spent a few afternoons there myself before I started working with my father."

They spent a few minutes on the bird-call signals, then Alain left, satisfied. *This is going to be great.* He thought about his new allies. For a spur-of-the-moment decision, it seemed a good one. They were both enthusiastic and cooperative, although sometimes the communication seemed to fly so fast between them that he felt left behind. It

19

must come with being twins. They also seemed to accept his leadership, which was important. *Not that I have to be leader, but I'm the oldest, and no matter who leads, a lot of time can be wasted if someone always has to argue.*

* * *

As he approached the top of the ridge that night he reflected on the difference between a plan and reality. It had been a while since he made the trip, and he had forgotten what a difficult climb it was. The Chateau de l'Aigle was a rugged crag jutting up behind the town, its dry and crumbling ridges spreading out across the valley floor and blending into the stony fields at its base. Half way up a shoulder jutted out to the south, where some time in the far-off past someone had decided to build a chapel. Time and the vagaries of human politics had abandoned the sanctuary, and erosion had pulled the ridge away from under it, leaving the hulk teetering on a narrow crest. *One day this is all going to come sliding down the mountainside. I'd like to be here to see that. From a distance.*

The ridge was mantled with scattered shrubs, and tufts of grass and spiny bushes struggled to survive in between. The raw earth was carpeted with sticks, dead leaves, and several more varieties of thorn and cactus than he remembered. To climb it in half-darkness, trying to be silent, was almost impossible. He was glad he had come in plenty of time. He was relieved to reach the top, hot and sweaty, and find that he was the first there.

Approaching the summit on his stomach, he slid under a bush to peer across at the ruins of the old church. He watched for a long time, but nothing moved. He was debating whether he should scout around when he heard a crackling in the brush behind him. Hoping that the growing dusk would hide him if the wrong person was approaching, he pushed farther into the inadequate shelter of the bush.

When he saw the small figure worming up towards the crest he relaxed, pursed his lips and gave the "alert" call.

The figure stopped, waited, then answered.

Satisfied, he called out in a low voice. "Keep quiet down there! I could hear you a *lieu* away!"

Edmond said nothing, but proceeded at a slower, quieter pace until he was beside the older boy.

"Anything moving?"

"Nothing I could see. I haven't been here long. Where's Aimée?" He wouldn't be too disappointed if she backed out. *I don't want to be responsible for a girl out here on the lonely hillside at night with a criminal running around.*

Edmond's flipped a hand. "Oh, she's slower than me. She'll be here."

The two of them crept forward and stared into the deepening darkness. For a long while, nothing stirred.

"Do you think he's there?"

"According to our plan, he's down in the village right now, picking up his supper."

"I left a loaf of bread out real obvious. I hope he takes it and doesn't mess up anything else."

Alain was about to respond when he was aware of another shadow beside him. His heart jumped in his throat, but then he realized it was Aimée. Somehow she had slipped up on them.

His surprise made him speak brusquely. "Oh. There you are. We were discussing what to do next. We still don't know if he's at home or not." He had a sudden thought of how foolish they would look if they spent all this energy and there was no one in the old church at all.

Aimée shrugged. "If there's no one there, this has been fun anyway."

A good way to look at it. Alain grinned at his accomplices. "So shall we assume we are right and go over for a look?" He was gratified when they agreed at once. "We have to be even more careful, in case he's still there. Edmond, don't get in a hurry, now."

"Should we all go together?"

Alain considered. Any small noises they made would be less suspicious if they came from different directions. On the other hand, he had no idea what they were approaching.

"We would be safer to stay together."

Aimée's quick agreement showed how she felt.

"If you were staying in the old church, where would you be?"

After a moment Edmond spoke decisively. "The south wall at the far end. There's more stone left, and it curves around to keep the light of your fire hidden."

Alain tried to remember the layout. "And there's that niche in the wall to get into if it rained."

They nodded.

"So we come in at this end, on the uphill side." Getting agreement again, Alain set off along the western side of the ridge below the skyline, the other two following close behind. Last week's *mistral* had scoured the ground cover from the top of the *serre*, so they made good time with a minimum of noise. They scrambled through a gully and came down the side of the ridge where the old chapel perched.

The western end of the ruin was gone – undermined by erosion – and the corner of the north wall hung out over empty air. They kept low as they passed the opening and crept along outside the uphill wall. Approaching the gap half way down, Alain stopped and the other two slid alongside. They both looked at him.

This is it. If we've been heard, I might be sticking my head up only to get an arrow through my eye. That ought to impress Angélique. He slipped behind a small bush growing out over the broken stone and very slowly rose to look over the wall.

At first he could see nothing. The interior of the church was as barren as it had been for centuries, the flagstones all stolen long ago to build the village houses. Bushes and shrubs grew here and there, a large one half-concealing the corner where they expected their quarry's camp to be. It was even darker there, but as far as he could see, the *elgise* was empty. He lowered his head and turned to give a negative sign to his friends, then signalled that he was moving up.

Keeping in the shelter of the bush, he slid over the low wall, searching for any movement in the dark ahead of him. From this new angle he could make out a dull red glow that tinged a few protruding stones of the wall in that corner. *Where is that coming from? The sun is long set.* Then he saw an old fire, its coals almost dead, in a hollow below the niche. A jolt, half fear and half satisfaction, ran through him. *We were right! No shepherd would leave a fire burning in this dry country. Someone plans to return.*

If he has gone.

He looked back and made a gesture to join him, followed by a severe signal for caution. Then he crawled forward, his eyes searching every dark corner of the old building, his ears keen for any sound. All he could hear were the muffled crackling steps of the two behind. As they approached the fire it became apparent that no one was about.

The coals were banked, and the niche that had once held the statue of a saint now contained a small, dark object. Signalling the others to stay out of the faint firelight, he slipped along the wall and brought out a rolled bundle. After one last look around, they crouched on the dirt of the old floor and opened the cloth.

As he unrolled it, there was a loud clank. They froze, ears straining.

Nothing happened. After an agonizing wait Alain continued, more carefully now, the others holding out their hands to contain anything that might roll out.

Their haul turned out to be pitifully small. The old cloak harboured a tattered leather bag, a spoon and a cup. It was these last two that had made the metallic sound. The bag contained strange odds and ends, impossible to see in the dark: straps, buckles and odd bits of metal. The only recognizable things were a pair of rather scruffy lady's gloves and a square of cloth, which Alain suspected would turn out, when viewed in the light, to be a bright scarf.

"Let's put it back."

Alain nodded. "You're right, Aimée. We don't want him suspicious. And let's hurry. He could get here any moment."

Carefully but wasting no time, they rolled the bundle and replaced it as close as Alain could remember to its original position. Then they moved over to the side of the church facing down towards the village.

The middle of the wall had fallen away here, too, but a large and prickly bush made access difficult. They looked over, again careful to keep their heads off the skyline.

"He'll come up there." Edmond pointed to a line of bushes that marked one of the deep, dry watercourses eroding the mountainside. It passed along the opposite side of a small field that some time in the recent past had been an orchard. Sere, twisted trunks were all that remained. Above them the watercourse was not so deep, and a string of trees and bushes on what might have been an old path curved naturally into the ridge, approaching the church from the east along the mountain.

"Where shall we hide?"

Alain looked out again. "He might leave the creek and cut across the old orchard if he's confident. If not, he'll stay in the denser trees as long as possible, then come in down the ridge. Whichever choice he makes, he'll enter through the east end where it's broken down. One of us should stay near the ridge, and the other two closer to his fire in the west end of the church."

Aimée pointed to an old pine, more a bush than a tree, above the path.

"I like that spot."

It was not far from the path the thief would probably take, but it was getting dark, now. "That should be fine if you stay very still."

He caught a glimpse of white in her face. She must be grinning at him. "Did you hear me when I came up the hill?"

He grinned back. "I'll take the other end of the church, where it's open. I can lie behind those bushes, and if he comes my way I'll fade back down the mountain. What about you, Edmond?"

The boy pointed to the thorn bush blocking the broken wall, right where they were standing. "There's a hole under there."

His sister's eyes widened. "But that's within three paces of his fire!"

"*Vraiment.* I'll get a good look, won't I? Besides, if he comes for me, I can slip out underneath. If he's small enough to get through that hole, he's not very dangerous."

Aimée nodded. Alain stayed out of this one. *If she thinks it's good enough, I won't argue.* "So let's get ready. This may take a long time, so make yourselves comfortable." They rehearsed their signals once more, birdcalls ringing out among the ancient stones. Then they separated to their positions to wait.

3.   The Trap Sprung

Late Evening, June 6 1788

It took much longer than Alain had thought it would. He tried to keep track by the movement of the stars, but had no real idea how, so he gave up. Several times he was ready to quit, but each time he persuaded himself to stay awhile longer. Real birdcalls wove sleepily up the hill, and he hoped there were no nighthawks around.

A whisper cut through his thoughts.

"Alain! Something moving down there!"

He peered over the bush. Edmond had half-crawled out of his shelter and was waving at him.

"Not so loud! Are you sure?"

"Pretty sure! Where that old trail crosses the creek bed, and that stone wall makes a bridge? Looked like someone was climbing over it, then coming on up the hill."

"Give Aimée the signal and get back under cover."

A moment later, the call of a hunting owl drifted over the ruins. Another owl answered out along the hill, then all was silent. The moon hadn't risen yet, and a faint, even light glowed from the stars and the brightness in the west where the sun had set long ago. Again, the wait seemed endless. Then the owl up on the hillside called again. Aimée. Their quarry must have passed her.

Then things got mixed up. Immediately after, there was another cry, this one the warning. Then, it looked as if Edmond was out, because bushes crackled and a small figure was outlined briefly against the glow of the fire. Alain peered ahead, wondering what was going on. He was about to move forward when the warning call sounded from Aimée again, twice. Then all was silent.

There came a louder cracking of branches and more silence. Then the yellow light of flames sprang up. Someone had put wood on the fire. He heard a low, muffled cough, and again a small figure was outlined for a moment against the light. What was Edmond doing? Why had Aimée warned them off? He agonized over what to do. In the end, it was easier to do nothing. He could have ignored one warning, but Aimée seemed to be a very sensible type and he had to trust her. The cough sounded again, stronger this time.

He inched forwards, staring at the wall, trying to make out the flickering shadows on it. Then he blinked. All of a sudden – or maybe not so sudden, as he could not tell when it happened – a figure was sitting against the wall, half in the firelight. It was Aimée. She was seated comfortably, her back to the wall, her arms around her knees.

There was an explosion of sound, and a high voice carried through the ruins.

"*Sainte Marie Mère de Dieu*, protect me! Holy *Jésus et tous les Saints* help me now. Holy father, I have sinned, forgive me. Oh, my Lord, *c'est un fantôme*. Oh, Lord, forgive me my trespasses whatdoIdonow?" The voice croaked, then fell off into a fit of coughing, and a small shadow hunched over between Alain and the fire.

Then Aimée's voice came, soft and casual. "I'm not a ghost, boy. I'm as human as you are. Don't take on so. I'm here to help you, not hurt you. You don't sound in very good shape, boy. Are you cold?"

The shadow straightened. "You ain't a ghost, here ta punish me for my sins?"

"Heavens no, little fellow." She chuckled. "I've got sins of my own. I'm a girl from the town down there, and I've come to help you. Are you ill?"

"You're from the town?"

"Yes. The *boulangerie* at the foot of the hill. I think you know it."

"An' what if I do?"

"We left a loaf for you. Did you get it?"

"A loaf? Ya left a loaf out? And I didn't go that way tonight. Ain't that enough bad luck ta give ya *le lepre* and rot yer toes off." There was a pause. "Why'd ya leave a loaf out?"

"Because we thought you might be hungry."

"Who's we?" The boy looked around suspiciously.

"My brother and me. He's about your size. Maybe a bit bigger." She raised her voice. "Edmond? It's all right. He's a friend. You can come in, now."

She made it sound like the end of a game, and Edmond crawled out from under his bush. Alain took the cue and kept still.

The boy gaped. "*Merde!* You was right there all along, and I never caught on?"

Edmond smiled. "We had you figured pretty well. Knew where you'd be, where you'd walk, when you'd come."

"*Zut alors!* Ya didn't know I wasn't comin' by yer shop tonight!"

Aimée's voice cut off this possible conflict. "Are you alone up here?"

He nodded. "Takin' care of myself, I am."

"How old are you, anyway?"

"I'm eleven, I think, Might even be twelve."

Even given the effect of malnutrition in some city slum, the lad couldn't be over nine. *Well, if he really is taking care of himself, he might be ten.*

"*Oh, la vache!* You're not eleven. I bet you're not even ten."

The urchin gave a nonchalant grin. "Well, ya know, sometimes what's true gets all mixed up with what ya wanta be true, and after a while ya can't quite remember which is which. So ya go for a sorta half way in between, ya know?"

"A compromise, is that it?"

"What's that word? Compromise? Yeah, that's what it is. A compromise."

28

He seemed quite pleased with his philosophy, combined with the new word he had learned, and sat looking at them, smiling all over his grubby face.

Alain regarded the boy. *He is so easy with these older strangers. What confidence! Unless he has someone larger nearby...* He tried to look around, but his hiding place prevented him.

Aimée seized on this opportunity. "The truth does change a bit, sometimes. Actually, we do have another friend. *Un autre garçon.* Can he come and join us?

The fugitive peered around again, then waved an easy consent, a movement spoiled by another spate of harsh coughing. While his attention was distracted, Alain rose and approached the fire. The boy looked up at Alain's height, sudden mistrust oozing out of every pore.

"Ya sure that's alla ya? Don't have a bailiff hidin' round the corner?"

Alain laughed easily. "No, I'm it. I'm the only one left."

"All right, then, you can come and sit down."

Edmond leaned forward. "Where are you from?"

The boy paused, a thoughtful look coming over his face. "Oh, around and about. I move when I please, ya know."

"But you must have come from somewhere in the first place."

"*Bein sûr.* But I bin a lotta places since." He looked at them all, his smug grin returning.

"Marseille." Alain nodded.

The grin faded. "*Sacre bleu!* How'd ya know that?"

"Your accent. My father took me to Marseille two years ago when he went on business, and the fish sellers in the market talked like you do. I bet you come from fishing people." The boy's inflection was strong, and so heavily laced with *Provençal* that he was hard to understand at times.

"*Nom de Dieu*! I'd jump off a cliff before I'd go out in one of them leaky tubs. Nope, I'm just another rat from the gutters. I'm a landlubber, and proud of it."

Alain reserved judgement. *'Landlubber' sounds like a sailor's term to me.*

"Who're you folks, since ya know so much about me?"

Alain made the introductions. When the boy heard the word "*advocat*," his eyes narrowed.

"A lawyer's son, hey? Bet yer rich. Bet yer dad's got his silver all stashed away in banks in England and Austria for when th' revolution comes."

"Revolution?"

"Don't ya know nothin', back here in the hills? There's goin' ta be a revolution. The people, like me and my friends, we ain't goin' ta take much more of this. There's goin' ta be an uprisin', and it's comin' soon!"

If it hadn't been for the conversation at de Bardel's, Alain would have dismissed this as idle boasting. "And who is going to lead this revolt?"

"The people. The common ordinary people, like me and the baker's kids here. You better decide real quick whose side ye're goin' ta be on, lawyer's son, 'cause we're not goin' ta be easy on those who held us in slavery all these years while they lived in luxury. Them and their fancy balls and their big *chateaux* and their banquets and servants and horses and all."

Alain had to grin at the boy's tiny ferocity, but still he asked a serious question. "Where have you heard all this? It sounds a lot like treason. You could get in trouble with the king's officers, talking like that."

A hoarse chuckle escaped the boy's throat, his head thrown back. "Trouble with the king's officers, now. *Ma foi!* Why d' ya think I'm scroungin' my grub out here in the sticks, rather than back in my home town, where I'm knowed and respected?"

"I don't know. Why are you here?"

"Let's say I was seen too many a the wrong places at the wrong times. There's a lot goin' on down there that don't at first meet the eye, if ya catch my drift. So I thought about it, and what with Marseille gettin' too hot for me, I figured I'd head for Paris, 'cause when the revolution comes, that's where it's all gonna happen, and I'm gonna be in on it."

Alain let this idea sink in. Then he looked at the group gathered around the fire. "The question is, what to do with you now? With that cough, you're in no shape to travel, and you can't keep stealing from the townspeople. We aren't the only ones with brains. Once Antonin the bailiff gets involved, he'll find you."

The boy gestured with his thumb. "She said ye'd help me."

"I heard her. She didn't ask me first, but since she said it, that goes for all of us. But there is one condition. No more stealing."

"Easy for you. Ya got supper and a warm bed ta go ta."

"That's true. But you've got a cloak to wrap up in, and it's a warm night. I can give you what I brought for a snack, and we'll bring more tomorrow. But there's no argument. You steal again, we turn you over to the bailiff. Agreed?"

With a poor grace, the boy nodded. "I dunno what's the big deal. I only took a coupla things that the owners had lots more of."

"Hmm. I doubt if the owners see it that way. By the way, you didn't tell us your name."

"Jimmy." The single word was spoken proudly, as if they should have heard of it.

Edmond frowned. "That's not a name."

"Whaddaya mean, it's not a name? *Sacre bleu!* Ask anyone in the Canebière 'round the docks if that name don't mean somethin' to them!"

Aimée shook her head, her voice soft. "He means it's not a French name."

"Mebbe it ain't. I never did hear of anyone else with that name."

"What's your other name?"

"I told ya my name. Ain't got no other. Don't need one. Everybody knows who Jimmy is."

"Well, we do now. It's getting late and it's pretty dark going down the mountain. We'll leave you, and one of us will come up tomorrow with food, all right?"

"*D'accord.* Any chance you could bring some water? I bin lookin' for a watersack or a jug, but they're all put away real careful in this town. It's a long ways across the hill to that stream."

Alain knew from experience how difficult it was to cross the many small, steep gullies, all full of thorn bushes, that ran down the mountainside, and how their sheer dirt sides slid when you tried to walk across them.

"*Pas de problem.* We'll bring water. But it might not be till late. We have work to do." He stood, and his team followed him.

The boy shrugged. "If ya get here 'fore dusk, I won't have ta go scroungin'. That'll be fine with me."

Time to make my point clear. "And if we're late, you'll wait anyway. Remember, any more thievery, and we turn you in."

Again the shrug. "*Ça marche.* You're holdin' the tiller, I guess you get to steer for a while." He unrolled the cloak, checking his belongings and giving the others a threatening stare.

"By the way, you had better give us the things you stole."

"What?"

"If we put them back it'll take the pressure off and no one will be looking for you."

The boy clutched the bag to him and pulled back against the stones, looking more like a broody hen than a child. Aimée leaned down and laid a hand on his shoulder.

"You don't need them any more. We'll bring you some more. Better ones, even. Do you want the townspeople to be out looking for you? Keep the cloak. You need it."

At her soft touch the stiffness went out of the boy and he coughed again. Gently, she took the cup, fork, gloves and scarf from him. He rolled up in the cloak and lay on the ground near the fire, the old leather bag under his head, his arm wrapped around it. Alain and Edmond found more dry branches and laid them at hand while Aimée wrapped the loot up in her shawl. They bid Jimmy good night, but he ignored them and they set off down the hill in the dark.

It was tough going at first, but after a while they reached the fields that stretched their last, stone-scattered edges up the mountain, and they could walk side by side.

Aimée moved up beside Alain. "Are you mad at me?"

He glanced down at her face, a pale circle hovering there. "Should I be?"

"I thought you might be. But it all worked out, didn't it?"

"Can't argue with that, but it might help if you explained. Why did you warn us off? There was no danger."

"If I hadn't warned you, what would you have done?"

Alain considered. Then he nodded, even though she couldn't see. "As soon as I figured out how small he was, I'd have jumped him."

"Right."

"I see what you're getting at. And then he wouldn't have trusted us. But why do we want him to trust us? We had him. All we had to do was turn him in. We'd be heroes."

"Is that what you want?"

"Well, I suppose not. I can't see being a hero at his expense, poor little Rat. Can you imagine, calling yourself a rat and being proud of it?"

She chuckled. "I don't think he's a rat. More like a pigeon, the way he sticks out his chest and struts around."

"Do you think he'll be all right? That cough…"

She was silent for a moment. "You can never tell. As long as he keeps warm it should go away in a while. If it gets down in his chest it could kill him. I can't tell, right now." Her face screwed up with worry.

"Don't be upset, Aimée. He sounds pretty tough. We'll take care of him and put these things back, and he'll be fine."

Again he could see her face turned up to him. "Thank you, Alain."

"Why thank me? I'm not doing anything for you."

"You know what I mean."

When he thought about it, he probably did.

4. Hailstones

June 7, 1788

"You had better get up now, *mon chou. Papa* has finished his *chocolat.*"

Alain groaned and rolled over. Then as the maid's words sank in, he sprang from his bed in an abortive attempt to hurry.

"*Pas si vite*, young Alain. 'More haste, less speed,' as *ma vieille maman* used to say. Now I've laid out your suit, and there's hot water in the basin. It won't take you *un moment* to get ready, and *votre père* is in *une humeur très bonne* today. I haven't been looking after you all for these years without knowing exactly how long it takes you to get dressed in the morning."

"Ariane, you are an angel sent from heaven to help this poor sinner cope with the world. Now will you get out and let me dress?"

"And they say young girls are modest. Many's the time I cleaned your little…"

"Ariane! Don't be so rude. I've heard that story too many times. Go away!" The folds of his nightclothes muffled the strength of his protest as he pulled them over his head.

Her unperturbed step receded, another platitude, this one in her native *Provençal*, wafting back over her ample shoulder. He barely understood it, but it was something about people who party all night paying for it in the morning. And he had hoped that no one heard him come in so late.

Putting back the stolen items had been fun. Sort of fun, but also scary. *The thought of being caught, of the lawyer's son arrested. The thought of what Angélique's mother would have to say!*

But they had not been caught. It had been hard to find places where a stolen object could have been naturally lost, but obvious enough that it would soon be found. It would have been unwise to replace everything in plain sight. Mysteriously returned objects would have raised a superstitious uproar, with every peasant jumping at his shadow for weeks.

He stumbled downstairs collecting his thoughts, but his ready excuses died on his lips as he entered the dining room. His father merely looked up from a letter he was reading and nodded to Alain's place at the table. "Your chocolate's getting cold."

Grateful for small mercies, Alain slipped into his chair and reached for the cup. "What's on the agenda for today?"

The elder Jouvent put down the letter. "We have to go over the documents on the Montsaléon case again. I want to be positive that we have interpreted the various laws correctly." He slapped the letter on his knee several times. "I wish the king would get his lawyers together and write a common set of laws for the realm. It is so ridiculous, trying to write a contract that takes two or even three different sets of laws into account. I imagine it was fine in the old days, when people only had dealings with their immediate neighbours, but in modern times, with the new roads and all this mobility, the old, regional laws just don't work."

"At least it keeps us lawyers busy."

"But we could be doing so much more useful work! Besides, Alain, I have told you before not to make jokes like that. Too many people say that sort of thing in all earnestness."

Alain grinned and made the motion of shooting a pistol in his father's direction.

His father grinned back. "Caught me again, didn't you?" He leaned forward. "You know, if you are good at manipulating people's reactions the next step is to do it without them noticing. That way they can't fight you." He nodded knowingly and sat back.

Alain also put on a serious air. "Yes, father. I will remember that. The next time I provoke you, I will be sure that you don't catch on. It will be too bad, though."

His father raised his eyebrows.

"If I get good at it you will never notice, so you can't be proud of me."

As Madame Jouvent entered the room behind her son, a piece of bread bounced off the wall beside her.

"François! What is going on here?"

"Don't worry my dear. Just a small disciplinary action required to remind our son of his manners."

"Perhaps it would be good for his manners if he cleaned up the results of the lesson."

"Sorry mother. *Papa* and I have to go down, now. There is a great deal of work to do on the Montsaléon case. Ariane will be glad to clean it up."

"Alain!" The steel-in-velvet voice.

He winked at his father and bent over to scrape up the crumbs. "Ah, the humility of it all, forced to do servant's work while my parents recline in luxury."

His mother was fussing over his father's coat and tossed her comment over her shoulder. "A lesson in humility never did anyone any harm. Especially a young lad who doesn't need to get above himself. Now you two get down to the office. I'll be there in a few minutes. I have to talk to Ariane about lunch." She grabbed each of them by a lapel, and they turned in the door to face her. "And don't you think you're going to spend all morning nit-picking about the various laws *sieur* de Montsaléon is trying to bend. I know you enjoy it, but we also have real work to do." Ignoring their protestations of innocence, she kissed each on the cheek and pushed them out.

The three of them spent the morning working efficiently through a large pile of documents. Just after eleven o'clock Mme. Jouvent raised her eyes from her copying job. "All right, you two. I'm sure I can finish off here by lunch. You go and play in your case histories and files."

François sighed in exaggerated relief and reached for the appropriate papers, but Alain could not let this slur pass. "Mother, this case is very difficult. The transactions involve properties in three different provinces, and that means there are three separate sets of legal precedents to consider. If France had a unified legal system, we wouldn't have this kind of..." He wound down as he noticed his father pointing a finger at him in a shooting gesture.

"Don't even consider it." His mother smiled serenely but didn't look up from her work.

Alain lowered the ball of paper he had been poised to throw and turned to help his father. Peace reigned once more in the office of "F. Jouvent, Advocat et Notaire."

They were just sitting down to lunch when there was a persistent knocking on the downstairs door. Jouvent got up in irritation. "Now who could be so rude as to disturb us during a meal?" He stomped down and opened the door.

They could hear his brusque tone turn to one of mild surprise, and then his step returned up the stair, more slowly than his descent. "It seems we have the footman of Mme. de Charrette, who honours us with his dignified presence."

"Albert?"

"Is that his name? Albert very respectfully presents this missive to M. Jouvent Jr. and would consider it an honour to wait for any reply the said M. Jouvent would care to tender."

M. Jouvent Sr. saw his wife's perplexed look and put on an elevated accent. "Mme. de Charrette brought a footman with her. Very correct."

Alain, in the act of reaching out his hand, glanced over and was gratified to see a moue of distaste cross her face. Then his attention was occupied with the letter.

It was a single piece of heavy paper, folded twice and sealed. He broke the ornate pink wax, looking up at the mix of interest and anxiety with which his parents were watching him. One glance at the signature confirmed his suspicion. "Angélique." They both nodded, and he went back to reading.

The letter was brief, in a precise hand, neat but not flowery in the least.

"She's here and it's a beautiful day. Are we going riding?"

He looked up. The adults had not moved. "Angélique just got a new horse, and she wants me to go riding this afternoon."

His father's worried look deepened. "I'm not sure, Alain. I did mention the difficulties of getting too involved here..." He glanced over to his wife for support.

Alain looked at his mother as well, his heart sinking. In matters like this, the two of them were always in accord, and he had long ago learned the futility of resisting.

To his surprise, her glance slid towards the stairwell down to the office, and that displeased look reappeared. "No, François, I don't see a problem. Alain, why don't you write the young lady that you will be happy to ride with her later this afternoon. You might impress upon her that you have business to attend to. You can get away by three o'clock."

Alain headed for the office stairs, but again his mother surprised him. Getting up, she opened her private writing desk and extracted a piece of thick, cream-coloured paper, which she laid out, gesturing for him to sit.

With an exaggerated bow he did so, and wrote a short note along the lines she had suggested, very careful to be neat.

Gordon A. Long

She took the note, folded it and handed it to her husband. "Perhaps you would be good enough to close this with the family seal and send it off with Albert." She said the name with a touch of disdain, raising an eyebrow to her son, making sure she had it right.

He nodded, grinning with pleasure.

His father shrugged his shoulders. "I don't mind being the errand boy, for once." He disappeared once more. Soon a murmur of voices floated up the stairwell, and the door opened and closed again.

"I suppose you know what you're doing," was his only comment when he returned to his place.

"I suppose I do. There is no reason Alain should not go riding with whomever it pleases him to ride. His horse may not be a purebred, but I'm sure he rides it with as firm a seat as anyone."

The elder Jouvent had regained his humour. "As long as he doesn't expect his father to play butler too often."

"If Albert puts you off so much, I'll pretend to be the downstairs maid next time."

* * *

Once his mother had decided on something the wheels turned even more smoothly than normal. Precisely at three o'clock, dressed in a riding coat that was passable but not his best, Alain was standing at the big front door of Chateau Savournon. To his relief, it was not Albert who answered, but Angélique herself, dressed likewise for a rough ride.

She made a silencing gesture, but her eyes flashed. "Mother's not enthused about this whole situation, so let's not draw attention to ourselves." She led him around the west wing of the house to the stables, where a handsome, grey mare with darkly mottled flanks and black stockings stood by the mounting block.

Without waiting for the groom's help, Angélique flung herself on and with a flick of her wrist arranged her skirt over the sidesaddle. Alain swung up on his own brown horse, and for a moment their eyes met. Then Angélique tossed her head. "Where shall we ride?"

He shrugged, although he had a route planned. "Where would you like to go?"

She shrugged in turn, reining her horse out the gate. "I don't care much. I have already ridden the small paths around here to get Ocelle used to me, so I'm ready to try something more interesting. Do you have something in mind?"

Perfect. He pulled up beside her at the junction, aiming her horse up the road. "I imagine I can find a good trail. How about south past la Queyra, up through Jubeo Forest, to the Gorge of the Riou?"

She laughed. "Sounds very well planned, and I only recognize one of those names. Can we be back in two hours?"

"Easily, if that poor, city-bred horse of yours can keep up."

She regarded him under lowered brows. "I imagine it can keep up with that shaggy country-bred beast of yours."

Oops. "Angélique, I don't want any racing, or anything." *Or any fighting.*

She wasn't exactly disappointed, but something in her tone told him she was upset. "Fine. I understand. After all, she's a new horse."

"I guess we should take it easy until you're more familiar with her."

The two horses, side-by-side, trotted through the village, Alain enjoying the reaction of the people they met. Angélique was friendly and comfortable, speaking easily to people who spoke to her, giving a wave or nod to those who did not. When they reached the bridge before the hamlet of Gonillons a wagon was crossing, and Alain rode ahead so they could go in single file. Angélique had a bit of trouble getting her horse out on the echoing bridge but handled it masterfully. So Alain was in the lead when he rounded the corner of the first building and was confronted by a stocky, thick-necked gentleman of about twenty-five, dressed in high leather boots, a rifle over his arm. Two men in huntsmen's clothes stood behind him.

"And where are you off to, young fellow?"

"We're just out for a ride, *sieur* de Gonillons."

"Well, you make sure you stay on the paths. You youngsters, riding all over the fields, destroying the crops..." He stopped in mid-sentence as Angélique rode up.

"Why, good afternoon, my Lady. Is the boy taking you riding?"

She paused before replying sweetly, "Good afternoon *sieur* de Gonillons. Yes, we are out for a ride together. A pleasant day for an outing with friends, isn't it?" Her eyes flicked over the two servants.

The man seemed unaware of any irony. "Certainly my Lady." He bowed, his arm sweeping up and out. "Please, ride where you will."

"Thank you. I certainly shall." She lifted her reins and her horse, still skittish from the bridge perhaps, sidled, causing de Gonillons to step back out of the way. Angélique did not look back or apologize.

Alain kneed his horse to stay even with her. There was silence for a while, except for their horses' hooves thudding on the road. He glanced across at her several times; gradually the stiffness went out of her back.

They had reached the edge of the village and broke out into the open fields. The sun was warm, and the growing crops were losing their light spring hues, turning to the darker green of maturity. Alain picked a spray of blue flowers from the hedge, handing it to her wordlessly. She looked surprised, then smiled warmly and rode on, holding the flowers to her nose in her free hand.

They jogged comfortably along the road, enjoying the warmth of the sun and the beauty of the June countryside, but for Alain, it was not the perfect beginning he had envisioned. Perhaps his mother's attitude had made him sensitive, but he was put off by the suggestion that Angélique's parents were not keen on having her ride with him. And something was bothering her, too. Something about being careful. He kicked himself for the reference to her horse. The last thing he wanted was to draw attention to their class difference. *How to find out what's wrong without making it worse? I'll probably make it worse. There was also more going on than the polite surface conversation with Reynaud de Gonillons.*

But their unease was soothed by the gentle breeze, and soon they were chattering together about whatever came to mind. Talking with her certainly wasn't a problem. She was interested in everything, from the plants in the hedge to the people they met walking alongside it.

"What's that peak called? I always thought it looked so threatening, looming like it does over the valley."

He grinned. "That's Revuaire. He does loom a bit, doesn't he? Maybe because on the south side of the valley his face is always in shadow. That's my favourite mountain, standing out from the rest of the cliff like a sentry."

"Some sentry. I don't think I'd like to live at Pélissieres. Who needs a sentry 200 *pieds* tall looking over her shoulder?"

"Makes a splendid view for those of us who live on the other side of the valley, though."

"I've always wanted to get up there. Now, that view would be spectacular!"

"You can."

"Climb that? You must be out of your mind."

He grinned. "Oh, no. Just wait a while. You'll see."

She pushed for more information, but he refused to tell her, only promising that she would find out later in the ride. Finally she gave up and turned her attention to the scenery.

Soon the road left the populated floor of the valley and followed the edge of a gully up into the trees. They passed through the hamlet of les Queyras – not much more than a farm with its outbuildings and worker's cottages – and wound up through a denser wood of pine trees whose crowns spread out twenty or more *piedes* above them, leaving open space and a carpet of bare pine needles below. Crossing a low pass, they reached the foresters' station, a massive stone building with several smaller sheds around. They stopped there for a drink at the spring, but then mounted and pressed on. Alain was eager to reach the gorge area because the views were spectacular and he wanted to see her reaction.

He was not disappointed. As they rounded the corner and came out of the woods, she reined in her horse and sat, her mouth open.

"Oh, Alain! I never knew there was anything like this near Savournon. This is beautiful!"

He wasn't sure how so rugged a scene would seem beautiful to her sophisticated eye, but he had to agree it was impressive. Right in front of them the river, at this point merely a mountain stream, swung around a huge outcropping of rock that leaned over the water, its stratified lines twisted and eroded in fantastic, curved planes like a squashed layer cake. Downstream the flow, tame now in the summer's drought, trickled through a series of pools in the smoothly worn stone of the valley floor. Willows and other leafy plants grew in lush green clumps, a contrast to the thorny, arid hillsides above. To their right, the trail wound along a rocky ledge worn out of a softer layer of rock, and above it the hill sloped upwards to the blue of the summer sky.

"Watch the footing here. It's very smooth."

"Ocelle is not used to this sort of trail. Should I lead her?"

He slid off his horse. "Good idea. Then we can go right down to the stream."

They made their way to the water, laughing as the horses splashed right in to drink.

"We had better have our drink a bit upstream."

"Yes. *Eau de cheval* is a distinctive essence, but not to my taste."

They tied the horses to a willow and scrambled around the rocks, crossing and re-crossing the stream at will. Lower down they came to a place where the pools were larger.

"We used to swim in there when I was a kid."

"Wasn't it cold?"

"Quite. We only went in on hot days." He remembered the cool water on his bare skin, and tugged at his necktie. *I wonder if...*

"What's up there?" She was pointing to the west, where the slope of the hillside disappeared into sky.

"That's the back of Revuaire."

"It is? That's amazing!"

"Yes. This side is flat and slopes gently all the way to the top. Then it breaks off like a piece of cheese, and the exposed edge falls two hundred *piedes* straight down."

"You mean you can just walk right up the peak?"

"It's a hike, but it isn't difficult. There's no real climbing."

"Can we go up there now?"

"Not and be home in two hours."

She made a moue of disappointment, but didn't seem too upset. "Of course. We'll have to come another day."

That suits me fine.

They descended farther along the banks to where the stream dropped over a large slab of rock that had fallen into the canyon in ages past and was too hard to wear away like the limestone underneath. It was an impressive sight, but there was something more Alain wanted to show her. He led her downstream of the waterfall on the left bank, then turned back up the hill.

"Look in there, behind the water."

She peered in. "It's all dark. I can't see anything."

"Come closer. Look now."

"Oh, I see. There's a tiny grotto. Like in a fairy tale!"

There was a cave, not much over three *piedes* deep, its walls covered in ferns, small drops of water bejewelling each frond.

"I found it one time when we were playing 'brigands.' I hid in there for ages and the other boys couldn't find me."

"Isn't it awfully damp?"

"I almost froze, but it was a great hiding spot." He looked in. "It seems smaller, now."

They returned to the horses, then hiked up the stream past the stratified outcropping. In that direction the trail soon shrank to nothing, so they stopped. As they were turning to come down again, Angélique paused, her head cocked to one side. "What was that noise? Sort of a low rumble?"

He listened but heard nothing. "Probably the water. Sometimes you catch an eddy of deeper sound that you don't usually hear."

After listening a while they continued down the stream.

"There it is again."

Alain had heard it too, this time. Mountain bred, he had no doubt of the source. A mass of deep black cloud swirled over the top of Revuaire, an ominous growl issuing from its depths.

"I think we're going to get wet."

If she was worried, she was determined not to let it show. "Should we head for the forest?"

Alain was concerned too, with more reason. "The rain isn't that much of a problem, but a forest isn't a good place to be in a storm because of the lightning. We're safer down here in the river bottom."

They hurried back to the horses, and Alain led them to a spot where a layer of harder rock overhung the trail, affording a meagre shelter. "I guess the horses will have to get wet."

They snuggled in with their backs to the rough wall and pulled up their feet, holding the reins of the horses, which stood on a lower shelf, their heads almost at the level of the cave. The thunder hit louder this time, and the first huge drops of rain fell, splattering on the hot rocks.

Then for a while everything was noise and motion as the thunder raged and the rain battered. It was all they could do to keep the horses under control, and once they both had to go out in the storm to quiet Ocelle. Alain's horse had been through it many times before and although he wasn't happy at the closer strikes, he bore it well.

In the middle of it all, Alain heard a noise all farmers dreaded. "*Merde!*"

"What did you say?"

"I'm sorry, but look." He pointed out through the rain. A rattling sound rose through the rush of the falling water.

"That's hail, isn't it? Are we in danger?"

"Not us, but I hope this doesn't hit Savournon. A hailstorm at the wrong time of year will destroy the crops."

"Oh."

He wondered if she realized how serious that would be. *Probably not. How could she?*

"Tell me about it."

"What?"

"The hail. The crops. What does it mean to the people if the hail is bad?"

He described the effects of the loss of just one crop on people whose livelihood depended on the land. "They get two crops a year from this soil, but sometimes the field has to be left fallow to revitalize for a year. One crop lost means trouble. Two spoiled crops mean starvation and people dying in the final days of winter."

She asked more questions, and he told her more about the lives of the peasants. The hail faded out and the rain continued as they talked. They would watch the swollen, muddy, stream in silence for a while, and then Angélique would ask another question. She had an unending curiosity about life in the area, and after a while he couldn't help but comment. Her answer disconcerted him.

"I'm working."

He said nothing, but waited for her to go on.

"I work too, you know. I spent several hours this morning organizing my father's business papers."

"You messed with his papers? He'll never be able to find anything!"

She looked piqued at this but then grinned. "You've seen his system too, have you? Don't worry. I have them organized so he can find things. It was easy."

"I never thought keeping the books was easy. My mother does it for us. I guess that's something women are naturally good at."

She gave an unladylike and derogatory snort, and he wondered what he had said wrong. *I meant it as a compliment. So much for my suave, mature image. Time to change the topic.*

"But what has working got to do with asking me all these questions?"

"I'm pumping you for information. This is my *seigneury*. I will inherit it all some day. You've listened to my father, I'm sure. I want to know all about the land, all about the people, so I can do a good job of running it."

"But what about your...uh...your husband? Aren't you going to get married?"

"Oh, I'm sure I'll get married, but that won't make any difference. I'm still going to run my land. Marriage won't change that. It didn't for my great-great-grandmother, and it won't for me."

There could only be one ancestor she was referring to. "Angélique de Lombard."

"You know about her? I'm named after her."

"Everyone here knows about Angélique de Lombard. They still tell stories about her. But I thought you would have been named after your grandmother."

"Well, sort of. She was named after Angélique de Lombard, too. But I was named after the original. Nana says so, and she should know. She's Angélique de Lombard's daughter."

"She is? And she's still alive?" He thought how this might sound, and laughed. "I mean, I know she's still alive, but Angélique de Lombard was so long ago, it's hard to think of her daughter still living."

"Oh, Nana's alive all right, and she'll tell you so if you have any doubts. Eighty-four this year, and still sharp. Have you met her?"

"How could I avoid it? She must be where you and your father get your ideas of how to manage the land. Twenty-one children of her own, and at her age she still knows everyone in the valley: who they are, who their family is and what they've been doing. But what did you mean about marriage not making a difference to Angélique de Lombard?"

"Well, her first husband died, and her baby too, within one year of each other. But she kept on running the *seigneury*. Then she married Charles de Rastel de Rocheblave." She made a face.

"Was he the one that got shot?"

"Right. And do you want to know something?" She leaned closer, to whisper in his ear. "He deserved it." She sat back in satisfaction, looking for his reaction.

He had no problem playing her game. He was honestly confused. "But the men who shot him were convicted of murder. They were supposed to be guillotined, but the king pardoned them. I bet Angélique was mad about that."

"I'm not so sure. It was all his fault."

"Whose fault? Her husband's?"

"That's the way Nana tells it. He wasn't a very pleasant-tempered man, I guess. He didn't get along with the de Genton brothers anyway, and when he saw them hunting on his land he got mad and told them to get off. Of course, they had the right to make a chase onto his land, just as he had a right to follow an animal onto theirs."

"Is that what Reynaud de Gonillons meant when he said to go where you wanted?"

She tossed her head. "De Gonillons! He doesn't own enough land to make any difference. But my great-great-grandfather lost his famous temper. He shot one of their dogs, and then he grabbed another gun from his groom and pointed it at François de Genton. What was the man supposed to do? Sit and wait to see whether he would get shot or not? He fired his gun, turned his horse and got out of there fast. He didn't find out till later that de Rocheblave was dead."

"So Angélique de Lombard wasn't angry at them for killing her husband?"

The evil grin looked very interesting on such a pretty face. "I wouldn't exactly say that. The king pardoned them, but he levied heavy fines against them, along with reparations to the grieving widow. She used the opportunity to buy them out, and that was the end of the de Gentons in this valley. She never remarried, and she ran the *seigneury* for the rest of her life."

"I'm sorry to hear that you and your illustrious ancestor take such a dim view of marriage."

She leaned towards him again, her hand touching that place on his arm. "Oh, no, Alain. I think marriage might be a fine thing. You must understand that in my situation, it does little good to dream about a fine prince carrying me off. Marriage for someone like me is more likely to be a matter of business or politics."

"And you don't mind?"

"Of course I mind! I would much prefer a handsome prince. But there are facts of life you can't duck away from. All this dressing up and flirting with men that I do in Grenoble may be fun, but it is also part of my business in life – to attract a good husband. That means a rich, powerful one. I get to play all I want, but sooner or later I have to pay for it. If I'm lucky, I'll get a decent man and we'll learn to love each other. If not, well, Angélique de Lombard managed, didn't she?"

"And you don't see that situation might change?"

She smiled sadly. "Not unless the world we know is turned right upside down. You have to understand that, Alain, if you are going to be my friend. That is how it is with me."

He looked down at her earnest face. Well, he couldn't ask for it any plainer than that. He nodded and turned away. This was going to take a lot of thinking. When he thought of her marrying, it bothered him a great deal. From everything he had read and heard, this could be love, and it wasn't so wonderful. *Maman always says that in ten years, it won't seem so important. Hah*! Right now, the trick was to do something about it. *How am I to handle this? Can I make her feel the same way? How*?

He thought of how his parents got along, but it was no help. They were such a close team that it was impossible to figure out how they worked together. They were certainly not matched. *Maman* was calm and ladylike, but with that unexpected streak of business. *Papa* was rougher, more easygoing: a great father, but so playful at times that it seemed like the family comprised a mother and two sons. But when they threw their weight into something, they threw it together.

He thought about earlier this afternoon at home. While Alain himself had been surprised at his mother's reaction, his father hadn't been. He had dropped the argument without word.

"Are you coming back soon?"

He looked around to see a pair of bright eyes close to his. Too close. The impulse to kiss her was too strong. He froze, and she backed away, an uncertain smile on her lips. "We were having a good talk, and getting things straight, I thought. And then you were gone. Just...not here."

"I was thinking."

"About what?"

He considered telling her. *Why not?* "My parents."

"Your father seems nice. What's your mother like?"

He shrugged, wondering about the proper words to use. "Well-mannered, also businesslike, I guess."

She made a small face.

He hurried on. "Calm, intelligent too, but with a sense of humour."

"Ah, that can make a great deal of difference."

"I think so. If I try to think of *Maman* without her humour, it somehow doesn't fit."

She frowned as if she was making a decision. Finally she looked up at him, the uncertainty showing in the slant of her head: turned away, as if expecting a blow. "What was her opinion of you coming out with me?"

"She thought it was fine. She wanted me to."

"She did?" The relief was so plain that he didn't want to go on, but he felt he had to.

"But not for reasons you will like."

"What do you mean?"

Alain took a deep breath. She had been honest with him. He had always been honest. *I don't know any other way to be.* "Angélique, I don't want to make you upset. I don't want any trouble between us. I'm having a marvellous time with you, and I don't want you angry with me."

She looked up with a puzzled frown. "What are you talking about? I'm not angry with you." She smiled briefly. "I'm having a marvellous time, too, but what's the problem with your mother?"

"Well, I suspect my mother was...a bit upset."

"So she didn't want you to come with me."

"No. She was upset at...not at you, but she didn't like the idea of Albert bringing the message. No idea why. It was my father who wasn't sure I should come. He...well, he doesn't think I should spend too much time with you," here it came, "because of... you know..." He cursed himself, but he couldn't bring himself to say it.

It seemed he had done the damage anyway. Her face went dead still and expressionless. Her voice held a level tone, but there was a hint of steel. "And your mother?"

This was crucial, but as to which answer would be the right one, he had no idea. He plunged on.

"Well, I think she was saying... um...sort of, 'My son is good enough to go riding with anyone he wants to, and to hell with anyone who says he can't.' At least, that's the feeling I got."

Her shout of laughter rang off the rocks, causing the horses to toss their heads and shift their feet. "I have to meet your mother!"

He jumped to the horses, pulling the reins firmly. It sounded like he had said the right thing, but he couldn't be sure why. He covered his confusion by fussing with the animals, calming them, wiping the saddles dry. "Yes, I'm sure you can meet her, if you want. But why?"

"Your father's fine. He's just being a lawyer. But your mother I have to meet."

She refused to say any more, and jumped to her feet, hailstones crunching between her boots and the rock. "The rain has almost stopped. Can we go home, now?"

Maybe I didn't say the right thing. "I suppose so. We'll have to be careful going up those rocks. We had better walk the horses."

She leaned over and pinched his cheek. "That's right. You take good care of me. My mother will be so pleased." A touch of bitterness had returned to her voice, and again he was confounded as to what she meant. *What is all this about mothers?*

With exaggerated care, she led her horse over the slippery bedrock until she reached the carpet of needles under the pine trees. "There. I made it, see?" She laughed and without help swung lithely up onto the tall hunter and sat there, the humour still on her face.

He had no choice but to contribute a confused grin. Mounting, he followed her up the trail.

5.   Rat's Nest

June 7, 1788

They made their way back down over the pass, the horses slipping on the steeper parts of the road. Lower down where the trees opened up they began to see people again, peasants out inspecting the fields for damage. Angélique insisted on stopping and being introduced so that she could find out about the crops, most of which had been touched by the hail, but not badly. Some of her questions were naive, but no one minded answering her. After each discussion she would quiz Alain about the man she had just spoken to, his family and to whom he was tenant. She was especially interested in the ones who rented from her father. Then they were in Gonillons. Alain noticed her eyes moving watchfully, but they passed through the hamlet without incident.

Just after they crossed the bridge into Savournon, Alain heard his name called. They reined in and waited while Edmond trotted up to them, splashing through the mud that had liberally spattered his trouser legs.

With a guilty start, Alain realized that he had forgotten about the boy on the hill.

With his usual brash charm, the smaller lad started right in. "Hi. You're Angélique de Bardel, aren't you? I'm Edmond Sarobert."

"Your father is the baker? Pleased to meet you, Edmond."

He bowed, smiling, then looked to Alain. "Uh...we should talk."

"I have to take Mlle. de Bardel home, then I can come back."

"Don't mind me. I will wait if you like."

"We are sort of late, and the storm..."

"It's not a problem. Unless it's something private?"

"Oh, no. Not really." He looked from her to Edmond. He would love to tell her about their triumph of the night before, but it was not entirely his secret, so he had kept his mouth shut. *But now that Edmond is here...*

Edmond grinned. "You haven't told her, then?"

That was enough opening for Angélique. She swung off her horse. "No, he hasn't, but it's too late. He has to tell me now. What is going on here?"

Alain dismounted too, glad to have his decision made for him. "Watch out, Edmond. The lady has the most inquisitive mind since Galileo. If you have any secrets, leave now."

"You trust her?"

"Of course he trusts me." She tied her horse to a nearby gate and stood, arms crossed, challenging them.

The two looked at each other. "Well, Alain, you start."

"Will Aimée mind?"

"The question is whether the Rat will mind."

"Is this a game? Aimée is your sister. Who's the Rat?"

Between them, they told her the story. As usual, she was full of questions, but finally she had it all. "So what are you going to do with him?"

"That's the problem. We don't know. We can hide him until his cough is better, but after that?"

"What does he want to do?"

"We haven't asked him. We only met him a few nights ago, and there have been more pressing things to worry about. For now, we are mainly concerned with keeping him hidden and fed."

"And from any more thievery." Edmond's face took on a thoughtful look. "He seems to steal more than he needs to. He just sort of...does it."

"You could be right. In any case, we have to get him down off that hill soon."

Angélique looked up to the ruin, high above the town. "He was up there this afternoon, in the storm?"

The two boys grinned at each other. "I bet that was some experience."

Angélique gazed at them, shaking her head. "You have no sympathy, have you?"

They assured her that he was safe, with a nice, dry niche to crawl into.

Again her derisive snort. "I'm guessing that he would be pleased if we bring him down. Preferably tonight."

"We? Are you going to help?"

"Of course. Why else did you tell me about him?"

Since his own reasons for telling her were more selfish than he would admit, he had to let that stand.

Their conversation was cut off by the approach of galloping hooves, and they edged their mounts to the side of the narrow street. Instead of passing, the rider yanked his horse to a stop.

"Why Albert. You have mud on your coat. Why are you hurrying so?"

The footman did not dismount. "Mademoiselle Angélique. Your mother commands you to return instantly. You are very late."

One glance at his companion's face and Alain looked around, half expecting to see ice forming on the puddles.

"Thank you for the message, Albert. You may return to the *chateau* and tell my mother you have delivered it. You may also take her a message from me. Tell her I am on my way home, but I am at the moment talking with friends, and that I will be along soon." She ticked off a finger for each point, ending with three fingers held in the air.

"Can you remember all that, Albert?"

"Yes, Mademoiselle." He started to rein his horse around.

"Albert?" Her voice was at the same level, but the tone had changed.

He froze, his head twisted toward her.

"You may go, Albert." She smiled sweetly, and he kicked the horse back into a gallop. She turned back to her friends.

Edmond stepped back, his eyes wide. "Ooh!"

She made a face. "My mother's footman."

"And your mother likes that sort of thing?"

She looked more carefully at this small boy who asked such pointed questions. "Yes, Edmond, I'm afraid she does." She tossed her head, the hair threatening to escape from under her tricorn hat. "So what are we going to do about the Rat?"

Alain was beginning to understand Angélique's problems and how she reacted to them. Still, there was no sense in making the situation worse.

"There's nothing you can do to help at the moment because first we have to get him off the mountain. We have a safe place for him, and when he's there we will tell you, and you can meet him if you like."

"Yes, you'll have lots of questions we haven't thought of."

"Yes, Edmond, I suppose I will." This time she used the gate to mount her horse, allowing Alain to hold its head. She might be tired after the long ride, but she was doing her best not to let on.

He mounted as well. "I'll be around to see you when the shop closes, all right?"

The smaller boy looked up impishly. "Don't get distracted, now." Then he turned to Angélique with a formal bow. "It has been a great pleasure to meet you, my Lady."

She bowed in the saddle. "And you, *monsieur.*"

They all laughed, and Edmond spattered off down the side street that led to his father's shop.

All too soon for Alain the two riders reached the *chateau* and pulled up in the stable yard. Angélique kept her horse close enough that she could touch his arm. "Don't get down, Alain. I have to deal with my own family."

"As does everyone. Thank you for a marvellous afternoon."

She allowed the groom to help her down, then turned to look back at Alain.

"Don't you dare leave me out."

He understood and nodded.

"And when you have a message, send Edmond. He would like it."

"I'm sure he would."

"*Au revoir*, Alain." She was gone through the side door of the *chateau* before he could blurt out any of his carefully planned phrases. *Oh, well. They probably would have sounded hollow anyway.*

Avoiding the looks of the groom and stableboy, he reined his horse out of the yard and headed home.

* * *

It turned out to be easy to get the Rat down from the Eagle that evening. He was pathetically eager to go. The storm had passed over the southern part of the valley, but he had seen enough lightning to give him a real scare. His hair was fairly standing on end as he told about his most narrow escape, where the bolts had struck on either side of the church, and he had felt the heat reflected off the walls. Alain saw no sign of any strikes nearby, but said nothing. It had been a harrowing experience for the city-bred lad.

The three boys slipped down the west side of the ridge into the gully, dodging the stone blocks that had tumbled from the ruin over the years. It was a cool, damp evening near dark and no one was about, so they walked boldly along the upper street until they crossed a narrow bridge. Backed against it was a tumble-down stone structure which had once been a house but now was open to the sky, its rafters and thatch long since rotted away, the bramble bushes crowding in where once people had lived and worked.

"*Zut alors!* Am I going to stay here?"

"*Pas du tout.* Watch." Edmond flattened against the wall where the bushes did not quite touch the stone. Following this natural passage, they reached the end of the building where one corner had fallen away, revealing a dark space. Edmond swung his feet into this hole, dropped and slid down a short gravel slope. Following, they pulled aside the old cloth that hung across the doorway and found themselves in a small, dry room built into the underside of the bridge.

The trickling sound of the stream announced drinking water near at hand, and a neat fire burned in a half-circle of rocks against the far wall. Smoke rose through a crack in the bridge foundation and disappeared in the darkness of the stone overhead. A pallet of straw filled the corner across the room next to the fire. Odds and ends and old utensils lay on various stones and ledges, making the place look homey. In the middle of this snug nest sat Aimée, looking pleased with herself.

"You mean this is all mine?" The young thief stared in disbelief, then turned to Aimée as if she were the one most likely to give him the answer he wanted.

She nodded happily, then went around showing him the various items she had brought, giving him tips on where to keep everything and how certain utensils worked. As she went on, his amazement grew.

"*Pas mal.* Where did you get all these things?"

"Oh, I scrounged them." The Rat looked even more impressed.

Edmond nudged Alain. "He thinks she stole them." Alain nodded, grinning.

When she finished, Aimée stood back and motioned for the small boy to take his seat on the straw. He did so with the air of a king taking control of his realm. The others made themselves as comfortable as they could on various bits of wood and rock.

"*D'accord.* I like this fine." The youngster looked around with a broad grin.

Alain clapped his hands on his knees. "Good. This will be safe for a while. The entrance is well hidden, and you can't see it from the road at all because of the bushes in the streambed. Even your fire is camouflaged. We'll bring you food, and you can stretch your legs in the evening and early morning when it's not too light."

"But Jimmy, no more stealing."

"Why would I steal?" The boy turned to Aimée with innocent eyes. "You're bringin' me everything I want."

She nodded firmly. "Right. Just remember it."

Now was the time. "The problem is, what are we going to do with you in the long run?"

Jimmy looked at Alain as if he was crazy. "I'm fine here."

"You can't stay here forever. Sooner or later, someone will learn about you. We have to find you a place to stay." Remembering what Angélique had said, he went on. "What do you want to do? Do you want to stay here? In Savournon, I mean."

The boy looked around. "Yeah, well, I guess so. I was headed to Paris, ya know?"

"But Jimmy, you've only come about fifteen *lieu*, and it's about seventy to Paris." Trust Edmond to have the facts.

"Yeah. I s'pose. But if I could stay here, like for a longer time, could you swing that?"

The other two looked to Alain. This was his decision. "I believe so. We must plan carefully, but now we have more help. Powerful help."

"Angélique?" Aimée sounded doubtful, although she must know about the afternoon meeting. This could be touchy, and Alain was wondering how to approach it when Edmond chimed in.

"Don't worry, Aimée. Angélique will be fine. She knows a lot and she's keen to help. She already had some good ideas. And face it; she's rich. If we need anything, all she has to do is snap her fingers."

"Who is this Angélique?" The eager young eyes flashed. The boy had not missed the word 'rich.'

"Someone who wants to help you, who is a lady, to whom you will be very polite." Alain turned to the others. "But that's another problem. Angélique can be very helpful, but she has a real disadvantage."

"Visibility." *As usual, Edmond puts his finger on it.*

"Right. She can't go anywhere without being noticed, can't do anything without comments being made. If she stops to talk to Aimée in the streets, someone will want to know why. On the other hand, she has advantages we don't. She has money. Also influence. If she can think up a good reason to want something done, it will be done."

"So what do we want her to do?"

"We don't know yet. We have to get together and talk it over. At least the pressure is off. Jimmy is safe here for a while, and now we can take the time to make good plans. Which reminds me," he turned to the younger boy, "I haven't heard you cough all evening."

The Rat gave out a very real cough, then grinned. "Oh, it's still there, but I have it under control. I'm tough. Takes more than a cough to get me down."

"Good. Just see that you stay out of the wet, out of sight and out of trouble for the next few days."

The thin body curled up in the bundle of clean rags that Aimée had found to cover the bed. *"D'accord, patron.* I'll be good."

At that, they left him smiling into his fire, his fingers twisting around the leather sack that lay against his chest.

They emerged cautiously from the old house, but the street was empty. Their paths home ran together for a while, and they talked as they went. At least the boys did. Finally Alain noticed Aimée's silence.

"What are you so wrapped up in?"

She started, then looked across at him. "Our problems are not over. Jimmy is going to get bored soon and do something silly."

"What do you mean? He's safe, warm, and has food coming. He doesn't have to do anything. You'd think that type of kid would take full advantage."

"Oh, he will, but that won't be enough. He's led an interesting life, and I bet he's never been in a situation where he had nothing to do for this long." She raised her eyebrows. "We have to keep a close eye on him."

"Our best bet is to find a legitimate place for him. Then we can worry about civilizing him."

The other two nodded, and they all stood, thinking. "Well, let's meet again tomorrow at noon and see what we've come up with."

The twins turned into the gathering darkness to make their way home, leaving Alain with a lot to think about.

6. Politics

June 14, 1788

They spent six days trying to figure out a solution to their problem...their several problems. First was to keep their fugitive fed. This wasn't difficult when the twins' father owned a bakery, and Alain could coax extras out of Ariane.

It was harder to keep the lad occupied. True to Aimée's prediction, he started to get fidgety after the second day. They took him out in the evenings, wandering the unused paths they could find, but there was little time between dusk and full dark to get far. He couldn't read, so there was no help there. One thing that did help was Aimée deciding to teach him his letters. The older boys tried as well, although with less enthusiasm.

At first it was hard to persuade her pupil that writing was a useful skill.

"What's the point of this scratchin' in the dirt with sticks? What good will it do me?"

She explained that then he could read books and find out what other people thought, what other places were like.

He shook his head. "If I want to know what someone's thinkin', I ask him, *n'est-ce pas*? If I want to see a place, I go there." He was rooted firmly in the here and now, and anything outside his sight or recent memory had little meaning to him.

Edmond came to his sister's aid. "It's a great way to send messages. Think of an army where the general has to give orders by voice and the messenger gets them mixed up."

The small boy nodded, and the lessons went better. His interest increased as the boredom set in, but it was not enough. They had to find something more permanent.

The other problem was Angélique. Alain suspected that she was suffering from the same difficulty as the Rat. After two days she sent a note, by a stable boy this time, asking what was going on. The tone was sharp; she was feeling left out. He sent a message back, not explaining anything, even though the stableboy couldn't read, but telling her that nothing was happening and suggesting they meet.

He wanted to drop in and talk to her as he would with any other friend, but he couldn't simply show up at the door for fear he would be sent off. There was no reason for her family to turn him away, but the thought of it kept him from going. After a few more notes they finally agreed to take a walk the next afternoon. As he received the last note, Alain tried to read some meaning in the stableboy's smile. He was either thrilled to be part of this romantic communication or amused to be running back and forth on such silly errands, keeping him from real work.

That evening when the group met at the Rat's hideaway they discussed again how Angélique might help, but came to no conclusion.

Jimmy couldn't understand the problem. "I thought you said she was rich? Then why doesn't she give us some money?"

"I doubt if it's that easy. Anyway, if she gave us some money, what would we do with it?"

The younger boy looked at Alain as if there was a spider on his ceiling. "*Sacre bleu!* Spend it. What do you think?"

Alain gave up.

The next day Alain called for Angélique. This time one of the other servants, a young village woman, opened the door.

"Well, Master Alain. Going walking with the young *mademoiselle*, are you?"

He found himself blushing at her warm smile. He mumbled something about keeping his father's clients happy, which she brushed off.

"*Bien sûr.* I remember when Jacques and me was walking out. You mind, young man. It wasn't long after that we was married." She beamed at him again.

"*Le bon dieu*, Madame Dufour, we're only going for a walk. Don't you go spreading it around town that I'm coming courting. She's only fourteen years old!

"Besides..." He made a gesture that took in the whole *chateau*.

The woman shrugged and shook her head, patting him on the back. "I'll go see that Mademoiselle is ready, though I'm sure she heard you knock." She leaned closer. "Just keeping you waiting. They do that." She turned and walked away.

Alain sighed. *Sometimes I wonder if anyone ever listens to what I'm saying.*

They strolled down the hill and followed the stream towards Pélissieres. As they walked, they tried to figure out what to do. Angélique wanted to know all about the Rat. She also wanted to meet him.

"I don't see how that's possible. Think about it. You're an important visitor. We don't get visitors that often, and everyone is curious. Wherever you go, someone will notice. If you tried to sneak into that old house by the bridge, the story would be around the town in half an hour, and your mother would find out about it in two."

She sighed, swatting at daisies with a small stick she had picked up. "I suppose. But what can I do to help?"

"The Rat says to give him money. He figures that'll solve everything."

She threw up her hands. "Everybody thinks that giving them money will solve everything. Even the king has been complaining that he needs more tax money."

"I gather he does. The royal treasury is empty, what with helping the Americans pay for their revolution, the nobles not paying their taxes, and keeping Marie Antoinette happy with her jewels and parties."

She shook her head. "Marie Antoinette isn't the problem. What is the cost of a few fancy dresses, compared to the thousands of *livres* the *seigneur*s owe on their taxes? I checked with my father, and he has paid everything he owes, but most of them haven't. Why does the king let them get away with it?"

"He doesn't have much choice. If he tries to collect, they all band together and say, 'No,' and then what does he do?"

"If we had a king with a backbone, he would find a way!"

"Angélique! You may be able to talk like that, but if anyone thought I said it, I could end up being the centre of attraction for the Saturday morning entertainment at the scaffold in Gap. I'd like to keep my head for a few years yet."

"Well, it's true." She looked chastised but not too repentant. "There are thousands of *livres* being paid in interest every month on the king's debts."

"Which doesn't get us any closer to a solution for our own problem."

"Alain, I like talking about the country's problems. Everyone should take an interest in what's happening in Paris and in the provincial government in Grenoble. If more people cared what was going on, France wouldn't be in such trouble. All most of them care about is filling their pockets with silver."

"That's an easy thing for you to say. Most of the people in this village spend most of their time getting enough money to stay alive. They have no time to worry about France."

"And since I have plenty of money, I have the leisure to think, is that it?" There was a dangerous tilt to her chin.

He ignored it. "Do you blame those peasants we talked to the other day for being concerned about their crops?"

"Of course not! But it's pretty naive of them to imagine that Father lowering the rents would solve all their problems."

"Wouldn't it help?"

"It's not that simple, and you know it." She was walking faster now, the switch slashing at bushes as she passed them.

"We don't make that much money on any one tenant. If we lower the rents we make no money at all. If we can't make any money to live on we have to sell the property and find somewhere to invest our money so we can live. If someone less charitable than my father buys the land, where are the peasants then?"

"But Angélique, your father is not a typical landlord. Next winter when you are in Grenoble, ask yourself what is happening back on the lands of all those well-dressed men who have time to go to all the parties that you attend. Ask yourself where they get all the money and how they know, or whether they care, what happened to their peasants who lost crops to the hail this summer."

She looked thoughtful, but not convinced, so he went on.

"And for many of them, their traditional revenues are not enough. They need more money, so they try to screw more out of their tenants. You would be astonished at how much of my father's business involves peasants taking the *seigneur* to court to get him to fulfill his traditional legal duties."

"What do you mean by that?"

"Well, to give you an actual example, last year the Bishop of Embrun, who is also the *seigneur* of that area, decided that he would no longer allow the peasants to cut wood in the forest of Batie-Vieille, a right they had owned by charter for centuries."

"Why would he want to do that?"

"Why do you think? So he could sell them the wood that was theirs by right!" He was catching on. *These obstinate questions only keep her from admitting the truth.*

"You want an example closer to home? The peasants of Savournon took your great grandfather, Jean Joseph de Rastel de Rocheblave, to court in Grenoble because he wouldn't keep the mill in proper running order. He also insisted on using the Veynes measurement system to weigh the grain instead of the local one, which allowed him to collect a larger fee for the use of the mill. And he increased the tax a young man had to pay if he wanted to marry a girl from Savournon, and several other smaller things, like hunting through their vineyards with his dogs."

"My father doesn't do anything like that!"

"Angélique, nobody denies that your father is a fair man. But you are avoiding the issue again. Look at it this way. If that hailstorm had destroyed a field of barley, the peasant has lost about a third of his annual income. What have you lost?"

"We have years when father tells us we can't spend much because the crops are poor!"

"I'm sure you do. But what does that mean? Not buying another dress? Not throwing a big party for your name day? For the peasant, it means his children will go hungry this winter!"

She turned to him, her eyes narrowed, her cheeks red, her hands in fists, rigid at her sides. She drew in a breath to speak, and he knew he had gone too far. In that instant, the thought flashed through his mind that here was the problem between them. *Here is where our minds can never meet. She will never understand what it is to face starvation. In a way, I'm glad it is going to end now. It will save a lot of agony later on.* He braced himself for the blast.

It didn't come.

She held that tense position, but then a change came over her face and she let her breath out slowly. She turned and continued along the path, her head bowed. He followed, wondering what was going on in her mind. Then she stopped and turned to him. Her brow was wrinkled. "It's true, isn't it? The cost of one of my dresses could feed one of those families for weeks."

"If the harvest is good, they can survive. It is the poor harvests that bring their problems to a head."

She thought this over. "So to be fair, if there is a good harvest, the owner of the land deserves his rent, but when the harvest fails, he should adjust it accordingly."

Alain found himself switched to the other side of the argument.

"It isn't that simple, Angélique. The peasants are always asking for lower rents for all sorts of reasons. Some of them are useless farmers and lazy as well. Many of them are shrewd operators. If they thought your father was going to give them any more breaks they would never pay anything at all. Just like the lords."

"Ahh. So the problem is to get the help to the people who deserve it and keep the others working at a profit for everyone."

"Sounds right to me." He turned and continued walking. "And your father does that quite well by keeping to his legal rights and responsibilities and helping out in individual cases where he can. No one has starved in Savournon."

"But not all landlords are like my father." She strode beside him, her head bowed in thought.

"It seems that most aren't."

Her head came up. "So our system isn't fair."

"It isn't. But nobody has come up with a better one, and if they did, the nobles and the king, not to mention the rich churchmen who are often the biggest landlords, wouldn't let it happen."

"That isn't fair, either."

"My father says that as long as one man has rights that another man does not have, life will never be fair."

She turned that over in her head, then smiled up at him. "I like that. So we need to have the same rights for everyone."

He shrugged. "I imagine it's not as simple as that, but it's a good start."

She walked on, her stride lengthening, and he could tell that she was pleased with herself. He watched her swing along, the sun gleaming through the few wisps of hair that had escaped from her beribboned bonnet, silhouetting her head in a halo of warm light. Then he hurried to catch up. "So you like talking politics, do you?"

"Is there anything wrong with that? Women are not supposed to talk politics, I suppose."

He was beginning to understand her attitude on that subject as well. He held up his hands in defence. "No, not at all. In fact, my parents spend a lot of time talking politics. My father especially, but my mother too."

She shook her head. "I wish my father had a better idea of what was going on. He just doesn't seem to understand."

"That's why he hires us. He has few legal problems, but he needs my father to keep him updated on what's going on in the world."

"My mother talks politics."

Don't sound surprised. I am best to be neutral wherever Mme. de Charrette is concerned. "She does?"

"Yes, but it has always bothered me, and I begin to see why. She doesn't discuss anything. You never get the feeling that she's listening to anyone unless they say what she wants to hear. I can't see her ever changing her mind about anything. She just gives her opinions. It's not the same as discussion."

I wish we could find a topic that doesn't feel so much like walking along the rim of Revuaire. "Angélique, what about the Rat? What are we going to do with him?"

They crossed the stream above the small hamlet of Pélissieres and turned south towards the foot of Revuaire, its rock wall towering sheer above the valley. He glanced up at the huge edifice. *Sort of like life. There's an easy walk to the top, but also a quick drop down.*

71

Angélique strode along, lost in thought. Finally she stopped and faced him "First thing, we make an entrance. We get him into town legitimately so no one will suspect he's been here for days already. Has the uproar about the thefts died down?"

"Mostly. Several of the victims have found their property. Some are suspicious, but there's nothing left to complain about. Edmond discovered an error in his arithmetic to account for the missing bread, which was rather nice of him, I thought. He is immensely proud of his bookkeeping. Getting the kid into town won't be too hard. Then we have to find him a place while he's here. Have you any ideas?"

"Could he do a bit of work?"

Alain grinned. "If you're thinking of hiring him for your stables, forget it. He'd have the nails stolen out of the door-posts before the first night was done."

"Ah, I had forgotten about that. We need something unusual to keep him interested."

"How about the foresters?"

"We might try them. Does he know anything about the woods?"

"I doubt it. That ought to occupy him for a while. It will also keep him out of the village and out of temptation."

"Fine. The foresters it is. We'll go riding one day, go around the long way to St. Genis. The others can take him there the short way, through Jubeo forest. I'll bring him home and say I found him on the road. A poor orphan, whose parents were migrant farm workers who died somewhere in the south." She walked on, that satisfied swing to her stride again.

"But don't you want to ask someone? What if the foresters don't want him?"

She turned to him and spoke with exaggerated slowness, as if speaking to a young child or a person who was not very smart. "Alain, if I say the foresters are to take him on, they will take him on."

Alain wondered what it would be like to have power like that over people's lives. *Frightening. You could do a lot of good, of course, but what if you made a mistake?* In this case, it was convenient.

"Great. What day should we go?"

They walked on, working on the fine details of their plan, and turned back when they had reached the abandoned *bergerie* high on the slope of Serre Clavel, with the gigantic wall of Revuaire looming over them. He grinned at her. "Funny to think that such an impossible cliff can be climbed by walking up the other side."

She shrugged. "It's a long hike, but the view would be worth it."

"Let's do it some day."

"I'm ready any time." She glanced at him sideways and strode off, her head high.

It was a different kind of time from their ride a few days ago. It wasn't such an up-and-down experience, but steadier, more comfortable. *Not so wonderful, perhaps, but satisfying in a different way.* Alain reached home that evening in a state of amiable bliss.

So it took a while before the extra bustle and movement in the house penetrated the haze of his thoughts. The reason came out at supper that night. His father, who had eaten little, pushed back his dessert plate and folded his napkin.

"I have an announcement which I would like you all to hear."

Alain glanced at his mother, but she just smiled. *She knows all about it, of course.* Ariane was standing nearby and turned to listen.

"There has been talk of calling the Estates together for a meeting. Well, it isn't just talk any more. You know what happened last week in Grenoble?"

"The parliament refused to pass the king's proclamations, and he sent his army to force them."

"Right. And the legislators sat on top of the buildings and threw roof tiles on the soldiers' heads. The fact that the king was willing to send troops against the parliament has opened many people's eyes, even people who originally didn't want the realm to change. Representatives from the three Estates will be meeting at Vizille on July 14 to discuss the present situation in France and to come up with some solutions." He paused and looked at his family, a satisfied smile on his face.

Alain nodded. "Well, it's not as if you haven't been pushing for this for months. It's great that they finally listened."

"Oh, it wasn't only me. Many others have felt the same way. Still, a few of us did the pushing, there's no denying. But there's more!"

Alain had rarely seen his father in such a state. He could hardly sit in his chair, and his glance roved around more than usual.

"Guess who is one of the representatives for the Third Estate."

"You?"

A look of mock disappointment crossed his father's face. "Don't sound so surprised. Why shouldn't I go?"

"Of course you should." He jumped up and put his arm over his father's shoulders. "I'm surprised that for once the other people thought the same way. That's great, *Papa*. When do we leave?"

"I'm sorry, son, but you aren't going anywhere. I'll only be away a week or so, and there is a lot you and your mother can do to keep the business moving. Politics is all very interesting, but someone has to earn a living for the family. We have a month to get ready, so it won't be difficult."

7. Upsets

June 14 – 25, 1788

He didn't see Angélique the following week. His father was anxious to get a lot of paperwork finished in advance, so they worked longer hours than usual. Alain didn't complain; he needed to build credit so he could take extra time for the proposed expedition to St Genis.

On Tuesday after supper the knocker sounded, and Alain answered the door. It was the same stableboy, with a letter in his hand and the same grin on his face. This time, Alain just grinned back. He read the note, which said, "Tomorrow afternoon," and sent a verbal confirmation.

Ignoring his coat, for it was a warm evening, he told his parents that he had to go out.

"Not visiting young ladies at this time of night, are you?" His father's eyes twinkled.

"No, just going down into the village to get some things for tomorrow. Angélique wants to ride south towards Montrond in the afternoon. Is it all right if I go?"

"I suppose. We must keep our clients happy." So his father hadn't given up on his worry. *Domage. Some things can't be helped.*

Alain strolled down to the *boulangerie* and caught the twins just closing the shop. "Care to go for a stroll?" He spoke casually, but he was aware of close regard on the part of M. Sarrobert. "Don't worry, I won't keep them out late."

The baker could hardly complain at the company his children were keeping, but he might be suspicious as to Alain's motives, considering the age difference. *Ah, bien. Nothing to be done.*

They slipped into the hideout, getting a momentary shock when there was no one there. They were discussing what to do when there was a scrabbling in the bushes outside and a thin face appeared in the doorway.

"I thought I heard voices. What did ya bring me?"

Aimée pulled out a cloth-wrapped bundle. "The usual: bread and cheese, with an apple for a treat."

The boy dug into the package and began to eat before he had fully unwrapped it. Alain met Aimée's eyes over the bent head, and they grinned. The little fellow was not over-trained in good manners.

"Did you ever learn to say thank you?"

The head came up, a grubby sleeve wiping crumbs from an equally dirty face. "Sure. *Merci.*" His head went back down.

Alain shrugged. "*De rien.*"

Eating at that rate the boy was soon finished, and the others could ask their questions. They had learned not to talk to him during a meal because he didn't bother to empty his mouth before speaking. The result was a spray of wasted food and unintelligible words.

"Where were you when we came in?"

"Out scoutin' around. If you keep low, you can move easy under the cover a those bushes."

Aimée looked concerned. "Don't let anyone see you."

"Don't worry. I'm good at not bein' seen. Just have to practise in the trees. I'm more used ta city streets."

Alain grinned. "I might arrange some practice for you in the forest."

The boy's face brightened. "Oh, good. Can we go now?"

"Not till tomorrow. But this is permanent. Angélique has got you a job with her father's foresters. You will be living with them, helping them in the woods."

The Rat thought about this, pulling at his left ear. "Sounds all right. Did you say a job?"

"Well, I don't imagine they'll work you to death, since you're a friend of Angélique's. But you had better behave yourself. Those foresters aren't a bad lot, but they won't put up with any nonsense from any city kid."

The city kid grinned. "Don't worry. I'll be good."

I don't think it's going to be quite that easy, but who knows?

The next night the city kid was installed happily, or so it seemed, with the foresters in their hut north of the *chateau* on the wooded slope between Savournon and the Col des Eyserrines, where the old Roman road cut through the mountains to the north.

It had been an easy ride back from St Genis, with the Rat perched behind Alain's saddle, chattering happily with Angélique, who was enthralled with his stories. She had impressed him by recognizing his name, telling him that Jimmy was English for Jacques. If he was aware of the hostilities between France and the country where his name originated it didn't bother him, as he told her tales about the English sailors he had met on the docks of Marseille.

They hustled him in for a quick interview with *sieur* de Bardel and were relieved at how well he remembered the story they had decided on. Before leaving the *chateau* they cleaned his pockets of the various trinkets that had somehow, to the Rat's great surprise, collected there. Then they took him up to introduce him to Aubin and his two sons, the foresters who looked after the cutting and planting in the woods of the valley.

On the way back to the *chateau*, Alain asked her what she found so interesting in the Rat's tales. "Most of those stories aren't true, you know."

She gave him a withering glance. "My life isn't as protected as all that. It isn't his marvellous deeds I'm interested in. It's the city. I was in Marseille last summer. It was beautiful: the blue water, the hazy sky, the palm trees. But that's not the city he was talking about. To think that while I was amusing myself with swimming and lying in the shade, he was living a life like that."

"I see what you mean."

"It gives a person something to ponder."

The next day was a long one in the office, as were those following. It wasn't until Saturday that he got a chance to take Angélique for another walk. This time she wanted a tour of the village. He made no comment but led the way, wondering what she was doing.

That set the pattern for several days to come. Alain managed to go with her when he could, and she went alone a few times. She would walk around, stopping to be introduced to everyone they met: talking, listening, sometimes asking quite personal questions. However, she seemed to take it for granted that she had the right to ask them, and everyone answered freely, most of them even telling the truth as far as he could tell.

After a while he caught the pattern. First she would ask general questions about the person and his or her family. Then she would move on to occupation. Only after they were chatting comfortably would she delve into the real purpose of her questioning: income, education, taxes and the problems of life in the community. The days went on, and they walked when the frequent thunderstorms permitted. After several more hailstorms, the answers she got became more frightening. The winter of 1788 would be a hungry one.

She dodged any questions about her intentions, so he stopped asking, preferring to listen and keep his thoughts to himself. After all, he couldn't complain about the task. She was as friendly as ever, and he could sense their relationship growing closer and more relaxed. He had long since given up on the dream of making some grand gesture that would impress her, his realistic streak telling him that he had a much better chance in simply becoming a good habit she wouldn't want to break. Looming on the horizon was her eventual return to Grenoble.

In fact, he couldn't understand why Mme. de Charrette was still in Savournon. She rarely left the *chateau,* only to go into Serres once a week to visit with acquaintances. She did not associate with anyone in the village; there was no one of her social level available. Since she had never stayed here so long before, he could only wonder whether there was something in Grenoble she was hiding from. Surely the minor unrest of the 'Day of the Tiles' wasn't serious enough to chase her away. He never asked Angélique, because her mother was one topic they both avoided.

Catherine Jouvent, on the other hand, entertained Angélique several times. As he was going out, his mother would suggest that they come in on their way home for a cup of chocolate and a chat. Their talks ranged through a variety of subjects, including politics. Alain contributed little, content to sit back and listen. Angélique came off well in these conversations, and he wondered whether his mother was testing the girl somehow.

In any case, both of them seemed pleased with the results of the conversation, and that was enough for Alain.

In return, Angélique invited him in to visit with her great-grandmother, old Mme. de Dillon. 'Nana' didn't walk fast, but her mind moved at a rapid pace. She had a dry sense of humour and little regard for what anyone else thought of her.

They took a turn around the garden during the second visit and he finally got up the nerve to ask a question that had been bothering him.

"*Madame,* how did your father's family end up coming here from Ireland?"

She shrugged. "I suppose there was a time when being a Roman Catholic was more important than what country you were born in. Especially when Oliver Cromwell brought his form of religion to Ireland." Then she said something else completely unintelligible, grinning at their stunned faces.

"That's Gaelic. I'm not sure exactly what it means, but the last part is about changing with the times." She raised her head with a disdainful sniff. "Which some people around here might do well to listen to. Notably your mother. Sometimes the woman talks as if she is back in the seventeenth century." She looked up at Alain. "Even I wasn't born, then."

Angélique stopped. "Nana, I don't think you should speak of my mother like that."

"I have paid for ninety years for the right to say what I please."

"Nonetheless. You show a poor example to the younger generations if you refuse to treat your own grandson's wife with respect."

"In that case, I hope you will accept my apologies. I have no wish to induce a lack of respect in the young folks. There's enough of that happening with no help from me."

She turned to watch her step on the rough stones, but Alain could see the hint of a smile. *I doubt if respect for anyone is high on her list of priorities. Or ever has been.*

Aimée and Edmond went along on their walks sometimes, and Alain was impressed by their knowledge of the people and workings of the village. In fact, Alain began to understand that he was a part of a very special group. He mentioned it to his mother one evening in late July, when his father was in Vizile.

"I seem to be moving in strange company this summer."

"I noticed."

"I don't just mean Angélique."

She smiled. "The other three as well."

"Three?"

She turned from the counter where she was preparing the next day's dinner. "Alain, In case you didn't notice, your parents aren't stupid. M. Sarrobert came to see us last month when this all started. We all knew something was going on. He may have been concerned that it involved you and Aimée."

"Maman!"

"Alain, he is the father of a very mature little girl who has no mother, and his concern does him credit. It wouldn't do any harm for you to remember her maturity. She has feelings too."

Alain digested this in silence. He worried about how Aimée might feel, but had no idea how to deal with it, except to be sure that he didn't encourage her.

"It didn't take long to figure out what was going on. Your father is a lawyer, and we had most of the information you did. When the boy finally showed up and you already had him disposed of, we were impressed. Such a child, too. How is he managing, by the way?"

Alain leaned back and smiled in relief. "He's doing well, considering. He only ran away once, when the chief forester gave him a hiding for stealing his hat. Heaven knows what the kid was going to do with a hat twice the size of his head. It was probably the eagle feather in the band. He still swears it got into his bag by mistake. Of course, he went straight to the *boulangerie*, and Aimée talked him into going back on his own. He'll make a great forester. Or gamekeeper. You've never seen someone move so quietly through the woods."

His mother set a pan of peas and an empty bowl on the table in front of him. "And what do you think of the Sarobert twins?"

"They're impressive." He glanced at the bowl, then at her unyielding back. He decided not to argue and started shelling. "Aimée couldn't get into the parish school because she was a girl, so Edmond taught her everything he learned every day, and now she reads and writes as well as he does. Of course, nobody does arithmetic as well as Edmond, not even me. But still. That takes determination."

"And what do you think of Angélique, now?"

"What do you mean, 'now'?"

"Now that you have got past the pretty picture and found out what she's really like."

He stared at his mother. "So that was the plan."

She looked innocent, concentrating on the garlic she was dicing.

"You wanted me to see her a lot so I would find out what she was really like. Well, it didn't work. I like her just as much as before. More. She's not like I thought, all pretty and pale and sweet. Well, she's pretty, of course, and often sweet, but in fact, she's pretty tough inside."

"I like her, too."

He stared at his mother, smiling back at him. He would never figure her out.

Then she leaned over the table and put a new pod into his hands, and the smile disappeared. "Alain, do you understand what your father has been saying for the past few years?"

He resumed his work. "You mean politically? I have an idea. I've heard it often enough."

"But do you believe it?"

He shelled a few more peas before answering that. "I guess so."

"You mean you believe it because he says it, and he's your father. Well, that's a start, I suppose. You should try to believe it because it is true. Because his ideas are fair for everyone."

"That's what Angélique believes, too."

"Hmm. Soon there may be a great test of what Angélique believes."

"What do you mean?"

"What are your father and the others doing in Vizile, right now?"

"Talking about the troubles of the realm, I guess."

"I can tell you more than that. They are meeting in Vizille because the king won't let them meet at the parliament in Grenoble, and at this time they don't want to do anything illegal. They are meeting against the king's wishes, and they are discussing ways to limit the king's powers. They will also try to limit the powers of the nobles and take away a lot of their privileges. How will Angélique react when her special status is taken away?" She raised her eyebrows and pointed.

"Huh…?…oh." He resumed shelling. "Until recently, she wasn't aware of it. She has been working on the problem."

"In encouraging you to meet with Angélique, I was taking a risk. With things as they are now in France, there is no place for the friendship of a girl like her with a boy like you. She could never marry you without a scandal. She moves in a society into which you can never enter. There are advantages that you can never access, like the government positions that you cannot apply for, because you are not of noble blood. Your father and I, and many like us in the Third Estate, do not consider that is right. We are doing everything we can to erase those differences. To some extent, I was using you as a weapon to break down the barriers. In doing that, I risked your happiness."

"Maman, I did what I wanted. You didn't risk anything."

She smiled. "Thank you, but a parent doesn't see things that way. Perhaps I couldn't have stopped you, but I still feel responsible. As it is, I am not too displeased. You have formed a precious friendship. In the years to come anything could happen. *Le bon dieu* knows, I'm not arranging marriages for you yet!"

"I hope you never do! That's one privilege I'm sure Angélique would be happy to get rid of."

"Even if it means getting rid of all her wealth, as well?"

"How could that be?"

Catherine put down the knife she was using and stood looking at him. "Alain, what we are talking about here is changing the way France has been for centuries. Many people will not want to change. Many people will want to change more, and faster. There will be conflicts of one kind or another. Look what happened to Britain's colonies in America." She strode across the room, looking out the window. She stood there a long while, and he wondered what she was thinking about.

Then she turned, walked back to him, and sat. "Once change starts, it develops its own momentum. Some people would like to take all the land from the church and the nobles and give it to the peasants. What if those people get into power? Will the nobles and the king let it happen?"

Alain sat there, stunned. Until now, the idea of change had been merely an idea – interesting to talk about, to plan. The possibility of warfare throughout the realm had not sunk home.

She reached across the table and took his hand. "I don't mean to frighten you, Alain, but..."

He covered her hand with his. "Don't worry, Maman. I'm not frightened. Just very, thoughtful. This is more dangerous than I ever believed, isn't it?"

"It could be, and it is best that we are all prepared for whatever happens."

"When does *Papa* get home?"

"We don't need to worry just yet. The king is allowing this meeting to take place, and he won't interfere. He's not a very decisive man, the king, and this show of strength will hold him back, at least for a while." She stood and collected the shelled peas, sweeping the table bare with a whisk of a cloth. "You know, you need to practise more."

"Practise what?"

"Working and thinking at the same time. You took as long to shell the peas as it took me to chop this whole ratatouille."

* * *

Alain's father returned two nights later, with fatigue lines in his face but an air of triumph in every motion.

"We did it!" were his first words as he entered the door.

Alain and his mother crowded around, with Ariane getting in the way trying to take Jouvent's travel-stained coat.

"We did it! The king has called the Estates du Daphine to meet in Romans on August second. For the first time in 160 years! Serres is sending five clergy, six nobles, and nine from the Third Estate. We are going to demand a meeting of the Estates General. We are going to demand a whole lot of things. It's going to happen, Catherine. He'll have to give in. He's weak and his treasury is empty. He needs our cooperation, and to get it, he will have to pay. Pay in power. It's going to happen, just as we planned!"

With a mighty heave, he lifted his wife off her feet and spun her around in a circle before putting her down. She was beaming as hard as her husband. Alain watched them. *Here is something I can never be part of.*

Then his father turned to him and threw an arm over his shoulder. "History's in the making, lad, and we're in the middle of it! What do you think of that?"

Laughing together, the three of them crowded up the stairs into their home.

The next day, Angélique left for Grenoble.

Early in the morning she sent an urgent message to Alain, asking him to come as soon as he could. It was enough unlike her that he excused himself from breakfast and returned with the messenger.

This time she invited him in and took him to the small sitting room where they had met the month before. He looked around. How different it all looked, now that he knew the people who lived here.

She got right to the point. "Maman says we're going back to Grenoble today. Some kind of news came last night, and she said, 'At last they have things straightened out. We can go home, now.' and told Albert to get the big coach ready first thing in the morning. What is going on?"

Alain swallowed his disappointment and told her of his father's announcement.

"Oh, Alain, that's wonderful. Your father must be so proud. The king will have to give in, won't he?"

"But it won't stop with the king. My father says they will take the privileges away from the nobility, too."

Her mouth straightened, her lips pressed tight together. "Good. It has to be done."

"But that's you! I mean your father, at least. You may lose a lot of your income."

She looked at him, shaking her head. "Alain, haven't you been walking with me for the last month? Haven't you heard what the people say?"

"Well, yes, but I wasn't sure you did."

She threw back her head, and that loud laugh came, the one that always surprised him so much. Then she threw her arms around his neck and kissed him, just on the cheek, but a definite kiss. He had the brief impression of her soft lips, and the pressure of her body against his chest, then she was standing back, her hand in that familiar position on his arm, looking at him seriously. "Alain, if I had to be as poor as Aimée and Edmond in order to live in a place where everyone was equal, I would consider myself fortunate. If I had friends as good as I have here, I would be in heaven!"

He stood, staring at her, unable to say anything. Finally he said the only thing that was on his mind.

"But you're leaving."

Her hand dropped. "Yes, when Maman gets it into her head to go, there's no sense arguing." She looked up at him, smiled brightly. "Don't look so sad. I'll be back. Now that I've been here, how could I not come back?"

"But when?" He hadn't meant to sound so forlorn. He had meant to be off-hand, casual. He hadn't meant to be so honest.

Her smile faded. "Please don't be upset, Alain. It only makes it harder. I won't be back for a while. Not before next spring, I suppose. Tell the others, will you? Tell them I'll be back." *As if telling more people will help make it so.* "Tell the Rat I send him a big kiss."

"I can't do that! He'll throw something at me. You know how he hates to be kissed."

She gave a wan smile. "That way he'll be sure the message comes from me. No one else would dare. I have to go, now, Alain. I do." She started towards the door.

"Angélique..."

She turned back, staring at him, waiting. He couldn't say it. *Gone until next year!* His resolve firmed. "Angélique, you...you kissed me before. With no warning. I didn't get much chance to enjoy it. Could you...ah...could we...?"

She glanced to the door, returned to him and looked seriously up into his face. "Do you know what you're doing?"

"Yes. I do. I know exactly what I'm doing."

"Good." She stepped forward and kissed him gently on the lips. As she stepped back, one hand reached up and touched his cheek, just as gently.

"Good-bye, Alain. I...Good bye."

She spun and left the room. He stood there, wondering what she had meant to say. *What if she meant...?*

A dry chuckle whirled him around. "She's a fine girl, my Angélique, but she should know better than to leave her young man without showing him to the door." The old lady hobbled up to him, took his arm. "Come, young Alain, and I'll play hostess. There are a few things an old lady can still do to help out."

He bowed hastily and held the door open for her. "Yes, Mme. de Dillon. We…I…didn't see you there."

She chuckled again. "Oh, I just walked in. You two were feeling much too sorry for yourselves to notice me." She held him on the front steps of the *chateau* and looked up at him, her eye firm, though her hand shook on his arm. "Don't you pay any attention to me. I'm just an old lady, and my eyes don't see much."

Alain squared his back. "There was nothing happened that I wouldn't be proud to have anyone see."

Again that harsh chuckle. "*Bien joué*, lad. You practice up on me so when the time comes, you can do a good job of telling the people you really want to persuade. Now on your way, young Alain. Tell your father he did a fine job this week, and I hope he does more in future. Oh yes, and the next time you are here on business with your father, you come and have a chat with me. Old ladies sometimes have bits of news to pass on."

With a wink, she turned and limped back inside, leaving a bemused young man to turn away and walk slowly homeward.

Grenoble

November 5, 1788

My dear Wife,

Good news! I will be following this letter home in a few days, at least for a visit. This has been a short session, but much has been accomplished. Someone has been doing a lot of arm-twisting since our conclave in September, and ideas are moving faster. There are also a few changed representatives, especially in the Second Estate. I suppose some of them decided they didn't want to be politicians after all, preferring to stick with what they are good at: parties, scandal, and spending money for frivolous reasons.

By the way, can you imagine how our neighbor, Reynaud de Gonillons could have got himself in as a representative from the Second Estate? Oh, I admit he's a vital young man, with a certain rough charm. Cutting quite a social swath in Grenoble society, I hear.

What bothers me is that I can't figure out what he's after. Sometimes he sides with the nobles, then suddenly he will vote with the Thirds on a related issue. Maybe he's not sure himself what he wants. He wouldn't be the only one!

Alain, Angélique wishes me to send good wishes to you and her "other friends". She says you will know whom. I met her outside the Assembly yesterday. She had been watching from the visitor's gallery all day! She must be having a boring time this winter. I certainly wouldn't want to watch this circus the whole day, if I were a young lady with parties to go to.

The weather has been clear and cold here in Grenoble. I can't wait to get back to the warm South.

With affection,

François

Grenoble

January 12, 1789

My dearest wife,

Success! Well, at least modified success. The king has decided to call the Estates General together in Paris this summer. After almost 200 years! Dauphinée will be sending 24 delegates (we wanted 30): four clergy, eight nobles, and twelve from the Third. Several people here, quite influential ones, want me run for one of those twelve positions. A tempting idea. How exciting to be part of the making of a new France!

We are making good progress on the Provincial constitution, and a committee will be meeting in February to outline a plan of legislation for the Estates General. They will be sending a questionnaire to each village, asking for the people's concerns. Sounds democratic. The Sun King must be shivering in his grave!

Angélique de Bardel was at the Assembly again today. She told me it was the best diversion in a boring town. She provided some of the entertainment herself; after she left me, Reynaud de Gonillons waylaid her and said something, I wish I knew what. She turned on him and gave him a calm but thorough dressing down, ending with a comment to the effect that if he spent more time in the Assembly where he was supposed to be, and less time chasing around the bedrooms of Grenoble, maybe he would have a better idea what was going on in the real world.

She said that loud enough to turn a few heads, then marched out with her nose in the air. He slunk off. I felt like applauding, but I'm not sure it was wise of her. He's not the type to take a public slight easily, and he does have friends.

Ah, the impetuosity of youth! Sometimes I wish I had the nerve to tell some of these people what I think of them. With fond affection,

François

8.   Catching Up

May, 1789

Alain straightened his back and stretched, dropping his notebook on the wagon seat beside the driver. "Is that all there is?"

The man looked down, shrugged. "Do you see any more? I ain't got but one wagon, and that wasn't full, I know. Maybe the king'll send more next month."

"Next month! We have people starving right now." He gestured at the small mound of sacks in the shed. "This will only last a week."

The wagoner shrugged again. "The king's got his own troubles, from what I hear."

Alain could feel the anger start. "But this is why he has all the problems! If he would consider the people of France instead of lounging around in his palace at Versailles, he might figure out what was best for his realm."

The man grinned. "Maybe you ought to go up to Versailles and tell him."

"That's what my father is doing right now."

"*Ah, oui*, the Estates General. A good start, but it'll never amount to much. Jawin' and arguin'. A good prod with a bayonet is what they need up there. And it'll come to that, you mark my words." His jaw snapped shut, as if he had said too much on the subject. Then he tossed his head towards the seat beside him. "Climb up, *monsieur*, and I'll give you a lift back home. It's on my way out of the village."

Alain locked the door and climbed up to sit on the wagon seat, looking at his notes and wondering how they could divide such a small amount of grain among so many families.

He still hadn't come up with any solutions when the driver pulled up at the law office.

"You're doin' a good job, young Jouvent. Many people'r thankin' you for their daily bread this spring." With that the driver cracked his long whip over the backs of his oxen, and the heavy wagon rumbled away.

A glow of pleasure filled Alain. It was an honour to be given the job of organizing relief supplies, though he only got it because no one else had wanted such a difficult and thankless task. They were sorry now. He had badgered and pleaded, once riding all the way to Gap to talk to the *Intendant* himself, with the result that the supplies had increased. Up to now. *This last load is going to be a problem.*

"She's back! She's back!" The lithe figure tearing up the street towards him was no longer the waif they had found up on the mountain the summer before. Still small but no longer so thin, the boy was dressed in a sturdy outfit of rough working clothes, looking every inch the forester's helper. But his face was still dirty. Alain reached out and tousled the already-tangled hair. "Who's back, you ragamuffin? Why aren't you out cutting down trees or something?"

He knew very well who was back. She had told him in her last letter that she was coming. Still, it gave him a pang of pleasure to hear someone else say it.

The boy's small chest rose, his head tilting. "We brought down a load of that new walnut we cut last winter and put it in the dryin' shed at the carpenter's. I was just gettin' back on the wagon, and there she was. *Sacre bleu!* She kissed me. On both cheeks, right in front of all the men. Did they laugh! She looked at them and said I was the only one who deserved it." Jimmy strutted a few steps. "Anyways, she said she was glad to see me, and she sent me to say hello to Aimée and Edmond, that she'll be over to see them tomorrow, and to tell you you're invited over any time this afternoon." He was ticking the points off on his fingers, and Alain could picture Angélique telling him the messages.

"Well, *merci bien*. You came to me first, and now you're off to tell the others? I can tell by your grin that you're going to cadge another *brioche* from Aimée. How do you do it, having all the ladies love you so much?"

He cuffed the boy on the shoulder, sending him racing off again.

Angélique was with her father in the main reception room. When the smiling servant let him in through the ornate doorway, she looked up and a pleased smile crossed her face. As she strode towards him he wondered how he had ever though of her as delicate and pale. Then she was in front of him, grasping his shoulders and giving him the traditional three kisses: left cheek, right cheek, then left again. He was overwhelmed by the familiar fragrance, the softness of her cheek against his, the faint touch on his face of the curls that rolled across her forehead.

He gathered his wits. "I guess I really count. The Rat only got two kisses."

"If I had given him one more, he'd have died of embarrassment."

"More likely burst with pride. You've raised his status immensely with the men in the wagon-yard."

She laughed freely and turned towards her father, with whom Alain shook hands. "Alain and I have a lot to discuss, *Papa.* Would you excuse us?"

De Bardel looked pained. "I thought you were going to re-organize my life this afternoon. How will I put up with the agonies of suspense for another day, wondering what else I've been doing wrong?"

She laughed again, and Alain noticed, with an irrational surge of jealousy how she placed her hand on her father's arm. "Don't worry, *Papa.* You have been doing very well. I'm sure I won't have to change much this time." Her hand swept the room, and Alain saw that the business papers had spread even more than last month. "It's a good thing Maman didn't come this time. Think of the changes she would want."

Her father waved them out of the room and returned to his desk. They walked together across the main hall to their usual sitting room.

"Nana tells me you have been very busy this spring."

"Your great-grandmother has been very helpful. It was her idea that I go see the *Intendant.* I don't know what was in that letter she gave me, but he certainly listened to me after he read it."

"I imagine she reminded him of some indiscretion he pulled when he was ten years old. You know how she always knows all about everyone."

"Well, it worked. That time. We still haven't got enough supplies to keep everyone fed until the first crop comes in."

"Alain, the king has no more money. Every *sou* he spends for relief supplies is borrowed. An incredible amount of the public money is used to paying interest, and it's getting worse.

"Because of the poor harvest last year, the price of bread has risen. Because of that, people are spending all their money on food, and not buying anything else. So factories are closing because they can't sell their goods, putting people out of work. People out of work can't buy things, so more factories close. It's a terrible cycle, and the only way to break it is to spend more money, which the king doesn't have because the nobles won't pay their taxes!"

The colour rose in her cheeks, and she calmed herself with an effort.

"But we don't have to talk politics so soon. How have you been? How are your father and mother?"

"I haven't been doing much. Father getting elected to go to Paris for the Estates General was a big thing for us. I was surprised at how many people appreciated what he has been saying and doing for years."

"Hah! 'A prophet is without honour in his own country.' How is your mother coping?"

He laughed. "She's thinking of becoming a lawyer. Often she looks at some paper or other in the office and says, in a surprised voice, "I can do this!' Between the two of us, we're keeping the clientele quite happy. How about you? How was your winter in Grenoble?" He wasn't sure he wanted to hear the answer.

"It was fascinating! I was so disappointed when the Assembly was over in January and we had to go back to dreary normal. Your father is impressive. He isn't one of the leaders and he doesn't speak often, but when he does get up, they listen because they have learned that he will say something important and well thought out. Something a lot of them should learn to do."

There was no delicate way to lead up to this, so he just said it. "And Reynaud de Gonillons? What happened with him?"

Her lip went stiff, and her eyes narrowed. "That piece of horse-dung!"

For once, Angélique was not pretty. No pretty at all. He was proud of her.

"The fool went to my father and asked for permission to court me. Can you imagine?"

Alain could very well imagine. *I don't understand why the men aren't lined up to court her. Maybe I shouldn't say that out loud.*

"My father said perhaps de Gonillons had better ask my opinion. That must have set him back a bit. But he came anyway, and asked me, rather awkwardly I thought, if he could court me. I was polite to him out of sympathy, as I could see the situation was outside his experience. I told him that I wasn't interested in being courted, thank you *monsieur*, as my life was much too busy for that kind of thing.

"He couldn't understand. Being rejected must be outside his experience as well. He told me that he was willing to wait until I grew up some, and that he would keep an eye on me until then. I told him that would not be necessary and not to waste his time, as I was not anticipating a change of heart. He looked knowing and left. After that, he kept showing up with a proprietary air wherever I went. People were beginning to notice, and he may have persuaded them that there was an arrangement. When I found that out I realized I would have to be more blunt. I explained to him in words of one syllable that I took no pleasure in his company, and he should not envision having his eyes or any other part of him on me. It seemed to work. He hasn't bothered me since."

"Father wrote to us about that. He was worried. De Gonillons would be a bad enemy."

"I suppose I shouldn't have done it, at least not so publicly. But that was the only way to get through to him. I got what I wanted. It remains to see how much I'll have to pay for it."

"It's too bad he's your next door neighbor."

She laughed grimly. "Don't worry. If he tries anything here, my father will have him horse-whipped. *Papa* may seem like a softy, but he won't stand for any nonsense. That's why de Gonillons tries his tricks in Grenoble, when *Papa* is down here at home."

So Savournon is 'home' now!

"But let's not allow our first day together to be taken up by that man. Talk to me about Savournon. How are Aimée and Edmond? How is Jimmy?"

He laughed. "Aimée and Edmond go their own way as usual. The Rat has settled in, finally."

"What do you mean, finally?"

"I didn't want to bother you with it, but I had to go up and remind the head forester that *Mademoiselle* would be deeply grateful if he would be patient with the young scamp. He burnt down one of the huts, making lamps with some alcohol he got his hands on. The foresters must be distilling their own brandy up there, and most of the anger was about the lost drink, not the burnt hut. Anyway, the Rat is now an expert at building wooden huts. Aubin gave him plenty of practice."

"But after that he was all right?"

"Shall we say the problems have been minor. I doubt if he notices what he does half the time. He picks up anything small that he sees, including things from people's pockets. It can be quite annoying, although one of the foresters said the other day that it's comforting to be sure that if you lose something you always know where to find it."

"It sounds as if they like him."

"Everybody likes him. It's living with him they're not so sure about."

At that moment there was a discreet tap at the door that led into the domestic area of the house. After a brief wait the hinges creaked and Françoise de Dillon hobbled into the room. Alain was on his feet in a flash, but she waved him away.

"Don't bother with me. I've been making my way alone for twenty years now and need no one fussing over me." Her sharp eyes turned from one to the other. "On the other hand, why shouldn't I allow a young man to fuss over me? Doesn't happen too often at my age. No reason young Angélique should get all the attention." She lowered herself into a chair and her eye settled on her great-granddaughter.

"Notice how I've been learning manners? Notice how I knocked before I came in this time? Is that not *comme il faut?*"

Angélique laughed. "Yes, Nana. Much better. Now that you are being polite, the young men will be around here in droves. Whole flocks of them. Won't you be pleased?"

"Flocks and droves? Sounds like a bunch of sheep. Don't like sheep much. Seen too many of them. I like the ones with a bit of individuality."

Then she was hauling herself to her feet again and moving towards the door. "I thought I'd drop in. With your mother absent, the *ancêtre antique* is all that's left to keep an eye on you." Her bright eyes regarded them both once more and chuckled. "As if that would make any difference." Then she turned and went out, and they heard her voice, drifting back to them before the door closed. "Sheep. Stupid animals. Follow each other off a cliff if you let them."

Alain and Angélique exchanged a grin. The girl needed no apologies for her "ancient ancestor." Not where Alain was concerned, anyway. The old woman was his best ally.

A warm glow built slowly in Alain as they talked on. This was what he remembered of last summer: the comfortable, intimate conversations, theirs alone, which could never be taken from him. He told himself that she must be feeling the same. How could she possibly ever want to give this up?

Then reality stole in. *The better question is, how long can such happiness last?* He dragged up the nerve to ask and was happy that he had. She planned to stay the whole summer.

"I have been making myself indispensable on purpose. With your father away in Paris, *Papa* needs someone to tell him what's going on in the realm. And since Maman would never believe that I could be of any use in that way, I am going to be so helpful with the paperwork, which he doesn't like much anyway, that he will beg to have me stay. That kind of thing she understands. So I will be here for several months!"

"That's wonderful!"

She made a small grimace and faced him squarely. "Not as wonderful as it might be. I have been thinking very seriously this winter, and I have come to a decision."

"A decision?" Something in her manner chilled him.

"You are very special to me, Alain. You must know that. You will be for all my life. But this is not the time for mistakes." She counted the points off.

"One: I am young. The girls my age in Grenoble are playing at love, but it is only girlish silliness. My time for romance will be when I am old enough to handle it.

"Two: there remains the threat of an arranged marriage. I am not about to get myself caught up in a situation out of a tragic ballad.

"Three: this whole idea of romantic love is misleading. If two people are going to spend their lives together, they had better have something more stable to go on than the wild emotions of their youth. Couples who are happily married and stay happy are those who grow to love each other. Look at my parents, for example."

Alain glanced at her. In the first place, she rarely talked about her mother. In the second, he couldn't dream up two more poorly matched people. To his eyes, it seemed to be an arranged marriage that lasted for political convenience only.

"You think that they are so different, that they don't get along. Well, it even surprises me sometimes, but you are wrong. It was an arranged marriage. My mother comes from an old family, but one with little resources left. I'm sure it was considered a great comedown for her to be married to a 'country squire.' You haven't heard that expression? It's from England – a mildly insulting term for nobles like my father who stay on their land and spend little time in court.

"However my father makes a lot of money running his lands properly, and my mother's people have connections, so the marriage was a good one for both families. While I was still a baby they developed our style of life. Maman and I live in Grenoble, and *Papa* divides his time between us there and his duties here. There is a great deal of respect between my parents. Even living alone in Grenoble and visiting in Paris all these years, I'm sure my mother never... well, you're aware of what goes on at court."

His cheeks felt hot. He had never considered such a thought in regard to his own parents. It was inconceivable.

He found it hard to understand Angélique discussing the concept so casually.

She went on as if she hadn't noticed. "They do love each other. When we are together, they laugh and joke and sometimes embrace." She looked up sideways. "Yes, they actually touch each other in my presence."

His mind blanked. A smart reply was called for, but nothing came. Resentment stirred in him, that she could make him aware of what an outsider he was. This must be the kind of casual talk they had in the drawing rooms of Grenoble. If it was, he wanted no part of it. *I don't consider myself the prudish middle-class type, but on the other hand, there are limits of decency...*

"I'm sorry. I've offended you, haven't I? You went away again. Please don't do that. It makes me feel very lonely."

She was manipulating him, but it was nice that she cared enough to want to.

"You were making a point about marriage."

She smiled in relief. "Oh, yes. I got off the topic, didn't I? I was trying to say that people should get married because they know each other, their personalities match and they know they can live together happily for all their lives."

He nodded. "I can understand that. I doubt that it works that often in practice, but it sounds good."

"And you sound like a lawyer discussing a case. You're not much fun sometimes."

There was an awkward silence.

"Well, I'm like this sometimes. I guess we'll see if you can get used to it."

Her smile returned. "I'm used to it already." She stood, all business now. "And I have something to show you." She led the way deeper into the house. Alain had only been in the library of Chateau Savournon a few times. He remembered being impressed by the sheer number of the books and the variety of the titles, wishing he could get his hands on some of them. Now, in the middle of the floor stood a wooden crate, the top off and the gleaming aura of new leather spilling from inside.

Angélique turned and stood between him and the crate. "Alain, I want you to know I thought deeply about buying these. The money could have been spent on food for the hungry villagers. But I decided that this was a purchase that would help more, in the long run, than a sack of grain today." She stepped aside, and he looked down into the box. It was stacked with a matching set of volumes, a few individual books with different bindings scattered on top. He picked up one of these.

"Voltaire." The book was not new, and it fell open to a page that was soiled, as if from many hands pressing it flat.

"*I need not say which is most useful to a nation: a lord, powdered to the tip of the mode, who knows exactly at what o'clock the king rises and goes to bed, and who gives himself the airs of grandeur and state, at the same time that he is acting the slave in the ante-chamber of a prime minister, or a merchant who enriches his country, despatches orders from his counting-house to Surat and Grand Cairo, and contributes to the felicity of the world...*"

"The man puts his finger on the problem, doesn't he?"

She gestured to the other books.

"Rousseau, *Discourse on the Origin of Inequality*. My father has that one." He checked the names of several others. He raised his eyebrows. "Rousseau, Voltaire, Montesquieu, Diderot. All the Philosophes. A great deal of heavy reading, here!"

"But important! Do you understand what they say?"

"In general. Not that I've read most of them. *Liberté* and *egalité* of man, to put it in a nutshell. That means no privileged upper class, no censorship, equal rights for everyone. No buying 'offices' from the king to become a nobleman, either, I suppose. They like the English system of government, where the king is restricted by Parliament in what he can do, especially in the spending of money. My father is a great admirer of theirs, as you might guess from his politics."

"You sound so casual about this." A small frown.

Not a time to act superior. He smiled. "It's because I have heard these things discussed all my life. The newness has sort of worn off."

She brightened. "Then you'll be able to explain them. I must admit some of the points they make seem obscure at times. Will you read them with me?"

Invite me to walk barefoot to Paris. "Of course I will, but don't expect me to understand them all, either."

"Don't worry. We'll figure them out. Now look at what else."

He looked down at the matching set of volumes, their bright new leather inviting his touch. *This, I can be enthusiastic about.* "Diderot. *The Encyclopaedia.* Fourteen volumes. That's half a set! How did you get your hands on this?"

"Influence is useful sometimes, and money well-invested pays in the long run. Aren't they marvellous?"

He picked a random volume and opened it. The new paper crackled, and he held it with reverence. It showed pictures of people plowing fields, with the various tools numbered and labelled. The following paragraphs told what the tools were and how they were used.

"Knowledge."

"All that the modern world can gather together."

He ran his finger over the spine of the book. "It's a funny thing. To be able to buy knowledge. That you can own something like this."

"But you can't. You can't own knowledge. It should be free. Everyone should be able to learn. That's what this *Encyclopaedia* is all about."

"Edmond would die to get his hands on this."

"So would Aimée. Why shouldn't they get their hands on it?"

"You wouldn't mind?"

"Why should I mind? Didn't you hear what I just said about knowledge being free?"

"Angélique, you can't have the village children running in and out of the *chateau*. Me being here is bad enough. Your mother will have a conniption."

She stood facing him, the blood rushing to her cheeks. "Alain, that is the most narrow-minded, middle-class thing I have ever heard you say. How can you call Aimée and Edmond 'village children?' When you label them like that, you put up as big a barrier between yourself and them as there is between the Estates at the Assembly."

"I was trying to look at it from your mother's point of view."

"I would prefer to hear it from your point of view. I have been hearing my mother's point of view all my life." She relaxed, and a smile played in one corner of her mouth. "Besides, my mother isn't here, is she?"

She was like that. The fire flared up, then was gone. *I must always remember to wait, to stay cool until the mistral is calm again.* He allowed himself a wry grin. *Of course, the mistral blows for weeks, sometimes.*

And so, as the fields ripened under the increasing warmth of the summer sun, Chateau Savournon experienced the tread of plebeian feet, as the lawyer's son and the baker's twins shared the wonders of the *Encyclopaedia* with the daughter of the nobility.

Unfortunately, another ripening was occurring. One likely to develop a more sour fruit.

Paris

July 15, 1789

My dear wife and son,

I mourn for France. The progress we were making may all be spoiled. The situation has gone completely out of hand here in the capital. Mobs of poor people are roaming the streets doing what they wish, and the king seems powerless to stop them.

Yesterday, they attacked the Bastille to free the political prisoners inside. It was a useless gesture, as there were only a handful of prisoners held there, none of them for crimes against the realm. However, the people got together in thousands, went to the armouries and took weapons – rifles, powder, even a few cannons – and stormed the Bastille.

Of course there is no chance that an undisciplined mob could ever take such a fortress, but the governor's orders were unclear and he tried to bargain with them. They took advantage of this, and someone let the doors open.

The result is a few poor soldiers killed, a few undeserving criminals freed, and the mob running loose in the streets, its power unleashed, snarling and snapping at anyone who even looks like nobility.

The only positive outcome, I suppose, is that the king and the two other Estates understand that the common people have power, and that they had better listen to us Thirds more closely.

I know Paris is different from the provinces, but with such violence happening here, I am concerned for your safety and I feel so helpless to protect you. I would come home to you, but these are important times for France, and we must do our best to direct this "revolution" to the best ends we can.

Please be careful. Do not take any threat or uprising lightly. Blood has been spilled, and more is likely. I don't want to frighten you too much, but I know you are both levelheaded enough to handle this.

Alain, you are almost a man, now. I am counting on you to take care of your mother through this danger until I can return.

Your loving husband and father,
François Jouvent

Post Script

More progress. We are now calling ourselves the "General Constitutional Assembly." We are going to write a new constitution for France!

9. La Grande Peur

July 25, 1789

Alain was the first to be aware of the trouble. Late in the afternoon he was returning to the office after delivering some papers to a farmer in the hamlet of les Girards, a few minutes walk east of Savournon. As he passed through les Gonillons and approached the bridge, he noticed a swelling murmur of voices ahead of him. Alert at once, he moved closer.

The crowd of men and women in front of the inn did not look disorderly or angry. In fact, as he got nearer and could hear the comments called out, it sounded like they were just plain scared. The people he could see were not those likely to cause trouble either: prosperous farmers and shopkeepers, clerks, men with small government jobs. There were even several women there with children clutched to them. *What is going on? News of the problems in Paris must have got here, but why would that make the common people so frightened?* He moved in and listened.

There were no real leaders, but a half-circle had formed around the inn door. Various people were trying to get the crowd's attention by calling out above the noise. Alain registered a few of these cries.

"I tell you, it's brigands. They've already taken Gap. They'll be marching here as soon as they've looted the town!"

"*Sacre bleu!* They'll kill us all!" A moan went through the crowd.

"The Duke of Savoy is attacking! He has an army massed along the border, and they have destroyed the fortress at Briançon and are marching this way!"

"*Oh, la vache!* What are we going to do?"

There was little immediate danger, either from the crowd or from the rumours they were spreading, so Alain slipped through and sprinted for the bakery. He didn't go far, as he met Edmond half way.

"What's going on?" The younger boy's eyes sparkled with excitement.

"Nothing yet. There are all sorts of rumours going around that someone's attacking, but nobody knows who. Where's Aimée?"

"She stayed with the shop. If we need her, she'll close up and come."

"Good. Let's go back to the crowd and see what's happening." It felt better to have company at a time like this. Edmond still hadn't grown much, but his quick mind would be more important than any amount of strength in such an affair.

By the time they returned the situation had solidified; the crowd was making up its mind. At least, leaders were emerging and plans were being thrown around. The boys listened, and the more obvious stupidities, like everyone taking what they could carry and running, were shouted down. Then someone had an idea.

"What are the *seigneurs* doing about this?"

There were several shouts of agreement.

"Why don't we tell *sieur* de Bardel? He can ask for soldiers to come and protect us."

"Yes! Let's all go! He'll have to do something. He's in as much danger as we are."

Edmond pulled Alain back to where they could talk. "Typical, isn't it? No matter what their everyday complaints, who do they turn to for help?"

Alain grinned. "Right. But now we can be of use. You skip as quick as you can to the *chateau* and tell them what's going on. If *sieur* de Bardel isn't home or you can't get to him, either Angélique or Mme. de Dillon will listen and you can get action that way. Tell them there isn't much time. This bunch won't move fast, but it isn't that far. I'll check in on

109

Aimée and my mother to see that they're safe, then come along with the crowd to keep an eye on things."

His plan worked well, with the small exception that neither woman would be left behind to be "safe." First Aimée, then his mother insisted on joining the crowd.

"Alain, you said there were women with children. This isn't a riot, it's a mob of frightened people, and the more of us who have heads on our shoulders, the better it will be. Come on, Aimée." Mme. Jouvent was pulling her shawl around her, and before he knew it, Alain was locking the door and hurrying to follow them towards the muttering of the crowd.

They came out of their side street as the mob approached, so they waited as the leaders passed, then slipped in behind them. At first Alain walked in the middle and his mother and Aimée each took one of his arms to avoid being jostled apart, but soon it became evident that such precautions were not needed and their grip relaxed. The people had strung out along the road, talking in groups. They were still worried, and every once in a while another stir would indicate a new story passing through.

"They're much quieter than before."

"Of course." His mother gave a wry smile. "Now that they have decided to dump their problems on someone else, they are much happier."

By the time the crowd reached the *chateau* they were quite calm. It helped matters that Charles de Bardel was standing on his front steps to greet them. Two other landowners, François de Pélissieres and Frédéric de Jourdas, were with him. Alain couldn't help but notice three foresters leaning on their guns off to one side, a small grinning figure in their midst flashing him a wave. The Rat had been ahead of everyone as usual.

In the open doorway Angélique and Mme. de Dillon stood, and behind them, to Alain's surprise, he could see Angélique's mother. *I had no idea she was in Savournon. Well, if she is the type to run from trouble, she picked the wrong week to visit.*

Several of the people in the crowd started to call out questions and demands, but de Bardel held up his hand and a shuffling silence prevailed.

"People of Savournon. I am aware of the stories of dangers that threaten us. At the moment that is all they are: stories. However, I have sent a messenger into Serres to find out what is happening there. He should return in about an hour, and then we will know."

"But what about until then? What are we going to do?"

"Since the rumours all seem to indicate that we could be under an attack of some sort, and since we have no soldiers here, I suggest that we take steps to protect ourselves. How many here can lay hands on a gun?"

A large number of shouts greeted this, and de Bardel chuckled. "I thought so. We are not so helpless as anyone might think, out here in the country. And I suppose you can also shoot them?"

An answering chuckle, grim in tone, ran through the crowd. Every man here hunted in the mountains when he had time, and perhaps on the *seigneur's* land if he could do so without getting caught. They were all good shots. They had to be. Powder and lead were expensive.

"I thought so. We will gather a local guard together here in one hour. Bring weapons and enough food for three days. I will provide as much powder and shot as I have, but it would be best to bring your own, as well. And," here he raised his voice, "Any of you that are my tenants, I will consider that every day you spend guarding our homes as one day taken off your duties to the estate."

There was a ragged cheer at this, then a low muttering, as the tenants of other *seigneurs* speculated on their chances of such luck.

"So I suggest you return home, my friends, and prepare yourselves. Those who are staying in Savournon, you may go to your beds, secure in the fact that we are doing all we can to protect you."

He waited on the steps while the crowd dispersed, the more enthusiastic moving with purpose, the rest gossiping as they strolled away. A group of local leaders remained, and these de Bardel invited inside. Alain's friends held a quick conference. Aimée and Edmond were returning to the shop, and Alain's mother could see no reason to stand around either.

The Rat was heading back into the forest with his men. True individualists, the foresters had no intention of marching off with a bunch of peasant soldiers.

Alain stayed behind to talk to Angélique, who was still on the steps waiting for him.

"Why is your mother here? Is she upset?"

Angélique shook her head. "Upset isn't the word for it. She came down here because the situation is getting ugly in Grenoble. There are no mobs in the streets, like Paris, but there have been incidents of noble people being harassed and even roughed up by groups of toughs. It took a lot of courage for her to leave the house and come all this way, but she heard about Paris." Her nose wrinkled. "The wonderful Albert was too afraid to come. Then she got here, and this happened. *Papa* doesn't think these rumours are true. What he has heard, though, is that near Paris, and in some other areas, the peasants have attacked the *chateaux*. They are taking the papers that list their *seigneurial* duties and burning them because that will mean they don't have to do those duties any more. In some cases they have burned more than the papers." She looked at her home and shuddered, and Alain could see her imagination providing flames shooting out the windows.

"I doubt we'll have that kind of trouble here. Everyone is too worried about these outside threats. What does your father have planned?"

"Thanks to Edmond's warning he was able to get something started. He will have to put together this local guard he is talking about and take them wherever the *Intendant* at Gap needs them. Maman is very upset about that. She wants him to stay and protect the town and us. I've never seen her so worried. Of course, things like this bother her quite a lot."

Alain refrained from commenting on what quality of character that indicated in most people's minds. "So our information was useful?"

"Oh, *Papa* is very pleased. Can you imagine if that mob had showed up during dinner, and he had come to the door with his napkin at his neck and said, 'what seems to be the trouble?' They would have no confidence in him whatsoever. As it is, they have the impression he's on top of things, so they go away happy, thinking everything is all right."

"Which it probably is."

"We can hope. Now I had better go in and calm Maman down." She turned back to him. "You're not going with them, are you?"

He felt that pang, deep in his chest again. "Don't want me to leave you alone?" He said it jokingly.

She smiled. "If they truly needed you, I would be the first to send you. But do they?"

"I have no gun, and no one has invited me. Besides, if the other stories are correct, it might not hurt to have some people around Savournon."

She nodded soberly, then smiled at him and turned inside. He started home, but in the yard he met men returning to the courtyard, hastily wrapped bundles slung on their backs. They wandered up, unsure what to do with themselves.

One of the men called out to him, and he walked over. "What's going on, M. Jouvent? What do we do now?"

Pleased at the respectful attitude, Alain saw that the men thought he had been set here to organize them. *There is no sense in bothering the seigneur. I will do what I can on my own.* With little idea of what the men needed, he would have to improvise. He raised his voice, and the other early comers strolled over to listen.

"I am impressed that you got back so fast. It does you credit. But now you have time. Why don't you check your equipment and compare with each other? There is time to go back and get anything else you think of. Then you should pack your belongings carefully. You will be travelling tonight, and you know how long it takes for an awkward pack to start digging into your back."

There were a few assenting comments and the men fell to opening their packs. Alain watched to find out who was the best prepared. On a thought, he dashed into the *chateau.* There was no one to let him in, but he didn't think it mattered. Taking a pen and paper from de Bardel's working desk, he went outside and started a list of the equipment that most of the men were carrying. This created a crowd around him, and the new arrivals naturally came there for instructions.

By the time *sieur* de Bardel came out again an hour later Alain had a group of men sitting on one side of the steps and the rest lined up with their packs while he checked off their names and their equipment. He handed the list over.

The *seigneur* glanced at it. "Don't give it to me, lad. Keep going." He returned the paper to Alain and strode towards the corner of the *chateau* near the storage sheds, where two servants had set up a keg of powder.

"When you are finished with M. Jouvent, come over here and fill your pouches. Alain, who may I have?"

Trying to keep his voice casual, he indicated the men who were equipped. They rose at his signal and lined up for the powder.

More men appeared, and Alain was too busy to be proud. It was discouraging how poorly provisioned some of them were, and he sent a few home for more supplies. However, some had brought everything they owned, and there was no use sending them away. He caught a servant who seemed to be doing nothing and instructed him to find what they needed from the stores of the *chateau*.

"You might want to check with *sieur* de Bardel first, but we can't have these men going off to fight for us with no blankets to sleep in!"

He noticed with delight that the servant went straight to do his bidding without needing confirmation.

In the middle of this bustle everyone froze as the hoofbeats of a running horse approached. A moment later one of the grooms galloped up and threw himself off his lathered horse. De Bardel hurried over and everyone else gathered around.

"The district agent, M. Astier, sends his respects, my Lord, and asks if you can raise a company of guard to help defend us." A murmur ran through the crowd at this confirmation of their fears. "There has been no certain word, but all agree that any threat will come from the east or north. He has gathered four companies and is marching north to Veynes tonight. He suggests you use the Col du Croix and join him along the way. They will be leaving Serres about now, I should expect."

"Fine!" This was not the harried man that Alain knew from his legal dealings. In this situation, de Bardel was confident and decisive. "We leave in a quarter hour. The kitchen has food for you. Alain, will you line the men up at the side door?" He winked. "Tell them to have their cups ready, too. Then come and talk to me."

Alain complied, pleased at how well the men followed his lead. Then he grinned at himself. *They are lining up for free food and a drink from the seigneur's cellar. They would follow a school child for that.*

Once he had finished that duty he looked for the *seigneur* and stood at his elbow until he had completed his discussion with the other two nobles. "Ah, Alain. A fine job you've done. Thank you very much." De Bardel took Alain by the arm and led him aside, lowering his voice. "I'm glad to see you coping so well, because I need you to do something for me."

"Whatever you wish, sir."

"I'm not happy about this, Alain." His gesture swept across the busy courtyard. "These alarms are only rumours. I wish I knew more. Wish your father were here, to tell the truth. From stories I have heard, the trouble may start much closer to home."

"I know what you mean. Angélique told me."

The man glanced sharply at him, then nodded. "Of course she did. So you know what to watch for." Again he indicated his small army. "This is a good bunch of men. Too good."

"Too good?"

"That's right. I'm taking all the best men out of the valley. I have to. I have my orders, and if there is an outside threat, the only way to meet it is with a combined front. However, I am not happy about whom I am leaving behind. That's where you come in. I am not unaware of your accomplishments, you and my daughter and your friends. I understand the value of knowing what is going on ahead of time. Tonight was a good example. You keep your eyes open and your head about you while I'm gone. If there is trouble, do what you feel is best. Your mother is welcome to take refuge here at the *chateau* if need be, but perhaps she would be safer where she is. The *chateau* may be the least safe place in the village. Don't count on the villagers or the other *seigneurs* for help. They will have their own problems. Just do what you can."

"Certainly, sir. You can count on me."

"I am, lad, I am. Everything important to my life is in that building right now, and I am being forced to leave it unprotected." He clapped Alain on the shoulder and turned back to his work. "*Le bon dieu* be with you all."

"And you, *sieur* de Bardel."

10. Real Fear

July 28, 1789

The small army gathered itself together around nine o'clock and marched away up the street to the cheers of the whole town. For a moment, Alain wished he were going with them. Then he thought of the responsibility placed on him by the *seigneur*. He looked around at the coming dusk and thought of them marching off through the darkness for several hours, then sleeping on the hard ground, only to get up and march again. He thought with guilt of his own soft bed.

When all had settled down, he made one last patrol around. It took him nearly an hour, but he was too excited to sleep anyway. As he walked, he looked at the various buildings in terms of how easy the village would be to defend. To his inexperienced eye, and considering the weapons they had left, it didn't look good.

Well, that wasn't the type of attack he was expecting. There was no one nearby who would want to harm the villagers. He directed his steps towards the *chateau.* Here, there were better possibilities. The central part and the east wing, constructed in the past fifty years, were a problem with their big ground-floor windows, but the old west wing, with its heavy door and slit windows, could be held by a few men with guns.

"Alain?" He jumped. A slim figure materialized out of the darkness beside the house. "What are you doing out here?"

"Why aren't you in bed?"

"I asked you first."

He laughed softly. "Your father told me to look after you while he was gone. I was just checking."

"He did?"

In the darkness, he wasn't sure whether she was angry or not. It was the sort of thing that used to bother her.

"That was nice of him. He told me to look after my mother."

"It must be awful for him to have to leave you alone like that. He told me that everything important in his life was right here."

"I told you so."

Is she talking about her mother? "I like the idea of people loving each other."

"So do I." She leaned towards him, and he felt the light brush of her lips on his cheek. "Good night, Alain,"

"Good night, Angélique. Get some sleep. Everything will be fine."

"You get some sleep."

"I told you first!"

Her soft laugh trailed off into the darkness, and he stood there, a long time, looking up at the stars and dreaming.

* * *

When the real trouble came it was so fast they had little time to react. Alain was sitting with his mother after supper two nights later, discussing the latest rumours. He was concerned because the stories of the burning of the *chateaux* had filtered out this far, and there was a chance someone might get ideas. He had been doing his best to discredit them as rumours, but they held more truth than any of the other stories spreading around.

There was a tap at the downstairs door, so light that he hardly heard it.

"That's Jimmy. There might be trouble." He slipped into his darkest coat and ran down the stairs. The Rat had been staying at the Sarobert's where he was more available if needed, so Alain was not surprised that he was the messenger. "What's going on?"

"Aimée heard some stuff in the shop today, and I bin watchin' the inn. There's some visitors tellin' strange stories, and there's too many people listenin' too good. Edmond says they're the wrong kind of people ta be listenin', so we better call you."

By this time they were near the inn and they slowed their pace and slipped in along the wall. The windows were open onto the square, so it was easy to hear what was going on inside. Especially when what was going on was so noisy. There were a few people sitting at the tables outside, but these paid them no attention.

There was a lot of loud talking, and Alain wondered at the tone.

"They don't sound like the usual crowd, do they?"

"I heard 'em like that before."

"You have?"

The small head nodded. *"D'accord.* Back home in Marseille, you hear a bar-full like that, you get ready for some real fun. Any moment there's goin' ta be a fight break out."

"I don't suppose a fight would cause us any trouble. They happen here once in a while."

"But if there isn't a fight..."

"What then?"

"Then the shoutin' gets louder and it means they decided to take it out on someone else. Sooner or later they all come pourin' out the door together. Then someone better watch out."

It sounded terribly logical to Alain. "I want to listen for a while. Will you get Edmond?" He considered. "Bring Aimée too." He hated to put the girl into danger, but she could be counted on to keep her head in an emergency. *Cool heads are what we need.*

The Rat was off down the street and Alain slipped onto a nearby bench, trying to sort out the noise issuing from the windows.

Someone was talking loudly now, and enough of the other drinkers seemed to be interested that the man's voice could be heard.

"Yep, they finally got tireda the oppression an' the poverty an' the starvation and they just up an' took what was rightfully theirs."

There was a general rumble of agreement.

"I say that's the only way there's ever goin' ta be change. Ya got ta take what ya deserve, 'cause no one is goin' ta give it to ya."

Another voice chimed in, this one more cultured, but lazy, as if its owner could hardly be bothered to speak. "I don't know, Julien. These don't look like the kind of people that have been oppressed much. They don't look like they're hungry enough. You need people who really want something. Not the kind that will be happy to take any scraps you give them, and 'thank you very much sir.' No, I doubt if these good people here are going to be able to do that. Too bad."

There was a general rumble of protest at this, building until any other comments the voice may have made were drowned out in the clamour. After a while the noise died down enough that the first voice could be heard.

"Well, Hubert, ya just might be wrong. Do you hear that? That's from the heart, my friend, from the heart. If they get the chance, no tellin' what they'll do."

"My friend, that may well be. But I don't see us staying long enough to find out if they have any guts. We got business to attend to in the South. Here, landlord. Fill the glasses of our friends, and we'll be on our way."

A cheerful shout greeted this statement, and a moment later two figures appeared in the doorway. Alain turned away but took a sideways glance at their faces. All he got was the impression that one face was thinner and the other more sun-browned. Then all he could see as they strode off was their backs, one taller, one broader. He was sure he heard the muttered comment, "Dumb peasants." followed by a laugh.

He wished the Rat was here to find out where they were going and who they were, but it didn't matter that much. They had done their damage. It remained to be seen whether it would be serious.

There was a momentary lull inside as the patrons indulged in the bounty of their departed benefactor. Then the talk started again.

"Me, not hungry enough? *Zut, alors.* I done my share of starvin' this winter."

"Me too. Think I'm not the man to take what I'm owed? *Sacre bleu!* Just watch me!"

This got general support. The noise level rose as several other boasts were thrown in.

It was time to leave. As the Rat had predicted, this bunch was not breaking up into fights. He didn't want to be there when they came out, and he was worried where they might be going.

He headed for the *boulangerie*, where he outlined the problem to his friends. "Any suggestions?"

"My foresters are up at the main cabin. I could bring them."

"Not yet. I could send anyone to fetch them. We need help from farther away. Edmond, you're light. Could you take my horse into Serres and see if you can find help? Jimmy, try Le Bersac, although if those two have done their job the *seigneur* may be in trouble there already. It isn't that far. Do you want me to find a horse?"

"A horse? Ride on it? You must be joking. I know where Le Bersac is. I can get over there and back with help in no time."

"Good. Any other ideas?"

"How about the townspeople? Those men in the inn are riffraff. *Papa* and the others don't feel like that."

"Probably true, Aimée. But will they risk themeselves to protect the *seigneur's* property?"

"I can try. I'll talk to *Papa* and then see if we can find other help."

"Good. Let's go."

As the three boys got to the main street they were startled by a sudden burst of sound behind them. Alain looked to Jimmy, who nodded. "They're out in the street, now. They may mill around if we're lucky, dependin' on how scared they are of the authorities. Then they'll head out."

"There are no authorities at the moment for them to be scared of. Let's get moving. When you are asking for help, stress the need for quick help. We don't need an army. We only need a few men with guns. Right now." He listened to the roar behind them. "Tell them Mme. de Charrette sent you. They'll listen to you then. We'd better get moving."

The Rat disappeared, sprinting away. The other two hurried to get the horse saddled up, and then Edmond was off as well. Alain stood, wondering about his next move. There wasn't time to talk to his mother. It would be better to check on the crowd's movement first, then warn whoever needed it the most.

He slid behind a shed by the road and waited. It took longer than he expected. The mob wasn't rushing. The reason became more obvious as they neared him. They had found a wine skin and were pausing every few paces to share it around and discuss their grievances. Then a newcomer would join them and the whole situation would have to be explained. Since the leaders had been drinking for quite a while and none would allow the others to explain, this took some time.

Alain watched the group pass, trying to see as many faces as he could. Many were what he had expected. The poorest daily labourers, several of whom didn't work any more than they had to. The ones he hadn't expected were the poorer farmers, the clerks, the rat catcher, the chimney sweep and the itinerant knife sharpener: those who eked out a living at the smaller jobs around the town. The same people, he thought with bitterness, who had gone running to the *seigneur* two days ago when they felt threatened.

The mob passed, headed for the *chateau*, and Alain had to act fast. Cutting out past the houses, he took the path along the fields at the edge of the village, stumbling along it in the dark.

When he reached the *chateau* he slowed, looking left and right as he trotted up the drive, but there seemed to be no one there. This was strange, because usually this was such a busy place. All he could sense was an eerie, waiting stillness. Lights burned in a few windows and that was all. There was no movement behind the curtains.

More cautious now, he stopped to get his heaving chest under control and listened. There was no sound behind him. Good. He had outrun those louts, who must have paused for another sip of courage along the way. But they would be picking up more assistance as well. A glow on the horizon caught his eye. It was in the direction of Le Bersac and was too bright to be the normal lights of the *chateau*. *Mon dieux! Someone has set a fire!* His caution deserted him and he ran again. Only when he reached the front steps did a new reality creep through the anxiety that hazed his thoughts.

Four stories of chiselled stone rose up from the heavy, panelled door, looming over him in the darkness. This was not the kind of house that you ran up to, screaming. That would only cause the women to panic. He must be calm. He would show a good example.

A faint call blown down the wind from behind him boosted him onwards. Smoothing back his hair with both hands, he approached the front door. He raised the heavy brass knocker and let it fall, then again.

He did not wait long. The door opened a crack; a slim hand reached out and, with surprising force, hauled him through. The door slammed. He spun about in surprise to see Anqelique, her shoulder to the door, a candle shimmering in her hand.

She tried the handle, making sure it was locked, then turned to him. He could see excitement in the flick of her head, throwing the heavy curls away from her face. "What's happening, Alain? The servants have all left."

He paused. This was not the panicky maiden he had expected. Despite the late hour she was dressed in a simple, heavy travelling gown and wore outdoor boots. A pair of plain leather gloves was tucked into her sash, and a shawl lay across her shoulders.

"Are you leaving?" The question sounded foolish the moment he had uttered it.

"That depends. Something is going on out there. If we have to, we are ready to go. At least I am." A touch of asperity lifted her chin. "I assume this isn't a social call. Do you have news? No, wait. Perhaps it is better if Maman and Nana hear at the same time." She spun about and marched down the main entrance hall, under the paintings of her ancestors peering down out of the moving shadows thrown by the candle.

After a stunned hesitation he followed, grateful for time to rearrange his thoughts. Ignoring the reception rooms on the right, she led him to the left, to their usual sitting room. He first saw Mme. de Charrette, who paused in her anxious pacing only long enough for a glance that dismissed him. She, too, was in travelling clothes, although hers were much less practical than her daughter's. He looked around the room and noticed Mme. de Dillon, perched on the edge of a chair in the dimness of the corner.

Angélique dismissed her mother's presence in the same way the older woman had ignored him. "Nana, Alain has news for us from the village."

Mindful of his manners even in this tense situation, he sketched a formal bow. "I hope I can be of some assistance, Madame."

The old woman looked up at him from her armchair, her dark eyes gleaming on either side of her large, hooked nose, reminding him of the raptor he had surprised, late one evening, in a tree near his house. It, too, had regarded him with that unblinking interest.

"Well, the boy has presence of mind. More than many, it seems." She shot a glance at Angélique's mother, who had stopped her pacing but was twisting her hands in the ties of her sash. "I have hopes that your story will contain more useful information than the anxious twitterings of the servants."

Alain took a moment to steady his spinning brain. Years later, the memory of this scene would calm and support him when, as a beginning lawyer, he stood in front of his first judge and jury.

"They are coming, Madame. They are not far behind me."

"Be specific, lad. Who? How many? Why? Give us details."

"I can't be precise, Madame. It started with a few of the local tipplers, overdoing their usual evening complaining. Two strangers added their radical ideas. I'm not sure whether they had a purpose or just stirred things up for fun before they left. A lot of others have now joined the mob, though. Mostly farmers and some workers from the town. From their talk, they want to get hold of the lists to destroy them so they won't have to fulfill their annual obligations to *sieur* de Bardel. I'm afraid there was talk, Madame," here he shot a worried glance at Angélique, who was leaning forward, listening, "of burning more than papers. Many of them are carrying...carrying torches, Madame."

"It's burning, is it? *Ma foi!* Who are they? Give me names."

Again she had him off balance. He tried to think. "Well, I recognized Hilaire the tailor, and Justin from Gonillons was there, as well as Léo, the smith's apprentice..."

He was cut short by a derisive snort. "Léo? Young Léo coming here with a torch? I'll find another place for his torch that he won't like so much."

There was an indignant exclamation from Mme. de Bardel.

The older woman grinned over at Angélique, her face wrinkling even more. "Some time about your tenth child you stop being so worried about maintaining a decorous attitude towards the human body and its functions."

Angélique answered gravely, unconcerned by this change of topic. "I am not planning on having that many children, Nana. But we are embarrassing Alain."

"Quite right, dear. Let's get back to the problem at hand. Now, this rabble of drunkards. They will be here soon?"

"I could hear them as I entered, Madame. If they did not stop to drink again, they would be here now."

"So we have little time. Marie-Françoise, you will go to the servant's quarters and see whom you can find. Someone will have been brave enough or afraid enough to stay. Send one of them to the forester's lodge. Aubin will be there, and his sons. Tell them to come immediately, and why. If there is no one, go yourself." She dismissed the lady as she would a servant.

"Angélique, my child, are you very brave tonight?"

The girl did not speak, only nodded, her eyes wide in the candlelight.

"Good. Someone will have to formally receive our guests. You and I are the only ones eligible."

Alain started forward. "But Madame..."

"You, young man, should not be with us. In the first place, it is not for you to be seen defending the *Anciene Regime*. I know your father and I know you. You will be of much more use to your country if you align yourself otherwise. Besides, I have another need for you. Are you familiar with guns?"

"Yes, Madame, I have hunted with my father."

"Good. You will take this. It is already loaded." Standing, she reached into the corner behind her and pulled out a beautiful fowling piece, its carved stock echoing the texture of the gnarled hands that held it out to him. She marched out into the main hall and indicated that he should open the double doors to her left. As she crossed the reception room she pointed to the windows.

"Both overlook the courtyard. Pick an appropriate moment to let your presence be known." She took him by the sleeve, turned him to face her. There was no denying the command in her eyes.

"Do not let them see who you are. I want no heroics. Besides," and a smile touched her wrinkled lips, "there is no reason to let them know that there is only one of you. If they rush us, shoot the first man forward. After that...?" She crossed herself, and her eyes glanced upward.

She moved to *sieur* de Bardel's desk, retrieved a sheaf of papers and left the room, turning back at the last moment to give him a friendly grin. As she left, he noted that she was not in travelling clothes. In fact she was dressed as if going in to dinner. He could not help but notice the suppressed emotion in her movement, and it didn't seem like fear.

He checked the windows, listening first to be sure that the mob hadn't reached the house yet. The farther opening allowed a clearer shot at the front door, so he pushed back the shutter but left the window closed. On an impulse, he opened the shutter of the other window and took an antique blunderbuss off the wall, leaving it along the ledge. Then he waited, alone in the creaking darkness of the old house. He tried to guess what the others might be doing, but could hear nothing.

He did not wait long before he saw a flickering of lights at the foot of the driveway and heard unintelligible shouts as the mob got up their courage to enter the lord's demesne. As the dark mass crawled along the drive, Alain tried to keep calm. What should he do? He should be alert for some action that might help. What would it be? The only thing was to watch, and perhaps something would come to him.

His eye was attracted to the torches. The most dangerous men would be carrying them. As they approached, he picked out the ones in front. A leader would be leading, urging them on. But there was no single torch that stayed ahead. It seemed to be just a milling mob, spilling forward rather than charging. That seemed good to him. With a determined leader, those in the house would have no chance. *Le bon dieu* knew what Mme. de Dillon had going in that devious Irish mind of hers, but she must have something planned, and it would count on brains, not force. He watched the crowd approach.

When they reached the top of the drive they slowed even more, and the shouting died down to a mutter. He could remember the effect the majestic facade had on him a few minutes ago. The men spilled into the courtyard, not spreading out as soldiers would, but huddled together as if for support. One cannon or ten sharpshooters would destroy them easily. His hand shook with the intensity of its grip on the stock of his gun, and he forced himself to relax and watch.

After a minute when nothing happened the voices increased, and a small group in the front pushed each other forward.

However, before they could get far, the great door opened. There was immediate stillness. Then, from the dark tunnel of the doorway, old Mme. de Dillon stepped forward. She stood straight and her step was smooth and even.

Considering the bent and ancient body Alain had seen this evening, he was amazed at how strong she looked. She walked forward with unhurried dignity. At the front of the porch she stopped where the height of the stairs gave her the maximum effect.

Angélique, taller, bareheaded, stood at her shoulder, her eye sockets black in the shadows of the lanterns above the door.

The old woman's voice, strong and clear, cut through the sputtering of the torches. "Gentlemen. To what do I owe the honour of this unannounced deputation?"

There was a shuffling of feet, and again the knot of men in the centre moved forward as if reluctant. He focused on them. That was where the rush would come, if it did.

"Well?" Her voice rang off the stones behind her. "Speak up. When has anyone ever come to this house with a problem and been turned away?" Heartened by this, the men began calling out, odd fragments of sentences floating over the murmuring of the others. The knot of leaders resolved itself into a front of men, their shouts rising over those of the mob.

"Please, please, gentlemen." The old lady's raised hand quelled the growing noise, and she stepped down two stairs. "One at a time. Have you no spokesmen? What do you want?"

"Our rights!"

"Freedom!"

"Equality!"

On the heels of these, out of the middle of the mob came a rock, which arched towards the right wing of the house, far enough from Mme. de Dillon to be no threat.

There was no compliance in her voice now. It cracked out like a whip. "Jean-Claude Ferrier. When your father came to me for money to start his own shop, he did not tell me he had a son who broke other people's windows." Faces in the crowd turned to the unfortunate boy, and he slunk behind his friends. Then all of them turned to the front again. In that brief lull, Alain shoved the second window open, noting happily how the hinges squeaked. Staying well in the shadows, he laid the barrel of the old blunderbuss out across the windowsill where the ancient steel picked up the glow of the torches. He then returned to his own window to watch.

The effect of this had been for the men in the mob to draw together even closer, and there was a shift to the other side of the courtyard. He could see heads turning towards old Madame Dillon, then towards the gun. Should he show the fowling piece now, or should he wait for a more needful time? While he considered, the moment was taken from him.

"Come, my friends. Let us be civilized about this. If one of you has, perhaps, a list of what you wish to discuss?"

A slurred voice came from the middle of the throng. "We're tired of talkin' and askin,' and not gettin' anything. Want our rights, and we're going to get them, if we have to take them! We want our freedom, and we want it now!"

There was a general murmur of agreement, and the crowd stirred.

This was the moment, and he banged the window open, sticking out the gun. The men shifted away from his position. He wondered how he could get over to the other wing. Better not to risk it. What if something happened while he was gone from his post? He settled in, listening to what Mme. de Dillon would do next.

"Ah, now we get to the flavour of the matter. I don't see much I can do about your freedom. You seem to be doing pretty well what you want at the moment. But what, specifically, do I have that might help you get your rights?"

Another voice, came, this time from near the front. "Madame, you have the lists of the duties we owe *sieur* de Bardel. We've decided we ain't gonna do them, and we want the lists destroyed!"

Old Mme. de Dillon laughed, high and mirthfull. "So it comes down to the same story as always. Ask a man what he wants, and at the bottom of it all he wants to do less work! All right, so I happen to have those lists here." She waved the papers she held.

There was a satisfied rumble from the crowd. "And if you like, I will give them to you. What you do with them is up to you. Now, who do we have?" She looked at them, then through the papers in her hands.

"Ah, yes." She looked up. "Pierre Léon." She made a show of turning the paper towards the light of the torches so that she could read it. "Three days per annum of road work, one *levre* of rye, a half *levre* of wheat and five hens on Christmas. Here you go, Pierre. Come up and get it."

A tall, thin man in a cloth cap came forward slowly, but straightened up as his fellows clapped his shoulders and cheered him on. He approached the top of the stairs and reached up for his paper. She held him there, his hand outstretched. She smiled. "How is your wife, Pierre? Has the new baby got any teeth, yet?"

He mumbled an embarrassed response and took the paper, stuffing it into his shirt. There were cheers from the mob, and someone called out, "Burn it, Pierre, burn it!"

The man's head came up, and he spoke distinctly. "It's mine, and I'll do what I want with it." He slipped back into the crowd, but cut straight through and headed down the driveway.

"Now, who else? Ah, here we are." She looked out at the crowd. "Jacques from the *ferme de pré*." Again she studied the paper. "5 days per year, 11 *ras* of oats. Very well, Jacques." A man from the front of the crowd bounded up the steps and stood beside her, grinning down with his hand out.

Alain noted him for later. This one would not be taken in by her manipulating the situation.

"Ah, but wait a moment." The old lady looked closer at the paper in her hand. "From the record here, it seems you have not fulfilled your contract for the past three years anyway.

Here." She thrust the paper at him. "The *seigneur* is not losing much on that one."

The man's triumphant smile was considerably weaker as he descended. He put the paper up to a torch with a flourish, but few watched him.

The old lady handed out several more papers without comment, then stopped. She looked out at the crowd, and looked through the papers again. She seemed puzzled. She read out names, waiting each time for a response.

There was none.

"Jean-Louis? Is he not here? He does fifteen days work, and must provide three sheep and three *levres* of various grains per annum. He should be here! What about Pierre Berger? And Andre? Where are these men? They are the ones who give the most to the *seigneur*. Surely they would wish to have their papers."

She looked around. "And what of the rest of you? Your names are not here. What can I do for you?" There was a pause, but no one spoke up. "I have done what is in my power. You must seek elsewhere for redress of your problems."

There was a muttering in the crowd, and Alain tensed, his gun barrel clanking against the stonework. Several heads turned his way, and the men began to drift apart. Those who had been given their papers were gone, and those remaining had lost their fire.

The decision was made, however, when two windows of the opposite wing were thrown open, and a short, stocky figure with a rifle half-raised started out from the doorway, halting only when Mme. de Dillon waved him back.

"You may return to your duties, Aubin. Our guests are leaving." There was a hint of steel in her voice and, faced with three more guns, the dregs of the crowd faded out of the courtyard, their torches melting onto the darkness. Only after the last man was out of sight did the old lady's stance relax. She turned and laid a hand on Angélique's arm.

"You can call them out, now, my dear." Her voice had lost its ring, but it carried as far as Alain's position. He heard Angélique's voice, raised but wavering, as he dodged the chairs and tables in the dark room, out into the dim porch, lit now only by the spill from the lamps above the door.

The old lady still stood two steps down. She was smiling up at Angélique, but turned to include him. "Well done, my children. Your assistance was invaluable. Alain, your sense of timing is impeccable. Have you thought of a career on the stage?" She regarded the three men in hunting garb leaning on their guns in the doorway.

"You, too, showed yourselves when you were most needed. I thank you for your speed. Is Mme. de Charrette here?"

The shorter man stepped forward, his hand touching his forelock in an archaic gesture of respect. "She was tired, Madame. One of us would have stayed with her, but she told us to hurry. The boy is with her."

"Quite right of her. If things had not worked out so well, we might have had much more need of you. But now, perhaps one of you would go back and escort her here. I'm sure she is not pleased to be out in the forest at night, even with Jimmy as company." She tilted her head. "Especially with Jimmy as company."

She looked up at them, standing above her. "And I would appreciate help getting off this step. My old knees can only be called on for so much in one night."

The two remaining foresters crowded forward, but she waved them off. "Give me your arm, young Alain. I would be proud to have your assistance. Again."

Her arm was light on his and she managed the two steps with little difficulty, but her breath came quickly with each lift, and he wondered how much pain it was causing her. When she reached the top she kept hold of him and took

Anqelique's arm as well. "And you, my dear. An interesting experience, *oui*?"

Angélique's smile was weak. "I can understand your knees, Nana. Mine are hardly working right now. In fact, they may spill me on the floor any moment."

"Well, they held you up when you did the most good. Ask your friend who had the most difficult job tonight."

Their eyes meeting over the old lady's head, the two grinned at each other. There would never be any argument between them on that score.

Mme. de Dillon stopped in the doorway. "You will spend the rest of the night here, young sir?"

"I...well, I shouldn't..."

"Ah. You have no luggage with you, and also your mother will be worried. Next time you visit me, young man, you must come better prepared." Before he had time to register what she meant, she had turned to one of the foresters, who was leaning on his rifle and grinning.

"Wipe that leer off your face, Aubin. I'm not so old I can't have young men visit me. Now trot along to the lawyer's and call for Madame Jouvent – politely, now, she might be worried – and get the young master a bag for overnight. Tell her that Madame and myself would feel better," again that raptor-like glance pinned Alain, "if we had a man in the house."

She chuckled, and he wondered whether she was laughing at him. Feeling his face getting red, he glanced over at Angélique. Had she heard? He caught her eye; she was smiling too, and he saw the pride in that smile.

11. Aftermath

July 28, 1789

There was a slow rattle of hooves, and a lone horse jogged up the drive. Edmond, seeing no trouble, allowed the spent pony to walk the rest of the way. When he reached the steps he reined in, looking up at them.

"*Papa* and Aimée are coming with some men from the village. Do you need them?"

Alain looked to Mme. de Dillon, and she nodded permission to answer. "They might as well come up, though they aren't needed any more."

There were six of them and none had firearms, though Sarobert carried a hefty staff in one hand. When they approached, Mme. de Dillon received them with dignity, thanking them for their concern. While they spoke, Jimmy's head poked out the main door of the *chateau*.

"What are you doing in there?" Alain cuffed the boy's shoulder. "You seem to have got around a bit tonight."

"I told you I would be there and back *toute de suite.*"

The villagers were leaving, and Mme. de Dillon surveyed the group that remained. "Angélique, your friends have been useful again tonight. Would they like to come inside for a moment?"

They trooped in, following the old lady into the back of the house. "The cook doesn't seem to be here to throw us out of her kitchen, so we can make ourselves at home. Marie Françoise!" Angélique's mother appeared out of a side hallway. There was a stain on the hem of her dress, and her hair was not in the perfect style that Alain remembered.

"We have guests, Marie. Could we find them some chocolate?" With a wan smile, the other woman moved towards a cupboard. Angélique and Aimée joined her, and soon a kettle was swinging over a newly stoked fire on the hearth.

They sat around the big work table, Mme. de Dillon at the head, and filled each other in on their respective stories.

Jimmy had not even made it to Le Bersac. "I knew there was trouble, even afore I got there. There was a lotta light and I heard shouts. When I got close enough to the village, I snuck up, slow-like, but I didn't need to. They was all standin' round a big fire in the centre of the square. Every once in while somebody would run up and throw somethin' in, and they'd all scream like mad. It was pretty scary, let me tell you!"

"What about *sieur* de Bersac and his family?"

A shrug. "The front door of the *chateau* was open. Didn't look like too much damage done, though. Coupla windows smashed. So I figured we wasn't gonna get any help there, and I better head for home and make sure your message got to my men."

"A good choice, Jimmy."

He preened a bit. "Good thing I did, too. Madame had just got there, and the men wanted to go, but someone had to stay and take care of her."

Mme. de Charrette was pouring out a cup of chocolate, and she placed it in front of Jimmy, ruffling his hair as she straightened. "Oh, yes. He took care of me all right. He talked my ear off all the way down the mountain." Alain was surprised to see the friendliness of her smile. What a strange conversation that must have been: the ragamuffin and the proper lady, alone on a night of fire and violence, stumbling through the forest in the dark.

The lady turned to Alain. "Who were those men who came later?"

Of course, she had no idea who these other children were. "Mme. de Charrette, I believe you have not met Aimée and Edmond Sarobert."

They bobbed nervously.

Her eyes shifted to Jimmy, who grinned back. "Oh, but I have been told all about them. Your father is the baker, is he not?"

They nodded, and after a moment of imperceptible communication between the two, Aimée spoke up. "That was our father and a few of the older men from the village. All I could find in so short a time. We could have got more, but we thought it better to come fast."

"Another good decision." The lady smiled. "I am sure Mme. de Dillon has spoken to them already, but I hope you will accept my thanks as well. It is reassuring that some of the people still believe in law and order."

The twins bowed again and mumbled their thanks.

Alain grinned. "What about Serres, Edmond?"

The boy shrugged. "Nothing. The town was bolted up tight as a drum. In fact, I almost got my head shot off when I rode up. Could hardly get the man at the gate to look out the postern. He wouldn't listen when I said we needed help. When I used Mme. de Charrette's name he got more polite, but said they had no help to send anywhere. And he was only the old geezer on watch. I never got to talk to anyone important. I was slower on the way back and kept my eyes open, but everything else was calm. I cut through Le Bersac, and they were still standing around the fire, sort of quiet by that time. So I came home. I hope the horse is all right."

Alain nodded. "He's fine. He wouldn't let you run him into the ground. He's a smart old pony."

"I must have a small visit with certain people in Serres," Mme. de Charrette's voice was tight, "To let them know how displeased I am that they should ignore my messenger."

"Now, now, my dear. They have problems of their own." The old lady waved her hand in a dismissing gesture.

"Yes, Maman. Perhaps there was no one left to come. All our men are gone with *Papa*."

"We managed to find six good men with no difficulty. Why couldn't a big town like Serres?"

"With due respect, Madame, it isn't the same."

"And why not, Alain?"

He gathered his thoughts before he spoke. It was important that she understand. *It is important that I make her understand.* "Here in a small village, the situation is not the same. It is more personal. We have known these people all our lives. They would not let *sieur* de Bardel's family come to harm if they could help in any way. Many were frightened, but once they were given something to do, when they knew the danger was real, they were glad to be here."

She looked at him, her head to one side. "You have put your finger on it, young man. Leadership. Oh, I agree that they love my husband, and well they should. But, as you say, they needed someone to tell them what to do. My family owes you a great deal."

Alain could see Angélique's proud eyes on him and he knew he was blushing. "But I didn't do anything. It was Mme. de Dillon and Angélique! They stood out in front and faced down a mob!"

A small explosive sound drew their attention to the old lady, who seemed to be holding back a laugh. "We were in no danger, young Alain. What man is going to attack an old lady and a pretty girl?"

Mme. de Charrette looked grim. "I'm sure there are many men who would, and many of those are about in France this night."

"True, my dear. But not here. Those were village men. They all knew each other, and I knew them. They would not have harmed us." She laid her old, gnarled hand over Angélique's.

"Well, Nana, I wish you had mentioned this before we stepped out there. I would have found it much easier to face them if I had known all that screaming and swearing and throwing rocks was just for fun."

The old lady caressed the girl's hand, her face serious now. "I had no time, child, and the danger was real. They had to be handled, that was all. It is more credit to you that you stood your ground when you were much less confident than I of the outcome."

Angélique's glance slid over to meet Alain's, then fell to her hands. She wasn't blushing, but he could tell that she, too was embarrassed.

He kept grinning at her until she looked up and returned his smile.

Mme. de Charrette rose. "We have reason to be proud of you all, and I will be sure to tell *sieur* de Bardel when he returns. Now, I believe I will retire."

The young people all stood, and she regarded each of them before turning and sweeping out of the room.

They all stared at each other. Then Mme. de Dillon chuckled. "She always did know how to make an exit." She lifted herself to her feet. "I, too, need rest. Angélique will find you a room, Alain. I'm sure you two young bakers will have no trouble making it home." She swept her eyes across the group. "A good start to a bad time."

With that cryptic comment she turned and limped out of the kitchen before anyone had time to bid her good night.

Angélique grinned. "And who knows how to make an exit?"

She and Alain saw the twins to the door. It was a warm, pleasant night now that the danger was gone, and when they listened they heard the usual sounds: crickets, small animals rustling in the hedges, the cry of a lamb.

"It seems clear, but take care."

Aimée smiled up at Alain. "Don't worry about us. We'll keep out of trouble."

Angélique took the other girl's hand. "Just remember that some of those men may be about. If you see anyone, go the other way."

"We will."

Alain felt that a comment was necessary. "What do you think? Did we do well tonight?"

They all looked at each other, pride shining in their faces.

"We're some kind of a troop!" It sounded strange, coming from Jimmy.

They said good night, and the Rat followed them through the *chateau*, as he was leaving in the opposite direction. At the back door, Alain looked down. "Now, my dashing young Rat. Do I have to check your pockets on the way out?"

The boy's feet shifted, but his face didn't change. "Who, me? Why would you need to do that?"

Just before he turned to go, Alain stopped him with a hand on his shoulder.

"You did well tonight, Jimmy."

Angélique stood beside him. "You impressed my mother. We're very proud of you." She leaned over to kiss his cheek, and this time he stood still for it. Then he stepped forward, slapped Alain on the shoulder and was gone in the darkness.

As Alain turned to go inside his coat touched the doorjamb, and there was a metallic sound. Reaching down, he laughed, bringing Angélique swinging around to face him. He brought his hand out of his pocket, showing the three silver spoons he had found there.

"He'll never change!"

"At least he returned them." She turned and led the way back into the main hall. A valise sat in the hallway, and Alain recognized it, picked it up and followed her up the stairs.

She led him to a bedroom in the east wing of the house. "We always have a few rooms made up for emergencies.

There doesn't seem to be a maid to turn down the sheets, though."

"You're doing a superb job of it."

"Thank you, kind sir."

She turned and faced him, her eyes huge in the candlelight, and he remembered how she had looked on the steps in the light of the torches.

"You were very brave tonight."

She put her hands on his shoulders. "It helped a lot, knowing that you were there."

"With a gun."

"No, just knowing." Her hands slid around his neck, pulling him closer. He put his arms around her waist, feeling how slim and firm her back was. She lifted her lips to his, her arms tightening, and he could feel her body pressing against him.

Then her lips were gone, but she stayed there, her head laid comfortably against his shoulder. After a while she started to move, but he stopped her. She leaned back a bit to look at his face. This time it was his turn to ask.

"Do you know what you're doing?"

Her eyes closed, and he felt a small shudder run through her.

Then she looked at him, earnestly. "Alain, right now, does anyone know?"

He had no answer. Then her arms went around his neck again, tight and trembling. He held her for a long while until the shaking stopped, stroking her hair with one hand, starting at her forehead, and running his palm along the side of her head and down her back in a long, slow, caress.

Gradually she relaxed, and they stood completely still. "Being a hero is not so much fun, is it?"

"I guess not." He kissed her lightly. "But it has its compensations."

She smiled, the old sparkle returning. "I hope you wouldn't take advantage of my weakness."

"Count on it."

They slid apart, and the moment eased away.

"Good night, Alain, and thank you again for being here."

He bowed in a courtly fashion. "At any time, my dear." He grinned, but he meant it with all his heart.

Then she was gone, and he went to bed to dream of what would happen if the door should slide open, and a slim figure in a lacy nightgown should slip through.

Paris

August 6, 1789

Dearest Wife and Son,

I hope you can imagine the agony of suspense I lived through before getting your letter that all was well. We hear so many wild rumours about the horrors happening in the countryside that it is much easier to understand why Charles de Bardel went haring off into the mountains, leaving you all unprotected. I am so glad that events had a satisfactory conclusion and I am very proud of Alain for the role he played.

In fact I received an interesting letter in that vein from Mme. de Charrette, from the safety of Grenoble. She praises your leadership and quick thinking in the emergency, but then in the next paragraph she worries whether this has led to a "new and dangerous intimacy" between her daughter and yourself. Rather conflicting sentiments, and I could tell that she was aware of the contradiction, which made her even less sure. I'm afraid Mme. de Charrette is quite confused with many recent developments. I doubt if the near future will be kind to her.

Of course, you are familiar with my views on the subject, Alain, and it grieves me to be away from you at this difficult time. I would recommend you to your mother for advice, but I am, likewise, aware of her opinion. Please be certain that it is only your happiness I am concerned for, wherever you find it.

We have not been without drama, here in the centre of the political controversy. Your experience with a mob has become almost a commonplace occurrence, here in Paris. Large groups of people roam the streets at any provocation (such as when the price of bread rises), screaming for their rights and threatening any who oppose them or look too well dressed. These mobs are starting to call themselves the "sans-cullottes," due to the full-length pantalons they wear. Giving a name to anything legitimizes it, and I am not pleased with this turn of events.

The one good result from all this is that the fear of the rabble adds to our political strength. It is terrible to use those mobs to increase our power. Will the results be worth it?

Last night (or should I say, the night before? We were up all night), one of the Seigneurs rose in the Assembly and suggested that the seigneurial right to strike coinage be done away with. Another, not to be outdone, rose and suggested two more privileges be dropped. Soon they were all on their feet, competing to see who could give up the most. The result is that all seigneurial rights have been abolished. It is a great triumph for the people of France. I only wish it had not come about as the outcome of such unpleasantness.

I hope our local men were pleased, when they returned from their fruitless expedition, to find that they had been appointed as the National Guard. They could be a stabilizing force in the coming months. Despite the circulating rumours about invaders, I much fear that France's largest problem will arise from within. With the closing of so many factories there are thousands of people out of work, and the rising price of bread has made them desperate.

In spite of my misgivings I am still thrilled to be part of this great process and I have hope that, when the Assembly creates the new Constitution, we will again have a basis for proper law and order.

Your loving husband and father,

François Jouvent

Paris

August 27, 1789

Dearest Wife and Son,

Freedom of opinion!

Freedom of speech!

Freedom of property!

Freedom from arbitrary imprisonment!

Freedom from taxation without consent!

Equality of opportunity!

Equality before the law!!!

France has entered the modern age. No, France has ushered in the modern age! The Declaration of the Rights of Man, passed by the Assembly on August 26, a day to go down in the history of the world! From the despondency of my last letter, my hopes rise again. The Nation, the Law, and the King, all in their appointed places, governing the people by their own consent. Now the right people – the educated, active citizens, those who pay the taxes – will make the decisions.

There was a huge ceremony, and we all planted trees of liberty to remind us of our vows to the Nation, the Law, and the King.

Now to the real business: making a constitution to run this great country.

Your loving husband and father,

François Jouvent

12. Women of the Revolution
October 15, 1789

"We won! We won!" Alain took the steps down from the doors of the Hotel de Ville in Gap two at a time.

Angélique stood waiting for him at the bottom. "I gather you did all right?"

"I told you. We won! My first case!"

She smiled. "I figured that out."

"Well, I didn't get to present the brief. M. Forgeron did that. But I collected all the evidence and I decided what would be used, and we won!"

"The whole street knows it."

"Is there something wrong with that? We were in the right, and justice has prevailed. Do you know how good it feels to be a part of that?"

She smiled again and reached up to touch his cheek with the back of her gloved hand. "I suppose it feels fine." Then she looked over his shoulder. "But I don't imagine they feel so wonderful."

A group of men in rough clothes came out of the same big doors, moving much slower. As they passed the two on the steps, they made a point of looking away.

"What did they expect? When you don't pay your rent, you get evicted."

"I suppose."

"Angélique, what's wrong with you? Paying all those dues left over from feudal times was wrong. Well, they don't have to pay them any more. Fine. But those louts," he tossed his hand over his shoulder, "stopped paying anything at all. They still have to pay rent. The right to own property is written in the Rights of Man. *Sieur* de Bersac owned the property, and he has a right to rent it out to whomever he pleases. If they won't pay rent, he gets someone else. What's wrong with that?"

She looked troubled. "I have no doubt that by law your client was right. The court said so. And I'm sure you presented a clear, forceful case, and you can be proud of it. But something is still wrong."

"Justice has been done. There's nothing wrong with that."

"In the narrow sense of legal justice, perhaps. But what about moral justice, what about the people of France?"

He stared at her.

"The Revolution, Alain. The whole of the Third Estate – the rich bourgeois, the lawyer, the poor textile worker, the peasant – against the other two. They all worked together. Much though your father may be wary of the Paris mob, it's a fact that they had as large an effect on the success as the politicians in the Assembly did.

"That balance is changing. The First and Second Estates lost. I don't mind that, because the system wasn't fair. But now another system is being set up, and who does it benefit? It benefits the rich, that's who. They may not be *seigneurs*, but they are still rich, and the poor are no better off than before."

They walked in silence for a while. "I suppose you're right, in principle. But what has that got to do with my case?"

"Looked at from one point of view, the rich are using the system to take money from the poor, the same as usual. It looks as if you just helped them. In this individual case, you and your client were in the right. But looked at from the poor man's point of view, it seems like nothing has changed. The only difference? Someone has told the poor man that he can make things change. If things don't, perhaps he will change them himself."

"Are you saying I should have let them win?"

"Of course not. I'm saying it's too bad the case had to come to court at all. Couldn't *sieur* de Bersac have settled this some other way?"

"Angélique, is your memory so short? While you stood guard over your *chateau* with your great-grandmother this summer, these same peasants were breaking into his home and taking his furniture out and throwing it on a fire. Not a good start for peaceful negotiation."

She shook her head as if to free something caught in her hair. "I suppose you're right. But it isn't fair. The poor people of France have just exchanged one master for another."

She brightened. "Speaking of masters, do you know what just happened to the king?"

"Something happened to him?"

"Oh, yes, it did. I was talking to some ladies I met. A few days ago, the women of Paris got tired of having no food to eat while the king and Marie Antoinette sat out there in that huge palace at Versailles, eating and drinking and having parties. So they went out to Versailles and got them!"

"Who got who? ...whom?"

"The women of Paris went out to Versailles and got the king and his wife and hauled them back to Paris. What do you think of that?"

Alain looked down at his companion, puzzled. "I think it's terrible, of course."

"I don't. I think it's marvellous!"

"Marvellous! A bunch of women laying their hands on the king of France and hauling him around wherever they want is marvellous? Don't you understand that according to the Declaration of the Rights of Man, the power of the nation is vested in the king and the government, and anyone who attacks the king is attacking the realm?"

"Well, if the government isn't doing its proper job, what can they do? The poor are powerless in your system."

He couldn't believe he was hearing this. "But it's not my system. It's our system. It belongs to the citizens of France! You can't start pushing people around, just because things aren't perfect."

"No, it doesn't belong to the citizens of France. It belongs to the lawyers and politicians who wrote the laws. Look, the Second Estate used to be the bullies. We used to run the system. We wouldn't let anyone else have any power. But we're not the bullies any more. You have the power now. But who else are you giving power to? Who can vote? Not the poor; they don't pay enough taxes. And what about women? What power have you allowed them? You need to make sure that you don't become the next set of bullies."

They were standing face to face in a main street, almost shouting at one another. He took her arm and continued walking. "All right, all right. I see your point. But you can't allow people to attack the king like that."

She walked beside him again. "But Alain, do you understand what it's like to feel powerless? To feel that there is no way you can change some terrible wrong that is being done? That's how those women feel. I know."

"Powerless. That's a new experience for you, I suppose."

She stopped dead in the street, forcing him to walk back to her. She looked at him without expression for a long while.

"Alain, the carriage will be ready in half an hour. If you still wish to ride back to Savournon with me, be there. I don't suppose we'll enjoy the trip, but it would be stupid to go separately."

What could he say? *Don't react. Think. With a little planning, I'm sure you can create a better way to bungle things than you could on the spur of the moment.* He stood watching her stiff back marching away from him. What was the problem now? *Well, there's no talking sense to her right now.*

What got into her? He had thought she would be so proud of him, winning his first case, and in the new courthouse in Gap, the new *prefecture* of the newly made *Departement des Hautes-Alpes*. It was so convenient that people didn't have to go all the way to Grenoble for their cases. It was so right, so thrilling to be in at the beginning of such an adventure. *This is how my father must feel, making new laws for a new country up there in Paris.* And now she had spoiled it all with her moodiness. *What if I had been protecting her income? I would bet she wouldn't be so high and mighty then.* He filed that away as a possible argument for next time. He slouched even more. Why did there have to be a next time? He hated to argue with Angélique. He wanted them to be a team, working together. Why couldn't she be reasonable?

He wondered if it might be jealousy. Her people had lost control of the country, and his people had gained it. That might be why she would be so critical. *Doesn't sound like the Angélique I know. Maybe it is her, though. Maybe she really is like that, and I just haven't seen it. Merde!* He turned and stumped up the street to his temporary lodgings to collect his luggage.

It wasn't an unpleasant trip home. As usual, by the time Angélique got back to the carriage she wasn't angry any more. However, Alain could tell that the issue wasn't completely settled. He supposed it was all right to disagree on some things. After all, his mother and father argued, too. Still, there was a certain restraint about their conversation, and it made him feel terrible.

He was relieved, two days later, to receive an invitation to go riding. The stable boy no longer smirked when he passed the note over. In fact, he now seemed proud to be allowed this job. Alain grinned at him. "Tell her I'll be along at the usual time, Eustache."

He went inside to inform his mother, whistling.

When he picked her up, Angélique, too, looked happy. "Where shall we go today?"

He took the diplomatic route. "This was your idea. Where would you like to go?"

"Let's go up to the Gorges de la Riou. It must be lovely there, with the leaves changing."

His heart jumped. The Riou had always held a soft spot for him since their first ride there. Maybe she felt the same and was trying to make things better. He smiled and spun his horse around. "Great idea!"

They broke into a canter as they left the last houses of Gonillons, but had to slow as the hill steepened and the horses began to labour.

"It's still warm for this time of the year, isn't it?"

Angélique's face was red, but she was smiling. "I suppose. Let's just be happy for this sunshine. It sure helps after last week's rain."

The fall storms had been pounding at them, with the south wind screaming up from the Mediterranean loaded with moisture. The streams were running muddy and full to the brim. Then would come a thunderstorm from the west and dump a lot more water. The road sounded squishy under the horses' hooves.

Alain wiped a splatter from his coat. "A nice, dry *mistral* from the north would be a pleasant change."

She laughed. "As long as it didn't last for a week."

They toiled up the track past La Queyra and started up the long switchback that led to the foresters' hut. Suddenly Angélique pulled up.

"What was that?"

The noise came again. A man's voice, raised in anger, then a cry of pain. Without hesitation, Angélique plunged her horse into the pine forest beside the road. Alain was quick to follow, and they trotted around the hillside in the direction of the cry. The horses' hooves made little sound on the thick, damp pine needles, and they heard several more cries as they approached. Angélique threw a worried look over her shoulder at Alain, then slapped her horse with the whip that hung on her wrist.

They both broke into a canter, dodging among the trees, headed towards the sound of pain.

They rounded a pile of boulders and came upon the scene. A young man in peasant's clothing huddled against the rocks, his arms protecting his head, while Reynaud de Gonillons stood over him, a stick raised in his hand. He looked up as they pulled in their horses.

Angélique took in the situation. "What is going on here?"

De Gonillons' lip curled scornfully, tossing his head towards a carcass lying nearby. "I caught this sneak poaching rabbits. He won't be so ready to try that again." He jabbed the man with the toe of his high, shiny boot. "Will you?"

Angélique went very still. Her horse twitched, but did not move.

"Poaching?"

"Yes, poaching. This scum has been shooting our animals!" He raised the stick and brought it down across the hunched shoulders. His victim cried out again and crouched down lower, trying to hide himself behind the rock.

Angela stood in her stirrups, leaning down over the man. "*Nom de dieu!* Where have you been for four months? The Assembly has cancelled all *seigneurial* rights. Now he has the right to hunt here. Stop that at once!"

De Gonillons sneered up at her. "You've been spending too much time in the slums, my girl. I might have known. Sneaking around looking for a place to bed down with your skinny bourgeois boyfriend. Well, you tend to your business, slut, and I'll tend to mine." He raised the stick again with more anger on his face.

He didn't have time to bring it down before the shoulder of Angélique's horse sent him spinning. She urged the animal forward, her whip hand raised. Alain was prepared for something like this. Spurring his horse beside hers, he reached over and grabbed the whip.

"No, Angélique!"

She struggled, trying to bring the whip free, and their horses milled, finally moving apart so he had to let go or pull her to the ground.

By this time de Gonillons had ducked away and was standing behind a tree, breathing heavily. "You watch yourself, you little hussy. You hit me with that, I'll pull you off your horse and teach you the lesson you need."

Alain pushed his horse between them. "*Sieur* de Gonillons. I suggest you keep in mind the legal situation. You have been seen by witnesses beating another man for no legal reason. You have made a threat of violence against the daughter of a local *seigneur*. I advise you that you are getting into deep trouble. It would be best if you left."

"Well, aren't we just the little lawyer?" Reynaud stepped forward, and Alain pulled the horse around to keep the bridle out of reach. "You listen, you young upstart. You start laying down the law to me and you'll get worse than that oaf got." His eyes turned to the left.

Alain, following his glance, saw the fowling piece leaning against the rock. He kicked his horse ahead, leaned down and grabbed the barrel. "You won't mind if I drop your gun off back at the road, will you? People have died in hunting accidents in these woods."

He rode away with the gun, assuming Angélique would have the sense to follow. She did. The young peasant and his rabbit were long gone as well. Alain led the way to the road, where he leaned the weapon up under a tree where it would stay dry. No one in the valley would ever touch that gun, with its distinctively carved stock.

"Why are you going back to the village?"

He frowned over at Angélique. "You heard what I said about hunting accidents. Wouldn't we be better off riding somewhere else? Besides, it will be much more pleasant riding through Gonillons with him still up on the mountain."

They rode along in silence.

"Why did you stop me?"

"Angélique, you can't go around whipping people."

"Why not? He deserved it!"

"I don't disagree. But it isn't up to you to decide that. The law must decide."

"Then I don't like the law."

"Angélique! You can't act like that any more. Our realm is changing. You can't run around whipping anyone you want to like you could before. If you do, you're as bad as de Gonillons."

She jerked her horse to a halt. "I never whipped anyone in my life!"

He looked at her, saw the narrowed eyes, the deadly pale face, and saw that he had gone too far.

"I didn't mean you literally whipped anyone. I just mean that attitude. Sorry, Angélique. I got carried away, I guess."

After a moment her horse moved on, and he took that as a signal that his apology was accepted. However, they did not talk, and when they reached the main road she turned towards the *chateau*. He made no protest and followed.

When they reached the stable yard he dismounted with her. She handed her horse over to the stable boy and turned to walk him toward the road. In front of the *chateau* she stopped.

"You understand, Alain, that I have made a decision."

This was not a good time to be hearing about any decisions.

"I have decided two things. First, I am becoming more and more aware of the fact that the poor people of France are in need of help.

"The second is that I am going to help them."

He stared at her. "You! How?"

The anger rose in her cheeks again. "Why not me? I'll bet that was the king's response when they told him that the women of Paris were coming to get him. He learned something, didn't he? Perhaps you, and the men who are running the Assembly too, have things to learn."

"What do you mean by that?"

"I'm not sure, but I am going to start working on it. I'm going back to Grenoble at the end of the week. I have already looked into joining a club there, a club that will allow women to speak."

"A club? A political club like the Jacobins?"

She hesitated. "The...the Jacobins have been very good about helping political clubs get started in the provincial cities."

"You are getting into a club that is allied with the Jacobins? You'll have to check once a day to see that your head has not been removed! Don't you know what those men are like?"

Her head came up. "They are the men who want true equality for the people of France. Not just equality for a few rich men to run the country their way."

"Angélique! My father and the other members of the Assembly are not trying to get rich!"

Her stance softened. "Your father is a good man, Alain. I don't want to fight with you. But you don't understand. Maybe some day you will. I must go now. Thank you for stopping me today. I never wish to think I would act like Reynaud de Gonillons. Come and visit if you get to Grenoble this winter."

She stepped forward and kissed him, formally, once on each cheek. Then she turned and walked up the steps.

Later on, he would come up with several things he could have said to stop her in her tracks. At the time, all he could do was stand, mute, and watch her slim, upright form stride away from him.

Paris

Sept 17, 1789

My dear Wife,

A short note today, and I will include a longer missive with the business papers, which I will send tomorrow if I can get time to see to them.

Political life continues to be hectic. The Estates meet daily, and we slowly (oh, so slowly) thrash through the material. So much of it is so new and so controversial that everyone has to get his teeth into it and shake it around a bit, then pass it on to the next speaker. We are at the moment quite divided (along the lines you might expect) on the topic of voting.

We of the Third Estate want every delegate to have his own vote. The Nobles and the Clergy, of course, want the old way, where each Estate only gets one vote. Since there are an equal number of Third Estate delegates to the other two Estates, you can see how much difference a head vote would make to us.

However, we are gaining a certain amount of support from the Second Estate.

Some of the more forward-thinking seigneurs realize that if we voted on a head-count basis they would not be restricted to siding with their antediluvian peers. We even have a few bishops who are starting to look at things our way!

Catherine, my dear, could you see about having my green topcoat sent? The nights are getting cooler...

13. Parting

Winter 1790

It was a cold winter for Alain, as was the summer that followed. Angélique wrote at irregular intervals. Pleasant, friendly letters, full of information and not much else. The only spark of emotion he felt was when she talked of the political situation. Then she waxed eloquent, and he could see her, cheeks flushed, head high, those few hairs curling from under her ribbon, telling someone exactly where he had gone wrong.

He soon gave up discussing his legal cases with her, because she never commented on them in response. In turn, he decided not to comment on her political views, which seemed to become more radical as the year progressed. The names of Robespierre and Marat appeared more and more often in her letters, which worried him, because all he had read and heard about these two was unsettling. He could see where she was getting her ideas, and it was a frightening prospect.

He never made it to Grenoble to visit her. The new prefecture in Gap was as far as he got, with his increasing legal work taking him there regularly. He devoured any new information his father sent, and as a result was well informed on the new laws and regulations as they were enacted by the Assembly. In fact, he started a separate set of correspondence with the elder lawyer, concerned with business. The family letters still came to his mother, but the legal ones were addressed to Alain.

He found himself more and more removed from the interests of the others of his age in the village; marriage, inheritance and the birth of new stock paled beside the mental stimulus of legal wrangling and his increasing worry about the state of the realm. Even the "Holiday of Federation" on the anniversary of the fall of the Bastille rang hollow to those who knew the true lack of significance of the occasion and saw how the tawdry decorations did little to hide the pinched faces brought about by two bad harvests and concern for the size of the present crop.

His one consolation came from the books Angélique had left in Savournon. The twins did not feel it appropriate to visit the *chateau* when Angélique was not there, so he took books home with him, and the three often spent an intense evening arguing the points made by the writers, comparing them to the political pamphlets that arrived daily from the larger cities. Aimée and Edmond were the only ones who seemed to grasp the problems his father wrote about. Maybe that was because of whom they were learning their politics from, but still, their active minds wrestled with the concepts and they refused to let inconsistencies go unchallenged.

Old Mme. de Dillon, whose agile mind had kept up with all the events of the Revolution, waylaid him in the library for conversations. She drew the line at the secularisation of the priesthood.

"The church should have nothing to do with politics," was her opinion on the subject.

"But the church isn't involved in the politics. The priests get their salaries from the government, and that's all."

She turned towards him, her eye aglint with predatory glee. "All right, young lawyer. Let me rephrase that. The government should have nothing to do with the church. The possibilities for the overuse of that power are frightening."

He thought it over, then considered it again. Then he grinned. "Will you be disappointed if I agree with you?"

The dry chuckle that was so familiar to him now. "A little. Shows you have sense, in any case. Just not much sense of fun. When are you going to bring your two friends to see me?"

"Whenever you invite them."

"Listen, young Alain. I'm an old woman and I have no time left to wait on good manners. Make an appointment if you must, but get those children to me in the next week. I have things to say and people to say them to." Her usual bantering tone was gone, and he looked at her in a different light. *Does she know something? She seems as spry as ever.* Well, it wasn't the kind of thing you could bring up in polite conversation. Better to do as she asked.

So then there were four of them, and the old woman's knowledge came in handy over and over.

Fall rolled towards winter again and the harvest was better, but still prices did not drop, the factories remained closed and unemployment continued high. During the coldest weather a family of vagabonds was found frozen to death on the road to Serres, and after that a bonfire burned every night in the village square. A distressing number of people huddled around it.

And still Angélique stayed away. She was now a leading member of a women's political club associated with the Jacobins. Many of the members did not have the benefit of a formal education, either in facts or in manners, and their meetings, she was pleased to tell him, sometimes got quite disorderly. He never wondered how a girl of her age could hold her own in such a crowd. He knew her well enough. As the winter progressed, her letters became fiercer and brighter, and she spent more and more time discussing politics.

Alain was torn between his father's deepening dissatisfaction with the situation and Angélique's dangerous ideas, which served to make things worse, not better.

Paris

...The problem is that our work in the National Assembly is getting further and further away from reality. We are supposed to be creating the Constitution, but we are forced to pass other laws in the interim that are short-term reactions to unmanageable pressures, and I fear we are making a hash of things. We can only ask the people to give us time to get the country straightened around, but the food shortages and poor crops aren't giving us that time. There is no solution within our power, and that means conditions will soon become desperate...

Paris

...Damn these royalist *emigrés* in Switzerland! The fools want to create an army to invade France and re-establish the power of the monarchy, but instead they are making things worse. They want to use the nobility of Austria, Prussia, and England to help them regain their positions, but allying themselves with our historical enemies loses them support here at home. Because of this, it has become a successful ploy in the Assembly and elsewhere to undermine an opponent by accusing him of helping the Royalists. In certain circles – especially the *sans coulottes* – the reaction is instantaneous and violent. The *emigrés* who left first are the selfish ones who never had any desire for the good of our *patrie*. They only consider themselves and their positions. Should they be successful enough to mount an attack, even when it fails they will have destroyed everything we are trying to create...

Savournon

   ...Angélique, I cannot help but agree that many of the points you make are true. Even my father would not suggest that the National Assembly is making a great success of running the country. However, I argue with the greatest passion against the solutions I am hearing, both from you and from the Jacobins and their supporters. None of the actions that you are suggesting will solve the problems of our patrie. They will turn the control of the nation over to people who have less knowledge of the skills required to run a government, and more desire to be in power.

   The country was too long in the hands of those who did not have the good of the people uppermost in their minds, I agree. But now the country is in the hands of people with the knowledge and motivation to make the government work for the people, just as the Revolution intended. The sans coulottes in Paris are acting like children in a tantrum, wanting instant success, not willing to wait or to contribute to the solution.

Grenoble

...hardly think those who are starving and demanding bread can be compared to children in a tantrum. They would love to contribute, but there is no work for them, and so no money to put food on their tables, assuming that there was food to buy...

Savournon

···an unfortunate turn of phrase, but the crops have been poor and there is a shortage of bread, and this is not the fault of the Assembly. The riots stop the equal distribution of what there is. The Assembly must be gi ven time to put everything right. If we are to survive, people must trust those they have elected to do what is best for everyone···

Grenoble

...Those in power have done little to earn the trust of the downtrodden. The lower classes still have too little power, and recent history teaches us that if you don't wrest the power from those who have it, nobody will give it to you freely...

Savournon

···I agree that the lower classes have had too little power for too long. However, this means that they have become too concerned with gaining power, and have no concern at all for what they might do once they reach their goal, and no idea what they might destroy in the achieving of it. This leaves them open to the machinations of those whose desire is also for power of the personal kind.

You have protested that those who took power earlier in the Revolution did not give the lower classes their share of that power. Perhaps we should question those who are arguing for more power now. How much of that power are they willing to pass along to the lower classes? Or to anyone else...

Grenoble

...We have covered this ground before, and it is unfair of you to suggest that I would wish to take power and keep it for myself. The poor need to have a say in what happens to them.

Savournon

... I am not talking about you, Angélique. You and many people like you are honest in your intentions, as are my father and many other members of the Assembly. I do not believe the same of those who are gaining strength in Paris. Mentioning their names would be unwise, because we are approaching a time when putting any such statement in writing could end at the Tribunal and the guillotine.

Grenoble

...How can you sit out in the countryside and suggest that we are too stupid to understand what is happening in our *patrie*? Here in Grenoble, we meet almost every day, and hear speakers who have just arrived from Paris and all over France. We know what is happening!

Savournon

···But what motivates those speakers? I receive my information straight from my father, and he has no intention of maintaining his power for any other reason than to create a new Constitution for France···

Grenoble

...You often find fault with me for being naïve and supporting those who do not have the good of the *patrie* in their hearts. I begin to wonder whether your father is not in a similar position. While no one doubts the purity of his motivation, I am sure there are many in that Assembly who have other goals in mind. The power has shifted from the rich of the aristocracy to the rich of the middle class, and the poor are left starving in the streets...

Gordon A. Long

Savournon

...When you reach the point of accusing my father, who has been at the centre of this Revolution from the beginning, of naivité, I see that we will never agree on this matter, and so I will write of other things.

For example, what about the schism in the Church? One thing we can agree on is that the Pope has no business in the politics of France...

Savournon

...Papa, I cannot understand why the Assembly has attacked the priesthood. That move has given the counter-revolutionaries a great deal of support from people of all backgrounds...

Paris

...The Civil Constitution of the Clergy was perhaps not thought through clearly, but you must grasp the pressure we are feeling from the threat of outside interference. All the kingdoms of Europe are against us, and the Church of Rome supports them. We cannot afford to have possible agents of the Pope holding positions of power over our people...

Savournon

   ···*Why did they pass the Le Chapelier legislation? Surely that will enrage the lower classes even further, removing their right to unions or guilds, often their only source of protection from those with more power.*

Paris

   ...Once again, the Revolution cannot have corporations of any form threatening the Constitution. No intermediary body should stand between the individual – now armed with his natural rights – and the nation, which is now the guarantor of those natural rights.

Savournon

   ···*It occurs to me that you and Angélique and many of those who are active in the politics of our patrie believe that protecting the power of those in power, or gaining power for those who are not, is more important than protecting the rights of individuals to liberté, egalité and fraternité. I cannot see any way in which this will not end up in a battle to the death for control of the government and the patrie, with the natural rights of all of us trampled into the mud.*

Paris

...Which is exactly why we need a king. As long as there is a head of state to mediate, these arguments may take place in a civilized manner. We have worked long and hard to create a constitutional monarchy, and we need to be given time to show that it will work. If we jump immediately into a republican form of government, I am afraid what you predict will come true, and then I grieve for France...

Grenoble

...Which is exactly why we need to get rid of the king and all those who toady to him. Only when we have a republican form of government, and the power is in the hands of the people will we achieve a fair distribution of the goods and services everyone needs...

14. Loss

May, 1791

So for better or for worse the winter passed, and in the spring the lambs were born, the fields greened and that premier flower of the Revolution, the Constitution, looked like it would finally blossom. The only question was how much damage had been done to the whole plant by the frosts of the winter before.

One day in the middle of May, the usual stableboy came knocking at Alain's door. "*Le seigneur* would like to talk to you, M. Jouvent."

"The *seigneur*, is it? I wonder what about. Wait while I get my coat, and we'll walk back together." It was probably a message or question for his father, but still, there was a possibility...

When he entered the reception room de Bardel used for business, the *seigneur* was standing and looking out the window where Alain had placed the old blunderbuss during *La Grand Peur.* He turned slowly when Alain entered, a question on his face. Then he rushed forward holding out his hand. "Pardon me. Wool-gathering, I'm afraid. You certainly got here quickly. Thank you. Come and sit down. I need advice, and you are the one to give it."

"Of course, *sieur* de Bardel. Whatever I can do to help." *How on earth could the seigneur need advice from a youth of my age?* He waited.

After another pause, the lord spoke hesitantly. "By now you are well acquainted with my grandmother?"

"Mme. de Dillon? Of course. She has been very good to me."

The man smiled. "And you have been good for her. I have not seen her so spry in years. It is..."

"I'm not so sure, *Seigneur*."

"Why do you say that?"

"The last time I came to visit, she seemed less...less *here* than she usually is. That's not logical. Just an impression. I'm sorry to interrupt."

De Bardel raised his hand. "No, no, you were quite right. And on the mark too, I might add. That is why I called you. A few days ago she took me into her sitting room and gave me an order." He smiled. "This is not unusual, but it was rather a strange order. She sat me down and told me to get Angélique back from Grenoble. Right now. That was all. No explanations, just get Angélique back.

"So I wrote to Angélique and suggested that her great-grandmother would like a visit soon. As you might expect, my daughter has a busy life, and she wrote back that she would love to return now, but that she had important business to conduct. Later on in the summer she would surely come.

"This news upset Mme. de Dillon considerably. Now, she didn't say she was upset, in fact, she wouldn't talk about it, but I have known her all my life." He smiled in reminiscence. "When *grandmère* is upset, you want prior notice."

Alain nodded, several thoughts spinning through his head.

"So now I can't understand what is going on. I thought you might put your finger on it. I don't want to order Angélique back for no reason. My daughter is not one to take such a summons lightly, especially these days. On the other hand, I have the old lady to consider."

If sieur de Bardel only knew who he is asking. "Perhaps I can speak to Mme. de Dillon? Maybe she will tell me more."

The *seigneur* almost jumped out of his chair. "Do you think so? I would be in your debt if you would try for me."

As he followed the *seigneur's* hurrying back, Alain reflected on how strange it was that such a capable man in some areas would be at such a loss in dealing with his own family.

Madam de Dillon was perched in her usual corner, a blanket over her knees. She looked up, irritated, as her grandson entered, then brightened when her sharp eye caught her visitor.

"So now we will get some action, will we? Go away, Charles, and leave us to make plans."

The *seigneur* made a helpless grimace as he passed Alain, allowing himself to be dismissed like a small boy. Alain tried to look sympathetic.

Then he regarded the old lady. *Same firm posture, same predatory eye. Thinner, perhaps.* "What is it Mme. de Dillon? What do we have to plan?"

"Nothing complicated. Is it so hard to get one girl to come twenty *lieu* for a brief visit?"

"Madame, in the case of this specific young lady, I couldn't guess how to start, much though I would like to."

"Aha!" Her head swivelled towards him. "Still like to, would you? I thought so. Well, you do it."

He shrugged. "Do you have any ideas, Madame?"

"I certainly do. I told you a while ago that I didn't have time to play around with manners. Well, I'm eighty-seven this year, lad. Does that give you any ideas?"

Alain, in his turn, looked at her sharply. The usual bantering tone was there, but there was a slight forward tilt to her head suggesting there were no games going on either. He answered her soberly.

"Yes, Mme. de Dillon. You need have no worry about it. Angélique will come. I will see to it." It was a solemn promise.

Her body relaxed, and her sardonic smile returned. "*Comme il faut.* You want a job done, you give it to someone who wants it done more than you do." She leaned forward. "Want her here too, don't you, young Alain?"

"You could safely say that."

The familiar, inelegant snort. "Nothing's safe in this world, young man. Sooner you learn that, better you'll cope. Now you have a job to do. Don't stand around being polite."

He jumped to his feet to bow over her hand. "Madame, I will bring Angélique as soon as she can get here. You may count on me."

The old head nodded in satisfaction. "Best thing you ever did, lad."

He turned and left, wondering whether it was what he was going to do, or something he had done in the past that she was talking about.

His conversation with her grandson was likewise short "There should be no trouble, *sieur* de Bardel. Could I borrow a pen and paper?"

He walked over to the writing table, set aside some letters and other papers and wrote a brief note. Folding but not sealing it, he handed it to the older man, who glanced at the contents, then looked up at Alain, shocked.

"Is this a trick to get Angélique back here?"

"I'm sorry, Seigneur, but I am quite certain that it is the truth." He stepped in front of the older man. "No, don't go running in. When she wants to tell you, she will do it herself. She didn't come straight out and tell me, just gave me enough hints. You know the games she plays."

De Bardel nodded, a sad smile. "Yes, I do. And a different game with each person. If she wanted you to know, she didn't need to say it out loud. It's strange to think of her dying, though. She looks like she always has. All my life she has looked like that. Just as old, at least to my eyes."

He shook his head, and Alain felt it was time to leave. "If you send that message to Angélique, she will believe it as I did."

De Bardel turned, all business. "How much time do we have? Should I send one of the grooms?"

"We can't be certain, but I wouldn't kill any horses. *Madame* didn't sound that anxious. And Angélique will act quickly. The regular post will do."

"Good. I don't know how to thank you, Alain. I didn't know what do."

Alain took a deep breath, then risked it. "No need to thank me, *Seigneur.* Having Angélique here will be enough for me."

The older man smiled. "Yes. A silver lining. It will be nice to have her back."

He made no other comment, and Alain left, his step lighter than it had been all winter. He plucked a small yellow daisy from beside the street and stuck it in his top buttonhole. *Angélique is coming home. But at what price?* His footsteps lagged.

* * *

There was a chair in the hallway, and he sat there for an age, his head spinning over and over the same paths, which led his emotions up and down like a high mountain trail. Angélique did not seem a whole lot different. True, she was dressed in the newer styles, not the old frills and lace of the *Ancien Régime.* She still looked beautiful, but there was a harsh edge to her that he had not felt before. Still, she had greeted him like an old friend, as warmly as could be expected under the circumstances.

Seiur de Bardel came out of the room and paced up and down. Then he stopped. "I have some things to arrange. I'll be back." With that, he disappeared upstairs.

After another, longer, wait the door opened slowly and Angélique came out. She was walking unsteadily, her eyes blinded by tears. Then she saw him and walked into his open arms. He held her, feeling the sobs shake her body. As he had done once before, he stroked her hair, slowly and gently, until she calmed.

"She's gone, isn't she?"

Angélique nodded, gulped and looked up at him. "She was talking to me, telling me some stories of her life, the ones she had always told me, her favourites. First, she told me what to do." A faint smile trembled on her lips. "She was never too shy to tell anyone their duty."

"What did she tell you to do?"

She glanced at him, her head tilted. "I might tell you some day."

Then she smiled again as if remembering. "Then she told me some other stories. Chosen to send me a message, I suppose. At least at first. Then she wandered a bit, talking about things I didn't understand. After a while, she stopped. Then she looked over at me, and said, very clearly. 'You wait with me, now. It's nice to have company, and I want it to be you.' I took her hand, and she held mine firmly. After a while, her hand relaxed, and I thought she had gone to sleep. She lay there, quiet, barely breathing. Then she squeezed my hand a little, and I realized that she was whispering to me. I leaned over, and she said very softly, 'Don't let them tell you what to do, daughter. It always seems easier at the time, but it doesn't work.' I looked at her, and her eyes were open again, looking right at me, full of life as usual. Then she closed them, and that was the last time she moved. A long time after, I realized..." she paused to gulp again, "...she wasn't breathing any more."

She raised her eyes to his face. "She's gone, Alain. Just like that. I was looking at her, and I realized that she was once a living, breathing, thinking, marvellous person. And then she just wasn't. It was all gone, all that life, and it will never return." She laid her head on his shoulder, her arms lightly around his neck, and spoke in a thoughtful voice. "I never saw anyone die, before. I wonder if she wanted me there because it would be good for me."

She straightened up and leaned back to look in his face. "I'm glad she chose me to be there. It was a great compliment."

"Yes, it was. I'm glad she sent for me, too. Of all the people in her life."

They smiled at each other: sad smiles, but proud.

The door at the end of the hall opened, and *sieur* de Bardel strode in, his face anxious. Angélique turned and walked toward him, softly but surely. Now she was in control of herself and was going to give comfort, not only to receive it.

"She's gone, *Papa*. She lay there and slipped away, and I didn't even know." The girl put her arms around her father's neck and pulled his head down on her shoulder. Alain saw the tears in the older man's eyes and turned away to allow them this moment in privacy.

He walked out onto the front steps and along the driveway, then turned to look back at the house. It was an ugly building, when you looked at it. Tall and imposing, *oui*, but with little ornamentation. Just thick walls, the rough stucco faded to grey: small windows with carved stonework around them. Only the ornate, panelled main door with the square stone pillars on either side contained a hint of artistry.

He wondered why he had ever thought the house so grand. *It wasn't the building itself that impressed me. It was the people inside.* No wonder that now, at this moment, he felt something was missing.

"No one ever does what anyone else wants them to, especially a worn out old woman." That was her final message for him. She had sent to him for a private word earlier that morning. He had been shown into her *chambre*, a small, plain room, to find her in bed looking old and thin but still full of life. She had smiled up at him.

"But if you will take my advice... No, I don't need to give you advice. Forgive me. After a life of raising children – first mine, then grandchildren, then their children – it becomes a habit. I can't help trying to get the next generation coming along, as well." She laughed quietly, an echo of her old chuckle. "No, I cannot give you advice, because you will not take it unless you want to. But one thing I can do. I can tell you when you are right." She moved her head until her eyes met his, straight on. "And you are right, Alain. Keep on trying. You are the right one, and she needs you. She knows that, whether she knows it or not." The old woman broke the eye contact with a smile at her own play on words, and her head relaxed back on the pillow. "Now go and find her, young Alain. I have advice for her too."

And he had found Angélique and sent her in to her great-grandmother's deathbed.

Now he walked back inside. The main hall was empty. He heard low voices in the reception room and looked in. Angélique and her father were seated close together on a low couch, talking. She saw him and motioned him over. He hesitated, not wanting to intrude.

"Don't be silly, Alain. Times like this, we need our friends. *Papa* was telling me about how Nana used to organize his life."

De Bardel smiled. "You know what she was like, Alain, always poking her nose into everything in the whole village. Well, she was even worse with me. She sent a friend of mine away once because the girl was not the right one for me. I was vexed at the time, I remember. I had liked that girl a lot. Turned out that she was completely empty-headed. Looking back on it, I have no idea what I saw in her.

"But that was *Grand-mère's* style. Interfere with everything. It didn't help that she was right most of the time." He leaned back on the couch and locked his fingers behind his head, staring at the ceiling. "Everyone relaxed when she stopped because she became too old to get around. You were her last project, Angélique."

"Me?" There wasn't a lot of surprise in her voice.

"Oh, yes. She was always efficient, your great-grandmother. She didn't have the energy to meddle in everyone's lives, so she decided to do a good job of meddling in just one. Since your mother turned out to be a disappointment to her, I suppose she thought she would do her best to make sure you turned out right."

"I see. And how well did she do?"

De Bardel looked at his daughter fondly. "I guess we'll know in thirty years or so, won't we?" Then his face fell again. "If any of us are around in thirty years. Our old world has been turned upside down lately."

Alain heard the familiar expression and his mind went back to that moment, three years before, in the thunderstorm. He wondered if Angélique remembered. He looked over at her. Their eyes met for a long, thoughtful moment.

* * *

If her death had been a small, private affair, Françoise Marie de Dillon's funeral was anything but. People came from incredible distances to show up at the churchyard and pay tribute. There were few members of her family still surviving or still in Europe, many having emigrated to the Americas, but friends from all walks and levels of life swarmed around.

Alain faded into the background, helping to organize the many visitors who had to be accommodated before and after the funeral.

He watched Angélique out in the centre of things, helping her mother play the hostess, gracefully receiving the plaudits and condolences directed at her family from all who attended. There was little doubt that Mme. de Dillon had made a huge impression on many people. *It seems to me that she made a great deal of progress in her "meddling" with her great-granddaughter.* Watching Angélique in her natural milieu was like looking up the face of Revuaire. He reminded himself firmly that there was another way up, slower but more certain. *I just have to pray that she's still at the top when I get there.*

15. The King Flees

June, 1791

"It's the king! He's gone!" Aimée panted up to the office, her hand shaking as she leaned on the doorjamb, fighting for breath.

A shock ran through him. "Gone? How? You mean someone has taken him, or he's gone on his own?" He ushered her in and she collapsed into a chair.

"Oh his own, I suppose. A rider got into Serres this morning, and the wagon driver who brings our flour told me. Apparently the king and his family just got into their coach and left Paris in the middle of the night. No one knows where they are or which direction they are going. One thing is sure. They are headed to join up with the Austrians and the *Emigrés*. Next thing, they'll be attacking."

"I have to agree with you." He was proud of Aimée's political knowledge. "There is nothing the king would like more than to have the Austrians put him back on the throne, on his own terms. What are they doing to stop him?"

"That's who the rider was. They have sent horsemen out all over France trying to find him. The problem is that the royal carriage has a head start, and they are afraid he will reach the border and be in the arms of our enemies before the messengers can catch up to him."

Alain sat, unable to think. "This is terrible. What a stupid thing to do! What is wrong with the man? With all the agitation against the regime, now he hasn't a chance."

"Well, that's his problem, isn't it?"

"Why Aimée. I didn't know you had such strong opinions. Have you been talking to Angélique?"

She ducked her head. "A little. But I've been thinking a lot. She is right about one thing. The present government does not represent a large number of the people of France. Why should we worry about the king, anyway? We don't need him!"

"It's not that simple. The problem is that the king has given arguments to the people who want the whole system changed."

"But there are problems with system."

"Yes, of course there are. But what is the alternative? Changing the way a country is run is a touchy job. To have slow change is the best, but there will always be some who do not get what they want, or not quickly enough, so they want to change some more.

"Since all new systems have their problems, they leave themselves open to these radicals to take over. Then perhaps their system doesn't work too well, so a more radical group takes over. You can guess the end of that."

She looked thoughtful. "So we should support the present system, because what might follow will be worse?"

"It is such a pleasure to talk to someone with a logical mind."

She blushed this time.

There was a pause while he got his nerve up. "Aimée, can I ask a rather personal question?" She looked at him, her face a mixture of anticipation and puzzlement. She nodded.

"I don't see you going around with boys a lot."

"Is that your question?"

"Well, sort of... you know, do you?"

"They're all so immature." She dismissed the town lads with a gesture.

"But surely there are others."

She shrugged; she was uncomfortable, but he must forge on.

"Aimée, you know that I love Angélique, don't you?"

She glanced up at him, and he could see the pain. He had been right, but it gave him no pleasure. Then her eyes dropped and she said nothing, sitting there, her shoulders slumped. There was a long pause.

"Well, I thought it would be best if we...got it straight..."

"I don't want to talk about it, Alain."

"But isn't it better..."

She got to her feet, fumbled with the door latch, her head down. When she got it open, she turned, and he could see the tears glistening. "There's no sense in talking about it. It won't change anything we haven't all known for a long time." Then she turned and stumbled out, leaving the door open, walking quickly down the street.

He hurried to the door and stood there uselessly watching her walk away, her head still down. *Another triumph of my skill and diplomacy. Merde! How could I have said it any different?*

"That was kindly done, Alain."

He turned to see his mother standing at the foot of the stairs.

"Was it?" The bitterness swelled in him. "She's one of my best friends. Is it kind to make her feel like that?"

His mother smiled sadly. "There are some things that you can't do much about, and being in love is one of them. Having someone in love with you is even worse in some ways. You two are old enough to deal with it. There isn't much you can do except be honest, even if it hurts. Aimée will appreciate that later, if she doesn't now."

He shrugged, and turned back to his work. He wondered how he could face her again.

"There is one point, though..."

"I must never take advantage of the situation. I've known that since the beginning, Maman."

His mother smiled. "I know you did. I was going to say that, should the situation change in the future, you could do worse for a wife."

He sat and looked at her. "Just when I figure out how your mind works, you say something like that."

"Part of my charm, son. Catherine the Inscrutable, your father used to call me."

"But you are no longer inscrutable to him, after all these years?"

She smiled again. "I still do my best."

* * *

It was Edmond who came with the next news. Over the past few years he had developed many contacts in the village and in Serres, and he often knew what was going on, here and in the rest of France, before anyone else. The smaller lad found Alain and Angélique in the garden behind the *chateau* a few days later. He was taller, now, but with the same restless vitality, and he vaulted the fence and started in without preamble.

"They've got him!"

No need to ask who. "Where? How did they catch him?"

"An innkeeper in Varennes recognized the king and sent a message for a detachment of the National Guard to come and arrest him. There was a troop of cavalry supposed to be waiting to meet him down the road, but the carriage was late and the Royalists had returned to their billet for the night. Anyway, the National Guard brought the whole family back to Paris."

Angélique's eyes gleamed. "Was there a riot?"

Edmond was equally enthused. "No! It wasn't a riot at all. It all went on in dead silence." He paused to let that sink in.

"They marched in like a funeral procession, with muffled drums and rifles reversed. The crowds stood silent and let the king feel their eyes on him as he passed. It must have been fantastic!"

To Alain's mind, the fantastic part was that the Paris mobs could be kept under control in any way, but he felt it a poor time to mention the point.

"And what will they do, now?"

"It sounds like a bunch of people want the king removed. I'm not sure what that will mean."

Alain felt their eyes turn to him. "The end of the Constitutional Monarchy. They will have to set up a new system, something like they have in America." He shook his head. "I'm not happy about this. This is a chance for some unsettling elements to take more power."

"How would they do that?" Edmond's agile mind was engaging the problem already.

"There are two main forces in Paris right now. The mob and the National Guard. At the moment, the Guard is controlled by the Assembly. The mob is controlled, if you can call it that, by the radical leaders such Marat and Robespierre."

"Will they fight each other, or what?"

"I guess we can hope they will."

Angélique huffed herself up. "Alain, that's not fair. The National Guard are the defenders of France. They are the first army drawn from the people. They are the power of the people of France."

"The problem is who leads them. Someone responsible like Lafayette, fine. But what if the...if someone radical gets into power? What if those radicals get authority over both the Guard and the mob? Can you imagine what they might do?"

Alain saw Angélique's nose lift, a danger sign he had learned to watch for. "Maybe the people in power need someone to shake them up a little. Maybe they need to feel the strength of the common people for a change."

Alain couldn't let this pass. "So the National Guard will be a positive force, will it?"

"Why not?"

"Even in Savournon?"

"Well, I should hope so. I understand why you're worried about the Paris mob, Alain, with your father there, but this is Savournon. We know these people, and they know us."

"Exactly."

"And why does that make you look so smug?" Angélique regarded him with a small frown.

"I'm not smug. I'm quite upset. Can you guess who is an officer in the National Guard of Serres?"

Edmond nodded. "Reynaud de Gonillons."

Angélique half rose from her chair. "What?"

Alain shrugged. "The very same. I can't tell what goes on in his head, but I suspect that he has decided on the winning side and he has moved to protect himself."

She sat there, stunned. "But he's an aristocrat."

"Not any more. Noble blood is a hindrance these days. So he joined the Guard and got himself elected an officer. I saw him out 'training' his men the other day. They looked like a bunch of kids playing with dangerous toys. And there he was in the middle, slapping backs and making crude jokes. Most of those fellows are young farm lads. Someone like de Gonillons treating them as 'equals' would make quite an impression."

Edmond looked sober. "We'd better watch that man."

"Perhaps he'll go off to Paris?"

Alain frowned. "I'm not sure whether I'd like that or not. If he stays, he makes trouble, no doubt about it. If he goes to Paris and has any success at all, he might make a great deal more trouble."

The other two nodded, and they sat in glum silence. Then Edmond got to his feet. "Well, I guess I'd better get back to work."

The spring was gone from his step as he left the garden, taking the more normal path through the gate this time.

Alain rose as well. "I'll go with you. I have some letters to write for *Papa*."

He took leave of Angélique, looking down into her worried eyes before turning away. *Tres bien. She needs to be a whole lot less confident of her beliefs.*

As he wandered down the *chateau* driveway with the silent Edmond, he wondered if he should say anything to Angélique about his problem with Aimée, but he couldn't imagine what to say or how she would react, so he let it drop. She probably had it all figured out anyway.

Angélique had changed over the past year and a half. She was more confident, if that was possible. She had always been good at giving orders before, but now it was different. She seemed to give orders less, as if it wasn't as important to control people any more. Now she was pushing her political theories instead. Perhaps she was learning to take control on a larger scale. He grinned to himself. *Watch out, France.*

16. Theft

July 1, 1791

"Come on, Foncé, come and have a taste." He held out the meat. The cat stretched out a big paw, furry and almost black: a tinge of grey on the end of each long hair. Then he pulled it back. The tip of his tail curled and his mobile ears tested for danger around him. Alain held out the meat again and waited. The young animal's huge yellow eyes focused on the food and he sidled, trying to get up the nerve to take it.

Finally Alain laid the scrap down and pulled his hand back. The cat crouched and slipped a paw forward, pulling the food to a safe distance to eat it.

Alain looked at the handful of scraps he had begged from the cook and considered his progress. So far, not much. He could tell that Foncé wanted to come closer but couldn't quite break through a short lifetime of caution. Alain held out another piece of meat. The cat moved in then stopped just out of reach. He stretched out tentatively, then pulled back. The mouth opened, spiked white points flashing, to give a small and plaintive "mew" for such a large cat. Alain grinned and dropped the meat, which disappeared. "Don't you ever take time to chew?"

Angélique had been watching this act with tolerant amusement. "The barn cats don't chew unless they have to. They prefer to bolt it down in large chunks."

"I thought of giving him a big piece to see how he handled it, but he might choke."

She laughed out loud. "Alain, that cat is over a year old. He's been catching his own food all his life. Do you think he will choke if you give him a big piece of meat?"

He shrugged. "I suppose not. It seems unfair of me to take the chance, just to satisfy my own curiosity."

The girl gazed at him. "You are strange."

He dropped another bit of food in front of the cat and looked at her.

She shook her head. "Always a lawyer. You have to follow your ethics, even when you're dealing with a cat."

He thought about that. "The way you act when you are dealing with animals shows what kind of person you are."

She seemed to be in a different mood today: more thoughtful, somehow, as if she was bouncing some idea around in her mind, adding new information, then trying it out again. He wondered, but didn't complain; it was an improvement over her political harangues.

"Alain, what does the Revolution need? Not at the top, in Paris, but down here, locally."

"Besides relief supplies if the harvest isn't good?"

She made a negative gesture with her hand. "That's the trouble. You keep telling me how you hate the radicals up there, but what do you do to make things better here? Nothing."

"That's not fair! I learn all about the new laws and try to explain them to people who ask. I distribute the relief supplies. What else can I do?"

"Reynaud de Gonillons is doing something."

His mouth was hanging open, so he closed it. "Are you comparing me to him?"

She shrugged. "No. But it does make a point. It isn't good enough to sit back and be a critic. Anyone can do that. The people with the power at the moment are those who found a way to make personal advancement out of it. I don't mean that you should be selfish like they are. Our friend down the road, for example. But you have to take what control you can or you will end up being left behind, or even worse, destroyed by those who do take power."

"Like de Gonillons."

"That's right. If you want to have an effect on the Revolution, do something. If you allow all the people like de Gonillons to take control, what will happen?"

"I see what you mean."

She smiled. "So what are you going to do?"

"No idea. Join the National Guard?"

She looked horrified, then realized it was his turn to be joking. "Not your best opportunity, in my opinion."

"There are no political clubs in Savournon."

"So?"

"I'm supposed to start one?"

She shrugged, as if it didn't matter to her. Again he wondered where this was leading.

Their conversation lagged, and Alain turned his attention to the cat. He held out his hands to show that he had no more food. The cat sniffed his fingers but pulled back when he tried to pat its head.

Then it stiffened, ears alert, and twisted away, ducking behind a row of shrubs and disappearing. A moment later they heard the distant thunder of the knocker on the front door.

"You have a very forceful visitor."

Angélique stood. "I would let the maid answer, but perhaps I should go myself." She had only taken a few steps towards the house when the door slammed open and Reynaud de Gonillons stepped out, in full officer's uniform, followed by a protesting maid.

He made no attempt at pleasantries. "I want to talk to your father."

Angélique paused before answering. "What about?"

"That's no business of yours, girl. Where is he?"

She tossed her head. "He isn't here, so I suppose it might become business of mine. What do you want?"

He took a step closer to her, looking down with a smirk. "Since I'm sure your dear mother isn't here either, I suppose it might. I want to talk to one of your servants."

"Who?"

"The one called Jimmy. Where is he?"

Angélique shot a glance at Alain. "Why do you want him?"

The man moved forward again, close enough to make her uncomfortable, but she refused to back down. Alain stood, wondering what he could do.

"Full of questions today, aren't you? You get this straight, *citoyenne*. I'm here on the business of the *patrie*, and you will give me answers, or I will bring the full weight of the law against you. Ask your tame would-be lawyer what that means. He must be good for something."

Angélique looked straight into his eyes. "Only a coward has to threaten. If you want Jimmy 'on the business of the *patrie*,' I'll send for him."

The smile of triumph started to spread.

"But he's up in the forest, and I'm not sure where. It might take all afternoon to get him. You will pardon me if I don't invite you to sit down while you wait. In fact, I am not inviting you to stay in my house at all. I will send for you when he is here. Perhaps you would like to leave now." It was not a question.

The smile stopped and an even less pleasant expression replaced it.

"Listen, my girl, you don't tell the National Guard what to do or where to wait. If I want to sit, I will." He took her by the arm and turned her towards a bench nearby. "Perhaps we will wait right here. We might have a pleasant afternoon, if you'll send the boy away."

The blood rushed to Alain's head and he stepped forward, then stopped. The man outweighed him by half and was armed: both sword and pistol. He hesitated, wondering what to do. De Gonillons grinned at his discomfiture. "Run along, boy. I'll let you go this time."

Alain controlled himself. He tried to keep his voice calm. "You're making a mistake, Reynaud. You have laid hands on a young lady in the presence of two witnesses." His gesture included the maid, still standing at the door. "If a legal action of assault is placed against you, I remind you that this is not some peasant boy you are manhandling this time. Her father is an old-fashioned man, and he will not hesitate to have you whipped in the village square if you continue. I somehow doubt that your 'friends' in the Guard will protect you in this case."

The man laughed, but he dropped his hand from Angélique's arm. "The time will come when I can do what I like, and no aristocrat or village lawyer will be able to say a thing. Don't you forget that, boy."

He pushed past the maid, then turned in the doorway. "You have that kid down at the *Mairie* for me in two hours or less, if you know what is good for him. I'll tell you one thing though. His thieving days are over." De Gonillons turned and strode into the house, leaving the door open behind him.

Alain noted how pale Angélique's face was. "Are you all right?"

She tossed her head, though her voice quavered. "It takes more than a bruised arm to bother me."

"Did he hurt you?"

"Don't worry about it. Thank you for helping me, Alain. I didn't know what to do."

He shrugged. "I didn't either. It was the only thing I could come up with. The lawyer in me speaking, I guess. I wish I hadn't said that about your father, though. I shouldn't have reminded him about your nobility." He tried to grin. "That was the angry friend in me speaking."

She took him by the arms, faced him. "Thank you for being a friend. That was what I needed."

Alain had a sudden thought. "Jimmy! What has he done now?"

"Why do you jump to the conclusion that he has done anything?"

"I suppose I should be glad you're argumentative again. It means you're all right. Let me try that again. I wonder what they think Jimmy did?"

"I'll send someone to bring him down here so I can ask him."

Alain nodded. "Good. I'll go and see what it's all about. Edmond will have information."

"Thank you, Alain."

"Don't thank me. He's my friend, too."

She gave him the warm smile that hit him just under the breastbone. "I know, Alain. And you're a good friend."

She turned and hurried into the house, calling out orders like a sergeant before a battle. His step light, Alain strode out the front door and headed for the *boulangerie.* He was worried about Jimmy, but it was so much better to be working on something together with Angélique again.

The twins were sitting in the shop looking over a book, as there were no customers. Alain's questions brought an instant concern to Aimée's face, but a look of comprehension to her brother's.

"Yes, that would be it. There was a customer down at the inn robbed last night. A rich fellow, it seems, in the iron trade. He had business with Olivier the ferrier and stayed in the village afterwards. Stood the men in the taproom to several drinks, I understand, so he's popular. For some reason, he went out to walk around town at about ten o'clock last night. Had his purse lifted while he was walking, he thinks. He didn't notice till this morning, went straight to the Guard about it." The boy's narrow face was worried. "And so de Gonillons thinks Jimmy did it, hey? I can understand why."

"Edmond! How can you say such a thing about your friend?"

He shrugged and looked at his sister. "He's a pickpocket, a good one, and too many people know it. If I was a Guardsman, he's the first person that would come to my mind."

"But Jimmy wouldn't do that!"

Alain shook his head. "I would hope not. He wouldn't be that stupid. One thing I can tell you, though. If he did it, he won't come down the hill. He'll be long gone."

Edmond nodded. "The problem is, if he didn't do it, how do we protect him? If de Gonillons decides to take revenge on Angélique through Jimmy, what can we do?"

"We have to prove him innocent. Somehow."

Aimée leaned forward. "But that won't be enough. If Reynaud de Gonillons gets his hands on him it won't matter if he's innocent or not. He'll beat him and say it was questioning."

"I can go with him. He has the right to a lawyer, and even though I'm not official yet, I can still go. That ought to at least remind de Gonillons that Jimmy has important friends. Why would Reynaud be involved in this anyway? A lost purse isn't the business of the National Guard."

Edmond gave a knowing look. "If anyone was buying drinks in the inn, it's a sure thing de Gonillons was there. He saw a chance to get back at Angélique and took it. Makes him look like a public-spirited citizen, too. Very smart."

The other two nodded. "I'll see what I can find out about the crime." Edmond was gone before Alain could answer. He looked at Aimée and grinned. "If anyone can find out, he will."

Aimée did not smile in return. Her eyes seemed darker than usual. "You be careful, Alain. That man doesn't like you either, and you can't say what he'll do."

"Thanks for your concern, but I'm not in any danger. As long as my father is in the Assembly, de Gonillons won't dare touch me."

She looked relieved. She got up and went to him, putting her hand on his arm as Angélique often did. In spite of himself, he jerked away, then cursed silently as he saw the hurt on her face. To make up for it, he spoke as gently as he could. "Don't worry so much, Aimée. We're a good team. We'll get Jimmy out of this."

"I hate it here. I feel so helpless. The rest of you can at least get out and do something."

"But I though you liked being in the shop!"

"Of course I do. But I don't like waiting."

He smiled. "Neither do I, Aimée." He considered staying for a while to keep her company, then decided against it. "I'd better be going. I want to talk to Jimmy the moment he gets down."

He strode back towards the *chateau*, angered at the luck that brought this awkward situation between them. It wasn't her fault she was in love with him. After all, he would be a good catch for a girl like her. She was too intelligent to be interested in most of the boys in the village, and not well enough placed to find anyone better. He wondered how to find a way for her to meet some other people. Moving to a larger town was out of the question. She would never leave her father. He put those thoughts aside as he knocked on Angélique's door. There was another friend who needed him now.

The stableboy had not returned with Jimmy yet, so Alain used the time while they waited by filling Angélique in on the facts of the crime.

She thought a bit. "But how could he have done it? He lives away up in the forest."

Alain shook his head. "The man was robbed late in the evening, as far as Edmond knows. Jimmy could have slipped away and been in the village in less than half an hour, done the job and returned without anyone up there noticing he wasn't in bed. They sleep and rise early. I hope they all stayed up late, or something."

They also discussed the problem Aimée had brought up, about protecting Jimmy from a rough questioning.

"I sent for Aubin, too. Could he go along too, as a witness?"

"I like the thought of having him there. That Reynaud is a strong fellow." He remembered his helplessness this afternoon.

"Don't look so upset. I didn't expect you to attack him and throw him out. He's much too big, and he had a sword and two other Guards outside." Angélique laid her hand on his arm.

Alain, the incident with Aimée fresh in his mind, snatched his arm away.

"What's wrong?" She looked at him with sudden concern.

He tried to reassure her, but it was difficult, since he couldn't very well tell her the reason. He was saved further embarrassment by the arrival of the Rat. A very dirty and tattered Rat, followed closely by Aubin, who wasn't much neater.

"*Alors!* When did you last have a bath? If you're trying to keep Angélique from kissing you, you've picked a good technique."

The boy grinned up at him. "What do you expect?" He jerked his head towards the forester. "Me 'n' Aubin just got back from a big trip."

Alain looked at Angélique over the boy's head and saw the hope in her eyes. "What kind of trip?"

Jimmy strutted, but without the usual springing his step. "A long one. Three days in the mountains. We had some business over at the Abbey de Mon Frère, and we took a swing over to Le Saix on the way. There'll be good huntin' over in the gorge there next fall."

"So where were you last night?"

"Oh, up in the hills back of Lac de Peyssier. We come down over th' Aujour this afternoon. Just got in when th' kid came for us."

Alain hid a grin. The stableboy was at least two years older than Jimmy.

"He said there was no time to clean up. What's goin' on, anyways?"

Alain ignored the question, turning to the forester. "Is that true?"

The man looked puzzled. "Of course, M. Jouvet. Like he says, I had some business up there and the boy wanted to come along. Kept up real well, too. We'll make a forester out of him yet."

Alain explained the problem to them.

Jimmy spat on the ground. "You mean I'm supposed to have lifted this mark's brass? In the middle of town where everybody knows about me? What do they think I am, stupid?"

They all grinned in relief. "No, Jimmy, they don't know you. But nobody ever gave the National Guard credit for intelligence." Alain sobered. "But we still have to get you through this questioning, remembering that de Gonillons hates Angélique, and me too, I guess. Sorry Jimmy, but your friends have got you in trouble for a change."

To his surprise, the boy seemed unafraid. "Ah, I bin picked up before. I put on a little kid act and whine and cry a lot. They never bother but to cuff me a few. I bin hit hunnerts a times."

Angélique's head rose. "There will be no putting on an act this time, and no one is going to touch you. You are perfectly innocent, and we will see to it that everybody knows."

The forester spoke up. "If we have to go down to the Mairie, should we get cleaned up?"

Alain shook his head. "It strengthens your story if you're still in your working clothes. I'll come along with a pen and paper and make a big show of writing it all down."

Angélique stood. "Right. Let's go."

"Um...Angélique, I doubt if you should be there."

"Why not? Oh. I see."

"We'll be fine, don't worry."

She saw them to the door and stayed there watching them leave.

The Rat looked up at Alain. "What was that all about? Why couldn't she come?"

"I suppose you should know, since it's partly the cause of your trouble right now. De Gonillons is interested in Angélique, but she won't have anything to do with him. He got rude, so she dressed him down in public. He's never forgiven her. If she were there watching, he would be twice as hard on you."

The boy nodded. "Well, it's a good thing she ain't comin' then, hey?" His grin was losing its spark.

He put his arm across the boy's shoulders. "Don't you worry. We'll be there the whole time. He talks to you, and that's all."

They took the path past the *boulangerie* to see if Edmond had any more information. He had, and it wasn't encouraging.

"That man is burned up and swears he'll never come back to trade here. That's got the local shopkeepers upset. He could provide more business for them. He wants action, and they want action."

Alain stood, reviewing cases he had heard in court. "Jimmy didn't steal the man's purse. That leaves two possibilities. Either someone else did, or it wasn't stolen at all. If it wasn't stolen it was lost. The easiest way to solve the problem is to find it. Since everyone is sure it was stolen, they haven't looked for it yet."

Edmond nodded.

"Make a real search, Edmond. Can you get the man to go with you and retrace where he went and what he did last night?"

"He won't come with me. I'm just a kid."

"Maybe your father will help. If the other shopkeepers are involved they will persuade the man. Come to the Mairie and tell us the moment you find anything."

"Right." With a slap at Jimmy's arm, he was off up the street.

The National Guard had their assembly room in the new Mairie, and there the three presented themselves. Reynaud was nowhere in sight, and the Guardsman at the door asked them politely to go in and have a seat. They remained standing.

The room was cold and undecorated. A long table stretched down the right side, spread with a plain green cloth, not too clean. One end was covered with papers, the other by the remains of a meal. Several plank benches were scattered around, as well as a few more delicate chairs, which, though battered and scratched, looked out of place. Alain wondered who had "donated" them.

Finally the door opened, and de Gonillons strode in. He took one look at the group waiting for him. "What are all these scum doing here? Get out, you two. I'll take care of this blemish."

He reached for the boy, who ducked behind his friends. Aubin shifted so the Guardsman's hand closed on the forester's beefy shoulder instead. The men's eyes locked, then Reynaud pulled his hand away, making an exaggerated wiping motion. Before he had time to speak, Alain broke in.

"We have brought Jimmy here to talk to you, to straighten this out. He was not involved in the theft of the money, but you can ask him any questions you like. Ask, but no more. You will not touch him."

"I won't, hey? Well, after I've arrested him, I'll touch him all I damned well please, and no lawyer's brat is going to tell me otherwise."

"But you will not arrest him, because he is not guilty of a crime. Why don't you ask your questions before you make a fool of yourself?"

The man was clearly bothered by Alain's confidence and the sturdy presence of Aubin. After a moment he threw himself into one of the better chairs, propped his boot up on the table and looked at them. "All right. We'll do this all proper-like. It won't affect the outcome." He gave a cruel smile. "So, you sweeping from the gutters. What story have you concocted to prove your innocence?"

Jimmy stepped forward, and Alain was glad to see that he was keeping quiet and polite. "I don't know what you're talking about, sir."

"Oh, you don't? And you don't know about a certain merchant's fat purse that went missing last night?"

"Not if it went missing here in town. I was up in the mountains back of Lac de Peyssier last night, working."

"Hah! And I'm supposed to believe that, I suppose."

"It's just like he says, *sieur* de Gonillons." The forester's deep voice broke in. "He was with me."

To Alain's surprise, Reynaud seemed discomfited, glancing at the Guardsman in the doorway. Then he blustered. "We don't use those feudal titles any more, in case you didn't know. The proper form of address is '*citoyen.*'"

"All right, *citoyen.* The boy was with me last night in one of our shelters northwest of the lake. Took us three hours to get down this afternoon. Are you suggesting that the boy slipped out of camp, ran to town, stole something and ran back, and I didn't notice?"

The man snorted. "You work for her too. You made that story up, messed up your clothes and come down here lying to me."

200

Alain saw the forester bristling. It was time to cut in.

"*Citoyen*, their story will not be hard to check. They had business at the Abbey up there. If they went through the Valley of the Maraize, surely people saw them, even talked to them." He looked over at Aubin, who nodded.

"It isn't possible that Jimmy stole the merchant's purse. I suggest that if you want to be helpful, you start looking elsewhere."

De Gonillons' chair came down with a bang. "So the would-be lawyer is now telling me my duties!" He rose to his feet and advanced. "Get out of here you vermin, and stop wasting my time."

Alain put his hand on Aubin's shoulder and pushed until the resistance eased. The man turned towards the door, but he never let the Guardsman out of his sight. Jimmy stayed blessedly silent, and they started to leave. However, they didn't quite make it out the door before Edmond rushed up, his chest heaving.

"We found it, we found it!"

"You did? Where?"

"Caught on a fence! Hanging there behind a board where no one could see it."

By this time they had moved into the street, and de Gonillons was standing in the doorway sneering. "You found it hanging there. How convenient. More likely you figured things were too hot, so you put it somewhere it could be found. I hope he counts his change."

Don't say it. Calm and in control. Be a lawyer...Merde! Why not? How can it change anything? He held the other man's gaze. "Do you know how pathetically weak that sounds?"

The Guardsman bristled, then sneered again and turned his back, slamming the door behind him.

There was a stunned silence while the others looked at Alain. He could feel his cheeks grow hot. He glanced around.

"How did you find it, Edmond?" There was no doubt in his mind that the boy had been the one.

"Well, how do you find something you lost? I thought we should retrace the man's path, if he could remember it. Everywhere he went, everything he did. Of course, he wouldn't have done it for me, but I persuaded *Papa*," by this time the baker had joined them, following his son at a slower rate, but no less proud, "that if Jimmy didn't take the purse, then it must be around somewhere. Face it. There's nobody else in town with the skills to steal it!"

They all chuckled, and the Rat looked sort of proud, but half sheepish as well. Edmond's father spoke up. "It was funny. It was the merchants who persuaded the man to retrace his route, but it was Edmond who asked him all the questions. 'Where did you go then, *citoyen*? How did you stand? Oh, yes, there's your footprint. Stand there, will you?' I was chuckling because Edmond sounded so much like he knew what he was about that he had that fellow following him like a lamb."

Edmond continued, more excited. "There was one place where he stopped to talk to someone for a while, and he said he leaned on the fence. Then he put his arm over this man's shoulder and slapped him on the back, and they all returned to the inn. Well, I looked over the fence, just at the level of his belt, and sure enough, there it was. It had slipped over the board as he lifted his arm, and when he slapped the man, he didn't feel the tug when it pulled loose."

Jimmy grinned at his friend. "A smart fence, that. It's one a our fav'rite tricks."

"So is the merchant happy?"

M. Sarrobert took up the story here, bursting with pride. "He was embarrassed, but he covered it up by being impressed at Edmond's mind. Said I had a bright boy, and would I be putting him out as an apprentice? I told him I hadn't considered it. He said to get in touch if I was interested."

Paris

July 17, 1791

Dearest Wife and Son,

As I sit here in my rooms tonight, I wonder whether this is the end of all our dreams. I have not given up, but I now begin to glimpse what might await us, and I grieve for France and all her people.

In the first place, the king's flight to Varennes has destroyed any chance of a constitutional monarchy, and spoiled the possibility of the new Constitution succeeding. The king's irresponsible action and the people's firm response has firmly entrenched in the popular mind the idea that the nation can be sovereign over itself.

In order to support the Constitution, the Assembly was forced to back the king. This goes against common sense and the will of the people, and thus has weakened the Assembly's power considerably.

And today we have reached the point where Frenchmen are slaying each other in the streets. How can we hold our great country together when we cannot keep the peace among ourselves?

The protest this time was over unemployment. Quickly, as it always does,

203

the mob formed. Several thousand people, chanting slogans, menacing everyone unfortunate or silly enough to be in their way. Two unlucky men took refuge under the Altar of Patriotism. The mob decided that the two intended to damage the Altar. So they dragged them out and hanged them. That's right. They took two innocent men – no one has even found out who they were yet – and hanged them from trees in the park.

At this point the National Guard marched in, but by now the mob was getting vicious. Lafayette lined his men up, but the mob was crowding closer and closer, getting up its nerve to attack. Then Mayor Bailly arrived. Seeing the gravity of the situation, he declared martial law. It had no effect. The crowd was still growing, with people rushing to see what was happening, then getting caught up in the anger.

Some of us hurried down from the Assembly to try to calm things down, but it was no use. No one could speak because of the noise, and the mob was in no mood to listen. They kept milling about, shouting to each other. Little swirls of men, and some women too, formed in small groups around some orator or other, who would catch their attention and fire them up. Then that group would surge to the front, to get caught up in the eddying mass again.

I was disgusted, but not surprised, to see Marat in the middle of it all. I only caught sight of him for a while, but he was one of those exhorting the crowd to anger. Odious little man. To think he was once a doctor, working for the good of humanity!

The situation was tense, as you can imagine. The National Guard was holding their position, but not doing anything. What could they do? This made the crowd braver, and they came closer and closer, taunting the soldiers and threatening them. Lafayette ordered his men to stand fast, but who are these National Guard, after all? Not seasoned soldiers, used to standing firm under threat.

No one knows how it happened, but the crowd must have pushed too close to one of the soldiers and he fired his gun.

Immediately the mob attacked. I couldn't see anything after that, because the other soldiers opened fire, and the square was a mass of people running all directions, obscured by the smoke from the muskets.

When it was all over the soldiers remained and the mob was gone, except for the bodies of the dead and wounded lying in the street and on the steps of the Altar of Patriotism.

I wonder what other sacrifices will be required before France is calm again.

I am sorry to burden you with my sorrow, but I feel I must tell it to someone, and it is important that you understand the gravity of the situation here.

How I wish I were home with you.

Your loving husband and father,

François Jouvent

17. Blowup

July 31, 1791

Angélique handed the letter back to Alain, and they sat there, silent. Finally she spoke, to herself, it seemed: half in anger, half in sorrow. "Horrible."

Alain nodded. "Sickening, isn't it."

Angélique still seemed deep in her own thoughts. "What kind of man could do such a thing?"

Alain looked at her. "Who?"

She looked up. "Lafayette. He would be the one who gave the order."

Alain was getting more and more puzzled. "What order are you talking about?" He looked at the letter again. "*Papa* doesn't say anything about any order."

Angélique's lip lifted. "No, he didn't. Even if he does know the truth, which I doubt – your father is so idealistic – he couldn't very well write it down, could he?"

Alain heard the suppressed vehemence in her voice, and couldn't help the slight start of anger in his own breast. He asked the question, but he already had a feeling what kind of answer he would get. "What order?"

"The order for the troops to fire, of course. You don't actually think someone fired without an order and started it all by accident, do you? Grow up, Alain."

"Why not? Those soldiers were frightened men, facing a mob like that. You saw what *Papa* wrote. They aren't exactly veterans. One of them must have panicked."

Angélique's head shook in exaggerated patience. "Alain, you treat this as if it were a chivalrous game. Take the larger view. What we have in France – still – is a situation where the rulers are in trouble because they have kept all the control, and all the money, from the rest of the people. The people of France won't put up with that any more, but these men haven't learned. So they send Lafayette out to show their strength by making an example of a few innocents. That's what happened in the Champs du Mars. We used to consider Lafayette a good revolutionary, but it seems he has chosen the other side. Worse luck for him."

Alain could only stare at her in horror. He knew where she was getting her ideas, but how could she believe them? *How can Angélique, my intelligent, thoughtful Angélique, be spouting such nonsense? She had better be put straight in a hurry.* He kept his voice controlled.

"And what should Lafayette have done, faced with such a situation?"

"Nothing. Those people are unemployed and starving. They have a right to let the swells in charge hear their complaints. He should have left them alone."

"Angélique, those 'innocents' hanged two men, for no reason except that they hid in the wrong place."

"You don't know that. You don't know what those men did. Maybe they were going to blow up the Altar."

"But that's what we have law courts for! You don't take people out and kill them without a trial. Please, Angélique. Be realistic."

She was unfazed. "Even Louis didn't order his army to massacre his subjects. That's realistic."

He started to reply that Louis was in contact with the *emigré* army, allied with the Prussians and his wife's relatives, the Austrians, who were poised on the borders of France, ready to invade. But that wasn't the problem. The problem was Angélique's strange beliefs. *Why is she thinking like this? There has to be something else going on here.* "Why do you need to believe this?"

Her upper lip quivered again. "I don't 'need' to believe anything! What do you mean by a nasty crack like that?"

"I mean that you wouldn't be saying such stupid things if there wasn't a good reason for it. You're too smart. So it must be worth it to you to believe this nonsense. I'm just trying to figure out what it is you need."

Up to now she had been detached. Now her voice took on a note of tension. "Oh, so now I'm stupid, and what I say is nonsense?"

He disregarded the danger signs. "I'm beginning to catch on. You've made your decision, too. You've decided who will win and you have jumped to that side. Just like Lafayette. But you picked the opposite side."

"Perhaps I have decided who is in the right and decided to support them. Perhaps I have figured out who the real enemies of France are."

"Enemies of France! This has very little to do with France. It has to do with Angélique, and how she loves to boss people around. I bet you have a great time at your political club in Grenoble. I bet they think you're something, with your fine education and your big words. You're a leader there, with all those semi-literate shopkeeper's wives. You know, Angélique, I'm beginning to see what the problem was with the aristocracy. There's a little too much Reynaud de Gonillons in you."

She stood up, but the usual rage had disappeared. She seemed cool, even cold, though there was tension in the tilt of her head, the line of her shoulder. "At least he has made a choice. There is a time to make a stand. Climb out from behind your lawyer's desk and make a choice of your own. The reality you keep harping about can be changed. But only by people who care enough to get out and do something about it. Not people who sit around and complain. Certainly not by people who join with those who want it to stay the same old way. Make a choice, Alain. Even choose to be my enemy. But don't sit on the fence any more. I have no respect at all for people like that."

He had risen too, a hollow, cold spot growing in his stomach. He was losing her. Perhaps it was just as well. *So she wants me to take a stand, does she?*

He shook his head slowly. "Angélique, I wish it were as simple as it sounds when you say it. I wish we could jump onto the right side and win, and it would all be over. I do. I'm not afraid to stand up for what I believe. But I don't have that much respect for taking a stand. People who take action simply for the sake of doing something are dangerous to everyone, because they are often wrong. This situation is much too complex to deal with that way. I know that, and you do too. Some day when you get it straight we can talk about it again. At the moment, I see no point in any further discussion." He turned toward the door, aware of how much like a lawyer he had sounded. *Well, that shouldn't be surprising.*

She held the door as he passed through, and there was genuine regret on her face. "*Aur revoir*, Alain."

He stood looking at her. She was still beautiful, but somehow he felt sorry for her; he didn't know why. *There was no other way. I had to say what I did. Perhaps some day...and perhaps not.* He could feel the cold growing inside him. It would be there for a long time.

"*Adieu*, Angélique." He turned and walked away down the drive, his head bowed. It didn't even occur to him to look back.

So for Alain the winter of 1791 began with an early frost. He thought back over the past few years. It seemed that every winter before Angélique went back to Grenoble they had a fight. *Does she have to do that to prove she doesn't need me before she returns to her other life? Or am I causing it myself for the same reason?* Whatever it was, this time felt different. It was more like she had made a decision, and their final battle had been just tidying up the loose ends.

Fortunately for Alain, other things kept his mind occupied. In early September, his father came home.

Jouvent stayed in Paris long enough to see through the elections at the end of August, then departed thankfully for Savournon. The new Assembly had formed and started its work. For good or for ill, the Revolution had started on a new route, a path more radical than its first hesitant steps.

And it wasn't a good time to start. The harvest of 1791 was fair, but prices stayed high due to the depreciation of the paper currency. A slave's revolt in San Domingo cut off sugar supplies. Worst of all, the army was desperately in need of better organization and leadership to confront the threat of foreign invaders on all sides.

Faced with these dangers to France, Alain told himself that his own small difficulties were meaningless. He threw himself into his work. His duties handing out the relief supplies over, he had been hired by the *departement* in its efforts to get the farmers to use modern methods to produce better crops.

18. Talk of War

February, 1792

Since his father had returned, Alain had more, not less work to do. The elder lawyer had made many contacts in Paris, and combined with his knowledge of the new government and its workings, this brought increased business their way. Merchants were making the ten-kilometre trip (he was getting used to the new units of measurement) out from Serres to ask his advice, and he, in return, spent more time in the larger town. As a result Alain and his mother were still taking care of most of the local business and helping with the expanded trade as well. They bought a new buggy and another horse so that Alain could continue with his side of things while his father dealt with business in Gap. Catherine decided that the office needed updated furniture in keeping with the new clientele they were receiving, and a few nice pieces appeared in their upstairs apartment, too. It was good to see his father successful after all these years, especially for his mother's sake, but it seemed a hollow victory.

Jouvent did his usual best for his clients, the old and the new, but he took little joy in it. Many times Alain would come into the office and see his father, pen held above the paper but not moving, his eyes fixed on something out of Alain's perception. He would react to his son's presence, often with a sad smile or a shake of the head, and go back to work.

The main thing that kept Alain busy, though, was the new work he was taking on with the local farmers. It seemed that the new revolutionary government had actually read the *cahiers de doleances* the communities had made out. The main problem with the farming areas, especially the poorer ones, was the lack of productivity of the land.

To combat this problem, a group of intelligent men put their heads together. They came up with as many solutions as they could and made these available to any who asked.

The difficulty was to persuade the peasants to change any small part of the way they, and generations before them, had lived their lives.

In spite of the evidence of the poor harvests, or perhaps because of them, it required all of Alain's diplomacy, plus considerable badgering and bullying, to get them to adapt to the changes. In the aid of his mission, he found himself in some interesting situations…

"So, young M. Jouvent. That's the first time you've helped with a calf birthing?"

Alain joined the farmer at the basin scrubbing the blood off his hands, wincing at the cold of the water. He grinned with relief. "I suppose it was obvious."

The weathered face broke into an answering smile, and a hard, wet, hand clapped him on the back. "I'll say this for you, lad, you learn fast."

"She's a fine heifer."

Jules turned his head back towards the doorway that led from the living part of his house into the livestock area. "Oh, she is, that. For all she's born early in the season. She'll be a choice animal. It'll mean an extra field plowed every year, more milk for the little ones," his glance took in his three grandchildren, lying scattered like puppies on the hearth at their mother's feet, "more cheese, more bread…" The man's hands encompassed the forthcoming riches.

Alain joined in the enthusiasm. "This calls for a celebration, then."

"A good idea, lad. Marie, bring us the wine bottle."

Alain glanced around the crowded, noisy farm kitchen. "Uh…perhaps not here?"

The man focussed on him. "*Mais oui*. You didn't come here to learn about animal husbandry."

Alain nodded. *"Animal husbandry" is it?* No matter how much he ridiculed "book farming," Jules put to good use the small learning he had obtained as a child at the parish

213

school. *This man is my best chance to gain a toehold with the other farmers.* "We got sort of sidetracked for a while. Why don't we go into the village? I'll stand you a glass at the inn."

Jules nodded. "Fine. A good place to discuss ideas." He looked at Alain sideways. "Their wine's not so good as mine, though."

Alain laughed. "I don't suppose the landlord would appreciate us walking in, plunking down a jug of wine on the table and calling for two glasses. You pay something for the atmosphere."

The peasant took up his coat and went to the door.

Alain rose. "Good-bye, Mme. Morel. It has been, as they say, an experience."

She waved her hand and smiled. "Glad to have you any time. Hadn't been you, it woulda been me out there tuggin' on that rope."

Alain turned to regard the younger woman. "And also you, Mme. Morel. It has been nice to see you again. I hope your husband is doing well in Provence?"

The girl, leaning over her babies, turned a jolly face up to him. "Oh, he's fine, M. Jouvent. Got a good job right now – three months or more, doin' the winter work in a vineyard."

"It must be hard, having him away all that time."

She shrugged with the peasant's fatalism. "Well, he sends money home regular, and that helps. Besides," she glanced sideways at him, "we make up for it the week he gets back."

Alain could feel himself blushing.

"Marie, you mind your manners." The farmer's wife looked up from stirring a pot, amused as well. "Now you've embarrassed the young man." The younger woman bent over and picked up a girl of about two and held her, smiling proudly.

Alain shook his head. The casual earthiness of these people didn't bother him much, but he didn't feel comfortable when confronted by it. Accepting his position as butt of the joke, he smiled at them and followed the grinning farmer out the door.

As they walked, though, the man became serious. "He makes a good wage, *mon fils.*" He sounded apologetic, as if the fact that his son-in-law had no land of his own needed explaining. "We'll have a new plow in the spring. Steel-shared." It needed no discussion. A daily labourer could make enough to support a family working 150 days a year, and someone with a good reputation could work much more than that.

Alain laughed. "Just waiting for the new calf to pull it!"

"Oh we'll give her a coupla years to grow up first."

It was a short walk through the frosty, stubbled fields from the farmer's house in Les Girards to the inn. On the way, Alain waved his hand over the bare ground. "You could have a crop in here."

"In this frost? What could grow?"

"Well, from what I've read, it doesn't grow much in the winter. But if you plant in the fall you take advantage of the rains to get good roots started. Then the crop lies dormant all winter. You can feed the sheep on it early in the spring and put in your regular crop at the regular time."

The farmer looked skeptical. "And the land wears out faster, 'n' I have to leave it fallow more often."

"That's the other part of it. If you grow a legume for one crop, it replenishes the soil, and you never leave it fallow."

Jules' bushy eyebrows rose. "No fallow time? Ever?"

Alain shook his head. "That's what the pamphlet says." *He knows what a legume is. Another year, and I'll have him planting them.*

"Huh!" A disdainful snort. "Another of your pamphlets. Have those academy sorts in Paris ever bin to the Dauphinée? They got any idea what the soil's like here?"

215

"I don't know whether they have or not, but I'm sure this isn't the only region of France with this type of soil. Why don't you try it? I might be able to get you some alfalfa seed," he glanced over at the man, "free."

Jules returned the sly look with a grin of his own. "Free?"

Alain raised open palms. "*Peut-être*. The agriculture people are eager to have someone try this out." They had reached the inn, now, and they found a table near the fire, which Alain hoped would stop his shivering soon. He ordered wine.

When they were settled, Alain continued his pitch. "Look, why don't we try a small field. Say big enough to feed that new calf of yours next spring when she gets old enough for grass. I'll..." he made the plunge, "I'll share the work with you for a year. All three crops. Then you'll see how it works."

The farmer regarded Alain's hands, soft and white compared to his own brown, hardened ones, the fingers curled to the shape of the plow and the hoe. Then he looked again at Alain's face.

"You're serious about this, aren't you?"

Alain was being offered an opening, a rare chance to slip a wedge into the solid wall of peasant prejudice. He dropped his hands from sight and concentrated on what he was about to say. "I have two reasons for wanting this. The first is local. I would love to see the people of this valley with better farms, more food, better homes, better clothes. If these new farming methods work – and they will – that will be the result."

"Charitable of you."

Alain knew the French peasant. Set in the ways of his ancestors and poorly educated perhaps, but not stupid. *A shrewd bargainer with a good eye for the advantage, both for himself and others.* He raised his hands, palms outwards, in a gesture of surrender. "New methods, new prosperity, people expanding their farms, buying land? It wouldn't hurt my business any, either."

Jules nodded, satisfied with motivation he could understand. "And what's your other reason?"

"*Pour la patrie.* Oh, that might sound emotional, but I would like to see France prosper. And France needs to produce her own food. We are in a time of great danger. All the crowns of Europe are watching us like hounds circling a stag, waiting for the slightest sign of weakness. There are armies at every border, waiting to attack."

"What'd ya say about armies?"

Alain looked over to the next table, where two other farmers were regarding him anxiously, their wine glasses forgotten in their hands. *Merde! This is how rumours start.* "I was talking in general about all the armies the other realms of Europe have at our borders. I was just saying how France has to be strong, to keep them at bay."

The shorter of the two men spoke up. "Aye, and that damned armya *emigré* nobles, sittin' there in Switzerland, waitin' for their chance to take back their land from us."

His friend waved a dismissive hand. "Ah, now don't start on that again, Jacques. What would ya have them do? Give up their loyalty ta the king and leave him ta be bullied about by them Paris ruffians?"

Alain wondered how he could steer the conversation back to farming, but his companion seemed interested in joining the other discussion. With a mental shrug, he reached for the bottle and filled their glasses again. *This might take longer than I thought.*

"I wonder whether we should be so worried about them. What if we attack first? Maybe we'd beat 'em all."

The other two looked at Jacques in astonishment. "Could we?"

The short farmer shrugged. "The enemy armies are fighting for nobles who continue to oppress them. We Frenchmen are fighting for our homes, for our freedom, for the Revolution. How many of those enemy soldiers wish they, too, could throw off the yoke of their aristocracy? I doubt if many of them 'ud fight too hard against us. 'Specially on French soil."

"But what if we lose?"

Jacques shrugged "Well, Jules, I guess we had better not lose. It 'ud mean the end of the Revolution, for sure. Back to working for the aristocrats. No, I figure we better get out and whip a few of 'em, and they'll leave us alone. The sooner we fight the better, says I."

Jules laughed bitterly. "I know why you want us to fight. You want us to lose, because then the king 'ud get all his power back."

The other man looked discomfited, but did not deny the charge.

Alain didn't want to offend anyone but he could not let this pass. "But Jacques, you have forgotten something. Those other kings won't be helping Louis for nothing. Sure, they want a king back in power, because even one free Frenchman is a threat to all of them. But if they were to beat us, they wouldn't quit until they had demanded concessions, territory and reparations. They wouldn't be happy until France was beaten down to be a second-rate power. If you think living under the *Anciene Regime* was hard, try living in a country impoverished and defeated in a war." He paused for a sip of wine, then waved the glass to make his point.

"Now, I don't disagree with you about the need for a king. You can't run a government without someone with the power to make decisions and see that they're carried out. The Assembly can make laws and set policy, but I don't see how they could run the country, especially if we had a war."

Heads nodded at this. "We need someone to make decisions."

The other farmer thumped his fist on the table. "Right! We had a decent harvest last year. Not great, but not bad. And do ya see the price of bread going down? No! And why not? Because speculators bought all the wheat and are holding onta it 'til the price goes up. We need someone ta stop that kinda thing." He sat back to let the innkeeper set another bottle of wine on the table. Alain's head was already spinning, but he couldn't very well refuse when the man refilled his glass.

Jacques became enthused. "There should be a limit set on the price of bread."

Alain waved a finger. "Wouldn't that mean a limit on the price you get for your grain?"

This stopped them, but not for long. "If it was a fair price and all the other costs were kept in control."

"If we got this war over with we could settle down and solve these problems pretty easy."

The taller man looked doubtful. "But do we have enough of an army?"

Jacques snorted. "Hah! There's enough riffraff in Paris ta make several armies. Put them fightin' someone useful for a change."

The others agreed to that. "*Oui.* They shouldn't be recruiting here. We need all our men ta run th' farms."

"You need more than that." Alain was pleased at the firmness of his voice, coming as it did from the fuzziness in his head.

"And what do we need, then?"

"We need our farms producing more for every hectare."

The two at the other table looked skeptical. "Hectare. That's that new measure a land, innit?"

Alain waved off the technicalities. "More crops per hectare and less work for the farmer to get them. How does that sound?"

Jacques gave a short laugh. "Sounds like the kinda dreams a lawyer's son 'ud imagine. Not me. What I earn, I make with my hands, wringin' it outa this rocky ground. I do my dreamin' at night when the work's done, if I get the chance."

"Oh, no, I'm not dreaming. You just watch Jules' upper pasture next year, hey Jules?"

The older farmer had been watching this exchange with the indulgent smile produced by several glasses of wine. "Huh? Sure. That's right, lads. You watch my upper pasture for the next coupla years. Extra crops, right, Alain?" He raised his glass, and Alain did the same, then the farmer emptied his at one swallow. Alain followed suit and nodded, hiding the burst of joy in his chest.

"*Mais oui*, extra crops. Year round! And guess what else?"

Alain joined the men as they leaned forward as if to receive some deep secret.

"No fallow land!" The farmer leaned back, watching the disbelief on his friends' faces. "That's right, you heard me. Crops year round, no fallow. And what's more..."

Alain suspected what was coming next and nudged the man's knee under the table, shooting him a warning glance. The free alfalfa seed was only a possibility, and not available to everyone.

Jules nodded with a conspiratorial wink. "You watch and wait, *mes amis*. You'll see." With that he heaved himself to his feet. Alain did likewise, surprised that he could stay there. The wine served at the inn was stronger than what he was used to at home. Especially on an empty stomach.

He reeled out the door, stumbled back in to square up his bill then returned outside. Jules was waiting for him.

"Well, lad, we gotta do it now, *n'est-ce pas*?"

"I guess we do."

The man laughed heartily. "It may be worth it to see you out there on the handles of a plow, come spring."

Alain raised a hand to his head. "Right now, I could handle anything with handles, as long as I could lean on them."

Jules laughed again and slapped him between the shoulder blades, a force almost too much for his wobbly legs to handle. "Go on home and tell your *Papa* that you're goin' to be a farmer this year. He'll appreciate that."

Alain looked up at the man. *Is he as drunk as he sounds?* His father would certainly relish the idea, but that was not what most of the locals would have expected. *I'd better remember who I'm dealing with, here. I might end up doing all the plowing.*

Then he started home.

The next morning, Alain slept in. To be more precise, he stayed in bed. His mother brought him a glass of water, all he could manage.

"You should be hungry, Alain. You didn't eat any supper last night." Her smile was all innocence.

He groaned.

"I'm sure you'll feel better later."

He seriously doubted if he would ever feel better, but had no energy to argue.

"I hope it was all in a good cause."

That stirred his brain. It had been in a good cause. He remembered vaguely that he and Jules had made a deal of some sort, but wasn't too sure what it was. He had been pleased at the time, however; he remembered that. Oh, well. He would remember later. Or Jules would remind him. Now he ought to work on Seigneur de Bardel. Maybe Angélique would help. He had a vague feeling that there was something wrong with that.

Not important. Whatever, he would see to it. If he lived through the morning. He drifted back into the sanctuary of sleep, away from the ache of his head, the beat of his blood in his brain, the foul taste in his mouth.

19. Declaration of War

April 20, 1792

Alain had many arguments on his side: the threat of war, the need of the Revolution to succeed, the new patriotism – not strong in rural France, but present to some degree – plus the general feeling in the whole nation that it was a time for change. All leaned in his favour. Now if he could only get this dratted ox to do the same.

"Haw there, you! Haw around there. Come on, turn, you foolish beast! *Merde!* To the left, the left! Whoa, not that way!" Alain dropped the reins and walked around to stand in front of the ox. "We aren't going home until sundown or we finish a good half of this field. Now, which will it be?"

Two placid brown eyes stared back at him. He somehow wasn't getting through. Sighing, he hauled the animal's head around and lined it up for the next furrow, then returned to his position at the plow handles. When he had started this job, he had expected trouble wrestling with the plow. He had no idea how difficult it was to get a simple ox to go where he wanted it. The farmers he had watched plowing never seemed to have any trouble with the animals.

He looked back over his handiwork. The rows weren't perfect, but there was a fair amount of dark soil turned over. At the rate he was going, it would be two days to finish. If he survived.

"All right, Bubu, let's try again. In a straight line, this time, please!" He flicked the whip, laying it inexpertly across the brown hide in front of him. The bullock snorted and moved forward with a distinct lack of enthusiasm.

The spring sun shone with surprising strength on his shoulders, and he raised his arm often to wipe the sweat out of his eyes. At the end of the next row he checked his hands. The old driving gloves his mother had insisted he wear had protected them. He remembered her amused expression as they argued.

"Alain, you won't prove anything by wearing your hands to rags. The fact that you have never done manual labour is not in question. It's enough that you're out there doing your share. Use the gloves."

He was glad now that he had given in.

Leaving the bullock dozing in the furrow, he walked over to the shade of a tree where he had left his bottle of water. There was someone sitting there in the dimness. As he came closer, his heart gave a lurch. It was Angélique. He hesitated, thinking of his dirty shirt, tousled hair and grimy face. Then he strode forward. *This is nothing to be ashamed of.*

She was sitting on a boulder, in immaculate dress as usual. The new styles suited her. He never had liked those huge silly hats and the hair all piled up. Her hair down around her face in curls gave her a softer look. He had known for a long time what pretty ankles she had, and now she could wear dresses that showed them off.

"Well, you're looking cool and comfortable today."

She smiled. "The opposite of yourself, I should say."

"Amazing what one will do for what one believes."

She frowned. "Your mother told me I'd find you here, but I'm still not sure why. She said you'd explain."

He grinned. "It's a matter of credibility. I can't expect these farmers to take advice from a lawyer's kid. I have to roll my sleeves up and dig in."

"Why do you need to give them advice?"

"It's part of my job. I'm supposed to be helping the farmers become more productive, to use new methods. Remember all those diagrams in the Encyclopedia? The government has gone farther than that. They have a bunch of experts writing pamphlets and giving lectures on how to improve the yield of our fields. My problem is to persuade these tradition-bound farmers to try some of the ideas. Hence the plow. Did you know that the bovine species was created to be an example of obstinacy to the rest of the world?"

She looked over at Bubu, lazing in the sun. "What do you mean?"

"Look at those rows. Do you see how they curve? When we come close to this end of the field, he assumes its time to go home and he starts to turn right. I've had to fight him around every time. But we're getting there. Either I'm learning to use the whip more effectively or my stubbornness is paying off. When did you get back?"

She tossed her head. "I got here the night before last. The house was in a terrible state, and I spent yesterday getting everything organized. *Papa* should keep a sharper eye on the servants. They run the place any way they like if you leave them to themselves."

Alain was nettled. "Why wouldn't they? If no one tells them any different, it would seem the natural thing to do."

Her head cocked to one side. "That's an interesting way of looking at it. I suppose you're right." She stood up. "But I didn't come here to keep you from your work with my little problems. I came to invite you for a visit at lunch tomorrow."

His heart leaped, but then she continued.

"I'm having Aimée and Edmond over as well, and Jimmy, of course. I thought it would be nice to get us all together again."

"That's great. Could you make it the next day?" He nodded his head in the direction of the field. "Unless old Bubu gets extra co-operative, I won't be finished before sundown tomorrow, and the seed has to go in as soon as possible."

She smiled. "Ah, the seasonal concerns of the land. This is impressive, Alain. I hope the farmers appreciate what you're doing for them."

"Jules does. The others will wait until they see the results. Some day after I'm dead they'll raise a statue."

She stood, the skirt of her dress swirling in an eddy of colour around her legs. "I'm sure they will. The day after tomorrow it is, then, at lunch time?"

She held out her hand, then her cheek for him to kiss – a friendly but cool gesture – and then turned and walked away, raising her parasol as she strode out into the sunshine.

He watched her go, a bitter taste in his mouth. So that was how it was going to be. All friends together, himself no different from the rest. He turned to his plow. Well, he had lived through this before. It was disappointing to be set back so far, but what could he do but accept it? *At least she seemed impressed at my work.* He wrenched the plow around and laid a firm stroke of the whip across the bullock's hide.

"All right, you beast. *Allons y!* This would not be a good time to develop a mind of your own. Now move!"

To his surprise, the animal did. Maybe it was getting the idea.

20. The Rat Scuttles Off

June, 1792

"Why do you keep feeding him? He's a barn cat. He'll never be tame."

Alain did not look at Angélique, but kept his hand steady, the food lying across his palm. The big cat slid forward, lifted the meat with his teeth and retreated to gobble it down.

"I'm practising."

"Practising for what?"

"Future romances."

She frowned. "I hope there isn't some kind of message for me in there. If there is, you might not live to regret it."

He shrugged. "I've given up trying to insult you by mistake. I've decided it's much more fun to plan it all ahead of time. That way, at least I can enjoy my success."

He looked up from his concentration on the cat. She was glaring at him with narrowed eyes.

Well, that got her attention. He smiled sweetly. *Now what do I do with it? Great planning, Alain.*

Their game was interrupted by the patter of feet. Edmond trotted around the corner of the *chateau,* his eyes alight.

"They've sent for volunteers from the National Guard to come to Paris."

Alain pulled his hand back from Foncé. At his sudden movement the cat jerked away, but he ignored it.

Angélique, too, looked interested. "How did you hear that, Edmond?"

The boy grinned. "Easy. I ran an errand to Serres this morning, and a mob of them came through. That Mireur fella brought five hundred all the way from Marseille. An unruly lot. The officers spent the night in Thiebeaud's Inn and sang that song of theirs so many times the innkeeper finally gave them a free round of ale if only they'd stop. A good thing the local Guard in Serres is a responsible bunch and kept them out of trouble. They're staying a couple of days to recruit, then moving on north."

"Are you joining?" Angélique smiled across from the vegetables she was weeding.

Not something she wouldn't have considered doing three years ago. A step forward, I think.

Edmond gave the question thorough consideration before answering with a shake of his head. "I wouldn't join the Guard. I would do better in an Engineering regiment. Or Artillery. I'd like to learn to sight in a cannon."

Angélique straightened, a look of horror on her face. "I was joking, Edmond. I didn't mean you should go!"

Alain grinned. "Don't worry. He's too young. Unless he wants to be a drummer."

"Oh. Well, that's a relief. Don't give me a scare like that, Edmond."

They were interrupted by a knock at the garden gate. It was Aubin, who bowed to Angélique and asked if he could speak with her. Alain controlled his smile. Ever since the Night of the Bonfires, the foresters had treated Angélique with respect. Even the depredations of the Rat had not changed it. The Rat! Alain noticed that the forester looked very serious. *What's he done now?*

"He's gone, Mlle. Angélique."

"Gone where?"

"Gone to Paris, if you can believe him, Mademoiselle."

Angélique and Alain traded glances.

"He was headed there in the first place..."

"And the National Guard from Marseille passed through."

"That's right, Mademoiselle. Somehow he heard they were in Serres, and he was gone."

Angélique's eyes narrowed. "You mean he just took off?"

The man grinned. "No, Mademoiselle. We might have made some progress with his manners. He came to me and said he was going. Easy to be polite, since there was nothing I could do to stop him. But he asked me, very earnestly, to tell you that this was his chance, and he had to go. He said you would understand."

Angélique smiled as well. "I suppose I do. It's too bad, though. We're going to miss him."

"Us too. He sure kept things lively up there."

Alain snapped his fingers. "Speaking of missing things, what did he take with him?"

Aubin's brow wrinkled. "Ah. It doesn't seem like he took anything that belonged to any of us. Only goods from the *seigneury*. Food, blankets and the like. You don't mind do you, Mademoiselle?"

"Of course not. We can't have him going off poorly equipped."

Edmond jumped to his feet. "What if he doesn't come back?"

Angélique looked at him in surprise. Then she smiled. "Oh, I'm sure he will. He's off for adventure. This is the one place in the world he's been treated well. I'll bet he finds life in the slums of Paris isn't as good as his memory of his life in Marseille. He'll be back."

Edmond nodded, satisfied. Alain was interested in Edmond's reaction. *I knew the two of them formed an attachment. I shouldn't be surprised at its strength. They have similar minds.*

"Is there anything more I can do, Mademoiselle?"

Alain watched Angélique turn on the power of her smile. "No, Aubin, you have done more than I ever hoped you could."

"Thank you, Mademoiselle."

"Is there anything my father should be told about the forests?"

He considered. "Nothing unusual, Mademoiselle. Do you remember Pierre Tolin having a problem last fall keeping his pigs under control? I told him that boy of his is too young to take care of three big hogs, but he wouldn't listen. Next thing you know, they're out in the oaks, picking up the nuts a week before they're supposed to be in there. We helped him get them home. Two days later, they're back in the forest again. Pierre made like he was upset, but I doubt if he minded too much. I told him if he let them loose again before the proper day they wouldn't be allowed in during the season. Well, that seemed to make a difference, and he toed the line all winter. At least I think he did. But now I see him and his son up in the brush under Revuaire. They said they was out looking for a stray pig, but we've heard that too many times. I bet they was going to steal some extra wood over their allotment."

Angélique shook her head. "There's always somebody who wants more than his share. We'll have to keep an eye on him."

"That's what I thought. Jimmy would have been useful. One of his specialties, watching people." He grinned. "Don't worry, Mademoiselle. We'll take care of M. Tolin. I told him he steps out of line again, I'll report him. Is that all right?"

"It should be, Aubin. It's not fair to everyone else."

The forester nodded, satisfied. "I'll be on about my work, then."

"Just let us know if you hear about Jimmy."

Aubin bowed and went out the gate, his back straight and his stride long and free.

Angélique smiled. "I'm glad Jimmy is at least learning manners."

Edmond made an attempt to be cheerful. "They're not likely to last, travelling with that bunch. More likely to pick up some of his old tricks."

"If he's going to Paris he might need them."

They all nodded soberly. It was difficult to imagine the life the boy would lead, there in the danger and the squalor of the capital. *At least he is trained for it.*

"Aimée will be upset."

"She's attached to Jimmy, isn't she?" Angélique paused. "I'll tell you what, Edmond. I'll go down and break it to her. She would prefer that."

He nodded. "That'll help some. Thanks."

"I'll go now. We can drop Alain off at his office. Time he got back to work anyway."

Alalin smiled and shrugged. She was right, as usual, although it hurt to be sent off to work when the rest of them were getting together. This was how Aimée must feel sometimes, tied to the *boulangerie* as she was.

* * *

"Alain, you've got to see this new journal from Paris!"

Alain looked up in surprise as the twins stormed into his office. "What is it, you two? Another political diatribe from Marat?"

"No, this one is facts..."

"At least it says it has the facts..."

"You know how they are. It might be true."

They were in fine form, their voices blending into a single line of thought.

"Well, let's see this work of art." He held out his hand. "Where did you get it?"

"A pedlar came through this morning, headed south. They're all over the place."

Alain glanced down the sheet. It was one of the many political pamphlets churned out by the thousands in Paris and the other large cities. Short, poor quality paper and ink, but sometimes important information.

But he had no chance to read it, because again the door banged open, this time to admit Angélique. She, too, was excited, but not indignant as the twins were.

"Have you seen what...Oh." She paused, looking from the paper she held in her outstretched hand to the paper in his. "You've seen it."

"Well, I was just starting. Why don't you all have a chair, and I'll glance over whatever has you all so fired up. What did they do? Execute the king?"

"No, they made a complete fool of him." There was triumph in her face.

Alain raised his eyebrows. "We all know how easy that is. Better if I read first and we talked after."

They all sat and shifted around until he finished. He tossed the paper on his desk and snorted. "Well, that's true to form, isn't it? He lets them invade his private rooms in the Tuileries, scare his family half to death..."

"And lets them put one of those stupid Phrygian hats on his head."

"And they sing that song they're calling 'The Marseilleise'."

Angélilque grinned. "I wonder if Jimmy was there!"

"It was his bunch that was singing it." Alain considered. "How did they get it named after them? It was written for the Army of the Rhine."

Edmond smiled. "The Rat probably stole that, too."

"But can you imagine?" Aimée was not in a joking mood. "They let that mob right into the Tuileries. Where were the soldiers?"

"Better question, which side were the soldiers on?"

"But he has his Swiss guards. And there are always a lot of Royalists still hanging around the court. Not all the nobles have left the country."

Alain looked at the pamphlet again. "It doesn't say much, but it sounds as if he either gave orders not to stop them, or didn't give definite enough orders, and the Guard couldn't act."

"Or gave no orders at all." Edmond snorted. "What's wrong with the man?"

Aimée's back straightened. "That's the king you're talking about, Edmond. Show respect."

"Hah! I figure he has to earn it!"

The girl glanced at her brother, but thought before she answered. "I suppose you're right. The day of respecting someone because of the accident of his birth is past isn't it?" She looked over to Angélique to make sure she hadn't hurt any feelings.

Angélique nodded. "Putting aside the basic problems with the *Ancien Régime,* it's the king's indecisive personality that has got us into all this. Not that it's such a bad thing. We needed those changes. But if he hadn't waffled around until it was too late, we wouldn't be in the fix we are now. We let him have his chance, and now he has destroyed it. I hope the new government coming in takes a lesson from this. I'm willing to give them the opportunity, but if they don't come up to standard, they won't last. There are alternatives."

Alain glanced at her flushed face and aggressive posture. *Now, what did she mean by that? I'm afraid I know.* He wanted to challenge her, but couldn't bear what might happen next. For once, he let it be.

21. The Convention

August 20, 1792

It was an angry group of men that met in the lawyer's office. Angry and afraid, Alain could tell. *Well, they have a right to be. The Jacobins have murdered the King of France.*

"What's going on, M. Jouvent? What are they doing, up there in Paris?"

Alain's father shook his head. "Hard to say, M. Cloutier. Killing people, I suppose. It's what they seem to understand."

"Oh, come on, M. Jouvent. It can't be all that bad. Surely there are good men in the Assembly who can keep those rabble rousers in line."

"I hope you're right, M. Sarrobert. But I have little faith in anyone being in proper control. Several have tried, but each one in turn has lost favour with the mobs. Of course they did. They couldn't give the mob what they wanted: free food and drink and the right to do anything they chose. Look at Lafayette – hero of the American Revolution, head of the National Guard, now fled to the army of the *emigrés*."

"But who is in power, François? Who is running the country? Is the Assembly still in charge, or is it this Convention?" Charles de Bardel was at the meeting, but not as the master this time. There was no pretense that he had any more ability to take charge than the rest of the local men. *It is my father they come to, my father who gives them the best answers they will get.*

"It's all up in the air, as far as I can see. This new government they call the National Convention will be different from what we had before, because they will try to function without a king. I suppose the king himself isn't essential to the running of the country, but there has to be someone. You can't do something like that by committee. It doesn't work. All arguing and nothing done. There will be yet another Constitution to make up the rules by which they will govern.

"The most powerful group of men at the moment call themselves the Girondins because their leaders come from the Gironde area. They are sane men, many of them from the provinces, like us.

Against them are the Jacobins, the radicals. They are the ones who demanded that the king be arrested, and they agitated the most for his execution. Their power comes from Paris, from the mobs of *sans coulottes*, egged on by Marat's wild writings and Robespierre's speeches, more frightening because they are so cruel, yet so logical. They call him *L'Incorruptible,* but his radicalism and his oratory worry me more than Marat and his ravings."

"So we have another government, another Constitution? How can the country continue to function and fight a war if things keep changing?"

"Is this government likely to be more radical than the last?"

"Will this government manage to keep power? What happens if they fall? Who will be next? These Jacobins?"

Jouvent held up his hands. "Please, my friends. These are the questions everyone is asking, all over France. I have no answers for you. I wish I did." Alain watched in dismay as his father's face lost its animation as the old hopeless look returned. "More precisely, I have answers to those questions, but they aren't the ones you want to hear. I am deeply afraid for our *patrie."*

There seemed nothing to say after this, and, one by one, the local merchants said their goodbyes and trooped out. At last only Charles de Bardel remained. The three sat in silence for a while.

"I don't understand, François. Why can't we just run the country, all pull together to get us out of this mess? Of course there are hard times, but I'm sure that if we shared everything around, we could exist through the odd bad winter without people starving to death. I have always done my part. I admit there have been inequities, and I am willing to change things to make them more even. Why can't we all do that?"

"I wish it could work that way, but I'm afraid there are too many greedy people who want to take their own advantage at the expense of others."

"That's not entirely fair, *Papa*."

The two men turned to look at Alain.

"I'm sure some are of that sort, but most of us would like to cooperate. We're just afraid that if we give up something the others won't, and they will laugh at us for being soft while they take our share plus their own. Also, other people have a different idea of what is fair, and who is to say they don't have a right to their ideas?"

His father passed his hand over his forehead wearily. "You could be right, *mon fils*, but the effect is the same. And then the ones who want power take advantage of the suffering of the poor to gain their support. So we get what happened at the Tuileries." He paused. "Those poor soldiers."

De Bardel seemed equally depressed. "I don't understand, Jouvent. If what you say is true and those people seize power, what is likely to happen?"

"Who knows? The only thing you can be sure of is that two types of people will be in danger: those they see as a threat, and those who have something they want."

"Like me."

"And me."

"And that means our families, too."

"These are men with hard hearts, Charles. They will not let any sentiment get in their way."

"That's good, then." He looked up to see the two Jouvents staring at him. "No, I mean what I did was good. I sent Marie-François away. She couldn't stand it – all the hatred and uncertainty. You may have found her hard, Alain, and she is very strong in some ways, but that is one thing she cannot stand. So she is in Switzerland. Safe."

"And Angélique?"

The man smiled, a mixture of sadness and pride. "Angélique has her own strength. She is a grown woman, now, and she will do as she pleases."

Alain breathed a sigh of relief, but his father's next words choked it off.

"This puts both you and Angélique in a delicate position."

"What do you mean?"

"If your wife is classed as an *emigré*, then her whole family is suspect. No matter how loyal to France you are, it places you in a difficult legal situation. There are things you can do, legal steps you can take to protect yourself, but I warn you, if the more radical parties take power, they will not allow any legal niceties to get in their way."

The *seigneur* looked frightened. "But what can I do?"

"You could leave as well."

"No. I have my land and my people to look after. I must stay." They were brave words, spoken with an uncomprehending stubbornness.

"I will come and look over your legal situation tomorrow. As I said, you can take steps to lessen the impact. Of course, those steps will reflect the old Constitution. We will have to deal with any new laws that come up. But we will do what we can."

They rose, and de Bardel took his leave. Alain stood in the doorway, watching him walk down the street, shoulders drooping, head low. "He just doesn't understand, does he?"

His father shook his head. "He is a good man, Alain, an intelligent man. But he is the product of too many years of the *Ancien Régime*. He cannot comprehend what is happening. In his life, a man's honour was almost as important as the size of his land. Now he is dealing with men who have no sense of honour, at least honour as he sees it. And you're right. He doesn't understand. He would be better to take Angélique and follow his wife. Things could soon get very difficult for people like him."

Alain shook his head. "Angélique wouldn't go."

His father eyed him with a frown. "What do you mean, she wouldn't go? Of course she would. She wouldn't want to and she would put up a terrible fuss, but she would go in the end."

Alain smiled sadly. "This is a situation that you don't understand. The freedom the Revolution has brought has made a great change in Angélique. Her father said more than he meant when he said she would do as she pleased. She is her own woman, and no one will ever tell her what to do."

"Worse for her."

"Perhaps, but it is marvellous, as well. She is being tempered by this upheaval, and is becoming something fine, strong and flexible."

"If she survives."

Alain sobered. "I am doing my best to make sure that happens."

His father nodded. "She will need the help."

Alain gave a crooked grin. "Whether she wants it or not?"

"If you can find a way to give it to her."

22. Slaughter

September, 1792

"It must be nice to have your father home again."

Angélique was making polite conversation to keep Alain entertained while he waited to discuss some legal business with her father. He knew it, but it sounded more like the old Angélique and he took advantage of it. His horror at what his father had told him recently, and his fear of what that might mean for France and for Angélique, were wearing him down. *Maybe just a bit of sympathy...?*

He sighed. "He has finished his legal work in Grenoble and returned, but nothing has changed. He's still not really home."

Her face filled with concern. "Alain, you haven't said anything before. What's wrong?"

"He left here years ago, full of hope, full of determination. He was going to do something, to make a difference to *la patrie*, to the world. Well, you have to admit he tried. They all tried. And they failed. I suppose certain people take that kind of failure harder than others. *Papa* is trying to be cheerful, and it's great that he's home, but he hasn't been the same all year. He's so unhappy, I can tell. He just sits there sometimes, and I'm sure he's back in Paris, wondering what he could have done to help it go better. Then he tries to be cheerful, to be part of the family, but it doesn't work, and that's worse, somehow."

Angélique laid her hand on his arm. *How long has it been since she had made that old familiar gesture?*

"It must be the change. He lived that dream for years. He was in the middle of great things, and now he's out of it. It's bound to bother him. He'll be back to normal soon. Besides which, I can't see why you call that failure. After all, they made great progress. They wrote a new Constitution, they formed a new form of government, they got rid of the king..."

Alain shook his head. "You still don't understand. They didn't want to get rid of the king. A government needs a head, someone with authority. They needed a king. You may have a low opinion of the system they made up, but it would have worked. Now, the government will be taken over by a bunch of those Jacobin hotheads. You haven't yet figured out how dangerous that is. Especially for you, a former aristocrat with an *émigré* parent. These people want to destroy everything my father has created, and they are willing to kill anyone who gets in their way. If that means nothing to you, consider where their power comes from. It comes from the Paris mob, who are a bunch of bloodthirsty savages. And it comes from the National Guard, many of whom aren't much different, only better armed. You worry that Reynaud de Gonillons might cause trouble here. Well, he's a sheep in wolf's clothing, compared to many of them."

Angélique sat there, unperturbed. Then she stood. "You're just upset, Alain, because of your father's sorrow. I'm sure you are overstating things. Certainly the Paris mob is an unpleasant group of people, but you must understand how they feel, being poor and helpless..."

"Forget it. We've been having this argument for years, and we just keep going over the same ground. I didn't push it before because I might have been out of touch with what was happening."

"But now?"

"Now I have read the journals. I have talked with my father. A lot. The things he has told me make my blood run cold. You have no idea what kind of people you are dealing with. You have never in your life seen the kind of person who will now be running France. And you will not understand until you hear the jail door slam how mistaken you have been. Nothing I can say will persuade you."

He tried to stay cool, because that was one way to get through to her, but as he heard his own words, and realized the truth in them, the old frustration boiled. "Nothing I can do will save you from this stupidity. Yes, stupidity! And I don't care if you squint up your eyes and get ready to say something horrible. If you are one of these people, then you're not the person I thought you were, and I don't care if you don't love me!"

He had said it, and it was too late. He had no choice but to continue. "I'm going to give you one last chance. I'm going to do something that I shouldn't, but this is it. One last chance."

He strode to the door and threw it open. "Come with me. You're going to talk to my father."

They walked along the street in silence. After a while, he cooled down enough to realize that the length of his stride was causing her difficulty, and he slowed. She had glanced over at him several times, but he ignored it. *This is out of my hands, now.* They entered the office.

François Jouvent was sitting at his desk, a pen in his hand, but his eyes were unfocussed. He came back to the present with a start as Alain and Angélique came in. A mechanical smile touched his face as he stood to take her hand.

"Why Angélique, how nice to see you. How is your father doing? I must get around to visit..." Then the strain on their faces got through to him.

"Is something wrong?"

"Yes, *Papa*, and you can help. I want you to tell Angélique what you told me last night."

Real concern woke in the elder Jouvent's face. "Alain..."

"Angélique is missing something, *Papa*. Angélique thinks that the Paris mob needs sympathy and understanding. Angélique thinks executing the king last month was a good idea. Angélique thinks that the Jacobins are a nice group of people, with all the right ideas!"

His father sat, shaking his head. "No, Alain. I'm sorry I told you. I just needed to get it off my chest. Her father would never forgive me."

"*Papa*, please. You worry that you failed in Paris, failed our *patrie*. Try to help someone, just one person, here at home. At least you can do that."

Then he received help from an unexpected quarter. Angélique stepped forward. "Please, M. Jouvent. I am old enough to decide what I will and will not be told. Do not hold back because I am a woman. What is this terrible thing from which I must be shielded? If Alain considers it is so important, then I owe it to him to listen." She pulled up a chair and sat, upright and firm. "Tell me."

"And tell me too, my dear. It is time you stopped trying to protect us from the realities of life. We will have to face them as well." Alain's mother stepped down the last flight of stairs from their apartment and sat, too, staring at her husband.

François shook his head, and Alain was concerned at how beaten he looked. "I don't have the energy to argue with you. I don't want to go through it again, but if you insist, then listen. Maybe you are right. If more people could see what was coming, maybe they could stop it."

He fixed Angélique with a shadow of his old, firm stare. "And if there is a young lady of the aristocracy who sees the Jacobins as the right people to govern France, she should listen very closely. You have already heard about the massacre of the Swiss Guard at the Tuileries?"

They nodded.

M. Jouvent continued. "I would prefer not to tell you what has happened since then, but perhaps it is better that you hear the truth, because the rumours will reach here from Grenoble as soon as I did.

"On top of all our other problems, we are at war. And the war has not been going well. The Prussians are attacking

Verdun, which is only 30 *lieu* from Paris, well inside the borders of France.

"And then the good people of Paris and a number of the National Guard decided that there were traitors who were undermining our efforts to win the war. They decided the offenders were in the prisons. Or something like that. Who knows how these people's minds work, if they work at all." He passed his hand over his forehead.

"In any case, they decided that it would be best for France if these people were out of the way. So they broke into the prisons and killed them all. Yes, all. The pickpockets, the debtors, the political prisoners. They set up a 'tribunal' and pretended to give each one a trial. Then they murdered them. Not with Dr. Guillotine's humane contraption. No, they shot them or stabbed them or hacked them to death with their swords. In places there was blood running in the gutters. That is not an exaggeration. The man I spoke to was there, and saw it." He glanced at each of them, as if to gauge the effect of his words on his audience. Satisfied, he continued.

Alain could see the old fire returning to his father's eyes, the old eager line returning to his body. With a spurt of joy, he watched his father lean forward, moving into his topic as he used to do when addressing a packed courtroom.

"And you think that is terrible, don't you? But deep down inside you can excuse it, because those men were criminals and at least some were traitors." He threw up his hands, palms out. "And you might excuse it, if it had stopped there."

He leaned forward, his voice dropping. "But it didn't stop there. Someone decided that the church was also the enemy of France. So they went to the convents and the churches. They set up their 'tribunals' in the courtyards, went through their mockery of trials and executed the monks, priests and nuns right there in their own sanctuaries. Again, the gutters ran with blood. The blood of innocents."

There was a shocked silence. Alain looked at his mother, whose face was pale. *This must be the first she has heard of these atrocities.* He looked at Angélique. She, too was pale, and he saw her swallow twice, as a person does trying not to be sick. Finally she spoke, her voice shaky and tight.

"Are you sure this happened, M. Jouvent?" It was a plea. *Say it isn't so; shield me from this horror.*

He looked straight at her. "I told you, I spoke directly to the man in Grenoble who was there. Do you want names? Jean-Antoine Savines." He looked over to his wife. "You remember him, Catherine. We spent time with him that summer in Embrun." Alain's mother nodded, and Angélique spoke again, softly.

"I met him once, in Grenoble. A nice, jolly sort of man, for a priest? I like him."

"Liked him. Past tense. He had the bad luck to be in Paris on September second, visiting at the Convent des Carmes."

"And they...?"

"Those are the people in charge in Paris now, Angélique."

Alain could see her fighting for air, struggling to find some reason, some sanity. "But...those are a bunch of street toughs and criminals. What have they to do with the Assembly?"

"Those street toughs and criminals are the Paris mob you have heard about. That mob is the power behind Marat and Robespierre. The Jacobins condone such activity because it increases their power."

She stared at him, horrified. "How can that increase their power?"

Alain's father passed a hand over his eyes. "Fear. The mob is a powerful tool because it is almost uncontrollable. It is a wild and senseless beast that the Jacobins can loose on their enemies. The fact that it destroys innocent people in passing means nothing to them. So everyone fears them, because any who resist will become victims of the *sans-culottes*. Power and fear." He shook his head. "There is worse to come."

243

He raised his head to look at them. "Yes, worse. The men in power now, the Girondins, are a sensible group of men. I know, Angélique, that some say they want to create a new 'aristocracy of the rich,' and that is partly true, but at least they are reasonable rulers. They will uphold the principles of the Revolution: *liberté, egalité, fraternité*. But they will lose."

"How?"

"They cannot cope with the situation that our country has been forced into, because there is nobody to concentrate on the running of the country. There needs to be an executive to make decisions, to keep the wheels turning. With the king gone, there is no one. The wars, the hunger, the inflation will continue. The people will become dissatisfied and look for easier answers. And they will find them. Oh, yes, Marat will give them the easy answers. Robespierre will show them leadership of the sort they demand. And then the beast will be turned loose in the streets of Paris and in the cities and towns of France."

For a long while, no one spoke.

Then Angélique got to her feet, slowly, as if in a dream. "I...I should go home, now."

Alain and his father rose too. The older man had come out of his fervour and he looked at Angélique with concern. "Are you feeling well? I'm sure Alain will see you home."

Her head came up; she straightened her shoulders, gave him a wan smile. "Oh, I'm all right. I just have some thinking to do."

Alain opened the door for her, but before going out he turned back. Wordlessly, he put an arm around his father's shoulders and squeezed. A weary smile crossed the older man's face.

Then Alain returned to his job of seeing Angélique home. As they walked, his concern grew. He knew her, knew her moods. He had never seen her like this. She walked listlessly, her eyes focused on nothing. *This is not only the horror of the bloodshed. She is not that delicate. This goes deeper.*

It wasn't hard to figure out, once he put his mind to it, watching her meander along the street. He had finally broken the wall of obstinacy that surrounded her. *But what will replace it?* It was strange that Angélique, so strong and forceful, had no confidence in herself. *She needs something outside herself to follow, and now she has lost it.*

"I wish I was a man."

That brought him out of his thoughts. "You what?"

She shook her head. "Oh, I don't want to be a man, not like that. What I mean, is, I want to have the options that a man has. I feel so useless!"

"What options?"

"Alain, how can I prove that I'm loyal? How can I do something for my country? If I was a man, I could go and fight."

He tried to lighten her mood. "Well, you could. You saw that pamphlet about Théroigne de Méricourt's Regiment of Amazons. If you wanted to fight, you could join them."

"Don't be silly. That regiment of women will never happen, and if it did I wouldn't join. I'm not a soldier. That was just an example."

"Should I join the army?" It was a question he had been pondering himself.

"Do you want to?"

He shrugged. "Not especially. But I want to do my best for my country."

"You should stay here and do what you are doing. Who would continue your work with the farmers if you leave?"

The thought came to him. "You could, I suppose."

"Me? You must be joking. Me behind a plow?"

"You wouldn't have to. You could persuade them much easier than I can. Say, why don't you come and help me anyway? I could use a persuasive voice from time to time."

"I might. But it's not something I'm very interested in."
They walked in silence a while. "I wish Nana was still here."

"So do I, but what help could she give you?"

"Someone to talk to. I always talked to her before."

"Talk to me."

"No, Alain. You have too much stake in things. You don't give me good advice or listen to me. You only tell me things that will be good for you, if I do them."

That stung. "Angélique, I want you to be happy. I'm not being selfish!"

She sighed, then stuck her hand through his arm. "I suppose you don't see it that way. Some day I may thank you for this, but I feel like I've been beaten around today, and when I look at the other end of the stick, who do I see?"

"Me."

"You see why you're not the right person to talk to."

"Then talk to Aimée. She's got a level head on her shoulders."

"I couldn't tell her how I feel. Sometimes when I see her so content, so sure of what she wants, and then she looks up to me as if I were someone special and I just want to crawl away and hide. If she understood how much I envy her, how much happier she is…"

Angélique, jealous of Aimée? This was enough to render Alain speechless until they reached the *chateau*. She turned to him, releasing his arm. "I'll consider your offer." It took him a moment to remember what she meant. "If you say I can help you, I could try." She shrugged her shoulders. "I can't see how, but I'll do my best." She tried to smile up at him, and the pain in that look was heartbreaking.

She mounted the steps and wandered inside, leaving him to stumble home alone.

* * *

In the following weeks Angélique began to ride with him when he went about his business, chatting with the farm women, asking them her usual questions and reporting their answers to him. It made a difference to his success, but it did not help his unease over her condition. He tried to talk to her about it several times, but it was like fighting smoke. She was there, she went through the motions, but she didn't seem to take notice. Alain began to wonder whether he would rather she believed in something, anything, rather than wandering around like a ghost. *The problem is, what will she choose to believe in?*

Angélique was in a dangerous position. The loss of her revolutionary beliefs had left a void in her life. *She is like someone who has taken a potion and will fall in love with whoever she sees first. My job is to find her a cause that she can become involved with. The problem is that she doesn't see my work as important enough for her energies. She wants something grander, more suited to her style. And I cannot provide that. No matter how I try.*

His mother gave him the only advice that meant anything.

"She is grieving, Alain. She has lost something dear to her, and it has left a void. At the moment, working with you is all she has. Did you know how good she would be at talking to the farm wives?"

He smiled. "Oh, yes. When I talk to the men and she persuades the women we get much better results. She's always good at talking to everyone." His face fell. "Except me. We don't discuss anything important anymore. Just work."

Catherine shrugged. "Count yourself lucky. She's talking to you.

23. Swiss Guard

September, 1792

At first Alain thought it was starting to rain. Then, as he woke further, he realized that the rattling against the glass was too loud and infrequent to be from natural causes. Getting out of bed, he edged the window open.

It was a fine night, a welcome coolness after the heat of summer. Yesterday's shower had cleared the air. There was no moon, but the empty sky and bright stars gave a touch of visibility.

Nothing.

A bird called, but that was all. He peered around and was about to close the window when the bird called again, more urgently. He looked out again and a third call focused his attention. *I know that sound.*

He caught a vague grey shape in the shadows, a pale blob of face looking up at him. Then came the cry of a nighthawk, the old warning signal. He waved, eased the window shut and dressed as quickly as he could in the dark.

Outside the house, he waited until the original call came again. He followed out into the back street.

"Edmond?"

"Can you come out?"

"I am out. What's going on? It's the middle of the night!"

"The Rat is back. At the old house by the bridge."

"Is he in trouble?"

"Yes and no. You go there. I'm going to get Angélique."

"Wait a minute. You can't just go throwing gravel at the windows of the *chateau*! Besides, she doesn't go to the bridge. We agreed."

"That was years ago. She's not an aristocrat now, is she? Besides," a dim grin in the starlight, "it's the middle of the night. See you at the bridge."

And Edmond was gone. There was nothing Alain could do but follow his instructions.

He slipped along to the old house, staying in the shadows as much as he could, but worried that he would stumble over something and make a noise. When he got there, he had to get up his nerve to move into the utter blackness. He remembered where the hole in the wall was, but the bushes inside the house had grown and their thorns had flourished as well. Hot and scratched, he was impatient enough when he reached the hole to drop down, not caring what was at the bottom.

The little room under the bridge was as he remembered it, including Aimée, bending over a low fire, and the Rat hovering beside her. What was different was the long figure that heaved itself up on the bed, and the flash of firelight on the blade of a sword.

The sudden movement made the two at the fire look up, and Aimée darted over to the bed. "It's all right, Hans. This is Alain. I told you about him."

The man half-groaned an agreement and allowed himself to be eased back. Alain moved forward slowly. "Who is it?"

"A friend of Jimmy's. He's in trouble, and Jimmy brought him here to us. We've got to help him, Alain. He's sick, too, with a fever."

"What kind of friend? What kind of trouble?"

Jimmy swaggered forward. The cheerful face Alain remembered topped a taller body, but the slimness was still there. "This is Hans. He's a soldier who ended up on the wrong side. He wants to get back to Switzerland, that's all."

"You want us to help an enemy soldier escape?"

"No, not an enemy. He's Swiss."

It all came together. "The king's Swiss Guard."

Jimmy grinned again. "Right on the mark, Alain." He turned to the man on the bed. "I told you he was smart."

The man raised his head and shoulders to look at Alain in the dim light. Then he nodded. "I am very pleased to meet you, M. Jouvent. I'm sorry to impose on you like this, but I'm not too steady on my feet and it's still a long way to the border." He looked to the Rat. "Has your friend gone to get more help? Is that safe?" He lay back, exhausted by this simple movement.

"*Oui.* Just one more. She's coming now."

Soon Alain, too could hear hesitant footsteps in the tunnel, and then Angélique entered. She had covered herself in a dark cloak, and she tossed the hood back as she straightened up, her hair fanning out in the firelight. There was an indrawn breath from the man on the bed, and the Swiss struggled to a sitting position.

"Perhaps I've died, and angel has come to take me to heaven?"

Alain felt a stab of pain in his breast. Angélique just smiled and held out her hand in a straightforward manner. "Sorry to disappoint you, sir. I hope it will be many years before I gain that status."

"Oh, I hope so, too." The man took her hand and brought it to his lips, and Angélique nodded decorously in response. But the effort was too much, and he fell back, his breath coming in gasps.

Angélique knelt beside him, her palm on his forehead. "He's burning up. Have you water?"

Aimée handed over a jug, and Angélique lifted the sick man's head. "Come on, now, you must be thirsty. Take a swallow at least."

The man drank, then drank again. When he signalled that he was finished, she laid his head down and gathered the rags around him. He lay back, allowing the two girls to fuss over him. When they were satisfied, they both sat back on their heels, and he looked up at them, grinning weakly.

"That's enough to make a man want to stay sick. Thank you."

Watching this from the other side of the room out of the way, Alain had a chance to assess this newcomer. He was about twenty or older. He seemed tall – although his position lying on the bed made it hard to tell – with considerable bulk around the shoulders. He was dressed in rags, but from the cut of his hair and the shape of his hands, Alain suspected that this was no mere soldier. And even the common soldiers of the Swiss Guard were an elite group. The man's cheerful attempts at gallantry in spite of his state of exhaustion grated on Alain, though it was petty of him. *How could I begrudge this man the attention after all that must have happened to him*? Still, it had bothered him to see how easily and naturally Angélique had accepted the kiss on her hand.

He laughed bitterly, deep inside. *I can imagine me trying something like that. She would look surprised and ask me why I was acting so silly.*

The Swiss swivelled his head to regard the small group, then at the Rat. "So this is your help?"

Jimmy's chest swelled, and Alain remembered fondly the peacock pride.

"I thought you said you had powerful friends. Now, I'm sure these are very nice people, these friends of yours, but how can they help me?"

Alain grinned to himself, watching as Angélique's back stiffened and Jimmy transformed from proud peacock to bantam rooster.

"Listen, you big lummox. This here is Angélique de Bardel, daughter of the main *seigneur* in these parts. Over there is Alain Jouvent, son of our representative to the Assembly in Paris. These other two are about the smartest people I've ever run across, and they can help you if they like and save your moderately fried skin, if they like. But if you think we're just a bunch of kids, you just check out who it was that brought you this far!" The boy's chin stuck forward.

The man sank back further on the bed. "I don't have the energy to fight with you, Jacques. I hope you're right. It would be too bad to get all this way and then not make it."

"Don't you worry. We'll get you out of here. We got friends and we got brains. First thing, is, we get you better. Then we'll talk about Switzerland."

The soldier looked near the end of his strength. "How safe am I here?"

"They hid me here for a week, once, when I was on the run. Nobody ketcht me then, nobody goin' ta ketch us now. Take my word on it. I ever lie to you before?"

A faint smile played on the pale lips. "Not that I ever caught you." Then the eyes closed, and the invalid relaxed more, pulling the tattered blanket around himself.

Angélique fingered the blanket. "Jimmy. Or should I say Jacques? This looks familiar. Just like the ones we issue to the foresters."

He squirmed, then a tentative grin started. "Yeah, well, you didn't want me to be cold, did you?"

She regarded him with severity. "That's all very well, but you used it, and you're going to have to pay for it." Her face broke out in an evil smile. "How about a great big kiss?"

This didn't faze him a bit. Straightening his shoulders, he swaggered across to her and stood with his face forward and his eyes closed. Instead of kissing him, she put an arm around his neck and pulled him down, running her knuckles briskly over his scalp. Before he had a chance to get a good protest out she pushed him away far enough to look at him. "Still not washing behind the ears, are you?"

He looked indignant. "*Comme il faut*. We got through the last week by travelling with a bunch of migrant workers, picking crops. You wouldn't expect anyone like that to be extra clean, now, would you?"

"You pretended to be peasants? How did you disguise his accent?"

"Easy. He didn't speak. I told 'em he was my uncle, and he was dumb and not quite right, you know. We kept his hands real dirty until they roughened up, and after that there was no problem."

"Didn't anybody ask who you were?"

"*Pas de problem.* The National Guard and me, we get along fine."

"Ah, yes, your friends from Marseille."

The Rat's reaction was not what they expected. "Hah! Bunch of slobs. They shoulda stayed rottin' in the slums. Give them a nice suit of clothes and a bed, and they roll it in a ball and sleep on the floor in the corner. Give them good food, they slop half of it on their shirt. And guns! They'd be better off usin' them as clubs. They weren't smart enough to find out which end the bayonet fitted."

Angélique's eyes met Alain's, and they shared a private grin. The Rat was getting civilized. Relatively.

Angélique made a final check to see that her patient was sleeping normally, then turned around to the fire. "Well, Jimmy, we're all here. Why don't you fill us in on what you've been doing since you left here this spring?

They settled themselves, and the boy from Marseille, with great delight, took the centre of attention.

"Well, as you know, I started out from Serres with the National Guard from Marseille. We took our time, stoppin' at any tavern that would have us. That bunch like a plaguea locusts cuttin' through the country. When we got to Paris, there was National Guard comin' in from all over the realm. They hadn't got nowheres to put us, so they gave us this big tennis court."

He grinned. "I found out it was the same tennis court where the Third Estate met to defy the king. 'Propriate, I thought. Anyways, we spent a bit of time gettin' the boys into fightin' shape, marchin' an' carryin' guns an' shootin' an' the like. 'Course, I didn't do none of that. I'm too young to be in the Guard. I made myself useful, takin' messages an' that sort of thing. It was great; I got to travel 'round Paris, take in the sights."

"But you didn't stay with the men from Marseilles?"

"*Aucune chance!* They was a rough bunch of buggers, and all they wanted to do was eat and get drunk and fight. They'd get in a fight with anybody, over anythin'."

Edmond had a knowing smile. "Like little things going missing?"

Jimmy gave his friend an injured look. "You think I'd be stupid enough to get caught? Asides, a few a them was pretty sharp fingermen themselves. No, I learned stuff here. Things that belong to your friends, you leave them be." He looked at Angélique. "That right?"

She laughed. "It's a good start, Jimmy."

"*D'accord.* Anyways, I got around a lot and I met a lot of people. I did real good at runnin' messages and I kep' my ears open, so I had lots of information. After a while I started picking up enough cash that I didn't want to leave it at the tennis court, so I moved out. At first I found a hole in a wall in St. Michelle, but after a coupla weeks I got enough together to pay for a room."

Edmond's eyes were wide. "So there you were in Paris, with a room of your own and money in your pocket, with all that exciting stuff going on? Did you see any of the riots?"

The swagger returned, in the tilt of his head. "See them? I'm the Rat from the gutter, remember? What better place to turn a coin or two than the middle of a riot? People come to a riot all unprepared, you know. They don't get up in the mornin' and say, 'Looks like a nice day for a riot. But first, I'll put on my hobnailed boots.' No, they hear the noise and they grab a stick and come runnin' in whatever they're wearin'. Never think to leave their purses at home!" He made an exaggerated picking up motion with his long, slim, fingers.

Then he turned to Angélique. "*Ah, bien.* That's wrong, too, but a guy's got to make a livin', and these political types aren't the kind to throw their money around, just because you do them a favour or two."

She must have decided that this wasn't the time for a moral lesson. "What political types did you do favours for?"

"Well, Mireur, to start with. I sorta got to know him on the trip north. I took a few messages for him, ones he wanted to be sure that they got into the right hands, you know? After a while I started ta get work from the ones I took his messages to. Then I got to run for the people they were sending stuff to. Didn't take me long to get a good cli-en-telle!"

"And did you keep working for Mireur?"

"Not like working. I had lots ta keep me busy, and he didn't need me much. You know, I figure he usedta give me jobs to be nice. But I kept droppin' round once in a while ta chat. Don't worry, I paid him back for his pa-tor-nage. A guy hears things, you know, and some things you hear is worth a lot to the right person."

"I'm sure Mireur was grateful."

"I guess he was. But that wasn't why I did it. I figure you gotta have some loyalty, you know. Ya gotta stick with yer friends." His casual wave took in those present, or perhaps the whole town of Savournon. It did not escape Alain's attention that his hand finished near the figure bulking the rags in the corner.

"So how did you get connected with the Swiss Guards?"

The Rat shrugged. "It was sorta by mistake. In fact, I was doing a lotta work for those Jacobin guys."

Angélique leaned forward, impressed.

"Yeah, they had a lot of stuff goin' on and they paid real good for information, too. But I didn't like workin' for them. They was...I dunno...too serious. Like they had only one thing in their lifes, and nothin' else mattered."

"Fanatics?" Alain ignored the look Angélique shot him.

"Yeah. *Fanatique*. That's the word. Anyways, you'd be surprised at how much contact there was between them and all the others, even the royalists. They're not so smart, you know. They think that because you don't know what's in the message, you don't know nothin'. But I figured out lots. If I took a message from a Jacobin ta another, and then the second guy sent me right away with a message ta some royalist type, I could make some guesses as ta what was goin' on. Guy called Mirabeau, for example...well, I could tell you stories.

"Anyways, I got sent ta the Tuileries a buncha times, and after they got ta know me there, it got ta be one of my regular trips, 'cause it's easier ta send a messenger who knows his way. After you get let in by the same guards a few times and spend your time waitin' for the replies you get to know 'em pretty good. After all, it's their job to know what's goin' on, and you can figure what it's like ta be standin' around on guard for hours a day. Bo-ring! So I kept 'em entertained, like, and we got ta be friends, a few of us. 'Specially him. He's a good type, you know. Nobility, as I guess you figured out. Younger son, makin' his fortune in the military. Anyways, we got along real well. When the trouble started, I hit right over there to see if I could help."

"Help? Wasn't the Tuileries under attack? You should have stayed away."

Alain grinned. *Trust Aimée to be worried.*

Edmond was more practical. "How could you help? Was there another way in?"

Jimmy grinned and pointed his finger, gun-like, at the other boy. "Ya hit it, *citoyen*. I slipped in an' out a couple of times. Strictly business, you know. Ya gotta realize that, while the mobs are shoutin' and the soldiers are shootin' at each other, their leaders're still talkin'."

"So I run a coupla messages back and forth, but I could tell that there wasn't no progress bein' made. None in the battle, either. These Swiss aren't no slouches, bein' hired 'cause they're the best. They had a buncha the aristocrats, them as was loyal to the king, helpin' them, and they was no sissies either. Lots of them been in the army, you know.

"Against them you got the Paris mob, with nothin' but their sticks an' cleavers. Then you got the National Guard. Some guys with guts, but the rest like my old buddies from the provinces. They didn't have much of a chance, to tell the truth.

"But the mob won the battle, didn't they?"

"Nope. They didn't win no battle. What happened was, the king lost it."

"Isn't that the same thing?"

"Well, the end was the same, but the way I said it puts the blame on the right guy. The king messed the whole thing up. Y'see, he was winnin'! What did he wanta go and surrender for? Not only that, but he told his men to lay down their arms. And whaddaya think happened then?"

Alain shuddered. "You mean he ordered the Swiss and the aristocrats to lay down their arms and give up to the mob?"

Again Jimmy made the gun sign, but there was no fun in his eyes this time.

"That's right. I dunno what he thought was goin' ta happen. Like everyone was goin' ta shake hands and go home?"

"What happened?"

The boy turned to Aimée, and Alain had never heard such bitterness in his voice. "What happened? This is the Paris mob we're talkin' about. Go on. Tell me. What did they do to all those poor guys?"

His intensity was such that the older girl was forced to answer, her voice a mere whisper. "They killed them, didn't they?"

"Damn right they did! Massacred them. Men who had laid down their guns. At least they killed the ones they could get ahold of. They wasn't all stupid, you know. I got some of them out myself, including Hans here. But that wasn't enough. The ones that got out, they started huntin' them down. All over Paris. You gotta know, these guys got a real problem. They've just escaped from a battle, lots of 'em are wounded, they're in uniform, and they speak with a accent. So the mob, and our dear National Guard, start killin' them in the streets. And if they made a mistake and killed someone else, well, too bad.

"I was pretty disgusted by this time. I had enough of Paris anyway. I mean, I like excitement same as the next guy, but this," He fingered his neck, "was gettin' a bit much. So I took Hans and hit for the provinces. He needed my kind of help and Switzerland was sort of the right direction for me, so we headed out together.

"Turned out headin' for Switzerland wasn't such a good move. Stands to reason they'd be watchin' those roads, since it's Swiss Guards they're huntin'. So we cut south, since I bin that road once, on the way up to Paris.

"Then I got the idea of bringin' him here. Figured we could cut over into Piedmont just as easy as Switzerland. When he got sick, I had no choice. I knew you'd help. So here we are."

He looked around the circle of his old friends, and there was no mistaking the plea in his voice.

Alain also regarded his friends before he spoke. "Of course we'll help." There were nods from the others. "Same plans as last time?"

Edmond's head came up. "It won't be so simple this time."

"Why not?"

"Politics."

Aimée followed her brother as usual. "Last time we were hiding from the local people, and the first thing we did was make sure they had no reason to suspect that anyone was here at all."

Alain nodded. "And now we have a National Guard who knows there are enemies loose."

"And they're ready to jump at anyone that seems to be an enemy to the Revolution."

"So we have to be more careful, that's all."

"Yeah, we're not just kids playing around anymore. We don't have that kind of freedom."

"But on the other hand we don't have to account for our time to our parents so much, so that will be easier."

Then the ideas started to flow like in the past, in their old patterns. Angélique and Jimmy with outrageous suggestions, balanced by Aimée's caution, Edmond's incisive mind equally fertile with thoughts and objections, Alain coordinating, organizing, keeping them on track. He noted Angélique's enthusiasm, and hope began to burn in his heart.

At the end of an hour they had a decent plan thrashed out for the feeding, nursing and safety of the soldier, with alternatives, backups and enough flexibility to cover such variables as the length of time it would take the soldier to recover from his fever.

Alain sat back, satisfied. "Only one more factor to consider. Will our guest agree?"

"Oh, he'll agree." The weak voice brought all their heads around. "I've been listening for a while. Can you do all the things you have been talking about?"

They looked at him blankly. The Rat elbowed Edmond. "He don't believe in us!"

Edmond's face took on an expression of sorrow. "He has n...o...o...faith." He stretched his words out dolefully.

The two of them shook their heads that such incredulity should exist.

Alain shook his head at this little act. "You've known the Rat for a while. Do you doubt his talents?"

The man grinned. "Well, it's hard to separate the fact from the fiction."

All the things he says he did in that short time. But his inside knowledge of political affairs! Yes, it was certainly hard to tell.

Angélique reached out and rubbed Jimmy's head affectionately. "I suggest you lean towards belief in most cases."

"And the rest of you?"

Alain shrugged. "We don't perhaps have the kind of talents Jimmy has, but we know the area and the people. Besides," he looked the Swiss straight in the eye, "we're what you've got. If you have any better ideas, we'll wait until you're a little stronger and discuss it again." He left it at that: a small challenge, couched in reasonable language.

The man nodded. "It seems the best thing for me is to put myself in your hands." His forehead wrinkled. "Of course, I'm feverish. This may be the stupidest thing I ever did."

Alain grinned back. "I guess when you wake up in a cell, you'll know."

Angélique interrupted this two-edged exchange by bustling over, Aimée close behind. "How are you feeling? Did we wake you up?"

The soldier lay back, smiling. "Not quite, although you do get enthusiastic, as a group. No, I feel much better. It must be something to do with being safe, even for a little while." His face became serious. "It has been a terrible week. Or more than a week, I don't even remember."

"Almost three weeks, M. Hans."

The man rubbed his head. "That long? I guess so. But how would you know?"

"News from Paris gets here in a week. Bad news in six days." Angélique reached out to lay a hand on his brow. "Your fever has dropped."

"I was on the mend already. Jacques has been taking good care of me. If he hadn't kept dragging me out into the fields to work every day, I suspect I would be much better."

"What? And waste our great disguises? Not a chance. Besides," Jimmy's grin became cruel, "I just had to see those lily-white hands of yours grubbin' in the dirt."

24. Escape

Late September, 1792

It was more difficult, now, to use the system that had worked so well hiding Jimmy. At first the Rat stayed with the soldier to help him while he was weak, but as soon as the man got strong enough to look after himself, they needed the younger boy to run errands. Alain and the twins were no longer children. They couldn't be seen running in and out of old buildings without questions being asked. So the job of keeping the soldier supplied with food and entertainment fell on Jimmy, to the mutual satisfaction of all. He staged another public "arrival" in town one day, and from then on he was free to come and go as he pleased.

And they thought they were doing fine until Sunday after mass. Alain and his parents were just leaving the church when he saw Angélique cutting in their direction. She seemed unaware of them, but her path intersected that of the elder Jouvent, and it was unavoidable that she would speak to him in passing. She shook his hand, passed a pleasant comment, smiled to Alain over his shoulder and moved on.

When they had walked down the street towards home for some distance Alain's father, looking bemused, glanced at him.

"Is there something going on that I don't know about?"

"What do you mean, *Papa?*"

"Why did Angélique pass me this note instead of speaking to you directly? I thought you two were long past that stage of your relationship." He turned his hand, and Alain saw a small fold of paper in it. He was about to reach for it when it disappeared. "At home might be a better place."

He looked at his father's face; there was no expression to read. Then the older man smiled. "I didn't spend three years in Paris without recognizing a conspiracy when I see one and how to react when I do."

Alain laughed in return – convincingly, he hoped – and tried not to seem like he was looking around with suspicion. The only people near were, like themselves, returning from church. Still, you never could tell.

When they reached their upstairs living quarters, his father handed over the note. It was simple but frightening.

The fox has been nosing around.

In response to his father's look, Alain shook his head. "It is something serious, *Papa*, but the less people that know about it, the better."

"Serious as in against the law?"

He looked at his parents' anxious faces. "I suppose it could be considered that. But it has to be done."

His mother stepped forward, her mouth open, but his father raised his hand. "If it has to be done, then do it. If you need help, ask." He turned away to take his coat off as if the subject was closed. Alain's mother remained where she was, looking at her husband and son.

She's feeling left out!

"Don't worry, Maman. We're being very careful." He wished he believed it himself. Angélique's message bothered him. His first response was to rush over to the hideout, but that would be wrong. *Surely someone is watching, even watching me. How to proceed?*

"Maman, has Ariane got the bread for supper yet?"

"I doubt it."

"Good."

He could see his father nod, as if to himself, as he left the room. Going down to the office, he penned a note similar in form to Angélique's, and told Ariane to give it to Aimée. She smiled knowingly and hurried off. He hoped that no one would stop her. It would be terrible for the old servant to get in trouble for carrying what she assumed was a love letter.

Nobody would do anything in a rush, but it was a good guess that everyone would show up some time near dark, each with thoughts of what was to be done. At least Edmond would have an idea. Aimée would have taken care of whatever preparations they needed. Angélique would also have a plan. The Rat would be there, a powerful asset on his own. That would be enough. It had to be. There would be no time for running back and forth. The man had to be moved tonight.

So as soon as the evening dimmed, Alain dressed in his darkest clothes and went for a stroll. When he reached the bridge, all was clear. He stood for a long time, peering into every shadow, but there seemed to be no watchers. Of course, there could be someone behind any of the small shuttered windows of the houses around, but that was a risk he had to take. He was about to start forward when a darker shadow slid through the doorway. Angélique, by the size, or Aimée. With one more look around, he slipped into the ruined house behind her.

Jimmy and the soldier were there, discussing things with Edmond. Aimée gone to arrange something, and Angélique was just settling herself on the old chair.

"I saw you come in."

She smiled. "You were standing beside the bush at the end of the bridge."

That worried him. "Maybe we came too early. If it was light enough that we could recognize each other, others could, too."

Her face became serious. "All the more reason to act quickly."

Alain turned to the group. "What are the options?"

Jimmy was quick. "Get the hell out of here!"

Alain grinned. "First and most obvious, but carrying dangers of its own. More?"

"The other end of the scale. Sit it out." *Trust Edmond to cover all the ground.*

"Move the two of you up to one of the foresters' huts. They would help."

"Any other ideas?"

"Disguise him as a stable hand at the *chateau*."

"Any serious ones?"

There were none. "All right. Which won't work? Run, stay hidden, stay disguised, move to the hut?" He ticked them off on his fingers.

Angélique frowned. "He can't stay. If they have any suspicions, all they have to do is come and look."

"But how much do they know? If they don't know where he is, moving him might reveal him." Alain often took the opposite side in these arguments to make sure the factors were all covered.

"We can't take the risk. If they do know more, he's caught."

"Are we all agreed?"

"Do I get an opinion?"

Alain turned to Hans. "Of course. I thought you would say anything you pleased."

The man grinned. He looked healthier now, and had tidied up his appearance as well as he could. He was a big, handsome, fellow and Alain liked him despite the threat he brought.

"You lot move so fast I can hardly follow. I agree it's too risky to wait. Where is this foresters' place?"

"I told you all about that. It's where I was livin' before I come here. You know, with Aubin and his sons. They're good sorts. They'd help out if I said so."

The soldier raised an eyebrow at Alain, who nodded. "What does everybody think of that idea?"

Edmond shook his head. "Too near town."

Angélique waved a hand to the side. "Too many involved."

"Well, that kills that one. What about the stables, Angélique?"

"Same objections but worse. I can't be sure of any of my people any more."

"It was an outside chance."

Alain reached out and punched Edmond on the shoulder. "To keep your reputation for having the most interesting ideas." He turned to the soldier. "Would you like to head for the border?"

The man nodded. "If it's safe, I would feel better getting out of France. I don't like all this running and hiding." His hand caressed the sword he wore. "I'm just a soldier. I'd prefer to have an enemy I can face."

"Let's hope it doesn't come to that. Now how are you going to travel? As a labourer, like before?"

"Yeah, I like that. I can put him back on th' end of a hoe. That'll be good for his strengtha character!"

Edmond ignored the joke. "I doubt it, Jimmy. No telling what information the Guard has, but they might have learned how you got here. How about as a rich traveller? Go for the extreme opposite."

"Being rich is too much an invitation to be harassed."

"Right. But he has to travel in the open. Nobody could get that far at night without being picked up by a patrol. They are keeping close watch on the border with Piedmont because of the fear of invasion."

Alain found himself depending on Edmond's knowledge, as usual. "So somewhere in the middle, then. But as what kind of person?"

"Well, we kind of thought..."

Everyone froze at the sound of footsteps in the passage. Edmond didn't turn. "Ah, there's Aimée with the stuff. As I was saying, we thought perhaps a merchant, travelling to sell his wares."

Aimée knelt and opened up the bundle she had brought in. "Sorry, it took a while to find a suit big enough for him." She looked shyly up at the big soldier. "But I think this coat will go around his shoulders."

He grinned down at her. "How did you know what to bring?"

"Edmond and I figured it out this afternoon. We only had to fix the details here tonight. All of us knew." She smiled again, bolder this time. "They've only been sitting here discussing all the other possibilities to make sure we didn't miss anything and to make you feel better. There wasn't any choice."

The big Swiss made a helpless gesture. "So let's not waste any more time. Where am I going, and how will I get there?"

Alain grinned. "Out the road to the east of the village, north of the *chateau* at Col de Faye, headed for the Vieux Chateau. There's nobody living there now. Then on to the forester's shelter at Beau Secours, up over the shoulder of Mount Aujour and on to the east. If you pass between Barcillonette and Esparron you can avoid any roads until you get close to Gap. From then on, you're out of Jimmy's territory, so use the roads. It's ten *lieu* or less to Piedmont from there. Three days' walk. Don't push it. Don't draw attention to yourselves. Beyond Piedmont we're not much good to you, but you're in safe country and you'll have to get yourself home to Switzerland."

The man changed into the tradesman's clothes Aimée had provided. They weren't a perfect fit, but they disguised his muscular shoulders.

"If I'm a tradesman, what am I trading and how do I find stock?"

Gordon A. Long

Angélique pulled a small but heavy purse out of her cloak and held it in her palm. "You're going to be a cloth merchant. I imagine you know enough about materials already to get by, and you can use your knowledge of the fashions in Paris to draw attention away from what you don't know. You should be able to pick up some poor-quality woven stuff along the way, then trade up when you hit a fair."

"Chorges, day after tomorrow."

"There you are. Once you get a load of good cloth..."

"Wait a minute." Hans was looking from Angélique to Edmond. "What was that about Chorges?"

Alain laughed. "Are they going too fast for you? If Edmond says there is a fair at Chorges, then that's where you go. It's not far from Gap. You'll make it there easily. Let Jimmy bargain for you. He'll get a good price, but not good enough to draw attention to yourselves."

Angélique continued as if there had been no interruption. "With decent cloth you can move along more confidently. It also gives you an excuse to stop over to trade again if you hear about trouble ahead."

"If a patrol grabs you before you get any goods, show the purse and make a big deal about the money you made, selling off all your stock. But it seems to me," Edmond gave his sister an apologetic grin, "you'd better find some new pants. Those don't look quite what a wool merchant would be wearing."

She turned her nose up and sniffed in her best shopkeeper manner. "It was all I could get on short notice. If you want a matching suit, you'll have to wait until Tuesday, I'm afraid. I have new stock coming in then."

They all chuckled and fell to discussing finer details. Alain noticed that the Rat was missing. Good.

In a few minutes, the soldier was ready to go. They used a blanket to construct a rough pack that was long enough to hide his sword, and he bounced it on his shoulder a few times.

"I can move fast with this if I have to. When do we leave?"

"When the Rat gets back. He's gone up to check on the streets around. Doesn't like to sit still for long, that one."

"Why do you call him a rat? It doesn't sound complimentary."

Angélique laughed. "That was his own idea. When he got here, he was quite proud that he came from the gutters of Marseille. He thinks rats have some good qualities."

Alain nodded. "The ability to survive in any environment being the most important one at the time."

The Swiss nodded. "And this time too. I won't complain. He's brought me this far, and I never would have made it by myself. You have all been a great help. If there is ever anything I can do for any of you, just get in touch. My family is Éahé, well known in Sion."

Angélique's face brightened. "Oh, I've been to Sion! We went up one summer when I was a girl. The Alps are so beautiful there, and it's a fine old town. Where do you live?"

Alain again felt a surge of jealousy as the two fell to discussing the town, searching for mutual acquaintances. He was relieved when Jimmy burst into the room.

"Men in the street over by the church. Four or five of 'em. Three more on the lower road."

"Anyone headed our way?"

"Not so's I could tell, but we better get movin'. You got everythin', Hans?"

"Yes. What about your things?"

The boy grinned and patted the bag that hung under one arm. "Everythin' I need, right here as always." He shot a glance at Angélique. "And a few I don't need."

With a wicked smile he held his closed hand to her. She reached out, and he dropped something into her palm.

"My earring! How did I lose that?"

Alain chuckled. "You'll have to stop kissing his cheek when you see him. He can't resist the urge to practise."

Angélique threw her arms around Jimmy. "I don't mind. You take care of yourself, now!" She tugged at her other ear. "Here, take both. You might need extra cash."

He nodded as if a good business deal had been concluded. Edmond paused in the doorway.

"I'm going. I'll draw them off, pull them north, then meet you two on the road to Jubeo if I can, go with you a ways." He slipped out through the door.

"Jimmy, you take Aimée and Hans out your own way. Angélique and I will stay here. If they come in, we'll try to delay them."

"Is that smart? That de Gonillons has got a problem with you two, you know."

"We'll risk it. There will be a much bigger problem if he catches Hans." He reached out and shook the soldier's hand. "Good luck."

The Swiss nobleman returned Alain's grip. "This group is very impressive. You have kept me alive until now, and it won't be your fault if I don't make it all the way. Thank you. It isn't much, but it's all I can say. If you ever need help..."

Alain nodded, a glow of pride pushing his jealousy out. This was a good man, someone who could have been a friend if time had allowed. He maintained this attitude while the soldier said goodbye to the two girls. The man spent no more time with Angélique than he did with Aimée, who was pleased and flattered by the attention.

"*Allons y. Vite, vite!*" The Rat was tugging at his friend's sleeve and they were out the door, but turning down the streambed to the right, crouching low to avoid the limbs of a spreading tree that covered their path.

The noises of their passage died away, and Alain and Angélique were left alone, standing in the centre of the room.

For something to do, Alain knelt to put more wood on the fire. "Might as well make ourselves comfortable."

Angélique sat down on the edge of the bed. "I suppose so. I hope it's a long wait."

The wait did seem long. Fearing what might come at the end of it, Alain could feel the tension rising in him. He wanted it all to be over, but the longer it took the better. They didn't speak much in case anyone heard them, and they were too concerned about listening for outside noises themselves.

When it came, Alain was so tense that he jumped to his feet. He looked at Angélique. She had heard it too: the sound of brambles plucking at cloth. Then a soft footfall on dirt. There was no doubt who would be the first man through the doorway, the one to get all the glory. Alain still didn't know what he was going to say. Letting others do the talking was the best plan.

The decision was taken out of his hands. Just at the moment when his eyes, riveted on the doorway, expected to see movement there, Angélique grabbed his shoulder, spinning him towards her, and threw her arms about his neck. Off balance, his arms went around her to steady himself. He heard a soft whisper.

"We might as well enjoy this." She lifted her face to his, and he kissed her, a long, lingering kiss. If their situation had not been so tense he could have joyfully forgotten all about it and lost himself in the scent of her hair, the feeling of her slim waist under his hands.

He was brought back to reality by an indrawn hiss of breath behind him. Turning, he faced Reynaud de Gonillons, a sword glittering in his hand in the fading firelight.

There was a tense pause while the man surveyed the scene. Alain had no trouble acting frightened. Angélique had turned away, hiding her head against his shoulder as if afraid to be recognized. He half-turned, sliding her behind him.

The Guardsman's eyes took in the two figures, then slid to the rumpled blankets on the pallet in the corner and he sheathed his sword, a knowing smile pulling at his mouth.

"So this is what the little hussy is up to when her *Papa* isn't looking." He stepped further in, looking around. Another Guard stopped in the doorway, a young peasant boy, peering in with interest. "Nice, snug, love nest you have here, Jouvent. Don't worry, I know who the little bird is." He reached out and shoved Alain aside. Stepping forward, he spun Angélique around, cupping her chin to raise her head.

She dropped her pose of shamed embarrassment and her eyes flamed out at him. "Get your dirty hands off me, you lout! What I do is my own business, not yours!"

He leered at her. "Not if you are doing something against the interests of France. Then it's my business."

She stared at him as if stunned. "The interests of France? What are you talking about?"

He looked around again, then returned his gaze to her. His hand still held her immobile and his forefinger slid a caress over her cheek. "Well, it may be that someone else has been using this place besides you. In that case, you may be clear of trouble. In that case, you could continue with your night's entertainment. Of course your partner might be other than the one you had planned."

Alain stepped forward. He had to be careful. It would serve their purpose to get the man angry. Not too difficult. The problem was not to get him so angry that he lost control.

"You've done it again, Reynaud." He put all the scorn he could into his voice.

The man's head swung towards him, although he didn't let Angélique go. "What have I done, boy?"

"You've pulled one of your stupid stunts in front of witnesses. If you're going to be a criminal, at least learn to do it right."

"Why you young pup!"

Alain shook his head. "If you're going to manhandle the daughter of a powerful family, you shouldn't do it with several of your men watching. One of them might be more loyal to his *patrie* than he is to you."

De Gonillons snarled at the young faces in the doorway. There were three of them now. "Get lost, you! I don't need you here."

"No, no, it's too late for that. They've already seen you, heard you threaten us. It's time for you to put your tail between your legs and run home." It was a risk, but he felt sure that the best way to make the man stay was to tell him to go. He hoped he hadn't overdone it.

As the back of his head slammed against the rock wall, he considered that he probably had overdone it. The enraged face so close to his was veined and mottled. A fleck of spittle hit him as the mouth opened to speak.

"Don't worry, you royalist scum. I won't hurt you much. Just a little serious questioning."

Alain could hardly force the words out, with his coat so tight across his throat. "Royalist? How can I be a royalist?"

"If you have anything to do with the fugitives hiding here, then you're royalist trash, and we know how to treat you!" The man gave him another slam, then dropped him. Alain staggered and stayed leaning against the wall for support until the room straightened out.

When he was able to see again, de Gonillons had turned his attention back to Angélique.

Alain motioned to the young Guardsmen in the doorway and tried to make his voice firm. "Bring that torch forward so that you can all see clearly. Watch carefully, so you won't have any trouble remembering everything when you are called to testify in court. Notice how hard his left hand is squeezing her upper arm. A doctor will testify as to the bruises that he has made. Notice that she made no threat before he attacked her, and that she is making no resistance now. This is a simple case of assault. A conviction, with all these witnesses, will be certain." He made his voice sound clinical to stop it from shaking.

"Note that at the moment he has only physically assaulted her. If his right hand should move any lower from her shoulder and touch her breast, for example, that would become sexual assault, and the penalties are much more severe..."

He skipped to the other side of the room as de Gonillons barged towards the door. The peasant boys disappeared. The man turned in the doorway. "There's more to this than it looks. When I find out what, my boy, I will be around to arrest you. Then we shall see how good a lawyer you are. If not, then I will keep this little secret between us until such a time as it is useful to me. Angélique, I doubt that your dear mother would be impressed to know what a bitch in heat her daughter is, chasing after bourgeois trash." He laughed loudly, spat on the floor, and spun out the door.

Angélique and Alain looked at each other. The sounds of footsteps died away.

"Are you all right?" Both voices sounded together, and they laughed shakily in response.

"Did he hurt you?"

She bent her arm experimentally. "Not much. How's your head?"

"My head? Oh, yes. I guess it's a little tender." He dropped his exploring hand to hide the dampness it had discovered. He wasn't fast enough.

"What's that? Are you bleeding? Come over here and sit." There was no denying her. He allowed himself to be pushed down onto the bed. She knelt, her fingers gently parting the hair at the back of his head, dabbing with her handkerchief. After a while she stopped. "It's not so bad. It must have been a sharp part on the rock that scratched you a little..." Her voice wound down and he felt her leaning against him more and more heavily. Then she began shaking. He turned, and she half-fell, half-sat on the bed beside him, burying her face against his shoulder. He held her as he had before, stroking her hair and murmuring soothing sounds, not thinking about the words he was saying.

"Don't worry. He's gone, and it's all over. He won't bother you again. I won't let him. I won't let anything bother you, ever again. I love you too much for that. Don't worry. Everything's going to be fine."

Suddenly the shaking stopped. She went rigid in his arms. She pulled her head back, stared at him. "What did you say?"

A shock went through him. *I said it. Well, it's too late now.* "I said that I loved you, and..."

Her hand stopped his lips. "That was it. That's what I thought I heard. You love me."

"Of course I love you. You know it. Ever since the beginning." He smiled, tried to make light of it. "Ever since, well... almost since Fripouille the lizard, but not quite. Then, I just thought you were kind of cute."

He looked down in to her eyes, which if it were possible, were growing larger. "Alain, Alain..."

Once again he found himself pushed backwards, except this time he hit the bed, and she was on top of him, holding him fiercely, kissing him, pushing her face against his neck. Her hair, breaking loose from its ribbon as it had always threatened to do, covered his face, his senses drowning in the smell and feel of it. She pressed against him, and he could feel her touch down the full length of their bodies. This was what he had dreamed of so many nights. His hands moved across her back and sides as he had imagined they would. She wore a thin summer dress, and it left little to the imagination of his exploring fingers. This was what he wanted. Now he would...

He froze. *And then what?*

"Angélique!"

She sensed the change in him and leaned back, a puzzled look on her face.

"Angélique, this isn't right. We can't. Not here, not now."

She stayed that way as sanity returned to her face. Abruptly she swung her feet around so that she was half-sitting beside him.

"Damn you, Alain Jouvent. Damn you, damn you, damn you!" Her fist beat time on his chest with her curses.

"Watch out. That hurts!"

She sat up and turned from him. "It should. You've just spoiled everything."

He straightened as well, taking her shoulders in his hands. "Why? I love you. What's wrong with that? We've both known it for a long time, but I finally said it out loud. I'm counting on you to love me too. I hope so, after all this."

"But Alain..."

He touched her lips with a forefinger. "We love each other. There's nothing wrong with that. Not now. Remember what you said, that day in the thunderstorm? Our world has turned upside down. Now we can love each other."

"You just don't understand!"

"So enlighten me."

"It all sounds so simple when you say it, but it isn't." Her mouth twisted in a bitter smile. "That's what you're always telling me, aren't you? That the simple solution is too shortsighted? Well, this seems simple for you, and maybe it is. But not for me. Alain, I know what you want. You know what you want. But don't you see, I don't know what I want? I've been trying to make a decision, and I just can't."

"A decision like the one you made last fall?"

Her head fell, then she looked up at him. "You could tell?"

"I've known you for a long time, Angélique."

She accepted that. "So you understand the problem."

"I can also tell what happened just now."

Her disbelief showed on her face. "I'm glad someone can."

"You made another attempt to make your decision. Not a very good attempt. You were going to get your emotions to make it for you. And I spoiled it all because I wouldn't go along."

Her hands went out in fists, a gesture of frustration. "Yes! What's wrong with you? I was willing to give you what you wanted, and now you don't want it. And I think I'm mixed up?"

He took her hands in his, forced her to look straight into his eyes. "Angélique, I've waited for a long time. Enough to allow each of us to decide that we are the right person for the other. That we fit together and can live all our lives that way. Remember what you said?"

"Will you quit quoting things I said when I was a child and tell me what's going on here?"

"Often you let your emotions make decisions for you. I've seen it happen, time after time. You make up your mind, but after you calm down you try to figure out if it was the right decision, the logical one. If you think it may not be, then you're in all sorts of trouble. Can you imagine how it would be if we had allowed that to happen here? And then you began to wonder if it was the right thing to do? Imagine the suffering. For both of us.

"No, I'm willing to wait longer. Now that your emotions have made their decision, I'm betting that your mind will follow along." He shrugged. "If I've made a mistake, well, I guess it's too late for me."

There was a long pause while she stared at him. Then she shook her head. "Alain, sometimes don't you wish you could just relax and take life as it comes, and not worry it to death first?"

" I sometimes do that, but I usually end up regretting it. I'll stick to my own style, thank you all the same."

She grinned. "You will, won't you? You never give up. That's one thing I like about you."

"Love."

"Love?"

"That's one thing you love about me. Go on, it's true. It won't hurt you to say it."

She threw up her hands. "All right. It's one thing I love about you. Are you happy?"

"Very. Now you have to kiss me."

Her brow turned down. "Alain, I didn't say it would be like that."

"Look. I have told you that I love you. In doing so, I have cancelled all my other options. In return, I get certain benefits. One of them is that I don't have to pretend any more. Since we both know that I love you," *it feels so good to say it out loud,* "we both know that I will be wanting to kiss you from time to time. So I'm allowed to ask. You can answer any way you like. That's your option. But be prepared. From time to time, I'm going to ask."

"Dammit, Alain, do you have to wrap everything up in a legal argument?"

"That's another thing you love about me. And, by the way, your language is getting rather strong, isn't it?"

"My feelings are rather strong at the moment. I'm sure I'll be back to my usual demure self once I get under control. But seriously, Alain, that's one problem I have. I can't see myself spending my life with someone who has to have a legal agreement to ask for a kiss."

"That's a problem?"

"Yes. That is a problem."

He shrugged. "Problem solved." Taking her head gently in both his hands, he kissed her. Not a long kiss, but definite.

"Now, I suppose there is nothing we can do to help our friends out there?"

Her smile faded as reality intruded. "I wonder if he caught them!"

"I doubt if anyone will notice us leaving here. I'll walk you home. We can stroll around on the way and see if anything is happening." They rose, and he put his arm around her waist. Not possessively, but just as if it were the natural thing to do.

She looked up at him. "We're not going to walk down the street like this."

"We're not in the street." He pushed her gently forward, and she preceded him through the door.

25. Jimmy's Return

Fall/Winter 1792

It took Jimmy three weeks to get back. He turned up at Alain's door one day looking even more scruffy than usual. Lying in the street beside him was a mess of what Alain at first took to be a pile of raw wool that had fallen off a cart. Only when he looked closer did he see the black nose and the dark eye that glimmered in the fur. "Jimmy! Did you get to Piedmont? And what's that?"

The boy shrugged. "*D'accord.* Even made money along the way. And this," he gestured, "is Vulcan."

Alain regarded the quiescent mop of fur. "Vulcan? As in the Blacksmith of the Gods?"

"Blacksmith of the Gods? That's what it means too? Great. I thought it was short for volcano."

"He doesn't look much like a volcano to me."

"Hah! Just wait till he gets going. I'm training him to do tricks. Made a handful in Gap on the way home, showing him to a crowd."

Alain was skeptical. The beast might have started his life white, but that was long ago. His grubby hair had developed a muddy tinge, culminating in a definite black around the paws and nose. Sticks and brambles were knotted in his long outer hairs as if he was trying to camouflage himself. It didn't work. Still, the eye looked friendly enough, and two ears might be trying to perk up through the tangle.

"So what happened with Hans?"

The boy swaggered his usual few steps before speaking. "Well, it was real tough gettin' away from town, as Edmond musta told you. But once we got movin' and got dried off it went better. That soldier sure knows how to walk, even when he was still weak. We got all the way to the border, and I sent him across. They're sure worried about invadin' armies comin' in, but they don't look so hard to see who's goin' the other way. Say, why don't you all come over to the *chateau*, so I can tell everybody at once?"

Alain grinned at the idea of the Rat now inviting people to the *chateau* as if it were his own. Well, perhaps as the hero of the hour he had earned the right. The boy snapped his fingers, and the bundle of fur on the ground exploded into a frenzy, bouncing around his master, barking joyfully. A proud grin, and the three were off down the street.

They sat in the garden at the *chateau* so that Jimmy could keep an eye on Vulcan, whom he didn't trust yet near the chickens and ducks. There they put together the events of the night of escape.

Edmond had created a minor distraction by waiting until the Guard came within sight, then showing himself a few paces away from the bridge. The soldiers called out to him, but he ran away, not too fast, up the road north towards Villelongue. Only two men had been sent after him, so he led them for a short distance then hid, allowing them to walk by him to continue climbing until they were out of the action. He hoped.

He had been on his way to rendezvous with the rest when he spotted a man standing on the bridge to Gonillons. Cutting back past the church, he caught the others just before they came in sight of the bridge. Aimée went forward openly to check who it was and whether he was still there. It was one of the National Guard and he saw her, so she had no choice but to walk on past him, stopping to talk long enough to distract him from noticing the rest of the party on the road behind her. Then she went home, knowing that her disappearance would be message enough.

The other three had been forced to take the road to Jubeo, hoping to cut across the fields to the Col de Faye road. Again they were frustrated by the sight, in the faint light from the west, of two men patrolling that road. As they climbed up out of the valley they began to hear noises behind them. Whether their presence had been discovered or not, there was a group of men following. They increased their speed and decided not to stop at the foresters' hut but to continue into the Gorges of the Riou, hoping the patrol would go elsewhere. They did not, but continued to follow at a rapid pace. The Swiss, still not recovered from his illness, found the climb up to the forest taxing, and despite the downhill path into the Gorge the soldiers were catching up. Edmond had been thinking as well as walking.

"I remembered that boulder you told us about, in the stream below the ford? First we stashed the bundles in the rocks nearby. It was quick work, let me tell you. We could hear the jingle of the soldiers' equipment by this time. I took the lantern out of the pack and kept going down the trail. The other two crawled into that hole behind the waterfall."

"Two of them?" Angélique looked aghast. "In that tiny, wet space?"

Jimmy grimaced. "It was cosy, that's for sure. We could hardly breathe. For a while we couldn't hear nothin' because of the sounda the water, but I could see out a bit. Then we heard this extra splashin', but there was no way of knowin' whether they was just crossin' the stream or comin' to get us. Then one of them gave a shout, and they all ran down the path."

Here Edmond took up the tale again. "I ran as quick as I could down the trail to a place where I could see the ford. When I figured the soldiers were at the point where they might spot Jimmy and Hans, I opened my lantern and started back up the trail, casual and slow. Say, it wasn't too difficult to look scared when six soldiers came running down the path at me waving their bayonets.

"First they asked where I was going, and I said home to Savournon from St. Genis. They asked me if I'd seen anyone on the path, and I said no. De Gonillons was leading, and he said I was lying. I said if there was anyone coming down the path, they must have stood aside in the dark and let me pass and they were long gone. He still didn't believe me, but he had to go on in case their quarry was ahead. He left one of his soldiers to escort me home, to make sure I didn't make any contact along the way. So I had to take the lantern with me."

"Leavin' us in the dark. Me'n Hans, we crawled outa that hole as soon as the soldiers started shoutin' at Edmond." He looked quizzically at his friend. "In fact, I figured they was doin' more than shoutin.'"

Edmond fingered his cheek where the bruises had almost faded away. Jimmy nodded.

"Anyways, we got out of there, up along the stream bed off the trail, takin' it slow, so as not to make any noise. Jubeo Forest's our territory, so I know it real good, and we hit the trail up over the Roc de l'Esculier with no problem. It was easier goin', too. Good thing it was a warm night or we'da froze, both bein' almost soaked through. Had to duck round the *chateau* at Col de Faye – there was lights on, even that late at night. We pushed on past the Vieux Chateau, slept a coupla hours in the brush near the foresters' shelter at Bonsecours, then hit out over the mountain to Barcillonette, just like you said. Took us the day to get to Gap. I went into town and bought Hans a pair of pants and a fancy hat to take attention off the rest of his clothes. He didn't like it much, said it wasn't his style. I told him that his style was now like a wool merchant's, and that was how they dressed. He had to take that.

"The fair at Chorges was great. We picked up a packa good wool – raw, but real clean. Packed it on to Embrun and sold it there, made a bita profit. Bought a coupla bolts of woven wool, rough stuff, but thick and warm, and packed it on up the road. *Merde*, is that Hans strong! Fell in with some others who was takin' winter supplies into Guillestre. They told us how much good wollen cloth was goin' for in Briançon, what with winter comin'. So we pretended that we were holdin' out for good prices farther on. Gave us a good reason not to trade with anyone.

"Well, wouldn't you know it, they was right! We got top money for our cloth, paid for darn near all our expenses!" Here he hauled out the purse Angélique had given him. It lay heavy in his hand. "Most of it's there. I had to spend a bit gettin' back." Alain could see his eyes shift over to where Vulcan lay camouflaged under a rosebush that had added its last few leaves to his decoration.

"You don't mean you paid real money for him!"

The boy's head went up. "*Pourquoi non*? I earned it and I like him!"

They all laughed. Angélique cocked her head in interest. "How did you manage to do all the bargaining? Didn't that look suspicious?"

"Naw, there's always a way. If you make what you do look like a flawa human nature, everyone accepts it. Hans played the lazy tradesman who would rather drink his glass and let the ambitious apprentice do all the work. I coulda made more, but I remembered what you said about not drawing attention, so I quit bargaining early. Still, we did pretty well, *n'est-ce pas?*"

Angélique poured the contents of the bag into her hand. Two earrings glowed on the top. "If you paid anything at all for that beast, you did pretty well. But what about Hans? Didn't he need money to get back home?"

"Him need money? Let me tell you, as soon as we got across the border – and that was real easy: just walk across with your goods, pay the tax and a little extra for the guard to have a glass of wine, and you're through. The French soldiers just wanted to make sure we didn't have no noblemen hiding in our packs!"

He laughed and paused. "...what was I sayin'? Oh, yeah, Hans and money. As soon as we gets across the border into a place called Cesana Torinese," Jimmy said this name with a lilt to his voice and a flourish of his hand that made them all laugh, "he walks into the first bank we see and writes out a note, signs it and next thing they're bowin' and scrapin' all over the place. And he's in Piedmont, not Switzerland! Let me tell you, that Éahé name carries a lotta weight. He gets all the money he wants, and the first thing he does is trot down to the tailor's for new clothes. Says he wants something that suits his sense of style, now that he's in a country where he could be himself. Let me tell you, his sense of style sure changed since his uniform in Paris!" He flourished his hand in a formal bowing gesture.

"So he thanked me again, and I come back. You know, it was hard to let him go. I liked him, in spite of he's nobility. I may just go up and see him some time. He invited me." The Rat stared around, daring anyone to contradict him. No one did. They all knew what the Swiss owed the boy.

"Was it hard getting back over the border?"

"Hard? You're forgettin', I was by myself, now. I slipped through so smooth they never even knew I was there." He ran his palms together in a long, slow motion, hands going in opposite directions. "Then I headed back. Took my time, checkin' out the country." He paused. "They ain't too happy over there, you know."

Alain's attention was aroused. "What do you mean? Politically?"

"Yeah, I guess you could say that. Nobody's talkin' much out loud, but you hear the comments they pass when they're alone with their friends, or they've had a few too many at the inn. They don't like the government a whole lot, but what they don't like worse is the whole country bein' run by that mob a *sans coulottes* in Paris. I figure if someone was to come along and say 'get rid of the lot, and let's go back to the king,' they'd be runnin' up from all over to kiss his..." he glanced at Angélique, "...hand."

She frowned. "You have been hanging around in tap-rooms with the wrong sort of people, young man."

He raised his chin, but there was a glint of humour in his eye. "How else am I gonna get the information? Ask to be invited home for dinner?" He gestured at his clothes. "I ain't quite ready for that, yet."

She hefted the bag of coins, looking around at the others. "I guess we'll have to take some of Jacques' hard-earned money and have the tailor run off a velvet jacket for him. Maybe then he will provide a higher class of information."

He didn't seem to move, but though she tried to jerk her hand back, it was no use. The purse disappeared, and no one could be sure where it had gone.

Jimmy laughed and elevated his nose. "Perhaps not, thank you my Lady." Then he dropped the Second Estate accent. "If I was wearin' a velvet jacket, where would I have put this?" He gestured at the table, and the bag of coins seemed to appear in his hand. "Better check them. Could be a bag of rocks."

Aimée grinned. "Jimmy, you brought them all the way back from Piedmont. I doubt if you'd steal them now!"

He turned to Alain. "Ain't it touchin' that someone could have lived all these years and still kept that much faith in human nature? And I thought that girl was smart! Now, Aimée, my dear." He ducked and her cuff bounced off his shoulder. "You gotta be nicer than that. If I was to take offence and go away, who would you have to boss around?"

Aimée sat back on her chair trying to look disgusted, but not doing too convincing a job.

"So what are you going to do now?"

Edmond's question echoed all their thoughts, and their serious faces turned towards the smaller boy. He grinned, refusing to be drawn in.

"Well, I kinda got an itch to do some more tradin'. I got a real kick out of gettin' all that money for nothin'. Well, not for nothin', akchully. We packed that stuff a good long way." He hesitated. "But for the moment, I'll be headin' back to the foresters. If Aubin'll have me, that is."

Angélique pinned him with her look. "And why wouldn't he have you back?"

Jimmy squirmed. "Well, when I left, I tried to be real polite, you know, but still, I wasn't s'posta take off like that. I mean, there was things we was s'posta to be doin' this summer, and I wasn't there to help. So maybe he don't see me as reliable enough to work with anymore?"

This last sentence was spoken like a question, carrying with it a look of appeal. Angélique tried to be severe. "And what about your duty to my father, who hired you when you needed a job?"

The boy's head dropped, and he scuffed the floor with his toe. "Yeah, I know. I guess I let you all down, huh?" He looked up at her through the fringe of hair that fell over his face.

Alain could tell that she was hiding a smile, but her voice remained firm. "I suppose my father will forgive you, since you did such a good job at saving Hans. As for Aubin, well, I guess you'll have to ask him."

The boy's face brightened. "Can I go up there now?"

She smiled. "You can do whatever you like, Jacques. You do what you feel is best."

He jumped up. "I better get going, then. *Alors*, I can't wait to see their faces when I tell them about my adventures!" He was almost out the door when Angélique's voice brought him spinning around.

"And Jacques, why don't you go along with the wagons when we send next spring's shearings to the market? You can make sure we get a good price for them." She paused to take in his joyful expression. "And is that any way to take leave of a lady?"

"Oh, no, Mademoiselle. I'm sure I forget myself in my joy." He glided to her and bowed over her hand. "I hope Mademoiselle will excuse my lapse, on account of my great pleasure in Mademoiselle's words."

He straightened, a challenge in his eye. Then he turned and strode with dignified pace to the door. Vulcan rose to follow him, and he bowed again and pulled the door closed behind him. There was a moment of silence, then they heard a high whoop and the patter of running feet. Everyone burst into laughter.

"He won't have any trouble with Aubin, will he?"

Angélique was checking that her rings and earrings were still in place. "Aimée, they love having him up there. Especially in the winter. It's a boring job at times, and lonely. Him with his schemes and his stories and even his petty thefts? It keeps them on their toes. When I told Aubin that Jimmy was gone on a dangerous mission, he was worried. Oh, they give him a rough time, but he needs it. They'll be happy to see him."

* * *

Angélique had brightened up, but it was temporary. The need to help the Swiss had boosted her into her old pace, but now he could see her slipping back. He had taken her out to show her the progress they had made on Jules' farm, riding in the carriage because...well, just because he wanted to. It Alain's opinion, this crop was one of his greatest triumphs. The harvest had been terrible that fall, but applying Alain's new techniques had kept that farm from the disaster that had overcome so many. Angélique made all the right noises and seemed duly impressed, but had not responded with any enthusiasm when Alain had thanked her for her help with the other farmers.

"Alain, I didn't do anything. I gave my opinion of what you have been doing, and you did well on your own with Jules before I even started. It doesn't look like much, but the others can't help but see the difference it has made to his crops this year. When they are all starving next March and he has a crop of alfalfa to feed his sheep on, they will look at him and think twice the next time you approach them with an idea. Yes, you have done very well."

"But don't you see how it helps to have you come around and talk to them? There may have been a revolution, but not in the hearts of the people here. To them, you are still the *seigneur's* daughter, and your interest carries a lot of weight. On top of that, you being very pretty doesn't hurt."

She smiled sadly. "I suppose that doesn't cut much ice with their wives, though."

He grinned. "Don't be silly. They like you, too, for some reason."

A fragment of her old spark appeared. "Why shouldn't they? I like them!"

"Why shouldn't you?" Then he became serious. "That's why I could use your help. You have a relationship with these people. They will listen to you. That, combined with the credibility I have been building, and we can get them moving twice as fast."

She took his arm as the carriage bumped over a rock. "I'll help any way I can, Alain. I doubt I'll be much use, that's all."

He didn't answer, torn by his thoughts. In fact, he felt that their relationship was developing nicely. She seemed to be slipping into the habit of spending more time with him, of allowing him the privileges involved in a more serious arrangement. But she did all this without a great deal of enthusiasm. Alain was in the difficult position of getting what he wanted, but not in the right way or for the right reasons. *The problem is, what if I do find her something to engage her interest? Will I lose her?* Grimly, he decided that he would have to take the chance.

He settled in to make it all happen. There were forms to fill out, letters to write. All the skills he had learned in dealing with the bureaucracy, all the contacts he had made in Gap and Serres through his work. He knew how it was done. He wrote letters, he badgered people. He even made a complete fool of himself a few times. *At least, that's how I feel about it. But they don't seem to notice. They expect people to abase themselves. I hate it, but if it works, I don't care.*

* * *

Finally, late in the fall, all his plans came together.

"Angélique! Look at this!" He burst in on her where she was sitting at her father's desk adding up accounts.

She smiled at his enthusiasm. "What is it that puts you in such a hurry that you track snow all over my clean floor? Have you discovered a way to grow grain on the mountainside? Give up. You'll never get any of the farmers to try it, no matter how well it works."

He glanced down. Too late. Most of the snow was already making small pools where it lay. That wasn't important. "No, it's the report from the government in Paris on the conditions in the *Departement* due to the poor harvest!"

Her face sobered, her hand gesturing towards the pile of papers in front of her. "From my calculations, I don't see that's anything to be excited about. We may be in for a very rough winter."

"Not as rough as you may think. Read it." He thrust the paper at her. As she finished reading, she shook her head, a look of surprise on her face.

"A half a million *livres* in aid from the government. That's more than we've ever received."

"Of course, that has to be spread over the whole of the Hautes-Alpes. But by rights, Serres should get a quarter of it. 125,000 *livres*. We can buy a lot of food with that! Think about it! And good seed for next year. Maybe we can find one of those new strains of wheat you can plant earlier in the spring. After all, if we're giving them the seed, they pretty well have to plant what we give them, don't they?"

Her hand waving in front of his face stopped him. "I fail to see the cause for such enthusiasm. Those are all good ideas, but how can you persuade the government bureaucrat who's in charge of all this money that it should be spent that way?"

He grinned, planted himself in front of her, hands on hips. "Not too hard. Guess who that government bureaucrat is?"

She looked up at him in amazement. "You? They won't turn over that much money to a twenty-year-old who isn't even a lawyer yet!"

He shook his head. "Of course not. My father is in charge, nominally. They have to trust him. But I'm running the day-to-day operations. I'm the one with the experience, remember? I've been through all this before, when we were doing it on a scrounge-what-you-can basis.

"Remember that visit I made to the prefect in Gap? The letter I took to him from your great-grandmother? Well, he remembered me. *Le bon dieu* knows how he's managed to keep his job, but I suppose those top civil servants are kept on because they are the ones who can run things. Anyway, he remembered, and when my father told him I would be the one in charge, he said it was fine with him, and he hoped I'd do as good a job as last time!" He shook his head and smiled. "Old Mme. de Dillon. She's still helping us."

Angélique stood and took his hands, a glow of pleasure brightening her face. "Alain, I'm so pleased for you. To have the opportunity to help all those people. I hope you do well." Her expression fell. "I'm sure you will. I wish I could do something like that. To help people, to make a difference."

"But that's just it, Angélique. I need you! I can't do it all myself. This will involve a lot of work. Assessing the needs of the area, chasing around to find the best prices on grain, seeing to cartage and fair distribution. The paperwork will be far more than I can handle myself. I'm allowed to spend a reasonable amount of the money setting up an office and hiring staff. I'll use our law office but I want you to come and take care of the accounts."

291

"But I couldn't do that! I don't have the training." She sat down again. "I don't know how to handle that kind of money. What if I made a big mistake?"

"Who has been handling your father's business for the past two years, one of the hens from the barnyard?" Alain threw up his hands. "This isn't like you, Angélique. You aren't afraid of things like this. Look, if you don't want to take the job, say so. Don't make excuses, just tell me."

She shook her head slowly. "There's not much business to keep me occupied around here right now. But I don't know enough. Consider carefully, Alain. You have been handed a great opportunity. You want to make the best of it. No hesitation, no mistakes. You need the best possible staff. Hire a real clerk, someone older, more experienced, to run your office. I'll come and help out as usual."

"I have someone older and more experienced. My mother. She's been handling my father's business forever. She'll help you if there are any problems." His pacing had carried him across the room. Now he returned to her, holding out both hands in appeal. "Come on, Angélique. Give it a try. If you find you can't handle it, we can make changes. But try it for a while, won't you?"

She smiled at his enthusiasm. "I suppose I can't resist such an offer. It's time I got out of my comfortable chair and did something worthwhile, anyway. If it has to be as an office clerk, then so be it. At least I can get along with my employer." She looked up at him from the corner of her eye. "Usually."

"Great! Why don't we go down to the office and we'll talk to my mother about arranging the furniture. Come on!" He grabbed her hand, lifted her off her chair. To his surprise, she came easily, sliding closer than he had expected, her arm going around his waist.

"Alain, you are such a dear!" She leaned into him, kissing his cheek, then moved past him to the door. He followed, his heart singing.

26. Government Inspector

April 1, 1793

Alain leaned back in his chair, stretched his stiff back. "You about finished?"

"I suppose so." Angélique straightened from where she had been bent over a list of figures. "They checked out twice. I don't know why I'm adding them a third time."

He grinned at her. *I won't mention the ink-stain on her cheek for the moment.* "It's because you love your job."

"Hah! Five years ago, if anyone had told me I would be a clerk and enjoying it, I would have...well, I would have given them a piece of my mind."

"It's fortunate you have such a good mind. You seem to give out pieces frequently."

She grinned. "Who have you been listening to, now?"

"Oh, stories do travel. What was that about the Rat yesterday?"

She put down her pen, the smile gone. "Oh, that was just stupid. Two of Reynaud's precious National Guardsmen were standing around with nothing better to do, and they stopped Jimmy in the street. Started on about how his name sounded English, and since we are at war with England, he might be a traitor."

"They must have been joking."

"Of course they were, but you can't let something like that get started. In these times, sooner or later it stops being a joke."

"So I assume you got into it."

"I told one of them that his sister's name was Marie, and perhaps that meant she was a friend of the Austrians, and perhaps we should haul his whole damn family in to question their patriotism."

"You said that? A bit strong, since he was only joking."

"I did." She tossed her hair back over her shoulder. "You can't let them get away with pushing people around, even in jest. They have to learn to mind their manners. Otherwise, a small joke becomes a big one, and it turns serious. Like little boys playing. It starts out in fun, but sooner or later somebody gets a bloody nose."

He nodded. "I suppose you're right. Are you saying that little girls don't do the same thing?"

"I suppose they do, but they're more subtle about it because their *mamans* taught them it was wrong to fight."

He grinned. "They learn later, do they?"

"They must."

"You did."

"Did you want me to let them hassle Jimmy in the middle of the street, just because they were bored?"

He shrugged. "No, I guess not. It seems a bad time to be stepping on people's toes, that's all. Oh, they needed it. It's just that we're treading such a fine line at the moment."

"And I'm not a diplomat. Not when I'm angry." Her grin came back. "They sure turned tail and slunk away, though."

He couldn't help but smile back. "I imagine they did. Two farm boys matching wits with Angélique de Bardel? Some contest."

"Alain?"

This sounded more serious. He looked at her.

"What is this inspector going to say when he comes?"

He shrugged. "I suppose he'll say, 'What have you spent the money on, and can you prove it?' And we can. So we have no problem."

"We don't? What about those changes I made in the accounting procedures?"

Alain wasn't so confident about that. Angélique's ideas, which she had found in one of her books, were not that far out of line with his mother's methods, and certainly seemed to do the job. But they were different, and thus a risk. "It all works, doesn't it? It balances and we can tell what happened to every sou. The worst that can happen is that he will ask us to redo our books using the old method. We could do it. We still have the information."

"But that would take weeks!"

He grinned. "And they would pay you for those weeks. What's the problem?"

"That would be a waste of money that could be going to feed people. And I can find something worse. What if we get a nasty inspector, and he takes it all away from us and gives it to another accountant to fix up?"

Alain's experience with the bureaucracy made him shrug and smile. "In that case, there's nothing we could do, anyway. That's one area where I agree with you. The Revolution hasn't changed anything. We've only exchanged one set of power-hungry bureaucrats for another."

"So a lot of it depends on what this man is like."

"Since when has the world been different?"

She slammed her hand on the table. "Why does it have to be like that? Why can't people just do their duties? It makes me so mad!"

"I know, my dear. I know."

* * *

It began in complete innocence. Alain told himself that.

The office was cramped, since they had added a small writing desk for Angélique and a cabinet for her files. Her desk backed on Alain's, and one afternoon it happened that he slid his chair back to stand just as she was getting up as well, and he almost knocked her feet from under her. He turned awkwardly to catch her, and they stood, frozen.

Angélique had matured over the years. Her hip, tight against his leg, was rounder than he remembered, and he revelled in the soft pressure of her breast against his chest. She did not move away, but looked up at him, and his breath caught. Then his eyes rose, and he saw that his mother was watching them from across the room.

His face burned, and Angélique pushed herself upright, her cheeks bright red as well.

"I...uh...I'm..." He glanced once more at his mother, who held his eye, then went back to her work.

He stumbled back to his desk, staring at a paper with no idea what he was reading, his sense of Angélique's presence behind him like a hot fire on a cool evening.

When he returned from seeing her home that afternoon he found his mother still in the office. She was reading something in an idle fashion, and he got the distinct impression that she was waiting for him. *As if I don't know why.*

Sure enough, she rose as he entered. "Alain, I've been meaning to talk to you."

"Yes, *Maman*? And what stopped you?"

"Privacy."

"Oh." He looked around the office. "We are rather crowded in here, now that there are four of us."

"Exactly. I have been watching you. And Angélique."

He frowned. "Why? We haven't been doing anything wrong."

"She is your employee."

"That's very good, *Maman*." His hand swept the crowded office. "She has been coming to the office six days a week for the past month. You two bump into each other about five times a day because your file cabinets are side by side. And you have thus deduced that she works here. How can anyone wonder where I inherited my intelligence?"

"You know what I mean." She stepped closer.

He looked at her. She was serious. He dropped his smile but not his eyes. "No, I don't."

She sighed. "She is a beautiful young woman. And if I say it who shouldn't, you are an attractive young man. It's a small office, and you are together here many hours every day."

"And I'm in love with her. Don't forget that small detail."

"Oh, I haven't. But now she's your employee."

"So? What difference does that make?"

His mother regarded him. "I had hoped you would be intelligent about this, *mon fils,* but let me put it another way." She took him by the lapels of his coat and stared him straight in the eye. "If even once during her time working here you lay a hand on her *comme ça,* I will take my riding crop to your *derriere.* Is that simple enough for your little mind?"

"But *Maman*! It's a small office. We're friends. How can you...?"

She shook him, once. "Have I made myself clear?"

He sighed. "Yes, you have made yourself clear. Do you think I wasn't aware of the problem? All day, every day?"

She patted his shoulder. "I know, *mon fils.* It must be very difficult."

"It is. But she has a reputation. I have a reputation. So do you and *Papa.* I'm not going to spoil everything by doing something stupid."

She raised her eyebrows. "You mean you may have inherited some of my brilliance after all?"

"No, only your good looks."

She smiled and patted his cheek. "That's my boy. Always knows what to say to make things right."

He sighed. "Except when it counts."

"Oh, don't worry about that. Girls always take it as a sign you're so madly in love with them that you can't think straight."

He regarded her seriously. "*Maman,* this is one situation where I can't afford to think any other fashion. No matter how I would like to."

She shook her head. "Logic is not the traditional way to win a girl's heart."

"Perhaps not, but it's the only one I have."

"And my mother told me I should never marry a lawyer." With that enigmatic comment she led the way up the stairs.

He turned to survey the crowded office, noting Angélique's writing desk so close to his. *There is nowhere else to put it.* Then he shook his head and followed his mother.

* * *

"Alain! I've got news!" The young lawyer stood in the doorway of his office and watched Jimmy swing down from his pony, Vulcan panting up behind to flop in a heap at his master's feet. Because of his new interest in business, the boy had become a great messenger, even if this meant learning to ride. It hadn't been as difficult as he expected, but he harboured a suspicion at the docility of a creature so much larger than himself. In his world such a situation was unnatural and therefore suspect.

"I thought you were in Serres."

"I was, but I came back as quick as I could. There's news!"

Alain was concerned. From the look on the Rat's face, it couldn't be bad, but still... "How is the relief operation there?"

"Huh? Oh, the relief. Oh, it's fine. That stuff you sent over to M. Laude must have been good. He read it, shook his head, and said something about new ideas. But he looked real pleased. No that's not what the news is about. There was a riot!"

"A riot in Serres? What about?"

Jimmy pushed past his friend to greet Angélique and Mme. Jouvent with great courtesy, but he couldn't contain himself for long. Swinging a chair into the centre of the room, he straddled it backwards, making sure their eyes were all on him.

"It was started by Jean Jacques and that Joubert character, who was angry because he couldn't get a civil certificate."

"No wonder they wouldn't give him a certificate. He's a deadbeat, a loudmouth, and a thief."

"Well, the crowd didn't seem to care about that. They roared and screamed, gettin' louder at everything he said. They went down inta the town and discovered they were locked out of the council rooms. Hah! Can't think why! They went for the key, but nobody would give 'em one. For a while it looked like they was goin' ta break down the door. The Gendarmes showed up, but they couldn't handle it. Wow, was they noisy! Chantin' things like *'liberté, egalité, fraternité'* and havin' a wonderful time. Then they go back up to the church, and Joubert gets up and starts rantin' again. He accuses the municipality of hoardin' grain, 'n' stuff like that. They tacked some kinda petition on the church door. I couldn't get close enough ta see. What a time! As I was leavin' town, a gendarme hit up the road towards Gap at a full gallop. I guess they'll send the sojers, now."

* * *

The Inspector-General turned out to be a tall, severely dressed older man with a long, clean-shaven face and a sad expression. He was carrying a bulky satchel, and he appeared at their door without ceremony in the middle of the morning on the appointed day. He announced himself as Alexandre Vincent, Government Inspector-General.

Alain's father ushered him in and introduced everyone.

"De Bardel. Related to Marie-François de Charrette, I suppose."

Angélique shot Alain a glance. Was this good or bad? "Yes, she's my mother."

The man made a clucking sound, shook his head. "A pity. But what could she do?" He shot a glance at Alain's father. "You're their lawyer. You did what you could with the property?"

The elder Jouvent nodded. "Everything is in order. But there shouldn't be a problem. She's only visiting in Switzerland because she's ill. She's not on the list of *emigrés*."

Vincent shook his head, the long face seeming even sadder. "Not yet, I suppose."

That seemed to be enough pleasantries. He slung his satchel onto the table and sat down, opening the case as he did so. He was well prepared, as the first paper that came to his hand was summary of their finances.

"So, Jouvent, you have been dealing with somewhat over 100,000 *livres* to cover the relief operations in this area. The reports you have sent indicate a higher proportion of money spent on the purchase of food supplies compared to administrative expenditures. On the other hand, you seem to have disbursed more than the usual amount on seed grain, of several varieties. Other than that, your activities fall within the normal range. Would you say that was a good general description of your project so far?"

"It sounds fair. As you can see, using my office makes for a lot of savings, and we only have one extra staff member hired. I'd like Alain to explain the seed grain."

"We'll deal with that in its time. Just thought I'd mention the important points before we started. First I'd like to take a look at your records."

"Of course. Mademoiselle de Bardel will show you."

Angélique brought the appropriate files over. There was a long silence while he looked through them. Alain and Angélique followed his progress, trying not to breathe down his neck. After a while, he stopped and went back over something, frowning. Then he nodded and continued.

After a while longer, he looked up at François.

"An interesting technique."

Jouvent made a motion towards Angélique. "You'll have to ask Mademoiselle de Bardel. The books are hers."

The long, dry face turned towards her. Alain could see her hands clench.

"What do you know about Reichert?"

"I...I have one of his books. It seemed a simple method, and it suited what we were doing so well." He seemed to be listening with interest, and she began to get enthused. "You see here," she pointed to a page, "it allows you to find out the total expenditure at any time, with a simple calculation."

He waved her hand away. "I don't need Reichert explained to me, young lady." Starting from the beginning, he looked through the file again, as if he was searching for something. Then he pounced.

"You see this point here, *Mademoiselle*? Why did you add all these?"

Angélique followed his finger, then shot a glance and a grimace at Alain. "I...well, I didn't quite understand the book at that point. It seemed like I was missing something. It didn't seem right that you could do it that easily, so I totalled it up, just to be sure."

A thin smile. "If you wish to follow Reichert, young lady, you must be prepared to follow him. All you had to do was take this total, here, and place it there. Then you add, and you can take your percentages from over here." He circled something, leaned back and looked up at her.

"Elegant, is it not?"

Angélique's face took on that flush that meant she was involved. "Oh, I thought you couldn't do that, because you had to take the percentages at one spot."

She received a wintry smile. "You are a bit short on experience with finances to start improvising. Trust Reichert. If he says do it, then do it." He gathered the files together. "Well, my friends. It should take me much less time to go over these than I expected, but there are many details to look at. I suggest you go about your business and leave me to it. I suppose if I have any trouble I can ask Mademoiselle?"

It sounded like a trick question to Alain. To his father, too, apparently. "The finances are Angélique's. Any questions about selection and distribution of grain are best directed to Alain, I believe."

Vincent swung towards him. "You believe? I was under the impression that you were in charge. Do you really know anything about this project?"

"The work is under my supervision in general, but I trust my subordinates. My son is more experienced with this kind of operation than I am, having handled the relief operations before, while I was wasting my time in Paris trying to keep this country under control."

Alain could hear the unconcealed bitterness seeping around the edges of his father's voice.

Vincent was unmoved. "Oh, I wouldn't be too upset, Jouvent. Your lot did a whole lot better than anyone has since, I would say. You laid a good foundation. Time to let others see what they can build on it. If the lad has the experience it will show. Leave me with these as I suggested, and I will see."

They all tried to work, but it was difficult. Every time their visitor started a new page or made a notation in his book, Alain and Angélique met each other's eyes.

Finally, Vincent pushed back his chair and put down his pen. "Well, I must say it looks good. I have a few questions on your contract system. You are being too loose with your suppliers, young man. So far they have lived up to their side of things, but one day you will run up against one who is less scrupulous. Then you will wish you had covered yourself with a firmer agreement."

He stood up. "I will allow you the opportunity to explain your actions later and I have suggestions for the future, but they are minor changes. We should be able to conclude this afternoon easily. That would give us time for a short stroll after lunch. This seems to be a mountainous area. Perhaps there are pleasant walks?"

After a tense but informative afternoon, Vincent refused their offer to stay the night. He said there was still enough light for him to make a *lieu* or so on his homeward journey. "You aren't the only one with a family waiting for you, Jouvent."

With that, he was gone, waving almost cheerfully, his horse trotting along to a light stroke of the whip. The four of them, standing in the road, turned and stared at each other, then burst out laughing.

"When he first walked in, I thought we were in for a rough time." Angélique chuckled. "What a dry old stick he looked!"

François shook his head as he held the door open. "I didn't tell you before, but he has a ferocious reputation. He has torn more than one poor bookkeeper to shreds."

"Well, he certainly liked it here. We couldn't do any wrong! He liked being served lunch here, instead of having to go to the inn. He loved walking up on the Aigle. He loved that coffee you brought back from Paris." Her mouth twisted. "Can't say I like it myself."

"It's an acquired taste. I enjoy it, now."

"He even liked my bookkeeping system!"

Madam Jouvent seated herself at her chair, leaning back in comfort. "Yes, Angélique, we've all been dying to ask. I didn't realize this Reichert was so revolutionary. He must be more advanced than I thought when you started using his methods."

Angélique walked over to her desk. "I didn't know he was either. I picked up his book in Grenoble one winter. You've seen me referring to it, I'm sure. Do you remember, Alain, the year I decided to make myself indispensable to Father? I found this book and looked it over to get an idea how you were supposed to take care of finances. When we started on this job, it all seemed to fit." She grinned. "I must admit, I had to ask Edmond a few times to explain the arithmetic."

"M. Vincent thought it fit. What was that list of names he gave you? You had such a long chat while we were walking, I was almost jealous."

"And well you should be. He would have loved to spirit me away from here. He was disappointed that I couldn't come and be his apprentice and learn how to do finances properly. It is a shame women have to go and get married and lose their chance to do something with their lives."

They all laughed.

"I told him my opinion about that, as you can imagine, and then we got talking about what a person could do. You know, with your life. To make a difference? And he gave me names of people to get in touch with, in Gap and Grenoble, who are doing things to make a difference. I'm to write to them and go and see them when I can, using his name as an introduction. He said they will be glad to tell me what they are doing and let me help if I want."

She paused and looked sideways at Alain. "He said something else. In his opinion I don't have to look too far if I want to help my *patrie*. A nation is built by people doing small things to help each other. Like we are doing here. He looks for people who are doing their best with no thought of glory, and he helps them to succeed."

She took a deep breath and looked at each of them. Her cheek flushed, and her breath quickened. "Do you know what the government is planning? To create orphanages to take care of all the children whose parents have been killed in the disturbances."

Alain looked at her. *The old, familiar signs. Could it be...?* "You see yourself running an orphanage?"

"Not just me. Look who we have. Aimée, Jimmy, you."

Alain grinned. *"D'accord.* Jimmy, teaching them to pick pockets. That's a good skill for an orphan."

M. Jouvent's voice rose to interrupt Angélique in the middle of clouting his son. "That sounds like a fine idea. I'm sure M. Vincent has the proper contacts. He oversees all the government projects, so he will know which ones are the best."

He grinned. "But for the moment, we have some celebrating to do. I must admit I was a bit nervous when he came down on me for not controlling what was going on. He was right. I have very little idea of what you are doing. I had been meaning to get it all explained, but there never seemed to be time, and there were no problems. But my trust was well founded. Come. There's a bottle of sherry that needs opening upstairs."

27. Emigré

June 8, 1793

"Well, *Papa*, it's finally happened." He threw the paper on his father's desk, turned and slumped in his own chair. "Delivered to us by our favourite National Guard Captain. He couldn't wait to gloat."

After a moment he looked over to see how his father was taking it. To his surprise, the older man was reading calmly, nodding his head. When he finished, he glanced over at his son. "There is little satisfaction in being proven correct in my predictions."

Alain nodded. "Exactly like you said."

"Close enough. This Committee of Public Safety gives the Jacobins power to do whatever they like. It was cleverly done."

"Yes. They made such a huge fuss about the threat to the Revolution that everyone got frightened. So they have bypassed the control of the Convention, because defending the Revolution has become more important than running the country. The Convention doesn't understand that the Jacobins can use those powers to destroy anyone who challenges their own rule. Including members of the Convention."

Jouvent rubbed both hands over his face, up and down. "Knowing Robespierre as I do, I can predict that, with the help of Marat, it will be a matter of months before he is an absolute dictator."

"The problem is what to do about it. Do you have any ideas?"

His father shook his head, side to side. "I have been a long time working on this, but I have no quick solution. I fear that we must go through a difficult time before the people of France, and especially the people of Paris, become aware of the danger of these men. But not yet. I have concluded that our country must experience a cleansing, and not a gentle one, before the population gets so tired of the tyranny that they rise above their fear and overthrow these savages. It will be a terrible period in our history and there will be many deaths."

"But what can we do?"

"What any man can. We will help when we are able, resist when we can, give in when we must. It is not a time to be a hero, Alain, though it may sound craven to say it. We do our best work by keeping out of trouble. A lawyer in jail himself is no use to his clients. A lawyer out of jail is much more effective, even a cowardly lawyer."

Alain made a sour face. "I don't like the sound of that."

"Neither do I, but my predictions have been accurate so far. Why should I be wrong this time?"

"But why don't we stand up to them? Why can't we throw them out of power?"

"Because now is not the time. We would not have enough support from the populace. We must wait until the people have had enough, until they are so afraid that they are no longer afraid. Then we must be ready. But for now, we wait and endure. And that will be very hard."

Alain's private opinion was that they should take action, any action, but there was no looming trouble to fight against, and he had no idea what to do.

* * *

Alain and his father were just finishing up for the afternoon when there was a knock at the door. It had been a busy day, and they were looking forward to a quiet evening. Alain threw up his hands in a 'what next' gesture and glanced through the window. What he saw made him hurry to admit their visitors.

"Seigneur de Bardel. What brings you here? Please come in." The older man entered, Angélique following. Both looked worried. Alain arranged seats and his father settled everyone formally. Something unusual was going on, and it gave them time to arrange their thoughts.

"All right, Charles. What has made you so upset?"

The *Seigneur* tried to smile. "Straight to the point, François? Get it over with. I must say, I appreciate it at the moment. The problem is, I must leave France."

Alain felt a shock run through him. *Leave France! Does he know what he is saying?*

"That may sound foolish, but I see no other option. My wife is in Switzerland, and she is sick. Truly sick. The doctors don't know what it is, but it could be serious. I have to be with her."

"That shouldn't be too difficult to arrange."

"Yes, but I doubt if I will ever return."

"Ah."

"I don't fit here any more. I tried, but I'm not a revolutionary. This upset in Paris...well, I don't understand it. I can't live with some *sans-cullote* in striped *pantalons* holding a knife over my head, ready to let it drop at a whim. I don't want to be here."

"That will create problems with your holdings. The moment your name goes on the list of *emigrés* your property is confiscated by the state. Trying to sell signals that you are leaving, and they will find a pretext to arrest you."

"That isn't the whole problem, M. Jouvent." Angélique looked to her father until she was sure he would not say it. "I'm not going."

"You aren't? That does make it complicated. You are aware of the danger that puts you in? You may still not be able to keep your lands, and the families of *emigrés* are likely to be arrested."

"M. Jouvent, I can't go to Switzerland. What would I do there? Sit around with the other aristocrats and make plans against my country? I have important work to do here. Ask Alain. I can't go."

Put on the spot, Alain stumbled over his words. "Don't ask me! I...don't want her to go, but I know how dangerous it is if she stays. It doesn't matter, anyway." He forced out a grin. "What Angélique decides, that is what she will do. Why don't we figure out how to arrange it?"

His father nodded. He knew Angélique well enough by now. "Let's look at ways and means, then. I hope you aren't in a hurry."

"My wife isn't in any immediate danger."

"Good. This hasn't caught me unprepared. I have been tossing around an idea and I would like your opinion. Listen and tell me how it strikes you.

"You can't sell your property. I have already explained that. Not all at once. But what if you were to distribute it to your tenants? Sell it to them, I mean, but not collect the money all at once. We could set up a co-operative group that would organize the farmers to control the finances, to allow them to pay something close to their present rents, take up the slack if they couldn't pay. The difference is that in the end they would become the owners."

"That would be like giving the land to them."

"You have already decided to give it up. If you leave, I can try to keep it in Angélique's name, but I can't guarantee anything. This way the land will be in the names of the tenants. If the Jacobins attempt to confiscate it they will be taking it away from the farmers. Very poor politics. They aren't popular around here anyway, and it would be stupid of them to create that kind of bad feeling."

De Bardel looked at Angélique. "It will mean losing everything we have here."

"Not everything. You should keep the *chateau*. It's not exactly a palace, and they can't begrudge you a place to live."

Angélique nodded. "I would like to keep my family's home, but even that I could bear to lose. It is more important that Mother and Father be together. Mother will never come back to France, at least not with things the way they are. So Father has to go to her. It's simple when you look at it that way."

I have to try. "Angélique, why don't you go, too? For a while. All this will blow over in a few months, a year or two at the most. I'm sure you would be fine in Switzerland with your parents. Hans knows what he owes us. He would find you something to do." He grimaced inside as he spoke. *Still, it is the best for her.*

She knew where his thoughts were going. "Why Alain, you don't want me spending time with a handsome Swiss nobleman, do you? I would have thought you wanted me here."

"I do want you here. But it isn't safe! Since the Girondins lost power, the men in charge in Paris are not to be trusted. And there are people around here willing to take advantage of the situation.

Look at those three in Serres, who call themselves the 'Triumvirate.' They pretty well took over the town, with their mob and the help of Barras and Fréron, those 'special envoys' from Marseille, threatening to send anyone who won't go along with them to the guillotine. They even got the official magistrates removed from office. It took two companies of soldiers to get the town under control after the riots they started in April. The town council finally got the Convention to clear the magistrates and arrest the 'Triumvirate.' But who knows what will happen next?"

"I thought we started this conversation by stating that I was staying, and that was it. We are wasting time."

He shrugged. There was no talking to her when she got that look on her face. *Why should I even try*? *Le bon dieu knows I don't want her to leave.*

She turned to the two older men. "Then are we agreed? M. Jouvent will set up the co-operative so that our name is no longer connected to the land. Then Father is free to go. I will stay in the *chateau* and hold on to it as long as I can."

Alain's father smiled. "You have a grasp of the schedule, at least. I will start on this right away and inform you as soon as I have something. We need to meet with the tenants first. Alain can go around and talk to them tomorrow. He is the one who spends the most time with them these days. After the meeting we can draw up the papers. Once you sign them you're free, Charles. We'll take care of Angélique here, don't you worry about that."

De Bardel stood. "I can't thank you enough, François. I hoped you would. I am torn, but I am needed in Switzerland, and frankly, I am not a whole lot of good here. You will do your best for Angélique. I just hope it doesn't come to that."

"So do we all. Now, you have given us work to do before supper."

"Right. Angélique and I will get out of your way." He turned to the door, and his daughter was there at his side as he walked away. Alain watched them go. The *Seigneur* didn't look sick, but Angélique treated him as if he were, walking with her head turned towards him her hand on his arm as if to steady him. Her loyalty was touching to see. *I hope we are not forced to regret this move.* He went back inside.

"So much for a quiet evening."

28. Orphanage

July, 1793

The *chateau* seemed empty: the rooms echoing and silent by turns. Alain followed Angélique into the library. "It is strange, having so few people around."

She shrugged. "With only me here we don't need all the servants. I kept the ones that have been with us the longest. I don't need them much, either, but I couldn't let them go."

"If the farmers keep up their payments you can afford to pay the servants. If we get the contract for the orphanage, we'll need them. Will they take to the different sort of work?"

She sat at her writing desk, leaning her elbows on the blotter. "After the upset of the past year and the past month, they're happy to have a place to live and work. Sort of like me."

He resisted the urge to put his arms around her. *Not here, not yet.* "Don't worry. This is going to be fine. When are the others coming?"

"Any time now. Aimée and Edmond already know about it. How will Jimmy react?"

"He should be pleased to help those who went through what he has experienced."

"I'm not so sure. He doesn't have much use for orphanages. Small wonder. From the tales he's told us, the ones in Marseilles are nothing more than an excuse for slave labour. Stale bread, smelly fish soup..." she shuddered.

"He'll join in. He's been a great help in all our projects."

"As long as he doesn't decide to teach them to pick pockets!"

* * *

"*Zut alors!* I ain't havin' nothin' ta do wit' no orphanage!"

Alain glanced over at Angélique, then back to their small friend. When he was upset his accent deepened until he was hard to understand. There was no mistaking his feelings, though. "Why not, Jimmy? I thought you would be happy to see orphans with a place to live."

"Yeah, but not in no orphanage. Them places is worse'n prisons." His eyes slid towards the door, then to Aimée. "You ain't gonna put me in no orphanage, are ya?"

The baker's girl smiled. "No, Jimmy. You have it all wrong. We're not putting you in it. You're going to help run it."

"Whaddaya mean?"

"You're the perfect person to help Angélique run her orphanage. She has no experience with children like that. She doesn't know how they think, what they need, what they're afraid of. You know all about those things."

"Yeah, well, maybe I do."

Alain laid a hand on the boy's shoulder. "Of course you do. The orphans will be happy to have you here. A lot of the other orphanages are horrible places, are they?"

"You bet they are. I wouldn't wanta go inta one a those. I wouldn't even walk in the door."

"Right, and now you can make sure our orphanage isn't one of those places. You can talk to the children. They'll trust you. Then you can tell Angélique and Aimée if there's anything wrong, and they can fix it."

"Angélique and Aimée?" He looked at the two girls. "You're gonna run this place?"

Angélique nodded. "Madame Jouvent will be in charge, but we'll be doing all the work on a day-to-day basis. We need you, Jimmy. Will you help?"

"I dunno. Who are these kids gonna be? I ain't wipin' no babies' butts."

Aimée laughed. "You don't need to worry about that. We won't be taking any babies. Just children of school age. That's our main reason for getting the contract. We have educated people to school them as well as look after them. I'm going to teach Reading and Edmond will do the Arithmetic. Angélique will handle the Science and other things. We don't have that planned yet."

"Hmph. Well, maybe. Aimée's good at teachin', that's for sure." The boy thought a moment. "Where's these kids comin' from, anyways?"

Angélique's face glowed. "There have been a lot of orphans created by the Revolution. Their parents have died in the uprisings and rebellions, victims of the guillotine or as soldiers killed in the wars. That's why the government is setting up new orphanages. These children desperately need a safe and comfortable place to live." She reached out and ruffled Jimmy's hair. "They aren't all tough enough to survive on their own, like you are."

"Huh! I wouldn'ta survived so good if I hadn't come acrost you lot."

"Well, there you are. Everyone needs help, support, and a family."

The boy looked around the group. "That's what you lot are, ain't ya? Yer my family." He burst into laughter. "Who do I gotta call, 'Maman'?" He shot a glance at Aimée. "I ain't callin' you nothin' like that. Not that you won't be great with the kids."

Aimée ducked her head, her cheeks reddening.

Jimmy winked at Alain and turned to Angélique. "I guess it's gotta be you, then."

"Only as long as you treat me with proper respect."

"So, we shoot that idea down in a cloud a feathers."

Angélique regarded the rest. "Then that's it. Everyone agrees?"

They all nodded.

"Then we'll finish the paperwork tomorrow." Angélique looked around at her staff. "Edmond, you have the best contacts in the village. You start looking into our food sources. We'll want good quality at a fair price." She glanced at Jimmy. "No three-day-old bread and fish soup, right?"

"Yeah, we'll be talkin' about that."

"Aimée, you need a head start on the school curriculum. I have contacts in Grenoble you can write to. Alain..." She frowned at him. "...what are you going to do?"

He raised his hands in a warding gesture. "I imagine I'll be doing everything you haven't figured out yet."

She slapped his hands down. "And doing a wonderful job of it, if you know what's good for you."

He smiled. Inside, he was glowing. *She hasn't looked this enthused for months.*

29. Conscription

Aug 30, 1793

A tense group of townsfolk gathered in front of the Mairie that hot August afternoon. A strange collection, if you didn't know why they were there. Small groups of people, mostly families, each bunched protectively around a young man or two. Conscription had come, and today was the lottery. At last M. Morel, the local Justice of the Peace, stepped out of the front door. The crowd went silent. "*Citoyens et citoyennes.* As you all know, our great nation is at war. All the monarchs of Europe see France as a threat to their safety, as they should. The fact of our existence, free men in the midst of slaves, is a beacon of hope to the oppressed populations of their empires.

"That means we must fight. They are not weaklings, these tyrants. They have the arms. They have the men. Paid soldiers who are fighting for money, not for freedom. But fighting men nonetheless. And to oppose them, France needs her own soldiers. Good, honest patriots like you, the young men I see standing here. Men who will carry the fight for freedom across Europe. Men who will stand for France when she needs them!"

A small cheer rose, and the Justice smiled. "I have here the list of eligible young men. Please signify your presence when I call your name."

He read them out, and at each name another cheer went up. To Alain, the whole scene was bizarre. *People are applauding as if these are children getting an award for scholarship, rather than young men risking their lives.* When his name was called, he stuck up his hand and was gratified by the acclaim he received. Blushing, he turned away. Angélique squeezed his arm. "They really like you."

The end of the list came soon; Savournon did not have that many single men between 18 and 25. Then the Justice continued.

"Not all of these young men will be asked to join the army to fight for France. The Convention, in the Decree of August 23, has made up the quotas, and Savournon must send five. As a way of choosing, all the names will be put into this box. I will select the first five names that come into my hand. Those will go, and the rest will make their patriotic contribution at home."

The next few minutes were a blur to Alain. As the names were read, he could feel both his arms gripped firmly. Angélique on one side and his mother on the other were holding him as if they could keep him there. His father stood nearby, face rigid. The twins hovered close, Aimée shooting him anxious glances. *They all look so worried.* He felt sorry for them.

As the names were drawn and read aloud, the cheers grew louder, part in adulation of those going, and part in relief for those who were spared.

Then it was over. The crowd gathered around the unlucky chosen, slapping them on the back as if they had won something, offering drinks in the taproom. A few women hiding their tears were disregarded in the scuffle.

Alain disengaged the hands that held his arms. Angélique smiled up at him in silent thanksgiving. His mother had regained her poise. Slipping her arm into her husband's, she led the way homeward.

As he turned to leave the scene, a red, snarling face pushed into his.

"So the lawyer's kid didn't get conscripted, hey? How did you fix that, you coward? Some farm kid goes away to war while you stay and get rich. How convenient." Reynaud, his hand on his sabre hilt as usual, was planted in front of him, daring him to push past.

Alain moved to avoid the man, but Angélique refused to budge. "Fine words, coming from someone who has bought himself a nice safe job close to home, intimidating poor farmers. Why don't you show how brave you are and

317

volunteer to fight for real, instead of playing toy soldiers with your fancy uniforms and your swaggering? Why is it that the Revolution seems to be an excuse for incompetents to gain power? Something to do with the way the scum always rises to the surface when the pot gets hot." Angélique's voice had risen, and there was a general chuckle among the people around them.

Then Angélique started walking, straight towards de Gonillons. He stumbled aside, and she sailed by, her head in the air. Alain glimpsed the surprise on the man's face, wiped out by a snarl of rage. Then they were past, leaving their enemy spitting in their wake. For the next few paces, Alain's shoulder muscles twitched with the thought of an angry man with a sword behind him, but nothing happened.

Angélique's nose came up. "Don't worry. He's too much of a coward to start anything."

"Not here in public."

"Bah! Not anywhere." Flushed with her anger and her victory, she marched on, and Alain and twins followed.

It was a silent group that stood around outside the office. No one had much to say, but no one wanted to leave. Then, in a calm and quiet voice, Edmond exploded the bomb.

"I'm going to enlist."

They all turned and looked at him. Angélique stepped forward. "But Edmond, you're only seventeen. You can't join the army yet."

"Only for a few more months. I can lie about my age. They don't care. As long as you want to go, they'll take you."

"But why?"

He shrugged. "France needs me. You heard the man. We're being attacked by every power in Europe. If we don't win, we'll be crushed."

Angélique turned to Aimée. "He's your brother. Can't you..." She stopped at the dumb misery on the girl's face. Aimée had known about this all along.

"You're being selfish, Angélique. You don't want me to go. Nobody wants friends going away to fight. But look at it from my point of view. Everyone here is doing his share, accomplishing important things to help the country run, and I'm just hanging around helping in the *boulangerie*, where I'm not even needed."

Alain pondered his friend's words. After all, he had thought this through himself. "Have you considered that with the rebellions in Lyon and the Vendée, you may end up fighting fellow Frenchmen?"

Edmond nodded, frowning. "That's a risk I must take. It's a fine distinction, but I don't plan on killing anybody. I'm not going out and joining the infantry. I wouldn't be so good there." He grinned and flexed the muscle in his scrawny arm. The lad had gained his full adult height, but not a whole lot of weight. "I got in touch with that merchant, the one who lost his purse? He's the kind of man who has contacts, and he always said he would help me if I needed it. Sure enough, he found me a great place. I'm going to be in Signals."

Angélique looked confused. "Signals?"

Edmond's face took on his patient look. "Yes. Not everyone in the army fights. One of the most important parts of warfare is knowing where the enemy is and deploying your troops in the right places. In the mixup of battle, good communications are crucial. The Signals corps sends the messages."

"That doesn't sound so dangerous."

"It's war. Anyone can get shot. But this sounds interesting: codes and flags and all sorts of stuff like that. I'm leaving with these recruits tomorrow, but I go straight into a special training session. I'll write to you and tell you all about it."

It was impossible to ignore the pride and enthusiasm on the boy's face. Angélique flung her arms around him. "Edmond, we're all so proud of you." Then she laughed. "Trust you to find something interesting to do in the army."

Alain stepped forward and shook his friend's hand. "I'm proud of you, too, Edmond. You'll get in with those signallers and soon you'll be making up new codes and new ways to send messages. Before they know it, you'll be running the show."

Mme. and M. Jouvent added their congratulations and went inside, leaving the young people to talk in the street. Edmond's enthusiasm carried them for a while with a hysterical gaiety, but soon it wound down and there was silence.

Edmond shrugged. "I...have a lot of things to get ready for tomorrow."

"You'll want to spend the evening with your family, then. We'll be there tomorrow to see you off." Another squeeze from Angélique, and Edmond was ready to depart. As he gave his friend a one-armed hug, he noticed Angélique laying a sympathetic hand on Aimée's arm, exchanging a silent communication.

They stood at the doorway and watched the twins walk away, Aimée with her arm around Edmond's shoulder. For once he didn't pull away, even though they were in the main street.

The two then returned to the office and sat down. There seemed to be nothing to say.

Finally Angélique broke the silence. "There is another inspector coming, Alain."

He jumped on the new topic with relief. "We didn't do too badly with the last one. What does this one want? Something to do with the seed grain?"

"No, no. It isn't about your business. This is for me. For the orphanage. He wants to look at my plans to make sure we will treat the orphans properly, not steal all the money for ourselves, that sort of thing."

"Sounds fine to me. What's the problem?"

"I've had two letters from this man and I don't like the sound of him at all. He has made up a list of regulations, which I swear is longer than the rules we had to follow when we were distributing the relief money! This sounds like the type of bureaucrat who loves to make things difficult, just to give himself a feeling of power."

"It wouldn't be the first time we've run across that."

She shook her head slowly. "Alain, what good is the Revolution, when all it has accomplished is to bring all the worst people into positions of power? I mean, what kind of person would make it difficult for orphans to find homes?"

"*Papa* says it's a stage we have to go through. There is a type of person who would make up his own little empire if you gave him a dunghill to supervise. Those people find ways to get into power when things get turned around. After a few years their incompetence will have a chance to show, and we'll get rid of them."

"I suppose. It's just so hard that we may not have our project approved, and just because of him!"

Alain regarded her, noting how her back slumped. "I liked it better when you got all upset about things like that."

She looked up. "No, you didn't. You used to get all worried that I would make a scene. You still do. Aren't you happy that I've learned to give in a little?"

He walked behind her, put his hands on her shoulders. "I guess I should be. But don't ever lose your fire, Angélique. It's something you have and I need. It's what makes us such a good pair."

She leaned back against him. "We are a good pair, aren't we?"

"We proved that this winter."

She reached up and took his hand, pulling him around in front of her. "Are we a good pair in other ways too? Not just at work?"

"You've known my opinion on that for years."

"And it hasn't changed?"

"Why would it?"

Her hand swept the office. "Daily contact, everyday drudgery. At first when we were friends my mother was against it. But my father said that I should spend time with you, that the novelty would wear off. At least that's what he said to Maman. I doubt if he believed it himself. She said it was a risk, but all right. And they allowed it. Good thing, too." A flash of the old stubbornness.

"Isn't that funny? My parents thought the same way. Didn't work, did it?"

She shook her head. "Not at all. Or perhaps it did. It allowed us to make decisions based on reality, not on some romantic notion."

"Don't lose the romantic notions completely, Angélique."

"Alain, I had my fill of romance. Every winter in Grenoble I went through the motions with the romantic young men. The parties, the daring secret meetings, the flirting, the games. It was fun, but it was no way to decide on a marriage partner. No, I want to make up my mind for other reasons."

"You told me that years ago, up in the mountains in a hailstorm."

"You remember everything I said, all those years ago?"

"And everything since. About us, anyway."

"Amazing. Why?"

"Because it was necessary to my campaign."

She looked at him directly, then her regard drifted over his shoulder. "And how's your campaign going, these days?"

"As usual, I suppose. Slow but sure. You tell me. How is my campaign going?"

She said nothing for a long time. Then she spoke slowly, avoiding his eyes again. "What will happen if you win, Alain?"

"What do you mean?"

"You have spent all this time chasing a dream. What if winning the dream means the end of the interest?"

"Angélique, that's the biggest bunch of nonsense I've ever heard. It's you I want, not the chasing. Every time we had a fight and you went away I was sick for weeks." He paused to think. "Angélique, why do you have to keep putting obstacles in front of yourself?"

She moved to stand close to him, inviting an arm around her, which he provided. Her voice came softly, her head down. "I guess I'm afraid to make a mistake." She turned but did not move away, looking up at him. "Alain, all my life I was told that my parents would find a husband for me. I hated it and I complained bitterly, but it was comforting in a way. Now I have to make that decision for myself, so it's hard. What if I get to choose like I want to and I make a mess of it? How will all my protestations sound then? Not only will I have an unhappy marriage but I'll look like a fool, too. At least under the old system I would have had someone else to blame."

He sighed. "Angélique, you are so strange. In every other aspect of your life you rush ahead, all fire and attack, and I have to hold you back, calm you down. Yet here, the part that's supposed to be emotional, you're cold and calculating. You have life backwards."

"Maybe. But that's the way I am." Her head rested on his shoulder.

"No surprise to me." They stood without speaking. Then he broke the embrace, took her by the shoulders and looked her in the eye. "Why are we having this conversation?"

Her eyes dropped. "Well..."

"Angélique, look at me. Have you made a decision? Is that what you're trying to say?"

"Well, I've been doing a lot of thinking, and..." She stopped.

"Angélique, this has been a battle between us for so long, you feel you're losing somehow by giving in. It's not so. It's never been a battle between us. It's between you and yourself. I've only been helping out. So you can't lose. Have you decided that we should get married?"

Her head came up. "You've never asked me to marry you."

"I haven't?"

"Never. There was a whole lot of talk about love and being suited to each other, but never marriage. Why not?"

It was his turn to look down. "It wasn't the time. I guess I was afraid to put it that way. If you said, 'No,' well…"

"So you never asked."

"You weren't ready to answer. Why make it worse?"

"So when are you going to decide that it's time?"

He threw up his hands in despair. "I've been waiting for you for all these years, and now it's all my fault because I didn't ask!"

She smiled, too sweetly. "So?"

"I suppose I ought to do this right in spite of you." He took a deep breath. "Angélique, I love you. Will you marry me?"

She looked up at him, the play gone from her eyes. "I have been thinking a lot, and I have made my decision. Yes, Alain. I love you, and I want to marry you. I may have known it for ages, but now I know it for sure. We'll be very happy, don't you think?"

It was a moment he would remember for the rest of this life. She lifted her arms around his neck and pressed against him, her lips raised for his kiss. They stood that way a long time, warmth suffusing them. After a while, they leaned back and looked at each other. Then she laughed and pulled him close again, and he laughed too.

"I love you, Alain. I have so often wanted to say that."

"Why didn't you, you goose?"

She ignored the insult and thought over the question. "It wouldn't have been fair. I wasn't sure how much I meant it. And you were always so serious, I just couldn't."

"Well, thank you for your concern. It shows how much you loved me, even then."

"Perhaps. It doesn't matter now, though, does it?"

"No. You can tell me you love me all you like, now. Please do. Feel free."

"Don't push me. I'm not in practice."

He grinned. "I can wait. I've had plenty of practice. But now we can get down to business."

She raised her eyebrows.

"We have spent too much of our energies on this problem for the past few years. Now we can turn all our attention toward our other projects and work as a real team."

"I thought we were doing pretty well, already."

"Oh, we were. But it's going to be better now. Just watch. Let that inspector come. Bring him on. We'll face him, together."

"Together." They embraced again.

"Am I interrupting something?"

They separated with a guilty start to see Alain's mother standing in the doorway. Then he remembered and pulled Angélique closer again. "Nothing important, Maman. We were just deciding to get married."

"Oh. It's about time. Well, I came down to tell you that lunch was ready. When you are finished, come on and eat." She turned and started back up the stairs again, leaving the two in the office looking at each other in stunned surprise.

Then she turned back and rushed to them. "Alain, Angélique, I'm so happy for you." She gathered both of them in a warm hug. "You sounded so casual about it I couldn't help but tease you. And by the way, your timing is terrible."

"What do you mean?"

"My dear, if Alain gets married he won't be conscripted into the army. We wouldn't have had all the worry this afternoon."

"But before this afternoon I wasn't sure. It was the idea of him in danger of getting killed that made me understand how I felt."

"Well, whatever the reason, I'm sure you'll be very happy." She took each by one hand led them towards the stairs. "I only have a simple lunch prepared, but I suppose we could have a bottle of the best wine. There was a sweet I was planning for supper, and we can have that now. You ought to arrange things better, you two. Give a person a few minutes' notice."

They all laughed and went up the stairs to where Alain's father and the maid were standing in the middle of the living room, puzzled at the racket.

30. Fugitive

September, 1793

Late one afternoon Alain's work was interrupted by the sound of carriage wheels outside and then a rapping on the door: not loud but insistent. Making his way through the cluttered office to the window, he pulled back the curtain. A sweating horse, its flanks heaving, drooped in the street and a familiar-looking man stood on the doorstep. His father glanced out, then motioned Alain to open the door.

The man stumbled in, his hair messed, his coat undone. Alain recognized him now. He was a magistrate in Serres, a former mayor of the town. "Jouvent. Thank *le bon dieu* you're home. They're after me, Jouvent. What am I going to do? You have to help me. Please! How can I get away?"

Alain's father led the shaking man to a chair. "*S'il vous plait*, M. Achard. Calm down. Who is after you? What has happened in Serres? I thought you had those problems all sorted out."

"Sorted out!" Achard stared into the fire, shaking his head. "Certainly we had them sorted out. We had those three troublemakers put out of the way where they couldn't cause any more riots, and the duly elected officials returned to their posts. But that couldn't last, could it? Not with the Convention riddled with Jacobins. Jacques somehow got word to Marseille, and those two hell-hounds, Barras and Fréron, came back again. They have turned everything around. I am to be charged with 'Unlawful arrest of patriots.' Patriots, *par le bon dieu*! Can you imagine anyone less concerned with France, and more concerned with his own hide than Jean Jacques?"

"Not unless it's that sleazy brother-in-law of his, Bravet."

"Well, there you have it, Jouvent. They are back in power and bent on revenge. Jacques has been 'elected' justice of the peace, their good friend Joubert is now a national agent, and they are sending Bravet to Paris to be a member of one of the tribunals there. Can you imagine? The fate of French citizens in the hands of a man who would cheat the municipality out of flood relief funds? That's democracy? That's justice?"

"Good riddance to him. Let us pray that he never comes back to the Hautes-Alpes to practice what he learns in Paris." Jouvent leaned closer. "But what brings you here?"

The former mayor stood up, began pacing. "I got word this afternoon. I'm to be arrested, along with Dr. Chevadier. That means I go to jail if I'm lucky. There is no such thing as a fair trial with those two throwing their power around. Hah! Democracy! I had to run, Jouvent. I can't let them catch me. Can you hide me?"

"I don't know, Achard. It isn't as if you slipped in here unnoticed. We aren't all decent people in this village, either. If you must run, I suggest you leave the carriage and borrow a saddle. Do you have anywhere to go?"

The man's bitterness showed through. "I suppose Lyon is my only chance. I can't believe it. Me, a patriot, going to the rebels in Lyon. Why should I be forced to do such a thing?"

"My friend, there is a madness loose in France, and I'm afraid it will get worse before it gets better."

Achard regarded Jouvent. "They told me you were taking on like Cassandra."

The lawyer smiled with a matching bitterness. "There's one difference, though."

"*Oui*. Nobody considers you mad. They all believe you."

"So far, I haven't been too far off the mark."

The discussion was cut short by the sound of galloping hoofbeats on the main road, approaching from the west.

"*Mon dieu*, they're here! What am I going to do?"

"There's nothing much you can do. Alain, get that horse and carriage out of sight. If no one who would talk has noticed you, it may be all right. We have ways of keeping you out of sight, don't we, Alain?"

Alain nodded. He knew what his father meant. "For a short time, anyway. I'll see to the horse, then get the others." He slipped out the door and led the horse around to the stable, pushing the light carriage in as far as he could. In the gathering darkness it would be fine, but a daylight search would be a different matter.

Shutting the stable door, he ran to the *boulangerie* to get Aimée. Until this moment, it hadn't occurred to him how much they all depended on her brother. However, she had the same brains, as he soon became aware.

"I'll go to the *chateau* for Angélique and Jimmy. He's been visiting more often since her father left, and he's there now. You could check what's happening in the village, and we can all meet back at your office. Does that sound good?"

He grinned. "Couldn't have figured it better myself. I imagine the messengers will have gone to Reynaud's headquarters in the *Mairie*."

She turned without another word and hurried off. Forcing himself to slow his pace, he strolled towards the centre of town.

Too late.

As he approached the National Guard building the door burst open and Reynaud de Gonillons came out strutting more that usual, if that was possible. Alain could hear the nasal voice clearly.

"I know where to look. He'll be with that snake, Jouvent. A *révisionniste* if I ever saw one. But we'll have to be careful. Do this all legal-like. Jouvent's an old fox, and his brat is even sneakier." He shouted to his guardsmen to form up ranks and turned to the two men who had followed him out of the building.

Alain didn't pause to hear any more. *Revisionist? He doesn't even know what the word means.* He scooted back up the street and cut for home at a run.

"Too late, *Papa.* They're already coming." He looked at the portly figure of the former mayor. "There's no way he can run, *Papa.* We'll have to do it the Paris way, not mine."

"We'll depend on the fact that these men are not liked here, and neither is de Gonillons."

"That means a crowd, *oui?*"

"As big a crowd as you can find."

"Right. Stall them for as long as you can." Alain whisked out the door and was down the street towards the *chateau* before the marching feet he could hear turned the corner. He met Aimée, Angélique and Jimmy hurrying towards him. He outlined the situation.

"We need everyone we can get. All the villagers, especially the loyal ones like your father and his friends, Aimée. Jimmy, you're the fastest. You get over to Gonillons and les Percevaux. Angélique: back to the *chateau* and Buissiere. I'll take this side of the village, and Aimée, you take the north side on your way back. Don't stop to argue with anyone. Just shout out that they're arresting Mayor Achard. He's not the mayor any more, but it helps. Let's go!"

He sprinted off without a backward glance. He moved as fast as he could, but even so there was quite a crowd gathered outside the law office when he returned. Aimée was there before him and gave him a wave as he strode up.

People continued to gather over the next few minutes, and the young National Guardsmen in the street began to look anxious, backing closer to the building, talking in worried whispers, their bayonets waving nervously.

Soon Angélique and Jimmy were there too, and the four of them stood where they had a good view of the door.

"I won't go in."

"You can do much better out here." Angélique held his arm firmly.

Jimmy was picking up rocks.

"What do you plan to do with those?"

The usual knowing grin. "A stone chucked at the right moment can have a great effect. Ya hafta be sharp, though. Ya gotta hit the right man. Sometimes it's a soldier you wanta hit, but sometimes it's the victim. Get the crowd's sympathies goin', you know? Don't worry. I bin here before."

"I suppose you have. Be careful."

The boy shot Alain a look of scorn. "Ya don't survive the streets of Marseille and Paris without a good idea of when not to stick yer neck out."

The door of the law office was wrenched open and Reynaud de Gonillons stepped out holding Achard with one arm twisted behind his back. There was a muttering in the crowd. He stopped and looked around, frowning. Barras and Fréron followed close behind. They didn't look upset at all. A voice at Alain's elbow put him in the picture.

"This is the kinda stuff they expect: arrests, mobs roamin' the street, all that. Watch, now. One of them'll start makin' a speech about traitors 'n' the Revolution."

A moment later, Alain and Angélique were both staring at the smaller boy in wonder. Fréron had stepped forward, filling his lungs.

"People of Savournon. *Citoyens*. Patriots. I am glad that so many of you have come to see the justice of the Revolution. Our *cher patrie* is in dire straits and needs all our help. The traitors and the royalists must be weeded out. An example must be made of the guilty. We must clean out this nest of parasites and make Savournon a true Revolutionary village." Jimmy nudged Alain and snickered, loud enough that the speaker heard him. It took Fréron a moment longer to realize that the crowd wasn't cheering, but he stumbled on. Gradually it became clear to him that this wasn't his sort of crowd. He slowed down at first, then stopped. He began to look frightened, shooting glances at the people around him. No one said anything; they just stared. Fréron backed up level with his cohort and motioned de Gonillons forward. The Guard Captain started to move ahead, but suddenly there were three large farmers surrounding him. A voice, gentle but loud enough to carry through the silent crowd, suggested he might be better off if he and his men went somewhere else.

De Gonillons went white. Alain could see his head twisting from side to side. He squirmed out of the group that surrounded him and signalled his men to back up against the building. But it was too late. By the time they got into a good defensive position there was nobody to guard. The street in front of the law office was crowded now, and all except the soldiers were jostling and moving. Somehow Achard got separated from everyone and disappeared. Alain saw the office door open and close. He circled through the edges of the crowd, headed for the stables.

By the time his father and the perspiring Achard came out the back door he had a fresh horse saddled. The man clambered up, and Alain's mother tossed him a cloth-wrapped bundle. He caught it, bemused.

"You won't want to stop tonight."

He nodded, started to say something.

"The speeches have been made, my friend. Time for movement." Jouvent slapped the horse's rump, and it carried its stunned burden into the dusk, headed east. "Good luck."

Alain's parents returned inside, but Alain cut out to the street. When he got there, the crowd was gone. He could see people wandering towards him from the road to Serres, so he went that way.

People were in high sprits. Several called out to him, and two slapped him on the back as they passed. From their attitude, something highly entertaining must have happened. He continued to walk.

Just above Pélissieres he met the bulk of the crowd returning with his friends in the middle. There was a roar when they saw him, and then he was the centre of a jostling, laughing mob, all shouting at him and shaking his hand. Angélique, her face glowing, slipped an arm around his waist and turned him around to walk with the rest. He looked over to see Aimée and Jimmy walking arm-in-arm as well. *How long has that been going on?*

They grinned at him. "How did we do?"

He had to shout to answer. "You tell me. What happened?"

"Tell you later!" The rest was lost in the celebration.

They turned off at the *chateau* while the rest of the crowd, shouting pleasantries, wandered back into the village. Once inside, Jimmy took charge of the story.

"After you left to get the horse ready, we moved in. I got ridda the rocks, 'cause I knew they wouldn't be no use. I started talkin' it up, about how as they didn't belong here, and we oughta run 'em outa the village. Soon enough everybody was sayin' it. We separated those two from the sojers clean as Angélique's best sheep dog could, and started pushin 'em, ever so gentle-like, towards the road. Aimée 'n' Angélique were right there, in the middle of it all, Aimée makin' sure nobody hurt nobody." He shook his head in wonder. "She stopped that big kid from Gonillons from throwin' a rock. Just stood there and looked at him, and he crumpled up and dropped it!" He put his arm around her shoulders, and she blushed bright red.

Alain nodded. "If either of them had been injured, even a little bit, they'd have been back with the soldiers."

The Rat nodded and continued. "Anyways, we kept nudgin' them, and after a while they got to the edge of the crowd. Seein' there was nobody in front of 'em, they started to run. Big mistake! They starts runnin', what'r' we gonna do but start chasin'?

"We chased 'em down the road, laughin' and throwin' stinky vegetables at 'em the whole time. Didn't stop until they was a coupla hundred paces outside the village. Then we let 'em go. They're still walkin', I bet. They'll be all the way to Serres before they'll find anybody to help 'em. Word spreads fast, you know."

His story was interrupted by a pounding on the front door of the *chateau*. Alain rose. "I'll get it."

A minute or two later he was back, looking grim.

"It seems we didn't run them out of town soon enough."

"What's wrong?" Angélique rose and went to him.

"That was our dear friend Reynaud. He demanded to speak to your father. He knows your parents have left the country, Angélique. He told me, with great pleasure, that in his new position as *justice de la paix* he would be rigorous in making sure the belongings of all *emigré*s came into government hands."

Angélique gave a strained smile. "He will be one angry man when he discovers how difficult that will be, and how little he's going to get if he does succeed."

Alain shook his head. "That new legislation has defined relatives of emigrés as suspects before the law unless they have 'constantly demonstrated their devotion to the Revolution.' Whatever that means."

"Angélique has constantly demonstrated her devotion to the Revolution." Aimée swung her hand around the small group. "Far more than the rest of us have."

He grimaced. "Well, she is going to have to keep doing so. Every time that man comes up against us we beat him, and every time he gets angrier. The only thing that keeps him in check is his own delicate position as a former aristocrat. I hope that he never gets so angry that he forgets to follow the law."

Their victory dampened, they sat in silence.

31. Feudal Parchments and Titles

Nov 1793

Alain was alone in the office, working on a brief that his father would be presenting to the new *chef-lieu* in Serres. The reorganization of the *Departement* had been another boon to the Jouvent business, as they could handle more work now that they didn't have to go all the way to Gap for court appearances. Alain was trying to do his best on this material, as his father had no time for it. Whatever Alain provided would be presented in court.

As a result Alain was irritated when he heard the strident knock. Closing his book on a place marker, he rose and went to answer. As he passed the window, he noticed two National Guardsmen in the street. He hesitated, then realizing that it was silly to be worried before he knew anything was wrong, he opened the door.

Reynaud de Gonillons stood there, complete with his uniform and sword. His hand held a piece of paper. His face held a look of gloating pleasure. He started to push past Alain, who gave back one step, then stopped.

"Be careful, de Gonillons. You have no right to force your way into the home of a citizen. Remember that anything you do here could be brought up in court."

The man paused, then thrust the paper at him. "This paper gives me plenty of rights, boy."

"What paper is that?"

"These are my orders from the Director of the Department in Gap, written November 17, instructing me to enforce with 'all possible zeal' the January 17th Decree." He began to read aloud with a great deal of pleasure and importance. "'We remind you of this task, and you must impress on yourselves without doubt to make sure that the pure air that free men must breathe is not infected by the pestilential odours of feudal parchments and titles.' What do you think of that, boy?"

Alain thought furiously. "Feudal parchments and titles? What are you talking about?"

"Since you don't know, lawyer boy, the Decree of January 17 calls for the destruction of all documents relating to the injustice of the *Ancien Régime.* Anyone caught in possession of these titles is not only breaking the law, but also under suspicion of wanting to bring back the *Regime.* It is my duty to destroy all these old papers, and I am here to find them."

"Looking for something in particular, de Gonillons?"

Reynaud drew himself up. "That name is a vestige of the feudal past. In the future you will call me Renaud Lafrance." The angle of his head changed as he said this, and Alain caught the distinct impression that the man was proud of this new name. *Does he really believe all the garbage he is spouting?*

"Trust you to switch to the winning side."

Reynaud moved in a flash, the back of his hand catching Alain across the cheek. "Watch your tongue, boy."

Alain balanced on his toes, his fists clenching. A red anger was rising in him, but he could see the man's hand toying with the hilt of his sword, a smile of anticipation on his face. Alain forced himself to calm down. Much though it rankled, physical satisfaction was out of reach.

"So what business does that give you with us, de Gonillons?" He said the name clearly, and with disdain.

The man's face reddened, but he made no further move. "You have records of cases from past years. You have been keeping copies of these feudal parchments and titles it refers to in the decree. I'm going to have a look through your records and weed out these signs of decadence."

"All of a sudden it's illegal to keep records?"

"If they contain reference to illegal situations, I guess it is. Now let me see your records, boy."

"But those are records of the legal work of most of the people in the village. They're confidential. You can't just go looking through all of them!" Alain could feel the desperation rising now. His opponent was enjoying this scene as only a bully could.

Reynaud smiled in mocking pleasantry. "Ah, but I can. When you do something illegal, you lose all those rights."

Alain hesitated. This sounded wrong to him, but he was unsure of the legal situation. Who could tell what new powers the decree had given to the National Guard? To his immense relief, his father's voice sounded from behind him. From the anger on his face, the elder Jouvent had been standing there for some time.

"I fail to see that any illegal act has occurred at this moment, de Gonillons." His father sounded cool, confident. "Unless it was your unprovoked assault on my son just now. I'm sure that a few of my papers fall in contravention of the new decree, and I thank you for drawing my attention to the matter."

He smiled, glancing at the orders. "The decree gives you the right to request to see any document you have reason to believe is illegal. At that point, I may show it to you, or I may withhold it, at which point I must give my reasons before the Tribunal for my action."

Jouvent stepped forward again, his chest brushing the paper that de Gonillons held in front of him like a weapon. "At no point in this process will a member of the National Guard be free to go through my papers, to pry out whatever dirt he wishes to use to his advantage." He moved forward again, and the man was forced to give ground. "At no point will you be allowed to look at any given document, as long as it is legal." He paused. "Especially if it regards the de Bardel estate."

He stepped forward again, reaching for the door handle. "I assure you that Alain and I will go through the files in the next few days and take care of the situation. Goodbye,

Seigneur de Gonillons." He held the door open politely, but the look on his face held no compromise.

The Guardsman hesitated, his mouth opening and then closing.

"I'll be checking on you!" was all he could manage.

"I'm sure you will. And I'll be checking on you. The powers of the National Guard are not unlimited. If you throw your weight around too much more, you may find yourself answering to your superiors." He closed the door in the man's face. Alain watched through the curtains as de Gonillons shouted his men into formation and marched them off.

He turned. His father was also watching.

"I'm not sure I should have said that, but I was upset at him for hitting you."

"Why shouldn't you have said it?"

"It's a choice. Do I leave him free to bully people until he crosses the line and we can prosecute him to get rid of him, or do I warn him and hope it will keep him under control?"

"You did right. Think of the pain he might cause while we waited for him to make a stupid move."

"It could be. Still, I hate to act in anger, even if I do have an idea what I'm doing. That man is holding himself on a very weak leash, and his political power is growing. How's your face?"

Alain considered. The numbness had gone, and his cheek was throbbing.

"Nothing serious. Just my pride hurt, I guess."

32. The Terror Begins

Summer 1794

Messidor, An 2

Alain was roused from his work by the sound of marching men in the street. Not many, but in step. *The National Guard. I wonder...* He moved to the window and looked out. Sure enough, four Guardsmen were strutting along, Reynaud de Gonillons at their head. He could see the officer shooting a smug grin as he passed.

"Father..."

"They aren't just out for a stroll. You hotfoot it to the *chateau.*"

"*D'accord.*" He was out the back door without coat or hat, taking the back street along the bottom of the hill to the outbuildings behind the *chateau.* Inside the kitchen door the cook stood wide-eyed, staring down the hallway to the front, where he could hear loud voices. One of them Angélique's.

"And what makes you think you can barge in here without even wiping your dirty boots?"

"This warrant makes me think so, little girl."

Alain stepped into the entry hall just as de Gonillons was moving forward. Seeing him, the Guardsman stopped, and Alain spoke before he lost the advantage.

"What is this warrant you're so pleased about? May I see it?"

"This warrant has nothing to do with you, lawyer boy." De Gonillons pulled it back to his chest.

"Well, since it seems to have my name on it, I gather it has something to do with me." Angélique reached out. With reluctance, he gave her the paper, which she then handed to Alain.

Alain glanced down the list. "Abetting emigrés, owning forfeited property. Aha! 'having maliciously and purposefully made statements attacking the sovereignty of the people to men who for the past four years have not stopped making the greatest sacrifices for liberty' *Mon dieu*, Angélique. You have been accused of calling someone names! I wonder who?" He nodded. "Yes, this is about what we expected."

"All right then..." de Gonillons reached for Angélique's arm.

"However, there seems to be something missing, *sieur* de Gonillons."

His hand hovered. "What do you mean?"

"The part that says you are supposed to arrest her."

"What? Of course I'm supposed to arrest her."

"Then it should say so. According to the charge, she is to present herself – herself, note. That means on her own – before the Revolutionary Committee in Grenoble on 25 Messidor,' Um...that's July 13, '...to give reason why she should not be arraigned before the Revolutionary Tribunal of Grenoble to make answer to these charges.' She has not been charged yet. She shall not be arrested."

De Gonillons' sneer came back, but his hand dropped. "And who thinks she's actually going to show up?"

"The Revolutionary Committee does, because that's what the letter says. Reynaud, you can't make up the law to suit yourself. Angélique has done nothing wrong, especially nothing that will allow you to get your hands on her in one of your cells. Now that you have performed your little chore you can run along." He stepped forward and realized that he was looking down into the man's eyes, which darted left and right, taking in the new breadth of Alain's shoulders. *I ought to do more plowing. It might be good for my health.*

"Well, I wish her the best of luck in front of that Tribunal. She will soon wish she had stayed home and dealt with me. They are a whole new level of the Revolution, and your little lawyer tricks won't have a whole lot of effect on them. They make the law, they don't bend to it."

"You dare to crow about the fact that France has fallen into the hands of those who disregard the laws that are enacted to govern and protect us. Where do you get your morals?" Alain felt the rage building in him, and he stepped forward again. "There is no room for such as you in this house, and soon there will be no room for you in France. It would be better for you if you leave!"

To his surprise, the Guardsman snarled and turned out the door, disappearing down the steps into the growing dusk, his soldiers stumbling behind him.

Angélique was beside Alain, her arm around his waist. "I hear Nana de Dillon cackling to herself."

He grinned. "She would have enjoyed that."

She laid her head against his shoulder. "We must take our small pleasures where we may. I'm afraid he's right about one thing."

"Yes. That Tribunal in Grenoble is a direct offshoot of the Jacobins in Paris, and I doubt if they have any respect for any law except the law of their own might."

33. Angélique's Hearing

July 12-13, 1794

24-25 Messidor, An 2

The de Bardel family had given up their apartments in Grenoble, so Angélique was staying with a friend of her mother's, a short, hospitable lady who treated her guest as a visiting princess.

When Alain teased the good woman about it, she raised her pointy nose and suggested that some people deserved the best, while others got what was coming to them.

It was comforting that his fiancé was staying in such amenable surroundings, and Alain went with his father to their business quarters with a lighter heart.

The following day was one for Alain to remember. 25 Messidor, An 2. He couldn't help but think of it as July 13, 1794 in the rest of the world, but he was in France, and Angélique was in danger of going to prison, and the unreality of the situation still hit him like a hammer to the chest when he thought of it. Which was often.

They picked Angélique up at an early hour to make sure that they were not late for the hearing, although the streets of Grenoble were hardly bustling. The citizens plodded about their business, making no eye contact and not stopping to talk unless necessary.

When she came out to the carriage she was carrying a valise. "What...?" Then he understood. "Surely you don't...?"

"I don't know what to think, Alain, and I want to be prepared. Much better to carry this all day and joke about it on the way home than not to have it and discover I need it."

There was no answer to that, so he put his arm around her and held her for the short journey to the Liberation Hall.

The huge room, with a few tall windows streaming shafts of light, was far too big for the intended meeting, which gave the whole thing a shadowy, temporary air, like children playing in adults' clothes. At the end of the hall was a statue of justice, holding scales in one hand and a sword in the other, the book of laws by her side. Under the statue sat the three members of the Revolutionary Committee, plainly dressed and dwarfed by their august surroundings. The Public Prosecutor sat to their left with his secretary and his papers. A Guardsman escorted Angélique to a plain wooden bench on their right. There were a few spectators in the benches that filled the rest of the hall, and Alain and his father, refused permission to sit with their client, sat at the centre in front.

When Angélique was seated the Prosecutor signalled to the clerk, who rose and stepped forward.

"*Citoyens.* Jules Prémery, Public Prosecutor before the Revolutionary Tribunal, states that, by order of the administrators of police, dated 17 Messidor in the year Two of the Republic, Angélique Diane de Bardel, having been accused of aiding and abetting those in enmity with the Republic, to wit those emigrés residing in Switzerland, contrary to the law of 14 Fructidor in the year Two of the Republic, and also of owning property forfeit to the state, and also having maliciously and purposefully made statements attacking the sovereignty of the people to men who for the past four years have not stopped making the greatest sacrifices for liberty, be required to show reason why she should not be brought before the Revolutionary Tribunal to answer for these crimes with her life, as is provided for in the law of 22 Prairial in the year One of the Republic.

"Consequently, the Public Prosecutor asks that he be given official notice by the assembled Revolutionary Committee of this indictment, and that on the basis of the foregoing, he be charged with drawing up this accusation against Angélique Diane de Bardel, for presentation before the Revolutionary Tribunal."

The clerk sat, and Alain met Angélique's eye. This was nothing new, merely a repeat of the summons.

The central Committee member nodded. "Could we hear the specifics of these charges, that the accused may answer to our satisfaction?"

The Prosecutor stood. "Yes, *citoyen.*" He turned to Angélique. "On the first charge, *citoyenne*, is it not true that your parents, Marie-François de Charrette and Charles de Bardel, now reside in Switzerland with the rest of the traitors encouraging the reestablishment of the monarchical government?"

Angélique stood. "It is true, *citoyens,* that my parents are in Switzerland temporarily. My mother is very ill, and my father has gone to give her support. I have with me documents from the sanitorium in Switzerland attesting to her condition. I deny that my parents are conspiring in any way against the Republic."

Alain held up the papers, and the clerk came and collected them.

The Prosecutor cleared his throat and looked to the Committee. They seemed to have no questions.

"On the second charge, *citoyenne,* is it not true that you hold extensive properties in the valley of Savournon in the *departement des Hautes-Alpes*, formerly the feudal estates of your family?"

"That is no longer true, *citoyen.* I have given over deed and title to all those former estates to the *citoyens* who work the land. I now only own title to my own home."

"Aha, but therein lies the deceit. Did your father not, in fact, sell that land to the former tenants, and does he not live in luxury in a foreign country, using French moneys to conspire against the *republique*?"

"No, he does not. The lands were turned over to their tenants on the understanding that they would pay, certainly. But that payment is to come over a long period of time, and neither my father nor I has access to the capital."

"But nevertheless, your actions must be construed as contrary to the weal of the *republique*."

"I think not, *citoyen*. Before the law of 22 Prairial in the year I, it was within my father's right to sell those lands to whomever he pleased and take any profit he could. Many of the landowners did this. In that case, the land went to anyone who had the cash in hand, leaving the present tenants, *citoyens* of the *republique* and productive farmers, without a living. Instead my father chose to accept a lower return to assure that those honest *citoyens* could continue to support the *republique* with their labours and support their families as well."

"And your family mansion? Surely you don't expect to live in your *Ancien Régime* luxury."

"My house in Savournon is hardly luxury any more. I hope the *republique* will allow me somewhere to live. As it happens, we have applied to house one of the orphanages the *republique* is creating to shelter the children whose parents have fallen to the guillotine and other accidents. The size of the house demands that sort of use."

"And have you been awarded this orphanage?"

"No, but I have every confidence we will, once this is all out of the way."

Again the Prosecutor looked to his masters, but received no orders. He cleared his throat and referred to his charge sheet.

"As to the third charge. Did you not, on 13 Fructidor, state that 'When you boil the pot the scum rises to the surface,' or words to that effect?"

"I may have said words to that effect."

The Prosecutor straightened his back and half-turned as if he was playing to the Committee behind him. "It is with the most violent indignation that one hears this woman speak such insults to men who for the past four years have not stopped making the greatest sacrifices for liberty; who on 10

August 1792, overturned both the throne and the tyrant; who knew how to bravely face the arms and frustrate the plots of the despot, his slaves, and the traitors who had abused the public confidence, to men who have submitted tyranny to the avenging blade of the law so that Louis Capet no longer reigns among them."

Angélique burst into laughter. The rest of the room fell deadly silent.

"I directed those words to and about a specific person. A self-important popinjay of a former aristocrat, a leopard who changed his spots to attain a soft position for himself as a Captain in the National Guard. Who struts around our village puffed up with his own importance, bringing down the reputation of the National Guard and the *republique* it should protect. The only sacrifice he has made for liberty is stuffing his growing belly into the uniform he does not deserve. That is whom I was referring to. No one else."

Please, Angélique. Stop now! It was too much to expect.

She swept the hair back from her face. "If there are others in this *republique* who have acted in similar ways, and I have no doubt there are, I leave it to them to judge themselves. I say nothing to them or of them. I count on the *citoyens* of the Revolutionary Tribunal to do their duties to rid our *patrie* of the real traitors who have abused the public confidence."

The echoes of her voice faded, and she stood, her hair flaming around her, her light panting breath the only sound in the room. Alain wanted to jump up and applaud.

There was a long pause, and then the Head of the Committee spoke. "Are there any more questions?"

The Prosecutor shook his head and returned to his seat. Angélique stood with her head high, looking at no one. The three Committee members put their heads together for a brief chat. Then the Head of the Committee rose.

Far too brief. I don't like this. Alain shared a worried look with his father.

"Thank you for your information, *citoyenne*. You have answered all our questions," he glanced over at François Jouvent, "and I have no doubt that your transactions were completed within the letter of the law. As it stood then. However, there are still grave concerns about your contacts with the *emigré* traitors outside our borders, and the inflammatory nature of your comments about members of the *republique*. This Committee does not feel qualified to judge such matters, and so it is our unanimous decision that the Public Prosecutor draw up these charges for presentation before the Revolutionary Tribunal. You are therefore commanded to stand before the Tribunal to face the consequences of these charges against you. Due to your association with the *emigré* traitors, you are considered a danger to flee, and therefore we order you kept in *la bastille de Grenoble* until such a time as these charges are prepared."

He nodded to the Guardsman who had moved up behind Angélique. "Take *citoyenne* de Bardel to *la bastille*."

Alain felt as if the wind had been knocked out of him. He sat, his mouth open, gazing at Angélique. She stood, her cheeks red, staring straight in front. Then she broke from her reverie. She glanced at Alain, shrugged and picked up her valise, holding it out with a rueful smile as she turned.

He understood the gesture. *We knew this might happen. I am not to let it get to me. I'm supposed to stay calm, stay in control. Be a lawyer. She needs a lawyer, not a milksop.*

But they're taking her away!

His thoughts swirled about that one agonizing fact as he stood, unaware of his surroundings, until he felt his father's arm around his shoulders, turning him from where he had been staring at the door as it closed behind her.

"Come, son. Now our work starts."

His knees weak and his lip trembling, Alain followed.

* * *

Once they were in the privacy of their office, the elder Jouvent sat his son down and pulled a chair to face him. "I won't try to fool you, Alain, this doesn't look good. Do you know what the Head of the Committee said to me?"

"Huh...who?"

His father shook his head. "I suppose you weren't paying attention. Just before we left, M. Fouquier took me aside. He knew all the details of Angélique's case. He didn't say it out loud, but his hands were tied. What he did say was, 'Don't let that son of yours marry her until this is all over'."

"Don't marry her?"

"Good advice, lad. If she is convicted, her family suffers." He raised a hand. "I know you'd be willing if it would help any. But it won't. She knows that; don't worry. But it was good of Fouquier to try to help. It goes to show that the people in the system aren't all violent and power hungry. There are a lot of decent men trying to stay alive and keep things running until this misery ends."

Alain buried his face in his hands. "It's never going to end."

His father slapped him on the back. "Oh, it will be over, don't doubt it. Our task is to see that Angélique is here when it is."

Alain raised his head. "What can we do? They won't let us stand with her. They won't let her have any counsel at all."

"Not in court. But we can do what we always do. Collect information. Find out names. Look for every crevice and cranny in the laws as they were, as they are and wherever they might not be looking."

Alain looked up at his father. "...might not be looking?"

"This isn't the Law as I taught you, son. This is the politics of power. We use anything and everything we can, legal or illegal. There is no honour in the enemy, and we do not have to treat them with the usual respect."

He picked up a pen. "Now, you have letters to write. Your first one is to Savournon. I want Jimmy here."

"Jimmy?"

"He's the most experienced agent we have, the best there is. He can do things you and I could never dream of."

"That he can. I'll start writing."

"Good. I have to go out now, because I have people to talk to. When you finish that, write a letter explaining the situation. This list," he wrote names on a sheet of paper, "give them the general outline. This list, you give all the legal details." He wrote a few names in a second column. "I'll sign them when I get back."

"I'll start right away." Alain sat down at his desk and uncapped the ink bottle.

His father picked up his hat and strode out.

34. Hero of the Revolution

July 21, 1794

3 Thermidor, An 2

Alain strode down the dark tunnel, trying to ignore the aura of misery that permeated the place. Angélique was waiting at the door to her cell.

"Look, Angélique. Aimée passed on a letter from Edmond. It's dated July 6. She got it the 16th. It got to me yesterday. That's three weeks ago, so he'll be even better by now."

"Better from what?"

"Read it. It's a great letter, and I suspect he's mostly telling the truth."

She gave a small grin. "Now you have piqued my interest. Give it to me."

He passed it through the bars.

Fleurus, La Belgique

July 6, 1794

My Dear Sister,

I want you to know that I am fine. I really am, in spite of the fact that I am writing this in my hospital bed. Forgive me if I wander a bit, but the laudanum they give me makes my brain feel fuzzy.

As you may have guessed, I was wounded. But before that, what a time I had!

My compagnie d'aérostiers was attached to General Jourdan's Army of the Republic, against the Coalition of English, Hanoverian, Dutch, and Hapsburg armies. That sounds like a lot of men, but just wait!

It was June 26, and the armies met in Fleurus, Belgium. I was up in the balloon, observing the enemy forces. It's wonderful! My balloon was called " l'Entreprenant." It was filled with hydrogen and attached to a long cable. They let us up over the battlefield, and we used semaphore flags to signal the troop movements to the generals, and wrote the messages and dropped them down. The Coalition troops were coming in five columns, and without us it would have been hard for our leaders to know where they all were. But we knew! We sat up

there like raptors on a crag and we
could see everything.

Unfortunately, it didn't take the
royalists long to figure out what we
were doing, so they started shooting at
us. Somehow one of the bullets set
the balloon on fire. Must have glanced
off a piece of metal and made a spark.
We'll have to work on that. Happily
for me, they were winching
l'Entreprenant down when it caught
fire. I waited as long as I could, but
it was getting too hot, so I jumped.
My lower left leg was smashed pretty
bad, so they took it off at the knee.
But we won the battle!

Another good part is that the
Army doesn't want me anymore, so now
I'm a " héros de la république," and
I'm coming home with a pension.

But I won't stop helping the
republique. I got interested in all that
coding and messaging. I have contacts
in the Army, and they'll be keeping in
touch. We've got ideas, and some of

them are working. I can stay home and still do my duty for France.

I'll be a month or so recuperating, but soon after that I'll make my way home.

Please tell the others I Am FINE, and tell them several times in a loud voice, because otherwise they won't believe you. Tell Angélique not to worry. They did a great job of the operation, though I wasn't so happy about it at the time. My leg is healing cleanly, and I can already get up and move around on my crutches.

Tell Papa I will still be able to clean the ovens and keep his books in order. I even got a new recipe for bread, although I don't know if the people of Savournon will like what the armée de la république eats every day. It is very nourishing when they can find the right ingredients!

Your brother,

Edmond

"Poor Edmond!" Angélique let the letter fall against the bars.

Alain grinned. "He seems to be handling it pretty well. Note the part where he tells us he is fine. You're not believing him like he wanted you to."

She smiled wanly. "He was always going to make his living with his head, wasn't he? I don't see him sitting in a doorway begging with his crutch propped beside him."

"How are things in here?"

"Oh, about what you'd expect. Everyone trying valiantly to keep everyone else's spirits up. Nobody from this section has been tried, yet, so we're all optimistic." She shuddered. "There was a terrible cry from along the hall yesterday. Sounded like several women. I can guess what that meant."

He shuffled his feet. Try as he might, he couldn't come up with anything cheerful to say, so he went straight to business. "Um...there's...uh...something we need to discuss."

"What is it?"

"Well, you won't like it but...*Papa* thinks you should sell the *chateau*. It would remove one charge against you."

"But what would we do for an orphanage?"

"Keeping you alive is the first priority. We can work on the orphanage after that."

She sighed. "Your father's right. Bring me the papers to sign. You know, I might have expected to be terribly sad about it, but right now, it just doesn't seem important. Set a price so it will sell quickly."

"Don't worry. We'll get a good price for it. We need that money for the orphanage."

"Thank you, Alain. It helps to know that you're looking after me."

"And I will for a long time to come."

There was a long silence as they both stared at the blank stone walls in the flickering shadows of the lamps. *I have to think of something to cheer her up.*

"I've done a lot in the past few days."

Her head came up, and she tried to smile. "What have you been doing?"

"Well, we have a two-pronged approach. The first uses the legal system as any lawyers would. We have to work our contacts. *Papa* knows people at the highest level, from his legal work and his recent politics. My assignment is our personal friends." He snapped his fingers. "I just realized that I should have asked you. Is there anyone from your days with the political clubs that could help? Surely the people you know are more involved in the current government than any of our acquaintances."

She shook her head. "Most of them have quietly disappeared, and I wouldn't dream of bringing them into this. The ones who stayed on and are in power now became even more radical, and will have nothing to do with a traitor." She looked up at him. "Just as you predicted."

Her sadness sent a pang through him. "Being right doesn't enter into it. If there was any way I could make it different..."

Her finger on his lips silenced him. "I know, dear. I shouldn't even bring it up."

He searched for another topic. *Nothing. Everything I think of leads us back to where we are. In a dark prison, with even darker prospects.*

"What was the other prong?"

"What?"

"You said a two-pronged approach."

"Oh. Yes." He pulled her in closer. "The illegal system."

She pulled away, frowning. "Alain..."

"No, no, not that illegal. We're making all the other contacts we can to find out what is going on." He leaned even closer to whisper. "Our enemies are not using the proper channels. Why should we? Reynaud de Gonillons will show up here sooner or later. He has to, because his testimony is the most crucial. If we can discover him doing anything illegal, it would harm his case a great deal. So we're looking. You'd be amazed at how many people of all sorts *Papa* has crossed paths with. Those he defended in court, for example." He grinned. "Some of them several times."

Angélique's head came up. "I like that. Why should we play by the rules? Have you made any progress?"

"Nothing, yet, but don't worry. You know how we work. We keep coming up with ideas, and sooner or later one of them will be successful."

She leaned her head against his shoulder where he pressed it between the bars. "Don't make it too much later. I'm not looking ahead too far right now."

He tousled her hair. "And I've saved the best plan for last. We sent for Jimmy."

"What!"

He held his finger to his lips and nodded. "It was *Papa*'s idea. 'Send for the expert. He's the one who deals with these people.' What do you think of that?"

"Your father is a very smart man, and I'm suddenly a whole lot more confident. When is he coming?"

Alain shrugged. "He could be here already. He never was one to announce his arrival."

She smiled, the first real show of humour he had seen for days. "When you see him, give him my usual greetings."

"Two big kisses? Hardly appropriate. He's grown up a lot."

"He's still Jimmy. It's the only way to keep him in line."

He saluted. "Your wish is my command, *Mademoiselle*."

"Don't you forget it. Away you go. You have work to do."

* * *

Back at the legal offices, the elder Jouvent was deep in a pile of letters that had arrived from Paris the day before. When Alain came in, his father looked up, shaking his head.

"I don't like this, son."

Alain's heart gave a lurch. "You haven't liked anything you've heard, *Papa*. What is it this time?"

"This Law of 22 Pairial. It's turning out even worse than we thought it would. There is no more questioning of suspects. They go straight to trial. No cross-examining of witnesses, no evidence for the defence. And the only punishment allowed is death. They've sent over a thousand people to the guillotine since they got that law enacted."

"But Angélique isn't guilty!"

"And that could still be the verdict. But it all depends on who is on the jury, and whose friends they are. Remember, this isn't the legal system we set up. It's a farce created to keep the autocrats in power."

Alain sat slumped in his chair, head in his hands. "How could such a thing have happened, father?"

His father shrugged. "The difficulty of instilling the ideals of free will and enlightened government on an uneducated populace not ready for it. Gives those with ambition free rein to manipulate it as they will."

"But when you and the others made the new constitution didn't you consider all this?"

"Every step the *republique* has taken in this Revolution has been a step away from the ideals we started with and a step towards the cynical exercise of power for the sake of power. When the people of France understand this, they will also realize that the men in the Committee for Public Safety have no feelings of *fraternité*, and will never allow anyone else *liberté* or *egalité*. Only at that desperate point will the people band together and throw these frauds out."

"Well, we can't wait for that to happen. We have to get Angélique free."

"Alain, there is a time to act but also a time when there is little you can do. This is one of those times. The actions of those in power must play themselves out. Once again, we will do what we can. We cannot keep Angélique from the Tribunal. However, we may be able to stall, to play for time. I am working at the highest levels I can."

"And I'm doing nothing."

"You are lifting Angélique's spirits. From what I gather, she's doing the same for all the people in there with her. That is the most valuable work of all."

"So I do nothing."

"That's right. And most important, you do nothing that might jeopardize Angélique's chances or your freedom. Do you understand me?"

"Yes, father. I just don't like it."

"Neither do I, son."

* * *

It was not possible to live in fear for so long. Day after day, night after night, the feeling gnawed at Alain. He went through his duties, he ate, he slept, but it was always there, ready to pounce, ready to send a thrill of pain through his chest. He wondered what it must be like for Angélique and the other prisoners. It could only be worse.

What Alain saw in Grenoble frightened him. He remembered the city as being bright and friendly. Now he saw a city in fear. The *tricolore* brightened many public buildings, but to him the blue and white faded into the background, leaving the swaths of red like streams of blood running down the faces of the houses.

People in the street hurried past in a businesslike way, their shoulders hunched. No one met anyone's eye. It was as if a plague stalked the street, and everyone was afraid to make contact for fear of becoming infected.

Angélique was surviving. She and some of the other women had been moved out of the *bastille* to a nearby convent, and that raised her spirits. They were still in a basement, but her cell had a small window, high in the wall, and they were allowed an hour in the garden every afternoon. She was nursing somone who was ill, but the woman died. Alain could see this loss had a serious effect on Angélique, but she refused to let on. She spent her time organizing the other prisoners and trying to keep their spirits up. So far, there had been no convictions among their group.

"Of course not. Nobody here is guilty of anything except having the wrong enemies. As long as a little bit of justice prevails, we have a chance. Surely a few men of conscience still hold power."

Alain didn't tell her his opinion on that, as there was no sense in depressing her further. He looked at her in the dim light. She had lost weight, and her golden hair was not as bright as it used to be. However, she was neatly dressed, and her head held its usual aggressive tilt.

"Don't worry, Angélique. We're working on your case the best we can. There aren't any provable facts against you, and your work with the relief funds speaks for you. Your application for the orphanage counts as "constantly demonstrating your devotion to the Revolution," like it says in the Law of Suspects. If we could get de Gonillons out of the way the case would fall apart. We've been checking, but he seems to have been very careful this time. No slipups, no false moves. No reason to have him arrested. But we're still trying."

"He came looking for me."

"He did? Here? He's not allowed to do that."

"That's Reynaud. He does what he wants."

Gordon A. Long

"Did he find you?"

"No, but he knows I'm here."

"Well, he could get into trouble if he contacts you, when he's the one bringing charges against you. If he comes again, get witnesses and record everything. Maybe we can denounce him to the Tribunal!"

"I have confidence in your father's abilities, Alain, and you'll do your best. Just get me out of here so we can go on with our lives, *d'accord*?" She smiled. "We have a wedding coming up, and this is causing a great deal of difficulty in my planning of the occasion."

She sobered. "That is, if you still want to marry a criminal."

He reached out, took her hands, shook them. "Don't be ridiculous! You're innocent! There will come a time when having been jailed by this lot will be a badge of honour. Don't you worry. First we get you free, then we get us married. Right away. I love you, Angélique. More and more."

"I love you, Alain. I have for a long time. I just wish I'd figured it out earlier. Think of what we missed."

"You can't worry about that. Think of the future. We have a long time and a lot of things to do." He assumed a lecturing pose. "Now listen. I'm very busy at the moment, and you have time on your hands. I want you to come out of here with plans as to what we will do over the next few years. The orphanage will take a lot of our time. And just because you sold the land to the farmers doesn't mean your responsibilities are over. If they don't get proper production from the farms, they won't make their payments and we won't get paid. So get planning, my dear. Use this time wisely."

She laughed, then. Several heads turned, and he could see weak smiles responding to her. "You make this sound like a holiday I'm not supposed to enjoy too much."

He held her hands again, let his eyes rest on her. "I have to go, now. It's good to hear you laugh. I love you, and I'm going to get you out of here."

She moved close to the bars. "You do what you can. And if you can't..." Her voice failed, then went on. "If you can't, then don't blame yourself. I got myself into this. There are enemies you can't fight, and fights you can't win. I love you Alain. Now go."

"I love you." That was all. He turned and walked up the dark hallway towards the freedom of the open sky.

35. Desperate Plans

Late July, 1794

He was in the Rue des Imprimanteures one day picking up nibs and ink when a familiar voice sounded at his elbow. "Say, *citoyen,* can you send me to a good lawyer?"

He kept walking, his face turned to the front. "I might recommend someone. If he's allowed to be seen talking to you."

He felt a tug on his sleeve, then Jimmy clapped an arm across his back. "Good to see you, too."

He gave his friend a full hug. "Have you been here long?"

"A couple-three days. Bin lookin' around, getting' the lay of the land. Got myself a job."

"You did? Will you have time for that? *Papa* and I have some things we want …"

"Oh, I already done a lot of what you need. And this is a good job. It's in a convent."

"Not the convent where Angéliqe…"

"That's the important one, wouldn't you think? I'm in the kitchen. Helpin' the baker, wouldn't you know?"

"That's marvellous!"

The boy shook his head. "I hate that place, Alain. It's too dark and…unfree."

Alain shuddered. "I'll agree with you there."

"And they don't bake bread half as good as we do at home."

Alain grinned down at the lad. "It's 'we' and 'at home,' now, is it?"

Jimmy's head tilted. "Aimée and me, we got an arrangement. Once we get a little older we'll make it official. Her *Papa* don't mind. He's happy to have the two of us. 'Course, I'm up in the forest a lot with Aubin. You know what's bin happenin' up there?"

It fitted, when he thought about it. Jimmy had always basked in Aimée's fussing attention, treatment that would have driven Alain to distraction. He slapped the boy on the back and turned them towards a chocolate shop. "Let's sit down and you can tell me."

When he was seated and had taken his first sip, the young forester shook his head, foam flying off his upper lip. "Those darned peasants. You know, they was only allowed to take so much per year from the *garigues*, put their pigs in the forest for so long, all those special rules from the *seigneurial* days? Well, turns out chuckin' all those rules wasn't such a good idea. They're in there all the time, and nobody's stoppin' them. Ground's all eaten bare, trees chopped down all over the place. I tell you, in a coupla years there's gonna be no forest at all. See how they like it then. No wonder there's bin all the famine. They ain't doin' nothin' right any more."

The boy hitched forward. "Now what's the real story? What kinda chances she got?"

Alain winced. "I was hoping you'd be able to tell me. I know the legal situation. She's mostly innocent. Yes, her parents could be classed as *emigrés*, but we've pretty well dealt with that. It wouldn't send her to the guillotine, in any case. The only problem is her insult to de Gonillons, and how he's managed to blow that up into a slander of the leaders of the Republique."

"So it comes down ta who's got the most clout. Who has everyone afraida him the most."

"Or has the most powerful friends."

"Huh. De Gonillons don't have no friends. Not here in Grenoble. Allies, yes. Muchual interest, that sorta thing. But he's gotta pay 'em off with somethin', and he ain't got much any more."

"Are you sure about this?"

363

"I ain't bin on holiday the last coupla days. He ain't liked, that's certain, and he's spent too much time swannin' around Savournon and not attendin' to business here. Ain't bin buyin' enough drinks in the taverns. I'm sure he'll make that up, now that he's in town."

"He's been sniffing around Angélique already."

"Yeah, well it's official. Got himself transferred here on a temporary basis."

"To the *bastille?*"

"He's assigned there. Got rooms down in the city. You know how he works. He could get posted anywhere he wants. Like the convent."

"That's terrible."

Jimmy wavered a hand above the table. "Maybe, maybe not."

"What do you mean?"

"Well, I c'n read that Reynaud pretty well. I figured he'll come and gloat. We c'n catch him makin' contact with the prisoner he's testifyin' against, we c'n put pressure on."

"*Papa* and I already discussed that. How did you figure it out?"

"Stands ta reason." The boy looked around the shop. "I gotta go."

"Oh. All right..." he signalled the server.

By the time Alain had paid for their drinks, the lad had disappeared.

* * *

The convent was a pleasant site, high above the city on the same shoulder of the mountain as the *bastille,* but farther to the west, with a beautiful view out over the valley. A long flight of steps led up to a tall gate where the first sentry stood. Once over that hurdle, Alain walked across the courtyard to the cellar entrance.

A guard was seated in an anteroom inside, and there the visitor had to show his papers. If he were lucky – or unlucky – enough to be allowed in, he then passed through a gate and along a straight, narrow hallway that plunged back into the living stone of the mountain. To Alain it always smelled damp, with a musty hint of the tomb about it. Angélique's cell was on a corridor that branched off to the left. She was free to move around a series of rooms that led off a central area, divided by a line of bars embedded into the flagstones. Visitors were allowed to speak to prisoners there, in the full view of everyone, although the other prisoners and the guards usually stood aside to give Alain and Angélique some privacy.

Alain had just retrieved his papers from the anteroom guard and started into the first hallway when an officer with Captain's insignia stepped along beside him. He glanced up. The man was tall, well built, with a round face and long side-whiskers.

"You're Alain Jouvent."

"I am."

"A friend of Angéliqe de Bardel, I gather."

"I'm her fiancé."

"Hmm. If I might give you *un peu de conseil*, don't be shouting that around."

"Why not? It's true."

The man gave a sad smile. "Ah, young love. It may be true, *citoyen,* but it won't help either of you. These are times for keeping our heads down and our mouths closed."

"And what about standing up for those we love?"

"*Avec déscretion, citoyen.* Carefully. We are more useful that way."

Alain paused at the junction of the two corridors, but the man did not continue. "Is there something I can help you with?"

"No, no. Please proceed." He motioned down the corridor towards the cells. Alain had no choice but to lead the way, and the Captain followed.

Angélique was sitting at the bedside of an invalid but she laid the woman's hand down and strode over to the bars with a bright smile. "So you've met Alix."

Alain gave the officer a stare. "He didn't see fit to introduce himself. It seems these are times to keep our heads down and our mouths closed."

The officer laughed. "*Vraiment, citoyen.* They are." Then he sobered and turned to Angélique. "Did you get the blankets?"

"We did, thank you."

"Five of them?"

"Four."

"Hmm. I'll deal with that." He nodded to Alan. "Nice to have met you, *citoyen.*" He gave what was almost a bow to Angélique, "*Citoyenne,*" then strolled back up the corridor.

Alain looked at her with raised eyebrows.

She smiled again. "That's right. A nice guard."

It was good to see the smile. "I'm glad you recognized the benefit of returning the courtesy."

"Well, I was a bit sharp with him at first. But he laughed at me."

"What?"

"That's right." She tossed her head towards her cellmates. "And then they all laughed. It was the first time everyone had laughed since I had come here, so what could I do? I laughed, too."

Alain shook his head. "That, I would have liked to see."

"He's a good man, Alain. A good man doing his best in a bad job. He helps us however he can."

"And it seems you help him. Happy prisoners are easier to keep."

"That's rather cynical."

"Just realistic. What was that about the blankets?"

She shrugged. "Some of his men are stealing things. The reason I met him is that he and Jimmy have been making sure the extra food we paid for is getting to us."

"Trust Jimmy to have the right friends."

It was one of the more positive visits he made, and he left feeling, if not happy, at least less depressed than he had been for weeks.

* * *

The next day, Alain contacted Jimmy. They did not meet often, trying to avoid suspicion on any observer's part, but today he had a package for the boy, sent by Aimée. Alain grinned despite his black mood. It was nice that some of his friends had something to be happy about. Times like these, you had to grab what cheer you could, when you could.

As soon as they were seated in his rooms he handed the parcel over, and Jimmy tore it open. "I knew it! Cake!" He set the paper-wrapped food aside. "Say, there's a letter in here. Aimée knows I don't read so good. What's she doin' sendin' me a letter?" He puzzled over the lines for a while and then slid it over to Alain in disgust. "Can't make head nor tail of all those big words."

Alain glanced over the note. The second time he read it more carefully. Then he reached out and put the paper to the candle flame, holding it until it was completely burned, then stamping the ashes to nothing on the floor.

367

"What'rya doin? That was my letter from Aimée! I ain't never had a letter before."

Alain held up a warning hand. He went to the door and opened it a crack. The hallway was clear. He sat down beside Jimmy. "Aimée wrote something she shouldn't have, and no one could be allowed to read it."

"What'd she say?"

"That someone who works inside a building could go in and not leave again, allowing someone else to come out instead."

"Aimée said that?"

Alain grinned. "We always knew she was smart."

"Whaddaya think?"

"I think we need to do a lot of thinking."

Hammering at it until late into the night, they polished their plan. Well past midnight they sat back, stretching their aching bodies.

"How does it look to you?"

Jimmy shrugged. "I dunno. We gotta do somethin', and that's the best we can figure. All our other plans worked."

'It's simple, daring and needs only a bit of luck to succeed. But it's also risky. As long as there is a chance that Angélique will get a legal release, we'll hold off."

"Hey, I ain't anxious to put my neck under the guillotine for nothin'. We got a coupla weeks left before her hearin'. I'll need time to get the papers made up. I know a guy."

He slapped Alain on the shoulder and slipped out the door.

Alain went to bed, the plan spinning in his head, but he could find no obvious flaws, no possible improvements. Finally he slept.

36. Breakout

July 30, 1794

12 Thermidore, An 2

Then came the 12 Thermidor.

As Alain left the inn that afternoon, he was surprised to see the familiar face of Alix Duval in the crowd. He was about to speak out when Duval motioned silence, then strode ahead. Alain followed.

Strolling into a nearby park, the Guardsman paused to view a flowerbed. Alain stopped, not quite beside him.

"They came for her today." Alain's heart jumped. He spun towards Duval, who turned away as if to leave. Regaining control, Alain looked ahead again. "She isn't supposed to go to trial for two weeks! What's going on? What happened? Has it happened already?" He glanced over to see a reassuring grin.

"I...lost her papers. Couldn't be sure of the right prisoner. Couldn't release her."

"Will that get you in trouble?"

"It shouldn't. She isn't up for trial, so it isn't unusual that her papers weren't ready. So I sent them away." His voice dropped. "I won't be able to use that trick again, lad. They might be back tomorrow. They might not. Just thought you'd like to know." He started to turn away.

"Wait!"

The man hesitated, reluctant to turn back, and Alain thought what danger he had put himself in just to come here.

"I can't thank you enough."

"Good luck, lad." Then he frowned. "There was something wrong about the whole thing. If it had been her turn for certain, then a few missing papers wouldn't have stopped them." He shook his head. "That de Gonillons was there, or Lafrance, or whatever he calls himself. He had an air of desperation... like he knew something, and he was pushing hard for some reason...I don't understand. But it's not good. He was so officious. That sort often get what they want, days like this." Then he was gone, striding through the trees.

They had no choice, now. If they were going to use the plan, it had to be tonight. He needed no more discussion with Jimmy. The boy was primed.

That evening, careful to keep to Alain's usual visiting time, they started out. For once, the rambling stairway up to the gate did not seem long enough, although it felt good to burn off some of his nervous energy.

About half way up, Jimmy stopped.

"Are you goin' ta gallop all the way ta the top? This cloak is heavy, and I'm sweatin' like crazy! Take it easy. We'll get there."

Alain grinned. "Sorry. I forgot about that robe. We have to go sedately anyway, as if you were a priest." He turned and moved on at a more normal pace. Soon enough, they were at the gate.

Nervous as he was, Alain was afraid to change his routine, so he stopped to talk to Duval in the courtyard as usual.

The sergeant leaned on the balustrade looking out over the city. "It certainly is beautiful. I always like the evening watch. You see such great sunsets from here. I suppose that's why the church built the convent here. Convents are often in places with magnificent scenery. Open, free places. Too bad."

Alain looked sideways at the man. Was there a message in that innocent comment? He decided to fish. "I have no idea why the church did what it did."

The soldier chuckled. "Oh, I do. You'd be amazed why they did things. I'm not joking. It's quite possible they put this convent here because someone liked the sunsets. My brother was a priest. He used to tell me stories like that."

"He's a priest."

The soldier's face hardened. "Yes, he was. And he stayed a priest, to the last."

Alain didn't need to ask what "the last" was. "I'm sorry."

The man turned back to the sunset. "So am I. I had all sorts of plans at the end, when he was in prison. Ways of getting him out, including storming the place with my men. They would have done it. But in the end I was helpless. It's easy to have ideas, but it's not easy to do, getting someone out of a prison. Especially now with all the political upset. Everybody doing their jobs twice as hard, making sure that they don't make a mistake and get themselves in trouble."

Alain stood frozen, listening as if hypnotized. There was no doubt. He was getting a message.

"For example, a few of my men take a great delight in figuring out what escape attempts might be tried. It's a game to them. You can't blame them for it. It's a boring job, standing guard all the time. They haven't caught anyone yet, but I suppose they will. They haven't thought of the results; another victim for the guillotine, maybe even a friend. They're only young and thoughtless and doing their duty." The man shook his head and turned away in the gathering twilight, shoulders slumped.

Alain was standing alone, his hand half-raised in a gesture of protest or farewell. He glanced over to where the Rat stood, partly concealed in the deepening shadows. *What do we do?* There was no chance of them carrying out their plan now, but if they retreated without visiting Angélique, suspicions would be aroused. *Besides, she's expecting us. I have to be there.*

He gestured, and the two began the long walk across the courtyard towards the prison doors.

The inside guards, seeing Alain's familiar face, opened the gate with a cursory glance at their papers, and then they were through, walking down that narrow, empty hallway. He thought he had grown used to it, but now the enclosing feeling was back, pressing down on him. The damp smell he had come to ignore pushed at his nostrils with renewed strength, and his stomach writhed. He grabbed Jimmy's arm through the heavy robe.

"They've found out."

"What d'ya mean? They can't have. Nobody but you and me know about it."

"It doesn't matter. Alix just warned me. If we try it, we'll get caught."

Jimmy looked around. "Shouldn't we get out, then?"

Alain pulled him along. "We've done nothing wrong. We can have our visit and leave as usual."

Jimmy squared his shoulders. "We'll see."

"What do you mean, 'we'll see'?"

"Quiet. Guards." Jimmy tugged his hood forward, and they passed the two soldiers, attracting only a bored glance.

Then they were at Angélique's cell. She waited at the bars, her hands clenched white. "They came for me today. It isn't time yet, Alain, not for nearly two weeks. Why did they come for me so soon?"

"There's no way of knowing, Angélique. There's all sorts of uneasiness going around. Perhaps it's because the Jacobins' powers are beginning to weaken. They'll be thrown out, and all the people they arrested will be set free. We just have to get through the next few weeks, and you'll be fine."

He wasn't getting through to her. "But they came for me today. I won't make it through the next few weeks." Glancing down at her trembling hands, she gripped the bars tighter to still them.

"We have to wait, dear. There's nothing else we can…"

A sharp nudge in his back interrupted him, and he stumbled forward, reaching out. Angélique's arms came through the gate, and he held her as best he could, the bars hard and cold between them. Jimmy came around and stood to the side, shaking his head.

"When you two are finished we can get down to business. Tell her about it, Alain."

"Jimmy, there's no chance, now."

"Tell her about it. Let her make the decision."

"What are you talking about?"

Alain hesitated, and Jimmy poked him again.

"It's rather simple. Jimmy picks the lock. You put on the cloak and come out with me. His false papers worked coming in. They didn't look at them carefully, so there's no problem. We have papers for you to get you out. Jimmy hides in the building, shows up for work at the kitchen in the morning."

It didn't sound so bad, stated like that, but he felt compelled to include his recent conversation with the captain. When he had finished, Angélique shook her head, and he could see that she was smiling.

"What's so funny? It could work!"

She shook her head again. "Alain, you haven't been in prison like I have. Everyone talks about rescue and escape. Your plan has been tried many times, in many prisons."

"Did it work?"

"Sometimes it did, sometimes it didn't. Your trick of having Jimmy stay inside is a good twist. But it doesn't matter, now. We can't disregard Duval's warning. Just be thankful he was here to tell you."

Alain shook his head. "I don't think you understand, dear. If it was only a mixup and they came for you by mistake, that sort of thing can be straightened out. But this is Reynaud de Gonillons we're dealing with. Who says he was even taking you to the Tribunal? You wouldn't be the first person to disappear into nowhere at a time of upheaval."

Her face blanched, and she grasped the bars as if she were going to fall. Her voice came in a husky whisper. "I never thought of that."

"So we have to try. No matter what happens."

Her hands gripped the bars with force enough to whiten her knuckles. "No." Her head came up and she stared into his eyes. "No, you're not thinking like a lawyer. We can't let de Gonillons scare us into doing something stupid. Can you imagine how he would laugh if you were to get caught? We would all go to the guillotine, and he would have done nothing at all."

Her shoulders straightened. "Come, now, Alain. I expect you to do better than that. Keep your head about you."

"But if he comes again? Alix says a few missing papers won't stop him next time."

"Then...then I'll ask Alix. He outranks de Gonillons, here in Grenoble. He can come with us and bring an escort of some of his men, to make sure I get to where I'm supposed to go."

"Right. And if it's all a bluff to grab you, Reynaud will back down. But if it's really a summons..."

She shook her head, her hair flying into a halo. "Then I'll take my chances with the jury. After all, I am innocent. Well thought out, Alain. A good plan."

The Rat snorted. "I still think we oughta get you outa here. We gotta do somethin'!"

She turned to him. "Jimmy, you don't know what it means to me, that you and Alain are willing to take this risk. It has cheered me up immensely to know that you care so much."

"Of course we care!"

She reached through the bars and ruffled his hair. "And that's all you can do."

"All right. And if Reynaud de Gonillons is playin' fast and loose with the rules to get you tried aheada time, Alain can expose him and send him in front of the Tribunal himself!"

"Yes, after I'm executed he probably can. I would be happy to think you could manage that, Alain. Now away you go. Leave the false papers here with me. If they grab you on the way out, you'll have nothing to incriminate you. Alain, have your father do his best to keep the legal proceedings on track. I don't like these little surprises. Jimmy, you keep your ears open in the kitchen. You might hear something useful. I'm not averse to an escape. I just want it to be successful."

The boy grinned. "I'll leave you two alone for a while." He winked at Alain and turned his back.

Alain reached through again, and Angélique leaned against him as well as the bars would allow. As he stroked her hair, he was struck by the absolute unreality of living without her.

After a moment she stirred. "I'm sorry we never got that romance we planned."

"What do you mean?" He stared at her in mock ignorance. "What have we been doing for the last six years, planting potatoes?"

She shrugged. "Trying to build a new nation?"

He grinned and held her again. "Oh, yes. That too."

The guard was returning. Jimmy put up his hood and turned back to them.

After a few pleasantries, at least as pleasant as possible under the circumstances, they pulled themselves away. Alain looked back just before he rounded the corner. Angélique was leaning her forehead against the bars, both hands holding herself erect. She seemed so forlorn that he almost went back, but then she straightened and waved cheerfully. He could do nothing but wave back.

His mind was a turmoil. He felt disappointed and relieved, depressed and exhilarated. As they turned the corner he wasn't concentrating, and it was only Jimmy's hand on his arm that made him aware that there were three soldiers standing in front of them, hemming them in against the wall. "And who have we here?"

"What do you mean?"

"I mean, we want to make sure that those that goes in are the same as those that goes out."

"Oh." Alain glanced at his companion, to see that the boy still had the hood of his cloak pulled up. "Jimmy..."

The Rat pulled his hood back, smiling. "What's the problem, Jean-Louis?"

The soldier held his lamp closer to the boy's face. "What are you doin' here, Jimmy? What kind of game are you playin'?"

"No game, Jean-Louis. Just visitin' one of the prisoners. Wanted to find out if they was gettin' all the food we send up from the kitchen. They are gettin' it, aren't they, Jean? They aren't losin' any dainty bits on the way up the stairs? The ones they paid extra for?"

The soldier stiffened, but he backed up. "I dunno what you mean. Now you two better get out of here. I don't like what I'm seein'."

Jimmy seemed about to respond, but Alain grabbed his arm and hurried him along. As they neared the gate they could hear the marching boot steps of the soldiers following. Fighting the urge to run, Alain strode along the tight corridor, his hand on Jimmy's arm steadying them both. Finally, they were through the gate and out in the open courtyard. A whoosh of air beside him made Alain realize that he, too, had been breathing tightly. He gave his companion a taut grin, and they moved at the same steady pace across the courtyard. As they passed through the wall a dark figure on the wall above raised a hand to them. Alain waved back, and they trudged down the long staircase towards the relative freedom of the city.

37. The Final Fall

July 31, 1794

13 Thermidore, An 2

That night Alain paced the confines of his room in deep despair. He thought endlessly of the things he should have done, might have done, could have done. For a while he was determined to go the next night and try again. He thought himself resolved, but then he remembered that Jimmy could not show up in the robe again, and that Angélique had taken the papers. *I'm not thinking clearly. I haven't been for some time. What if I had got Jimmy arrested? Poor Aimée.*

He shook his head. There had been no good reason to give Angélique the papers. *She took them to keep me from using them.* For a while he was angry with her for not letting him sacrifice himself. How could he prove how much he loved her? *How can I let her die and live afterwards, knowing that I did nothing to save her?*

As the greying of the window indicated the end of the night, a touch of reason returned to him. Now it became clear, as Alix had told him, as Angélique had told him – his father had, too – there were times when there was nothing you could do. Nothing.

He wondered how he would stand it.

As the light strengthened, the usual city bustle began to filter through the shutters. Throwing himself on his bed, he fell into a fitful doze in which vague, unformed dreams full of shouting and fire flooded through his head.

He awakened later to the sound of real shouts in the street. He rolled over, tried to sleep again, ignoring the noise. *Just another riot.*

A strident knock at his door snapped him to awareness. He started upright in bed, staring around. He had heard no footsteps. *Surely if the Guard came for me, I would hear boots.*

Marching. They always march. Forcing himself to stand, he straightened his clothes, smoothed his tangled hair, steeled himself and made his voice strong.

"Who is it?"

"It might be a friendly barmaid bringin' a jug a wine, but it ain't. Open the door, my friend. I got news."

Alain flung the door open. "Jimmy! Don't do that! You scared the life out of me." Then his wits settled. "What's going on? What are you doing here? What if someone sees you?"

Another thought hit him. He grabbed the boy's shirt. "Angélique! Have they come for her?"

Jimmy smiled reaching up to pat Alain's white knuckles. "Yer girl's fine. That's not what's happenin'. Lissen!"

Alain obeyed. There was more noise from the street, now, but it wasn't the familiar mob sound, which always swept by and moved on. This seemed to be a general buzz of conversation, as if there were many people nearby, but standing around talking.

Jimmy pulled at his sleeve. "Come on out. You'll see what's happenin'."

Out in the street there was a different feeling in the air. It had rained during the night, and Alain took a fresh, cool breath. But it wasn't the rain. Something about the city had changed. He looked around, glanced down at Jimmy. The boy smiled and waved his hand at the crowd. They were different people from the usual mob. Better dressed, more women. Listening, he began to pick up a word here, a word there.

"...definitely fallen, that's what I hear..."

"...can't last another vote in the Assembly, they say..."

And a more gruesome dialogue, with evident relish, "...a different sort heading for Madame Guillotine."

"The whole lot of them, I say!"

As the last two speakers, chuckling in a grim manner, turned into the inn taproom, Alain turned to Jimmy in wonder.

"Are they really gone?"

"I guess so. Four days ago, near as I c'n figger. News sure travelled fast, din't it?"

"Then let's go!" He grabbed Jimmy's arm and began to tug him up the street.

The boy came along, shaking his head. "No sense."

"What?"

"*Bastille* 'n' convent's shut up tight as a drum. I went ta work, but it was all locked up. No one in, no one out. Guess they're stuck with second-rate bread today. Got a nod from Alix, up on the wall, so she's all right. Don't worry, he'll take care of her. No Tribunals today either. Maybe never. It's all over but the paperwork, Alain, and you're the man to do that."

"But we have to wait?"

"Nothin' changes, does it?"

A thought struck Alain. "De Gonillons. He's up in the *bastille*. What if he…"

"*Pas du tout*. Left town the moment the news came in. I went round to his lodgin' in the city, but he was already gone."

"But where?"

"Back to Savournon, I'd guess." The boy's accent became cultured. "I suspect he feels rather out of favour at this time."

"As he should."

"So now let's go."

"Where?"

"To celebrate. Find your *Papa* and lift a glass to Angélique's early release. We got orphans waitin' for us."

"That we do, Jimmy. Let's go find *Papa*."

38. Epilogue: Homecoming

August 1794

A quietly happy group rode the carriage home to Savournon that warm summer day. After the shouting and wild emotion of the crowd in Serres when the freed prisoners had returned, Angélique seemed content to lean against Alain's shoulder and gaze out the window. He was more than content that she should be there.

"Look, Alain." She was pointing ahead. A roiling black storm cloud had piled up over the peak of Mount Aujour behind the village, but a ray of sunshine lit the belfry of the church and warmed the soft grey stucco of the houses.

"Pretty place. Think you'd like to live there?"

"It would suit me."

"Then let's do that." He gazed out the carriage window. "Mount Aujour. Now that would be a climb."

Her look turned south. "Revuaire seems rather small, now."

"Nice view, though."

"We never take the easy way up, do we?"

"No, but we get there."

For a long while no one spoke, but Alain's head was full of plans.

Angélique looked up at him hesitantly and broke the silence. "Where is he?"

He knew whom she meant. "Gone."

Light flickered across her face. "Gone?"

"Yes. Just disappeared. He figured out what was coming before official word got out, which was why he made that last attempt to get at you. But time ran out for him. He must have been ready for months. It turns out he sold his family home as part of the 'Lafrance' masquerade.

"The sly fox always has another exit from his den. When I got back from Grenoble he was gone, and no one has seen him since. Many of them went to Argentina. The Guard lads say he talked a lot about America. It doesn't really matter to us any more."

"So he gets away, unpunished. That doesn't seem right, somehow."

He patted her hand. "You have to remember, he never did anything wrong."

She stiffened. "What?"

"Think about it. We did him the greatest favour possible. Every time he tried to do something illegal, we stopped him."

Her old, unladylike snort warmed his heart. "Wasn't that nice of us?"

He patted her arm. "If it makes you feel any better, I doubt if he sees it that way. Think of how angry he must be. But he's helpless, as always."

"And gone."

"That's right. And if he came back, he'd still be helpless, because the law has been re-established. *Liberté, egalité, et fraternité* have returned to our *patrie*."

She relaxed against him, lulled by the sway of the carriage. Then he could feel her body begin to tense.

"What are you worrying about now?"

Her hand reached back over her shoulder to brush his cheek, and he felt a quiet satisfaction that he could read her so well.

"Where am I going to live, Alain?"

Alain shared a smile with his mother.

"I suppose you're officially an orphan, so we could stick you in the orphanage..."

"Yes. I could stay there if we ever get it approved. That's where I'll be working, won't I?"

Alain's mother patted her knee. "For the moment, you're staying with us. It will make planning the wedding so much easier."

She turned toward the older woman. "But do you have room for me?"

"More than enough. With the expansion of the business the old office was too small, so we bought a new house. Didn't Alain tell you?"

"No he didn't. Whose house did you buy?"

"A very nice one. I'm sure you'll approve." Catherine would say no more, and Angélique, twisting around for a glance at Alain's grin, dropped the subject. With a tired sigh, she leaned her head against his shoulder. He noticed how white and thin her hands were as they lay in her lap. He stroked them as if he could smooth down the cords and veins that stood clear.

They turned up the drive to the *chateau.*

Angélique looked at him. He could hear the pain in her voice. "Alain, I don't want to go past there right now. Could we go straight to your house instead?"

He patted her hand. "Don't worry, dear. This is the shortest way to our new home."

Angélique sat back, looking puzzled. When the carriage pulled up in front of the main steps, she was even more mystified. Her hand trembled as she rubbed her forehead, and Alain was briefly sorry that he was teasing her like this. Stepping out of the carriage, he reached up and took both her hands.

"Just step down, Angélique. Trust me."

She looked down at his reassuring smile, then got out of the carriage. She stood there, her eyes going from Alain to the *chateau,* then back to Alain, a worried frown wrinkling her forehead. Then there was a snicker behind her, and she turned to see Edmond leaning on his crutches and Aimée arm-in-arm with Jimmy. Five children in uniforms stood proudly erect in front of them. The rest of the Jouvent family had descended from the carriage, and everyone watched her, smiles all round.

Alain saw her mind working. The old Angélique look stole into her face. She turned to him, the uncertainty disappearing from her stance.

"Alain Jouvent. Just where is this new house you bought?"

He shrugged eloquently. "Well, dear, I'm sorry, but there wasn't much choice. We needed something bigger than the old house, with more office space. And for two families, well, there was nothing else in the village. It's a bit elegant for an orphanage..." He gazed up at the *chateau*. "Lots of room, though."

She stamped her foot, colour rising in her cheeks. "Alain! Stop playing games! Tell me the truth!"

The whole group laughed. Angélique looked around. Gaetan and two other servants appeared from the stable. Aubin and his sons were there, lounging against the wall in their foresters' garb.

The front door opened and Emilie stood there beaming.

"Welcome home, Mademoiselle de Bardel."

Alain swept his arm forward. "Welcome to the new offices of *Jouvent et Fils, Advocats et Notaires.*"

"You bought Chateau Savournon."

He nodded.

"We're going to live here."

Another nod.

"But the orphanage...the Inspector..."

"We turned Aimée and Edmond loose on him. He couldn't stand against a Hero of the Revolution and that barrage of motherly concern. He also mentioned Inspector General Vincent twice. I'm sure he was worried about keeping his position with the change of government. The whole thing was approved a week ago, and the first of the children arrived yesterday."

Angélique's laugh rang out as loud and free as ever, but her smile had a wry twist. "It's just like I told you before, Alain. We had a revolution. We thought our world was upside down. But in the end, here we are. Nothing has changed!" He shrugged again, and they shared a long look. Then the rest crowded around her, talking and gesturing, and swept her into the *chateau*.

François Jouvent stood in the doorway looking back, and Alain's heart leaped at the pride in his father's eyes. He raised a hand in casual salute, and the elder lawyer nodded and turned inside.

Alain took his time alone on the front steps. His eye travelled up the rough facade, four stories of stained grey stucco. As he reached the door he ran his fingers over a cracked panel that needed repair.

Nothing changed? He smiled to himself. "Oh, yes it has."

Historical Characters and Events

The 1793 riot in Serres, which the nearest large town to Savournon, is a historical incident, and all the characters mentioned are real. All the other stories recounted about Serres are actual events. Former Mayor Achard escaped to Lyon and was executed when that rebellion was crushed in December, 1793.

All the events and people from the rest of France are historically accurate.

Françoise de Dillon, Angélique de Lombard and Charles de Rastel de Rocheblave were historical characters, and the 21 children Mme. De Dillon birthed is accurate. She died May 16, 1791. She had a grandson, Charles de Bardel, who was born in 1756. Angélique is his fictional daughter.

The French used the balloon "l'Entreprenant" for reconnaissance in their victorious Battle of Fleurus in Belgium on June 26, 1794. There is no evidence to suggest that it burned, although fire was a common problem with hydrogen balloons, and they did not come into common military usage.

Gordon A. Long

About the Author

Brought up in a logging camp with no electricity, Gordon Long learned his storytelling in the traditional way: at his father's knee. He now spends his time editing, publishing, travelling, blogging and writing fantasy and social commentary, although sometimes the boundaries blur.

Gordon lives in Tsawwassen, British Columbia, with his wife, Linda, and their Nova Scotia Duck Tolling Retriever, Josh. When he is not writing and publishing, he works on projects with the Surrey Seniors' Planning Table, and is a staff writer for <indiesunlimited.com>

More from Gordon A. Long

Other Titles by Gordon A. Long available at <smashwords.com> and <amazon.com>:

"Out of Mischief" World of Change 1

"Into Trouble" World of Change 2

"Mountains of Mischief" World of Change 3

"A Sword Called...Kitten?" Romantic Comedy with an Edge

"The Cat with Many Claws" Sword Called Kitten Book 2

"Why Are People So Stupid?" Social Humour with a Point

Look for Gordon's books, selected reviews, poetry and short stories: <airbornpress.ca>

Gordon's opinions on humanity are at the "Are People Really That Stupid?" blog: <http://airbornpress.ca/arepeoplestupid/>

Find all his reviews and his ideas on writing at "Renaissance Writer:" <http://airbornpress.ca/newdir/>

"Sword Called Kitten Serial" Free online: <airbornpress.ca/kittenserial>